THE SEER AND THE STARGAZER

ELLE DUNPHY AND CERIS THOMSON

Seer

"a person who says he or she can see what will happen in the future"

Synonyms: Prophetess, Sibyl, Augur.

Stargazer

"a person who is involved in astronomy or astrology"
Synonyms: Astronomer, Astrologer.

Astronomy

"the scientific study of the universe and of objects that exist naturally in space, such as the moon, the sun, planets, and stars"

Astrology

"the study of the movements and positions of the sun, moon, planets, and stars in the belief that they affect the character and lives of people"

Also by

Elle Dunphy and Ceris Thomson

The Segontium Sword

The Sibyls' Secrets

First published in England 2023 by Red L.A.
This edition published in 2023

ISBN (paperback) 978-1-7395748-1-9

Printed and bound in Great Britain
Red L.A.

For more information visit https://www.newmoontarot.co.uk/

The Six Moon Phases

"The moon symbolises life's ebbs and flows, beginnings, and endings. Eternal love stays the same. It doesn't matter what life throws at you, like the moon, you'll wax and wane alongside each other." Ceris Thomson

New moon a time to start manifesting the dreams you would like to help you achieve your Destiny.

Waxing moon keep wishing the dream, keep it alive, you know you can achieve anything you want. Visualise your new life.

Waxing crescent sliver in the sky means you are still setting up your manifestation.

Full moon, go outside make a wish on the full moon and thank her for bringing your intention to reality, share your intention with her and say thank you.

Waning moon is a time you push negative energy away from you. Get rid of what isn't working for you as it's time to walk away from whatever it is that doesn't serve you.

Waning crescent is a dark time, a quiet time, a time for divination, tarot cards, reflect on what you have let go.

Note from Nain: "Sort out the loose threads of your life, otherwise they will become unravelled."

For Martin, the other half of my soul,
For my girls, you make me whole,
For Nain and Taid, your story has been told,
For Bryn Gosol, your history can now enfold.

To Elle for writing this book and bringing a dream to life.
To my dear friend Marje, always remembered with love.
To Meurig, we will always walk on the Vardre.
And lastly to the Moon, for lighting the path.
Ceris xxx

For The Gill whose body is lost but whose soul lives on.
For my family, friends, and those in Ysbryd.
Ceris and Martin, thanks for an exciting adventure.
Elle xxx

Dear Reader

Does the past make us the people we are in the future?

Serendipity led me to shift my world view and guided me to encounter professional Welsh tarot card reader and past life regressionist, Ceris Thomson. We met during an online reading in lockdown when everything was topsy turvy. Ceris' psychic visions around me were both enlightening and enlivening in equal measure. With an immediate rapport, when lockdown lifted, we met face to face in Conwy and struck a wonderful connection, realising we had walked past life paths together. Everyone meets for a reason.

Ceris and her husband Martin introduced me to the embattled narrative of the Conwy Valley, where many people have been slain. Two thousand years ago Ancient Roman legionaries conquered the area, fought with Celtic tribesmen, commandeered the land, set out the structure of society, created forts, built networks of roads, and navigated the waterways to Chester and beyond. When Roman authority collapsed in the Conwy Valley, Gaelic tribes from Ireland invaded the region. The Welsh Maelgwyn family and their clans fought to recapture the territory. In the Sixth Century, King Maelgwyn created Deganwy Castle on the hilltop of the Vardre overlooking Conwy and built upon Pagan sites created by the Romans. At the foot of the Vardre, near an Ancient Roman site called Canovium lies Bryn Gosol Farm with its mythical underground tunnel to the Temple of Mithras.

Against the historical drama of this region, and with information regarding Ancient Rome from Martin Thomson, Ceris and I decided to embark on the adventure of a lifetime and write a book together, *The Seer and The Stargazer*, where all roads lead to Rome. The narrative is a fictional account of the life of a Welsh Prophetess, Seren a modern-day Seer who uses clairvoyance, tarot cards, magical spells, astral travel, and past life regression to depict the past, present, and future. In some cases, real life names, events and places appear but their use and reference within this book is entirely fictitious. The characters are imagined, except Julius Caesar whose life and battles have been dramatised for the purpose of this story. All other characters, events and locations are the product of the authors' imagination. The tale includes legends, time dimensions and addresses universal themes of heroism, hope, and love.

This story is dedicated to the amazing people we know.

Elle

2014

Chapter 1 – The Llanrhos Seer

Spirits have a perceptible presence to those who use their sixth sense.

To ward off evil spirits Gwen would throw salt outside the front door for protection, followed by a spit when someone with negative energy left her farmhouse. It made Seren laugh. The eighteen-year-old art student always felt safe and shielded by her wise nain.[1] Idiosyncratic Seren lived with Gwen and taid,[2] Tomos in Bryn Gosol Farm, a remote stone-built farmhouse set in seven acres of countryside nestled snugly under the voluptuous bosom of two magical hills dubbed the Vardre. To the right of the farm, across the cultivated fields and pastures, was the crenellated 12th Century parish church, Saint Hilary's, where Tomos was Church Warden. To the left was a tangled oak known locally as the Devil's Tree.

Often, as they stood on the Vardre to view the violent Irish Sea, Tomos would lay bare to Seren the kaleidoscopic historical identity of the area. He spoke about the legend of King Maelgwyn who created Deganwy Castle and Llywelyn the Great, the ablest Welsh political and military leader, who was supposedly buried on the site of their parish church. By the main door of Saint Hilary's church, any visitor could spot a large carved stone set in a niche in the wall, acknowledging Ancient Roman rule. Sightseers may even have been aware of recent excavations on Gwen and Tomos's land littered with Ancient Roman goblets, coins, spade blades and pottery

---

[1] Grandmother
[2] Grandfather

suggesting that their farm may have been built on an Ancient Roman villa site.

It was the legend of the twisted Devil's Tree which captivated Seren. Once in every hundred years the battles fought on the Vardre could be heard by church visitors. Tomos contemplated that the Devil's Tree held the souls of soldiers, including Roman legionaries. He claimed to have seen three warrior spirits by the Devil's Tree, standing ramrod straight, guarding the defensive, unmortared bulwark. Tomos had shown a photograph of the spirits to prove it. Seren often speculated if her taid had heard the conflicts. When others visited this vicinity, they would be unaware of the underground passageway between the parish church and Bryn Gosol Farm. Leading to a cavernous temple, it was rumoured to have been used by secretive Ancient Roman worshippers of Mithras. Only Gwen, Tomos and Seren knew of its existence. Mysterious Llanrhos.

Conscientious Tomos was as reserved yet inquisitive as Gwen was dynamic and compassionate. They lived across the fields from each other in Anglesey, grew up together, fell in love and married when he was 24, and she was 18. They purchased the farmhouse in Llanrhos with its outbuildings of barns, byres, and stables. For fifty years they worked with livestock and the earth, rising at cockcrow, using the secret underground passageway to attend church meetings before returning home quickly along the tunnel. They would arrive before the farmhands appeared for breakfast. The speed, noise and chaos in the kitchen could be perplexing, because within moments the muscle-bound farmhands would have platefuls of food before their morning shift began. Seren helped serve bacon, pork sausages, eggs, and freshly baked bread, while Gwen and Tomos fed the livestock. At lunchtime, Gwen would arrive in the kitchen to prepare more food, often lobscouse and scones. No-one was ever left hungry. Love was embroidered into the fabric of this time capsule. Seren deliberated that there couldn't be another place in the house in which to stitch a further thread of affection, except perhaps the back dining room.

Never quite certain that the tales recounted by Tomos were true, one thing was assured for Seren, her sixth sense presented the stubborn, persistent impression of a spirit presence around her in the back dining room. A Roman soldier who brought with him freezing chills, vile odours, and a *do not enter* feeling which generated hairs that stood sentry-like on the back of Seren's neck. Upon encountering him, she would run to Gwen, be held tightly against her gentle nain's olive skin, peek into her soulful flashing black eyes, and be assured of protection. Her nain had undeniably inherited talents which made her unique among contemporaries. Emitting positive energy, she possessed the magic and power of prophecy. Had she existed in Ancient Rome, Gwen would have been vaunted as a Sibyl, Augur, or Priestess. As it was, she lived in a farmhouse, in a tiny Welsh village, a glorious, industrious woman renowned as the *Llanrhos Seer*.

Squirms of people would visit the farm, usually in the evening, beseeching Gwen for her help, requesting guidance, seeking prophecies, asking to be *read*. The distressed, the bereaved, the hopeless, the betrayed, the curious. Gwen would say that at some point in life, everyone would be affected by strife. When she led an individual into the back dining room for a reading, Tomos's stern face would soften with pride at Gwen's humanity and effective use of her oracular gifts.

Seren could recall the momentous evening when she spied a waxing gibbous moon shining through the window which illuminated a clique of women in the farm's back sitting room. On the stone flagged floor, a black, wrought iron pot emitted intoxicating incense swirls. Gwen's back was against the inglenook fireplace, bright candlelight flickered in her hawk eyes as she observed seven brightly dressed strangers sitting in a semi-circle before her. Blue incense smoke twirled, coiled, and curled towards the honey-coloured oak beams saturating them with the aroma of sage. Seven young women peered apprehensively at Gwen who could discern the excitement at this ritual. Expectantly the spectators waited, hardly daring to breathe. The Llanrhos Seer was silent, calm, pensive. Seren observed proceedings unfold as the exotic Tarocchi cards were unveiled for divination. Self-effacing Gwen was the High Priestess of tarot card and tealeaf reading. The women were there to participate in individual interpretations of their tarot cards.

The elegiac ghost of a Roman Centurion repeatedly visited Seren in her nightmares. He roared for help she could not bestow. During daytime he appeared to her in the back dining room, a place she felt must be avoided as much as possible, but Gwen cherished the effervescent energy in the room and enjoyed holding her readings there, away from curious eyes. Or so one might think. A pivotal event occurred on the night the seven young women visited the farm, Gwen invited Seren to make notes for each of them while readings took place. Disconcerted, excited, Seren understood not to breathe a word about the readings. She was asked to sit beside the glittering glow of golden light which audaciously sneaked through one side of the back dining room door, and be an amanuensis, a scribe. Eventually Gwen would teach Seren everything she knew about divination.

"Give me five minutes. Seren will bring you, one at a time, to the back dining room."

With that, the prophetess left a discombobulated audience in the sitting room.

Gwen worked by candlelight and relied on heat from a log fire to warm her guests. Arthritic legs on an aged oak table wobbled slightly as she laid out her tarot cards in preparation for the first reading. An antique, black Welsh dresser with ornate carvings held a collection of crystals, candles, and incense diffusers. It was not long before Seren gingerly opened the door and announced Margie, a twenty-year old trainee nurse, whose face was slightly obscured by her red woollen cloche hat. Gwen motioned Margie to sit opposite her, which she did at the same time as removing her hat. Burnished brown hair tumbled around her fragile, pallid face.

"Choose twelve cards dear then pass them to me."

After a swift examination of the cards, Gwen looked up. "Your father is offering you yellow roses dear. He's been in the spirit world for ten years."

Margie gasped. "He has."

"I see a boy wearing a life jacket. He and his mother were rescued from a boat, but not the man. He passed when the boat capsized. Do you understand this?"

It was impossible not to observe the astonished hazel eyes as they gawked at Gwen. She had captured Margie's attention. Her family had recently migrated from Italy to Wales. Margie's widowed mother remarried following that tragic accident from which her younger brother was still recovering. They'd wanted to escape the memories when they arrived in Wales, therefore Margie hadn't told anyone about the incident. She'd even taken her stepfather's surname to protect herself. Her eyes met Gwen's and imperceptibly, she nodded. A fat tear bubble popped and ran down her cheek.

Silence.

"The man who rescued your brother and mother did so at great personal risk."

Stunned, Margie simply nodded.

"There's a blue uniform. You're a nurse."

Margie gulped.

"I am. I wanted to honour my father by living a life where I offer my time and support to people. It's kind of a thank you for saving my brother and mother."

"Don't worry about your exams dear, you'll pass them with flying colours."

Gwen smiled. Margie looked down at her slender fingers and quivered. She had been finding it difficult to concentrate on studying medicine.

"The dark man who wears black glasses and a signet ring. Do you know who that is?"

"Yes."

"He's got his own best interests at heart dear. Think about that. Try not to let him distract you from your goals."

Margie smiled.

"Thank you. That's advice I shall consider."

Gwen's kind eyes sparkled as she stared at Margie.

"I know you will dear. Bright blessings to you."

With that salutation, Gwen summoned Seren who escorted Margie to the back dining room, where she was greeted with a caterwauling of questions.

"What did she say?"

"Could it be true?"

"What did you think of her?"

"Did she tell you anything awful?"

"Is she scary?"

"Are you pleased you saw her?"

"What did you tell her?"

"Are you ok?"

Ironically the last question was:

"Did she ask lots of questions?"

Margie let out a long, audible sigh of relief.

"She's amazing. Scarily accurate and offering brilliant advice. Wait and see what's in store for you."

Seren smiled proudly. It was usually the same reaction when people had a reading with her nain. One word summary. Awe.

In the early evening warmth, candlelight waltzed crazily in a glass jar as Sofia entered the back dining room. Seren silently, but quickly, closed the low door. A pungent waft of lavender candlewax hit Sofia's nostrils, she sat opposite Gwen and realised that there were no exaggerated gestures here.

"Goodness young woman. You bring with you lots of energy. The candles are crackling."

"Do I? They are? What does that mean?"

"When your spirit guide is with you, the candles flicker."

"Spirit guide? I've never heard of that."

"It's a helper who's been selected to guide you throughout life. Now dear, shuffle the cards and pick twelve, then pass them to me please."

Gwen paused and looked away from her mind's eye images.

"Who's the Leo? Is it you?"

"Gosh, yes, it's me."

"You're a drama and dance teacher?"

"Yes, I love it."

"This younger man that you're involved with …."

"Bloody hell. How did you know that?"

Gwen smiled.

"He behaves like a child. This man has serious issues with commitment dear. Are you sure he's worth the effort?"

"I love him. Completely."

"Look here he is."

Gwen showed Sofia the Knight of Swords tarot card and continued.

"He covers himself in a suit of armour. You can't get through to him emotionally."

"Well, I can only try."

"Yes, you can only try my dear. Is there anything you want to ask me?"

"Yes please. Will he ask me to marry him?"

Gwen looked at the cards.

"There is no ring in the foreseeable future."

Sofia looked crestfallen.

"You must decide if he's worth your love and effort. Only you can determine that, but I sense your verve for life. Harness it. Focus on that."

"Thank you, Gwen" whispered Sofia. Her face showed pitiful disappointment.

Together, Sofia and Seren walked into the kitchen.

"Come on Sofia, help me prepare a quick snack for everyone. A cup of tea always helps."

Sofia wiped her tears and by the time she had composed herself, Seren had slipped into the front sitting room to deposit a large blue pot of tea, seven cups and slices of bara brith[3] for the visitors.

A brash breeze echoed through the farmhouse as vivacious Bethany chatted away to Seren. She'd volunteered to have the next reading. Vibrant colours shimmied into the back dining room to broadcast Bethany's arrival.

"Hello dear. Welcome. Please take a seat and shuffle the cards."

"These. Oh, what stunning colours. How many should I take?"

"Choose twelve please."

"I hope I choose good ones" exclaimed Bethany; she pondered carefully over each card.

"You're very spiritual."

---

[3] Welsh tea bread.

"I seem to know when events are going to happen. Yes, you're right. I'm spiritual. I find it a bit scary really as I don't know what to do with it."

"Work with Ysbryd.[4] The spirits. Learn to accept the spirit world dear. You'd be a wonderful spiritual healer."

"I've had readings. Well, I've had this reading and one other, but I couldn't offer that to anyone. I don't have enough confidence in myself to think that I could learn to work with spirits. Oh no, not me."

"The cards are telling me you're a gifted healer. You work with the elderly."

"Yes."

"You're very kind, thoughtful. You put a lot of time into helping the people you work with."

"Yes, but that's different. That's my job and I love it. I like working with older people. They don't belittle others the way people my age criticise. They've had life experiences and don't judge a book by its cover. I'm not confident and I'm not attractive. People wouldn't take to me."

"What have you got to lose if you try?"

"I don't know. I've never reflected on that. No, I couldn't do that. I'd be a failure. That would dent the tiny bit of confidence I've got."

---

[4] Spirit, Ghost.

"Nothing ventured, nothing gained dear. You'd be an excellent healer. Do you have any questions for me?"

"Why don't I have much success with men?"

Gwen glanced at the tarot cards.

"You fix people. You repair men. You solve their problems for them, then they move on. Look for someone who isn't broken."

Bethany pondered this last piece of information.

"You're right. I do go out with men who are needy."

"Choose your next boyfriend very carefully. Wait for a man who isn't always whining about his life."

Bethany's head bobbled as she laughed heartily.

"Do they exist?"

"Yes. There are lots of suitable men. Avoid the grumblers. The first man you do a reading for will ask you out. He'd be a good choice."

"Thanks Gwen. That's given me plenty to think about."

"Is there anything else you need to know dear?"

"No. I've got enough to be going on with. Ysbryd. Confidence. Men. Please don't give me anything else to consider."

Gwen smiled. "Ok dear. Lovely to meet you."

Seren led Bethany into the front sitting room and asked:

"Who'd like to go next?"

"I will please," said Alys. The sight of her would make a person gasp, with her insouciant air and lethal red smile.

Seren escorted Alys to the back dining room, then followed her through the door.

"Hello dear. Lovely to meet you. Here are the tarot cards. Please shuffle them carefully and pass twelve to me when you're ready."

Alys's head quivered as she concentrated hard on rearranging and choosing the tarot cards.

"There you are" she said with a presumptive air.

"You've brought a picture of your sister with you. You changed your mind about the first one and brought another one instead. You'd planned which one to bring and at the last minute changed your mind."

"The first one was too big."

"What still hangs behind the bedroom door?"

"A coat."

"It has hung there for a long time?"

"Yes. I was going to give it to charity, but I couldn't bear to let it go."

"It belonged to your sister."

"Yes."

"You have a bird tattoo in her memory?"

"Yes. A swallow."

"She's giving you bunches and bunches of sunflowers."

"I have pictures of sunflowers in my bedroom. They remind me of her. We used to have competitions to see whose sunflower would grow the tallest."

"Is there anything you'd like to ask me?"

"Yes please. Will my business be a success? I've just started a jewellery business. Will it thrive?" she asked grandiloquently.

Gwen looked at the cards and shook her head.

"The cards aren't showing me anything dear. They're not giving me anything at all. I'm sorry."

"What's wrong with them?" Alys asked expansively.

"Sometimes that can happen dear. It's not your time to be read."

"But I want to know how my business will fare" she insisted.

Gwen could sense that Alys was desperate.

"I'm so sorry dear, but the cards aren't giving me an answer. I'm not meant to read you now. The spirits must be blocking the reading."

Some people could be surprisingly poor at receiving that news.

"Come again in a few months' time. Maybe the cards will work next time" Gwen cajoled.

"Well, thank you" Alys replied airily, dismissively.

If she could have howled, Alys would have. Instead, she mustered enough vigour to leave the room as if on a mission.

Before joining the guests in the front sitting room, Seren locked eyes with her dignified nain, who said nothing.

"That was a complete waste of time. I don't know why I bothered" announced Alys to her stupefied audience.

Trepidatious, Diana, who was next to visit Gwen set her weary face and followed Seren.

"Hello dear. Please sit down. Goodness. Straightaway the spirits are giving me the name Agnes. Who's that, connected to you?" Gwen asked.

"It's my mother."

"And who's Robert?"

"Could be her uncle."

"Who went to search for a grave in France?"

"I did. I went in search of my great uncle's grave in France. I did that two months ago."

"Your mother was with you dear when you did that. Now, here are the tarot cards. Give them a good shuffle, pick twelve then pass them to me."

"They're difficult to shuffle. They're so big. Much larger than ordinary playing cards."

Gwen smiled.

"They are sometimes tricky to handle" agreed Gwen.

"Here you are."

Diana passed twelve iridescent cards to Gwen.

"You have a lovely husband. He's like Bear Grylls that man. He's a real family man. I can see him cooking barbecues, building tents, climbing mountains."

"That's exactly it. What a perfect description. He's an outdoor person that's for sure."

"He loves you. And your three children. You're all at the centre of his world. Do anything for you all. What a lucky woman you are."

"I know. Yes, we are all lucky" agreed Diana "but we work hard to be a family."

"I can see three children. Two boys and a girl. Those boys are as different as chalk and cheese. Your little girl loves dancing and horse riding."

"Oh yes. That's right. Hari and Ben are not alike at all and well, Esmé is a real stick of dynamite."

"There's another girl on the cards, with the name of a flower."

"We've been trying for our fourth child, but nothing has happened as yet."

"In the spring dear. A little girl with the name of a flower. Perhaps Lily?"

"We'd love that" exclaimed Diana. "Thanks Gwen. You've made my year. How on earth do you know these things?"

With that she walked around the table and gave Gwen a bear hug. *'She was probably taught how to do that by her husband'* ruminated Seren with a smile.

"Nearly there now" reassured Seren to her nain. She knew that tarot reading could be emotionally draining for Gwen. "Only two more visitors to see. Would you like a cup of tea?"

Gwen smiled wearily and nodded. This was not a relatively normal evening. She longed to sit beside her calming Tomos.

Seren delivered tea and bara brith to the front sitting room to dilute the poisonous atmosphere caused by Alys.

"Who's going to be the penultimate visitor?"

"We've decided that I will Seren" volunteered home-loving Luci.

She regarded the back dining room with hope and eager anticipation. As she entered the candlelit room, Gwen looked up benignly and spied bosky hair atop an elfin face.

"Good evening dear. Please sit down."

Luci vigorously took her cue.

"It's a braw evening."

"Ah, you're Scottish. Welcome."

Without invitation, Luci picked up the tarot cards and turned them over and over.

"They're beautiful. Have you had them long?" she enquired confidently.

"They've been in my family for generations. One day, Seren will own them."

By the low oak door, Seren beamed.

"May I shuffle them?"

"Please do."

"I'm full of expectation. I'm so delighted to be doing this but I'm not sure you'll find anything important to say to me."

Gwen smiled.

"Choose twelve cards dear and pass them to me face down."

Luci obliged.

"You were meant to receive a ruby ring. Did you get it?"

"No" replied Luci askance.

"Your grandmother. She's Elizabeth, right?"

"Gosh yes. How do you know that? It's caused me a great deal of unnecessary upset. My mother kept it, and my grandmother told me it was to be mine when she passed."

Gwen carried on.

"I can see that there's a split between you and your mother. Tell her that your grandmother wished you to have her ring. Your mother will pass it to you. It's been difficult for her to let it go as it reminds her so much of happy times seeing your grandmother wear it."

"I see. I thought she was being greedy."

"No. Sentimental. Not selfish."

"You live at home with your parents?"

"Yes."

"And you thought it wasn't worth upsetting your mother, so you've not asked for the ring."

"No. I haven't asked for it."

"You need to learn to be more assertive."

Luci looked doubtful.

"You love cats."

"Yes. I have three of them."

"You've got a beautiful singing voice."

"People tell me I have. I'm part of a choir."

"You like going to shows."

"I do."

"You've got a lot to offer and yet you let something hold you back."

"Hold me back? From what?"

"From living a happy life dear. I see a man around you. He's married. He keeps promising to leave his wife. He's NEVER going to leave his wife. He's too comfortable. He's afraid of losing half of his money and his children. In that order."

Luci gasped as Gwen continued.

"He's self-centred. He never puts you first. Your grandmother in the spirit world is telling you to leave him and get a life."

Luci pushed back her chair which scraped on the floor tiles.

"I'm no good on my own."

"You're on your own already dear. You hardly see him. A couple of kisses here and there is hardly a relationship now, is it? Think about what I've said. By February it will be over, and you can start a new life."

Astonished Luci stared at Gwen. There was now no doubt in her mind that she had been making wrong decisions. Based on what? Lies probably. Lies from him. Lies to herself. She knew what she had to do but doubted she had the strength to carry it out. Bleakly she looked at Gwen.

"You can do this young woman. Be strong."

For a few moments Luci sat awkwardly opposite Gwen. Uncomfortably aware of silence in the room. She wished to stamp her feet, cry, rail, protest but she did none of those things. Rising fiercely, she thanked Gwen, smiled weakly and left the room without a backward glance.

"Phew. Things have been intense tonight Seren."

"They have, but people need to know otherwise they go on blindly, don't they? I'll go and get the last person."

Whilst she waited, Gwen ate a piece of bara brith. Not the delight of eating with Tomos, but it would sustain her until she sat with him at the hearth.

Seren brought in Julie, a heathery, drawn young woman wearing the perfume of failure. Across the table, Gwen sensed an air of hopelessness.

Gently she asked Julie to shuffle the tarot cards.

"Pick twelve dear. That's it. Give them to me."

She smiled at Julie whose face adopted a more optimistic expression.

"Hmmm. Who's not speaking to you?"

"My sister."

"She kicked up a fuss about a funeral?"

"She did. She didn't want our mum to be cremated. She wanted her to be buried and now she's not speaking to me."

"Invite her round for a cup of tea dear. Her stance will soften."

Julie looked surprised, embarrassed, and guilty all at once.

"When your husband has finished renovating your house, you'll move. I see a new front door. Invite her before that otherwise the rift may be too wide to breach."

"I will. Yes, I'll do that. Life's too short, isn't it?"

"Your husband. I see him knocking down walls. He works with wood."

"He never stops working. He's so committed to his job."

"Who's Sheila?"

"His mother."

"She's passed?"

"Yes."

"She's handing him flowers. Seems an extraordinary thing to do, doesn't it? Hand flowers to her son? But it's for the three little spirits."

"Three?"

"Yes. I see three little spirits."

"You do?"

"Have you lost twins and a baby boy?"

"Yes. We're on our last round of IVF and I don't know what to do. What will happen if it's not successful? If we can't have children? I don't know what to do."

"Go for it. If it doesn't work, you will have tried. If you don't have one more attempt, you'll always wonder what might have been. You're a strong couple. Your husband loves you very much. Together you'll get on with life if this doesn't turn out the way you hope."

"We've been married for five years. We desperately want children."

"Take the opportunity to try again. You love each other. You can face this together."

"Oh Gwen. I don't know if I'm strong enough. Look at me. I look about a hundred years old."

"No, you've come this far. You are strong enough to face this. You'll rely on each other for support."

Sadly, Julie wiped away tears.

"Thank you, Gwen. Thank you for taking the time to see me."

"Come back and see me any time you're ready. Take care dear."

Julie left the room but not before she turned to Gwen and blew her a kiss of thanks.

The dim candlelight crackled. Gwen silently and gently drew breath recalling the evening's adumbrated events. An overwhelming sense of presage engulfed her. She inhaled the gentle golden glow of light that shyly peeped through the oak door and waited for the return of her granddaughter. Perhaps Tomos was right, she should take the occasion to speak to Seren about the visions which disturbed her so. Seren had much to learn, and she would, in time.

Chapter 2 – The Legate

The past makes us the people we are in the future.

"Just before we go to sleep, and before we awaken, is the time that spirits are most active. A delicate, ethereal, cobwebby caul can fall between the real and imaginary, sleep and wakefulness, the conscious and unconscious mind. When we dream, or daydream, we can witness the most startling of things. Remember that Seren" counselled her astute nain. "And know this. Most people die at those times. The Ysbryd come to help them cross over."

It was the heavy, double-edged sword with its ivory hilt, clutched in his huge taut right hand which immediately stabbed her heart, metaphorically speaking. As the commander of five thousand men, this Legionary Legate wore the deadly gladius on his left, drawing it ominously from a leather covered scabbard. Seren spotted the resilient carbon steel edges and short, triangular tip in the silvery moonlight. She flinched. An efficient tool for stabbing especially in the hands of this dynamic killing machine as he practised his routine.

'Tomos taught me that Legates existed in Ancient Rome, but they don't in modern Wales. This feels real, as though I could touch him, smell him and he wouldn't evaporate' dreamt Seren.

That evening the Vardre's enchanting bosom was thrust into a push-up brassiere which acted as a cushion for Seren to watch events unfold. At once she noticed his muscular frame, close-clipped black hair, stubbly beard, and broad shoulders. As her eyes shyly moved downwards, a Roman leather arming doublet lay on his linen undershirt and the finest woven tunic lolled softly upon his walnut-brown torso. For majesty, a thick leather skirt hid the top half of his chunky legs. Skilfully criss-crossing his enormous dusty feet were handcrafted, leather open-toed sandals. Heavy metal body armour, held together by vertical leather strips, a war-hammered shield, and a silver cassis with sideways horsehair, dented by a cacophony of shrieking blows, rested close by him. She knew his eyes were a dashing lovat colour, that he sported tattoos of a bull and eagle on his shoulders and the mark of Julius Caesar's elite Legio X Equestris on his left calf, because she'd seen him before.

Her sharp amber eyes were drawn to the twenty-six-year-old commander of Roman legionaries and his fighting silver-grey mastiff Cane Corso called Hercules, which accompanied him in peace and war. Five of his high-ranking Centurions joined him from the fort at Canovium. They sat around a gilt campfire discussing strategy and tactics for their next battle.

"We are the most feared warriors. An elite fighting force. We don't need to prove anything Titus."

"I don't want to lead the men into an unnecessary battle Marcus. Our warriors need rest and nourishment. They are tired and hungry. We must put their needs above our own. Always. They can be fractious if not fed" Titus said sagely to his Optio.

"For ten years you have fought skilfully. You've led us with courage Titus. The legionaries will do as you ask" added a solemn Gaius.

"They will Gaius. In the next battle with the Ordovices the men will need to be in close formation. That will disrupt and overwhelm the enemy. But our warriors are starving and can't be strong in combat. We need more food from the farm. We are all famished. The legionaries must be fed first. Lucius, will you organise for meat and vegetables to be brought from the homestead?"

"Yes Titus. The girl will help us" agreed Lucius.

"You mean Ceres, the one who's named after the goddess of agriculture?" asked Titus.

"Yes. Such striking amber eyes, long corn-ringed russet braids, and an air of flamboyance as she walks."

"Antonius, you've not taken much notice of her then?" joshed Titus.

Perched on the hill, a puzzled Seren held her breath as she listened in silence to the humming weave and weft of chatter between the Legate, Titus Marius, and his officers.

'They're describing me' she thought exuberantly. 'So, in this dream my name must be Ceres and he's noticed me, a Welsh girl. His name is Titus.'

A giddy gallimaufry of sensations quivered through Seren.

She had read about the Goddess Ceres, the ultimate goddess of life. Daughter of Saturn and Ops, sister of Jupiter, Juno, Pluto, Neptuno, and Vesta. This deity was connected to harvest, agriculture, fertility, and motherhood. She protected Roman plebians and promoted the rights of women. With a modest and sympathetic demeanour, Ceres aided mortals.

Seren recalled the legend of the Goddess:

When Pluto was shot by Cupid's arrow he fell in love with Ceres' daughter, Proserpina and abducted her to live with him in the Underworld. By torchlight the Goddess searched for her daughter, abandoning her responsibilities, leaving crops to die and mortals to starve. When Ceres found Proserpina in the Underworld, Pluto agreed to return her to the land of the living for six months of the year but only if Proserpina would live with him for the other six months. Proserpina agreed.

The Ancient Romans supposed that the four seasons were a result of Ceres' search for her daughter. When Proserpina was missing in the autumn and winter months, crops and people died because the Goddess was distressed. When Proserpina returned during the spring and summer months, Ceres rejoiced, crops and people thrived.

Seren dragged her mind back to contemplation of Titus.

A temperate man, as cool, calculating and determined as a crow leading a murder, assiduous Titus cut a solitary figure when she usually observed him under obscurity of darkness. Enjoying his own company, forceful with those around him, Titus was an esteemed, intractable man. His legionaries knew he didn't suffer fools. Handling intricate strategy, he assumed men were all equal and Titus planned in meticulous detail every conflict. He fought alongside his soldiers, laughed with them, went hungry with them. In the violence of their lives, they would die for him. As would he for them. Unconditional love.

Exhaling a long breath of air, Seren paused for a moment, and observed him again. She noticed that the world was never silent. Even the grass embracing the Vardre whispered softly *'return tomorrow on full moon'*. As she stood to leave, Seren wondered if Titus would ever feel unconditional love for the woman Ceres who lived in the homestead. This became Seren's ritual. Watching and waiting for Titus and possibly Ceres, in her night-time visions.

What followed were empty sleepless hours leading to the early arrival of tomorrow, the day of the full moon.

"You look tired Seren. Didn't you sleep well?"

"No nain. I have a lot on my mind."

"Be vigilant on the Vardre Seren and beware the coming Ides of March."

Startled, unsettled, and a little embarrassed, Seren reasoned she had shadowed her dreams. Surely her nain wouldn't know about them? From the kitchen window she watched her grandparents leave the farmhouse to feed the cattle and toil the land. Usually, she helped with those chores but today was her turn to cook meals. Before the starry evening appeared and Seren could make her way to the Vardre, startlingly Titus visited the farm.

A shortage of labourers meant Seren was alone in the farmhouse. She dozed in the kitchen whilst chicken soup gurgled over the wood-burning fire. In her daydreams she saw Ceres in the kitchen who was watching Titus's strapping frame striding down the lane towards the front door before time allowed for a check in the mirror. The Legate saved any embarrassment about Ceres' appearance by forcefully informing her of his men's hunger. Nothing could dissuade her from his appeal. Smelling freshly baked bread and hearing soup simmering heightened his appetite. Unused to dealing with women and hardly pausing to draw breath he pronounced stroppily:

"What food could you provide for my men today, Ceres? They're starving and need to be fed before battle. They require the sustenance of well-bred animals. I've been informed that you and your grandparents tend the homestead well."

Of tough character, Ceres replied:

"Livestock must be killed sir, and the vegetables collected which takes time. Your legionaries ought to help as there aren't enough farmworkers to toil the land. My grandparents and I cannot do all those chores between us. I'm working in the kitchen and could take turns with my nain to prepare and cook the food."

"I'll send some men to assist."

"Thank you. Would you like to eat now? We have soup and bread followed by blackberry and apple pie."

Titus admired the girl's freshness. An ingénue, her innocence appealed to this intense fighting man who enjoyed the combat of war, despite losing some of his soldiers. Hunger made his stomach rumble, there was no option but to acquiesce as Ceres busied herself around the kitchen and instructed him to sit at the oak table. Surprisingly, this brawny, belligerent man, surrendered completely to her. Without explanation, once fed, Titus left the farm but not before bending to kiss a blushing Ceres gently on the cheek and thanking her with a courteous bow. As an observer, Seren felt surprised that the Legate had kissed farm girl Ceres.

That evening, under the light of the full moon, Seren sneaked to the Vardre in heightened anticipation of observing lion-hearted Titus. Worshipped by his legionaries, living, and fighting beside them, the Legate chose to sit alone by a small fire and stared at the constellations from his lair. Solitude weighed heavy. Titus contemplated battle whilst images of beguiling Ceres smouldered and swayed in the orange firelight.

Witnessing how much better he looked after being fed, Seren silently observed this giant from the safety of a small distance. She wanted to shout out to him but didn't because she noticed the young woman Ceres hiding behind a hawthorn bush. Startled and intrigued, Seren watched the pair.

Almost thirty hours of sleeplessness had left Titus exhausted. He imagined that Ceres was close by, in the wood, considering his movements. Carefully his head turned slightly to the left. She *was* there. He felt her presence. Slowly he rose. Given the circumstances, Seren knew that Titus had spotted Ceres. Trying to escape would be foolhardy. Titus was a trained combat murderer, used to predatory conduct. Ceres would not survive. Seren observed as Titus prowled menacingly towards Ceres.

"What are you doing in the forests at this time of night? It's dangerous to be here. You could be killed" questioned Titus irritably.

The truth would out as her nain would say.

"I was watching you."

"Why?"

"You're interesting. And intense. And a little bit scary."

He laughed and said:

"At the farm, I saw how you felt about me. I saw it in your eyes. You can't hide. Your eyes reveal your soul."

Relieved, Seren watched as Ceres smiled and heard her say:

"I don't want to feel like this about you. It's not a choice I made. You have wheedled your way in as each evening I watch you on the Vardre" she confessed.

The Legate bent to kiss Ceres. She stood on tiptoes, face upturned, wanting to be kissed.

For twelve nights, as the waning gibbous moon dissolved into a waning crescent moon Seren visited the Vardre and waited for Titus to join Ceres on the untidy edge of a copse.

"Here, take this. I made it for you."

Titus handed Ceres a pugio fashioned with a mercurial golden amber handle.

"What do I need a dagger for?"

"We live in dangerous times. I'll teach you how to kill a man."
"On the farm I kill livestock. I'm used to slaughter."

"It's easy to butcher. Anyone can do that. To kill with dignity. That's also easy. I can teach you that too. Living with the memories of pinching someone's hopes, dreams, loves. Taking them away from their family. Seizing their future. Removing their life. That's what's challenging. Knowing that you have done that. Living with it during daylight hours, and watching it replay as you dream. That's chilling. Overseeing violent death."

"But you slay all the time. That's your mission. You lead men into brutal battle. That's why you're here. To take what isn't yours."

"I know, but I have a heart. I have sympathy for the ones who die."

"So how do you live with yourself?"

"I understand and trust Plato's explanations about the teachings of Socrates. He held that the soul is immortal, is repeatedly reborn and exists to be reincarnated in another until our lessons have been learned. Above all else, nurture of the soul is important. Our soul dominates our thoughts and must be attuned. It's our inner voice. Socrates obeyed his dreams, his mental visions, his inner voice, and I do the same."

"You murder people for their land and women."

"War is in our genes. It's what we do to make our country great. To make ourselves heroes. This is my fate, to lead my men and be revered throughout the lands."

"You believe in Destiny then?"

"I do. And freewill. And spirit guides who share our journey and take us to be judged when we die. Ultimately Destiny decides our fate. We must suffer to learn. Learning should not be an easy process. We need to fail, to discover from mistakes, to get things wrong. Only a fool doesn't learn from the error of his ways. Socrates esteemed the virtues of temperance, justice, bravery, liberality, and truth. I try to embody those qualities."

"It's brave to slay someone?"

"There are many types of bravery. Sometimes it's braver to walk away."

"You never have?"

"I prepare our battles to the minutest detail so that my men never have to retreat, but I always have a withdrawal plan."

Each evening he taught Ceres how to use a pugio to defend herself, afterwards they lay together, surging with emotion until sunlight shattered darkness. She grew to love this fearsomely multifaceted man. He promised her she would not want for anything.

Titus offered Ceres an amber ring, with the inscription TM, a tiny eagle and SPQR on the inside.

"I had this made for you. The amber is from this place" he said, looking around the Vardre. "There are shadows in the stone that are meant to be there. They represent the ghosts of life, the amber is brightness, the spirit of life."

"What does the SPQR signify?" asked Ceres.

"SPQR? Senatus PopulusQue Romanus, The Senate, and People of Rome" was his noble response.

Titus placed the ring on Seren's finger as a token of his affection for her.

"It's indestructible and will always belong to you" he said gruffly.

"Why amber?" For you, what's important about amber?" she questioned.

"It represents the sun. The sun god Sol is most significant, around him everything revolves. It's a talisman of protection which promises the renewal of life. Everything grows in the sun, and a little rain."

The thirteenth night Titus failed to appear. When he was absent on the fourteenth night Seren panicked, recalled her nain's foreshadowing, and feared for Titus and Ceres. On the Ides of March, as Seren observed Ceres trudge up the Vardre, out of the blackness a Roman Legionary screamed at Ceres not to enter the area. Seren felt the freezing chill which had filled Ceres' lungs. In the distance, the shrieks and yells of battles and slaying on the Vardre began to be heard as far as the farmhouse. The rancid smell of burning blood, flesh, hair, and sinew, the vile stench of death, illuminated the senses of both women, but only Ceres was living this life.

Titus had been wrong. Ceres *was* left wanting. What she desired was one more tiny moment in time with him. As she sat under the gnarled Devil's Tree, Ceres clutched the amber handle of her pugio and wept for the soldier of Rome she may never see again in this lifetime.

'*What would Ceres do?*' pondered Seren. '*Would she wait? Fight? Leave?*' Seren shuddered, terrified for Titus and Ceres.

****

These stinging, inexplicable images which propelled Seren through time and space disturbed her. She sensed the need to speak with her nain about them. She had made notes of her dreams about Titus and Ceres, held securely in a crimson leather box which Tomos had made for her a long time ago. When her tongue finally loosened, Seren approached her nain.

"I think I'm going mad nain."

"You do tlws,[5] why is that?" her grandmother questioned calmly.

"There are dreams or visions or something that I have which feel real enough to make my heart clunk, my lungs breathless and my skin perspire. Sometimes it's as if I'm watching myself participate in another life. I don't know if my life is being pushed in time from behind, or if I'm being pulled from the future. I'm confused and the visions frighten me."

Her nain smiled.

"My cariad[6] tlws. What you're experiencing is past life regression, darling girl."

---

[5] Beautiful.
[6] Love.

"What's that nain? I've never heard of it. My dreams and daydreams are startling. Are you saying they could be revelations?"

"When we dream or meditate our unconscious mind helps reveal recollections of former lives. Or can show us our future lives."

"Do you think it's possible I could have lived in Ancient Roman times? That I could have loved a soldier of Rome? That my name could be Ceres?"

"Yes, my darling. That's conceivable."

"And smell the battle, hear the shrieks of war, feel a man's touch, and long for him?"

"Absolutely."

"That's weird because when I have these visions, or dreams, or whatnots, it's as if I'm looking down at myself. How do I stop it, or do I carry on? I'm confused."

"Only you can decide that Seren. Sometimes the lives we've lived before, or the life we are about to live, can be particularly challenging to visualise. Parts of any life might be violent, cruel, sad. In life we encounter challenges, which may become more frequent and increasingly demanding as we step along our path. If we learn lessons from each test, we become more enlightened, and our pathway opens to reveal the extraordinary as we aim to become our higher self. It's all about learning lessons from the past to go forward into the future."

"Nain, do I need to learn anything about past life regression?"

"I can teach you all you need to know about it Seren. It's up to you if you ever use the knowledge."

"Will you teach me tomorrow please?"

"I will. Let's go to the secret tunnel, away from the hubbub of the farmhouse. I'll wrap you in a blanket to keep you warm and bring an amber crystal to provide a strong barrier against any negative energies. You'll be protected."

"Nain. Amber? In my dreams, or visions, or whatever they are, a Roman soldier gave me, as Ceres, an amber ring, and a dagger with an amber handle for protection. How strange. I have a feeling that Rome is important to me. Why would that be? I'm a young woman from Wales. What's the purpose of past life regression? To see if I've lived in Rome?"

"It's not necessarily to see if you have lived in Rome. We are going to see your soul's journey. Where your past lives have been. You may visit other lives before you arrive in Rome. Past life memories could be responsible for the wounds people carry around with them in this life. Feelings such as fear, rejection, control or hurt. It may be that you must learn lessons from past lives for instance, forgiveness, bravery, how to share or love unconditionally. We can all try to understand ourselves better if we witness the different lives we have led. Past life regression could open the way to that. Let's see what happens tomorrow Seren. Wait and see. There are many doors you can go through to unlock *different* past lives."

2014

Chapter 3 – Time Shifts Backwards

We cant change the past. We live in the now. We can change the future.

Seren and her nain heaved a stone flag from the farmhouse floor which led to the secret passageway. Struggling to carry lit candles, and nain's hawkstaff, the pair clambered down the steep stone steps and followed a long path to a musty place where the tunnel widened and revealed part of the hidden Temple of Mithras. Roman legionaries had secretly worshipped here. Dim carvings of Mithras slaughtering a bull and dining with Sol, the Sun God could be depicted on wooden pilings which held up the ceiling. Gwen led Seren down worn stone steps to the central nave as shadows in the northern alcove bounced and sprang nimbly.

One day, many years ago nain had found a piece of driftwood on Conwy beach which Tomos had fashioned into a hawk's head on a long pole. Nain had placed a blue appetite crystal in the hawk's eye socket as this stone helped her connect with angels, the spirit world and astral travel. She called it her hawkstaff. A little like Gandolf the Wizard, nain worked with her staff as it acted as an amplifier of magic. She used hers at the beginning of magic and stomped it on the floor 'to put energy into the ground'. When she had finished, nain would say 'the deal is sealed' by banging hawkstaff on the ground.

Soothing in manner, Gwen instructed Seren to lie in the nave and wrapped her in a Welsh plaid, handstitched red and black tapestry blanket so that she would remain warm throughout the ritual. By contrast, Seren was somewhat trepidatious.

"I'm a little afraid, nain" embarrassed Seren exclaimed, with a quick glance at Gwen "but curiosity is getting the better of me."

"Don't be fearful my cariad tlws. I'll be with you. You'll still hear my voice and feel sensations. I'm going to use my hawkstaff and when we start, I'll stomp it on the floor to put energy into the ground and when we're finished, I'll stomp it on the floor again and say, the deal is sealed by banging onto the ground."

Seren breathed deeply through her nose and exhaled through her mouth to calm her nerves, placing total trust in her nain.

"We will meditate before doing the past life regression. Make yourself comfortable now that you're lying on the nave. You're in control, you can stop at any time. I'll guide you. I'm going to stomp hawkstaff now" said nain and banged her hawkstaff on the ground "to put energy into the ground. Choose a spot on the ceiling and focus upon it. Breathe deeply to the count of five, hold your breath to the count of five, breathe out to the count of five. I'll go from ten to one. As I say each number blink your eyes."

Gwen carried on in this way until Seren reached a state of introspection.

"Can you see the steps?"

"Yes."

"As I count up to ten, walk up the steps, slowly" instructed Gwen.

Seren listened intently and sighed.

"Can you see a chair?"

"Yes"

"This is your safe space. You can always return to this chair."

"Thank you."

"There are several doors before you. Choose one door which is drawing you to it. Tell me the year on that door."

"The year? It's 1518."

"Good. Now open the door and walk through it into a past life. Tell me what you see, hear, and feel" instructed Gwen.

"I will."

"How old are you?" queried Gwen.

"I'm eighteen-years-old."

"What can you see?"

"Minstrels are playing instruments on a balcony. I'm at a vibrant dance in a grand manor. The characters are of Tudor times, and the succulent smells of charcoal roasted chicken, pork, beef, rabbit, and lamb dangle enticingly in the hot air. It's feels like I'm watching a film, can empathise with the actors and experience their sensations."

"What do you look like?" questioned Gwen.

"My hair is pulled back and pinned on top of my head in an orange and gold coloured velvet gable. Wearing a stunning orange silk top framed with gilded embroidery, and an amber seashell-shaped brooch fastened to it at the back of my neck, I'm twinkling in the candlelight. My skirt, of the same silk material and brocade, has a tiny, pinched waist with hoops around the bottom to increase its edge. It's called a farthingale which covers me from waist to toe. The suede orange slippers which embellish my feet are so delicate and soft they look like they'd enable me to dance all evening."

Gwen could hear the excitement in Seren's voice.

"Who are you with?"

"John my fiancé. With his white silk shirt, ruffs at the neck and wrists, a doublet with close fitting hose and brown suede boots, he looks adorable. I feel so proud of him. I know that he holds the honourable position of training peregrine falcons for King Henry VIII. That's why we're at the dance because he works with the King. They have become friends."

"What are you doing?"

"We are dancing together. The Galliard. John is so athletic he enjoys doing the high leap. He's amusing" responded Seren. "His lovat eyes reveal his soul. Steadfast John."

"Tell me about the atmosphere at the manor house."

"I know that we are having a great time together, but I have a premonition of foreboding. John calls me a witch because I experience such presentiments but there's an unpleasant ambience. Although I'm happy to be with John, I feel anxious. My heart is racing."

"What are you apprehensive about?" interrogated Gwen.

"The King. Henry VIII. He's disappointed. It's obvious, he's grim-faced."

"Is he unhappy with you?" persisted Gwen.

"No. Of course not! Not with me, nor John. There are half-truths, speculative comments and gossip around the room surrounding the King and his wife, Catherine of Aragon. When we speak privately, John says that the King needs an heir to his dynasty. He's afraid of conspiracy within the court, civil war breaking out, or a war with France if he doesn't have a son. He wants to secure peace within his realm. The couple did have a son, but he died within weeks of being born. They were distraught about their loss according to those closest to them both.

The Queen's Maid has apprised John that Catherine has taken to staying in her room. She finds it tricky to face people. The King demeans her, finds fault with her, is unsympathetic when she cries. They were both longing for this baby boy. Henry VIII does not understand that childbirth is very difficult and dangerous for women. Every time she becomes pregnant, Catherine's in danger of losing her life. She seems to willingly put her husband's ambition above her own wellbeing.

The court doctor confided in John because they hunt together, that there have been many pregnancies which resulted in heartbreak for the King and Queen. It is whispered around the court that if they have a daughter, she would be viewed as a weaker leader than a male heir.

John has told me that the Queen yearns to return to the warmth and brightness of Spain. To safely walk the impressive, dramatic gardens of the Alhambra Palace, to hug her beloved mother Isabella, but she cannot return. She is grief-stricken. The poor woman has endured so much loss around her. Her sister Isabella died in childbirth, her first husband Arthur, Henry's brother died soon after they were married, closely followed by the untimely death of her dashing father, Ferdinand. Such tragedy around that woman.

Henry believes he is cursed because he married Catherine, his brother's widow. Rumours around the court say that the King has a vile temper and is peevish. Catherine cannot speak to him without being shouted at outrageously."

"It's interesting to hear about the King. Can you see him now?"

"He's an intriguing character. Yes, I can see him clearly. There is much to tell you about him."

"What's he doing? Dancing?"

"No. He's not dancing. He's sitting beside Catherine who looks wan. The King is lustfully surveying a striking, dark-haired woman who's wearing a white dress adorned with elaborate gold detailing. John, who seems to know everyone and everything, says she's called Anne Boleyn."

"Do you want to tell me anything more about the King?" questioned Gwen.

"He practises falconry with John. The King is a keen sportsman and around the court he's known as an intellectual genius, but some say he's a braggart, egotistical and shallow."

"Take me away from the dancing" instructed Gwen. "Move on a few years. Are you and John married?"

Seren smiled beatifically.

"Yes, we are" responded Seren. "We have two beautiful children, William, and Agnes but my heart feels heavy with unhappiness."

"Describe to me what's happening in your life" probed Gwen "to make you sad."

"John is in terrible trouble. We cannot sleep or eat. We fear for his life."

"What kind of tribulation? What's happened?" was Gwen's rapid reply.

"John has been accused by one of the King's men of stealing falcons. It's an offence punishable by death. It's not true. He hasn't stolen anything. He wouldn't. But he will go to trial. The only way I can think of helping him is by pleading personally with the Lord Chamberlain on behalf of my husband. If John is tried and found guilty, he will be publicly hanged, we will be thrown out of our home. Not only will his life end, but so too will ours. Mine and the children's, we all love each other so much. John is the centre of our world."

"Who has accused John?"

"There's a loathsome little man in green breeches, who owns a huge manor house nearby. He covets me and wants John to swing. This odious toad is the one who has spread vicious rumours about my husband. John is incandescent with fury and threatening to beat the man which will make things worse."

Seren weeps and Gwen nudged her to shift along a few more years.

"Tell me what's happening. Is King Henry VIII still the monarch?"

"Oh, it's a mess. Yes, he's still the monarch and has caused all kinds of suffering in the realm. We are a Catholic country. Henry wishes to marry Anne Boleyn but cannot unless his marriage to Catherine is annulled on the grounds that she was his brother's wife. William Wardham, the Archbishop of Canterbury, had previously objected to Henry marrying Catherine on the same grounds, but he was ignored.

Catherine has claimed that Arthur did not consummate the marriage. John has been told by the Queen's Maid that Catherine has refused to move into a convent, rebuffed Henry's exhortations and has appealed to the Pope in Rome for his support. The Pope assists her because Catherine's nephew, Charles V, is the Holy Roman Emperor. Obviously, he will not agree to a dissolution of the marriage. Henry is putting pressure on the Archbishop of Canterbury to declare his marriage void. There is a lot of fear, tension, and disquiet in the kingdom.

"Move on a few years. Describe what's happening."

"King Henry has been in ebullient mood. He caused a significant spiritual split with Rome to make himself Head of the Protestant Church of England and divorced Catherine of Aragon. Poor woman. John says she was devastated. She's been ostracised and can't even see her daughter, Mary. He has married Anne Boleyn, and a baby girl has been born to them named Elizabeth. Henry is still a dissatisfied, unhappy person. He appears to be perverse. He has everything and yet he has nothing. I feel that Henry will never be content and that for all her coquetry, Anne will not be joyful either."

"Move on a few years. What happened about the accusations flung about John?" questioned Gwen soothingly.

"Thankfully, the King saw fit to intervene with our terrifying ordeal. Henry VIII and John are expert huntsmen, applying patience and skill. They are firm friends. They have hunted together using gyrfalcons and peregrines for years. The King was aware of John's honourable character. He grasped that John would not be imprudent. He is not a thief! John's a good man. A respectable man. He focuses on his family and his work. Nothing else. Henry VIII pardoned John. That was the correct thing to do. Undoubtedly."

Seren is prodded by Gwen to say more.

"Tell me what happened after John was excused."

"We never felt able to settle in the house knowing that the toad lived in the hall in the neighbourhood and might, at any moment, upset our lives again. My ministrations helping women in childbirth and providing potions to the locals began to make John anxious too as there was much disquiet about what some call *witchcraft*. I'm hardly Homer's enchantress

Circe, portrayed as turning men into swine, lions, or wolves by using herbs and potions. Although I do admit to using special skills with remedies and words, *that's all*. I don't curse people. I don't have a *familiar*. By that I mean, no black cat, no rat, and we are escaping the toad! We are anxious because spiritual beliefs are at the forefront of everyone's mind since the break with Rome. As for the toad who lives in the hall. That sinister man developed boils on his face. They'll never recede, but they arrived naturally one day because of his poor blood circulation, nothing to do with me!"

Seren chortled.

Gwen could not refrain from asking Seren to explain how she helped people.

"In modest ways. My nain passed on to me an ancient grimoire. I burn sage to *smudge* rooms and use salt to ward off evil spirits. Those neighbours who feel anxious receive a concoction of pollen dust extracted from the spikes of the lycopodium tree to settle their nerves. For mental exertion, sleeplessness, or wounds I brew arnica leaves in a charcoal pot and if someone is suffering from headaches, a mixture of the white flowers and leaves of the bryonia plant works well. Goodness, I suppose I do sound like Circe, but I promise, I don't take revenge! I try to work for the highest good.

John was correct. We needed to relocate. He believed that idle blethering could have brought us down. We had navigated that choppy channel of unfathomable depths once before. Although I was viewed as a respectable member of our village, using my healing skills for the benefit of others, if there was one complaint about me, if I were to be accused of witchcraft, I might have been investigated and possibly strung up. In many ways it's laughable because I've never caused miscarriage, inflicted death on livestock or humans and never cursed anyone. After much deliberation we decided to move, away from the influence of the carbuncled louse landowner who'll never find a suitable wife!"

Gwen smiled and asked, "Where did you relocate?"

"We've not been here very long. An aunt of John's very kindly secured a role for him as gamekeeper based at the Bodysgallen Watchtower in Conwy, Wales. We uprooted ourselves. We packed a cart, took our two children and two dogs then left without a trace. We bumbled for days along muddy dirt tracks."

"What is your new home like?" questioned Gwen affectionately.

"We live in a hidden outbuilding which is attached to the narrow five-storey watchtower. The tower is used as a lookout to prevent attack on Conwy Castle. Inside the tower is a stunning anti-clockwise spiral staircase which can be unforgiving if we are on the fifth floor and remember that we've left something on the ground floor! The fortified side walls keep our home warm and cosy. It's a special place.

John is accountable for taming and training peregrines and gerfalcons, safeguarding them and their quarry. He's responsible for managing the fecund Marl Woods around the watchtower, tending the fertile soil, and rearing sheep. John frequently comes home exhausted, but I try to help him cultivate the land as much as possible, by growing vegetables and herbs.

He's got another enormous undertaking which is to protect a range of wildlife from poachers in the forests. Oftentimes the pilferers are quarrelsome, aggressive, irrational. It's understandable. This is not a land of fairness for all. The pilferers live in an impoverished makeshift rural community, they're often cold, hungry. They're trying to protect their families and provide for them. They're proud people. Falconry is a sport for the rich the results of which are not used to aid the destitute. John understands the locals' plight. If there are plenty of deer, pheasant, and grouse, he has permission to kill a few and pass them on to the inhabitants of Conwy and surrounding areas."

"What are your children doing?" was Gwen's automatic reaction.

"Our daughter Agnes, well, she is married to a gentle giant, who is a gentleman. They live in a house near us on Llyn Owen-y-ddol and have two gorgeous, mischievous daughters. Our beloved son, William, who works with his father, is about to marry a wonderful local lacemaker named Clare. We are ever so excited."

Seren gave a spontaneous cry of delight.

"Sometimes as I walk towards the house along the hedged walkways that John's created to hide the watchtower from prying eyes, I can't believe our good fortune. I often climb the spiral staircase because the views from the watchtower, over Snowdon and the Conwy Estuary leading to the Irish Sea, are spectacular. Our home is near a delightful village called Llanrhos. We are happy. We are settled."

"It sounds as though your life is going well after the mishap with John and the fright with the frog" said Gwen tenderly.

"It's time to find the chair Seren, go back to the chair."

After a few moments Seren exclaimed: "I've found it."

"Good. Sit on it. I'm going to stomp hawkstaff *now*" said nain and banged her hawkstaff on the ground "the deal is sealed. I'll count back from ten to zero. When I say zero your eyes will open. You will return to your current life."

An ashen Seren began to re-emerge from her meditative state. Bone cold, despite the warm blanket, she shivered.

"How are you feeling my cariad tlws? Your face is luminescent" commended Gwen. "Is there something you have learned about yourself during that past life regression?"

"Nain, I expected to visit a past life and see Titus, the Roman Legate I mentioned to you, and Ceres, but instead I visited Tudor times and shared my life with a man named John. It's confusing. John had the same colour and shape of eyes as Titus. He was fearless like him too. I felt as though I loved John with the same depth that I felt for Titus. Could John have been Titus but in a different era? Is that possible?"

"Interesting. Yes, cariad tlws. That's conceivable."

"And in that life, the Tudor life, I learned about injustice."

"Yes cariad. You come from a long line of resilient, powerful women, all passionate about helping others."

"In my Tudor life I created potions for others' benefit. John called me a witch. Why didn't he call me a healer or a midwife? Why a witch? Is it because I experienced feelings of foreboding? Nain am I a witch? Is that one of the lessons I needed to learn from Tudor times? That I'm a witch?" Questions tumbled out of a bewildered Seren.

"A white one, darling girl. A gwrach gwyn.[7] A white witch. One who will learn to work for others' highest good."

"Tell me about a gwrach gwyn. Are you one? We've never spoken about witches. I need to understand."

"That explanation cannot be summed up in five minutes cariad tlws. I hope you will find the story illuminating when it's told, but let's leave that for another time. We must return to the farmhouse, away from this chilly, damp air. You need a hot drink, a biscuit, and a bath. In that order! Come, your taid will be anxious about us."

"Please will you tell me soon nain. Let it be soon. I'm confused."

"You need time to percolate the past life you've just experienced Seren. I promise we will talk about things soon enough."

---

[7] White witch.

2014

Chapter 4 – A Gwrach Gwyn?

Is our mind shielded from greater awareness?

Stuck in thought, Seren arrived at Bryn Gosol having spent the afternoon on her own. She spotted her nain at the back of the farmhouse, carefully picking nettles in her herb garden.

"You look windswept Seren, what have you been doing?"

"Wandering the Vardre. Thinking. Collecting spring water in this bucket. It'll be a full moon tonight nain. I'd like us to make moon water together please."

"Take these nettle leaves into the kitchen. Bring to me four jars from the pantry."

Seren did as asked, washed the nettle leaves then burst into the fully stocked larder and grabbed four clean jam jars.

"Here you are nain."

"Excuse my dirt riddled hands" her nain replied, as she wiped clumps of earth onto her green apron and took the containers. "I'll hold the jars cariad tlws, you pour the spring water and as you do, think of the energies of the Moon Goddess Luna."

Seren did as requested, closing her eyes for a moment. Even so, she didn't spill a drop.

"We can put them here on the stone windowsill Seren, outside the kitchen, as it's going to be a clear evening. Grab four crystals and we can put one in each jar."

Thanks to her nain's orderly nature, several crystals were in various glass pots near the olive-green back door, just behind the holly bush. There was a holly bush outside the front door too, close to the lavender, '*for protection*' as her nain would say. Once, she had told Seren that medieval knights tucked holly leaves into their garments for protection before they went into battle. Secretly Seren thought this was an extreme form of self-harm and wondered if the knights were prickled to death. Seren chose four crystals and showed them to her nain.

"Oh, citrine. The juicy colour of sweet honey. A great choice for rituals as it brings with it vibrancy, happiness, increases confidence and sparks the intellect. Pop it into this first jar."

With aplomb the crystal plummeted to the bottom of the clear glass container.

"Oh look, the purple of this amethyst crystal matches exactly the thyme in my little herb garden. Did I tell you Seren that amethysts help promote vivid dreams and visions? This little crystal also improves psychic ability and intuition. Put it in" said her grandmother handing Seren the second spring water filled glass jar.

"Maybe that's why I saw the Legate so powerfully then, I'd been handling amethysts" exclaimed Seren as she turned and placed the jar on the stone windowsill .

"Could be. What else have you brought cariad tlws?"

"I chose moonstone because I think it stimulates passion, true love, encourages prophetic and pleasant dreams."

"Correct. It's a very powerful crystal. It enhances the world of women. Pop it in."

The luminous crystal bubbled its way to the bottom of the transparent glass jar.

"Which one is next Seren?"

"Selenite."

"Why have you chosen selenite?" probed her nain.

"I'm not sure. It just appealed to me."

"Interesting choice Seren. It helps calm the mind and open prophetic pathways. It dispels negative energies and is an aura cleanser."

"Yes, I thought I'd heard you say something about it dissolving negative energies given off by other people. Is it linked to the Goddess Luna?"

"Yes, that's right. Well remembered. It helps with spells! Drop it in here."

The virtually transparent crystal plunked to the bottom of the fourth jar. Seren checked they were securely placed on the windowsill.

"There. They're lined up like sentries now. Ready to absorb the moonlight. Thanks, nain."

"Great choice Seren. Well done. The water can bathe overnight in the light of the moon. Tomorrow, we can add the moon water to our bath water to enhance our spiritual energy. I think I'll use some of it to clean the steps and floors for protection. We'll boil what's left over to make moon tea. Would you like to help me pick some rosemary, and thyme? I'll wash and dry the leaves for cooking, and probably use some in my tinctures."

"Are you running out of ingredients for your potions?"

"Yes. I've been using a lot of the herbs we picked last week in my cooking. Did I tell you that the y Tylwyth Teg,[8] the faery folk, love thyme?"

"You did."

"Always consider the faeries Seren. And remember, with witchcraft, harm none."

"I will always consider the faeries. You used to read *The Magic Faraway Tree* to me which inspired my love of faeries and sparked my imagination. I'll try not to harm anyone with my magic" responded Seren, smiling brightly.

"Everyone has the capacity to be spiritual Seren but not everyone uses their skills."

Gwen looked closely at her granddaughter who was often deep in thought. She had observed Seren in the evenings as the young woman sat alone outside and stared at the moon and stars. Gwen worried about her.

---

[8] The faery folk.

"That's enough gardening for today. I'll have a quick wash, make a pot of tea, and bring some bara brith into the front sitting room Seren. Go and light the fire before taid returns home and we'll have our drinks in there. We'll go into the kitchen when he's back."

Seren did as she was asked, snuggled onto a faded pink flowery chair, watched the orange light of the log fire transform to blue, then orange again. Mesmerised. She had a million questions to ask her nain. She even had questions about questions. Thoughts tumbled over each other in quick succession fighting for supremacy in her consciousness.

"Thank you, nain for making the drinks. My turn tomorrow."

Gwen smiled. "Seren" she said quietly "you feel as if you're in a fog, you've always been an inquisitive girl, surrounded by witchery. Tonight, your induction can truly begin."

Seren looked excited.

"I've always wondered why you have so many candles there" replied Seren pointing to a large Welsh oak side table.

"Candles are very important for a gwrach gwyn. A white witch. We have altars, and this is mine but there are no set rules about what should be on an altar Seren."

"No set rules?" queried Seren.

"It's up to the individual witch what they do and use, but I'll share with you what *I* do."

Seren rarely asked for anything and a sense of glorious anticipation welled up inside. Her cherished nain was sharing long-held secrets. Witchy secrets. And she couldn't wait to hear them. Seren sat up in the pink chair eager to have her nain's buried treasure revealed to her.

"On my altar are elements of earth, water, air, and fire. These are represented by objects. I also have a little faery figurine and an image of the Goddess Circe."

"What's the earth represented by?" enquired Seren.

"A crystal, but it can be a rock or stone."

"And the water can be embodied by what?"

"Well, a bowl of water, obviously, or in my case a seashell because we live near the sea."

"And air?"

"A feather."

"Oh, I wondered why you had a feather on the side table. I thought it was from one of the cushions. The candles represent fire. I get that. But why are there different coloured ones on the altar?"

"Green usually brings prosperity and money to a business."

"I'll remember that when I set up my own business" exclaimed Seren.

"Do. I burn a green candle with our farm business in mind. Yellow brings fun, laughter, pizazz, good luck, and vitality. And the house is always full of that."

"It is. If I ever get an interview, I'll light a yellow candle for good luck" responded Seren.

Gwen smiled.

"White is to support spirituality and lit to honour the Goddesses."

"When we light a white candle on Imbolc, that's to honour Saint Brigid and mark the beginning of spring?"

"Right" agreed Gwen. "Purple is for divination and clairvoyance."

"I'll need to light a purple candle to help me become as wise as you nain and to help me guide others" said Seren.

"That would be a positive thing to do cariad tlws. A brown candle is used for healing animals."

"In lambing season that's why you have a lit brown candle in here. I often wondered why brown because it's not an eye-catching colour."

"Orange candles are to help with the law and legal matters."

"I hope that I never need to light an orange candle nain."

"Me too cariad tlws. A blue candle is lit to help heal people."

"For when they are sick?"

"Yes. Consider that people may be physically *or* emotionally sick."

"I'll remember."

"The pink candle is for unconditional love. True love. The kind of love where you want the best for someone else. It fosters independence. It's the love taid and I have for you. We know that one day you'll leave us. And that's the correct thing for you to do. You'll be secure knowing we are here. Unconditional love is forgiving mistakes, but not accepting harm to yourself if those lapses hurt you. Before we finish, remind me to tell you a spell to bring in your true love."

"Great. I can't wait to find out that spell. I'll use *that* one for myself. A red candle. Is that for trouble?" challenged Seren.

"No. Not at all. It's for lust, a different kind of love. A devil may care love."

"I'll try and avoid that kind of love then."

Gwen smiled "sometimes, you might wish for that kind of love too."

At that moment Tomos opened the oak door which interrupted their conversation.

"Taid I'm learning about what a gwrach gwyn does."

"Are you now? You're in excellent hands then. I'm home, obviously, and I'll be doing the crossword in the kitchen so don't worry about me. I see there's sailors' stew which I'll warm for us and I'm going to pinch a slice of fresh bread before we sit and eat."

Tomos was relieved that quiet Seren was animated about her witch's initiation. He backed out of the room and closed the door.

"The various diffusers nain that you have here" Seren pointed to the side table. "What do you use the different essential oils for?"

"Well, I put lavender at the front door for protection of the home. I roll a green candle in basil which should help the farm, and us, to prosper. Thyme and honeysuckle, I use both for the faery people, to attract the pixies to the house, which is especially good to protect little children. If you roll a candle in an essential oil, it changes it. It gives the candle more *umph* but use one oil at a time. My favourites are basil, lavender orange, thyme, honeysuckle, ylang ylang and sage."

"So, basil adds power to a green candle?" asked a surprised Seren. "What about lavender essential oil rolled on a candle?"

"Well lavender can sharpen the mind, strengthen pure love, and encourage fertility."

There was no silence in the room. Absorbing everything, Seren was so eager to find out more from her nain that her interrogation continued unabated.

"Orange, thyme, ylang ylang and sage. What does orange do then?" said Seren.

"Adds oomph, brings prosperity, joy and success."

"Wow" exclaimed Seren. "And thyme?"

"Well, that's needed for courage and ambition. You can use it in your clairvoyance and when honouring your ancestors, particularly those who have passed on their powers to you."

"I will nain. I'll honour you. Forever."

Gwen glanced at Seren and burst out laughing.

"Ylang ylang? That's an unusual name. What's that used for?"

"That's a very special essential oil. It eliminates fear, depression, anxiety, stress, and sadness. It resolves disputes and promotes serenity."

"I'm using that one!" exclaimed Seren.

"Would you like to know about the properties of sage?" Gwen asked.

"Yes."

"It's for good health, longevity, purification, wisdom and protection."

"I'll definitely need that" responded a sage Seren.

The ground had shifted for Seren. She was being schooled in new practices. Her life would change. Up until this moment she had not realised her innate power. Seren walked to the altar and picked up a little white mesh bag, tied with white silk ribbon.

"What do you usually put in the little bags nain?"

"Various items cariad tlws. Sometimes I place basil in a bag to bring money to the holder, with a white candle for protection, a shell to represent water and rose quartz for unconditional love. I give my little bags to people because it leaves a little bit of me with them, and signifies I'll see them again. I also leave them in places I visit which indicates I will return. I'm sure people think I'm bonkers, but I'm not."

"No, you're not! You're thoughtful, kind, wise" exclaimed Seren. "You do lovely things for people which are appreciated. Nain you asked me to remind you about the love spell. I can't wait to hear about it and practise it."

Gwen laughed.

"Be careful what you ask for and never ask for anything that will cause harm to others. You can't wish for a married man cariad tlws otherwise terrible things will happen. Is this for you to find your true love?"

"Of course" replied Seren.

"That's known as a soulmate. You do realise that don't you?"

"I've never heard of that. A soulmate?"

"It's a unique bond between two people. They appear together in different lives. It's two people coming together down the mists of time, in the chain of human spirit, who fit together perfectly. That's how you recognise each other in this life. The timing and circumstances will be right when you can be with your soulmate. Now. Here's the spell:

Roll a pink candle in an essential oil that you like, perhaps opium, orange, rose. Sprinkle a few herbs such as lavender, rosemary, or use rose petals, around the bottom of the candle. Put sugar on the candle holder for sweetness. The holder could be a shell, mirror, or candle container. When it's a full moon and the energies of the Goddess Luna are at her highest power, light the candle and say – 'Please Goddess of the Moon, bring in the love of my life. I am here waiting for him, and I am ready. I will harm none as I'm doing this'.

Use the spell wisely cariad tlws. In fact, let me teach you about circling yourself with protection. I don't want any harm to come to you."

Appreciative. Thrilled. Seren shifted in her seat, captivated by the new streams of ideas as they flowed from her nain.

"It's the intention behind the spell. It is all made in love."

"Teach me how to encircle myself please."

"I always cast a circle to open any area I am working in. I pull a circle around me."

"Oh. How do I do that?" queried Seren.

"Stand up and do as I do. Use your finger. You could use a spoon or a wand."

"A wand. You've got a wand? Never!"

"Don't tell anyone! People will think I'm potty. Right. Put your hand up towards the sky and say:

'By the power of the sky'

"Turn to the right" ordered Gwen.

'By the power of the sea'

"Turn right again."

'By the power of the earth'

"Turn right again."

'By the power of the trees, cast my circle.'

It felt as though they had danced together. Seren laughed. Tonight, her nain had infused her with an effusive, wonderful, entrancing spirit. She loved it.

"You must remember to close the circle when you've finished Seren. To do that repeat the incantation but turn left instead of turning right."

"Fantastic. That was exhilarating. Is there anything else I need to know?"

"Oh, lots and lots and lots but for tonight I'll tell you this. Our soul is immortal. It's repeatedly reborn and exists to be reincarnated in another until our lessons have been learned. Our soul dominates our thoughts and must be attuned. It's our inner voice. Above all else, nurture of the soul is important."

"Nain, that's what Titus told Ceres" exclaimed Seren. "The Roman Legate. In my visions. You too believe that to be true?"

"I do. The soul holds a complete record of everything that has happened, is happening now and will happen for every person during each different life, short or long. Your taid told me even Einstein believed that every moment of our past still exists. He thought that our past wasn't accessible but that it survived, somewhere. Einstein also said that we don't all experience the same time because we travel along the time dimension at different rates. He called it *spacetime.*

Have you heard people say that you're an *old* soul? It means your soul has been reborn many times. The other evening, we accessed your soul's file through meditation in the Temple of Mithras. What if Einstein was partly correct Seren? What if our past, present, *and* future endure in different dimensions of time, and we *can* access them when we meditate, or through people who have a gift? The gwrach gwyn gift. And what if gwrachod gwyn[9] are guided by others from a different dimension?"

Stupefied, Seren stared at her nain.

"Wait nain. Let me get this clear. So, there's an ethereal spirit called a soul? When it's created, the soul goes on a journey, in different physical bodies, throughout time, until it has learned all life lessons? Then what? A soul becomes a God or Goddess? A deity? With powers greater than those of ordinary humans? And does all of this make up the stunning fabric of the universe? Our universe? And some people have the gift,

---

[9] White Witches.

the power of retrieving different dimensions of time, to view the soul's journey, to help themselves or others?

"Yes. You've summed it up perfectly." Her nain smiled. "An excellent evening of learning!"

Seren laughed. "Nain you amaze me."

"Listen to your internal voice Seren. It's important. It will always guide you in the right direction."

"Are the Gods known as Destiny?"

"Yes."

"Could Destiny intervene in someone's life?"

"Yes."

"So, the past does make us the people we are in the future?"

"Exactly."

"And sometimes Destiny gives us a shove?"

"Yes. Inexplicable synchronicities will occur in people's lives. That's Destiny intervening."

"And *you* nain, have the power to see along the timeline, and guide people if they come to you, because you can access the past, present, and future?"

"Yes."

"And those are powers that you've gleaned from past lives?"

"Yes. And I have guardians to protect me. And we also have different life paths. We can choose which dimension we travel along."

"Do I have guardians?"

"You have. Another time I'll teach you how to bring them forward."

"Right. You need to pause there before I can take in any more information."

Gwen smiled.

"You're right. I've hit you with too much. You've absorbed a lot. You've already awakened your awareness and are aligning with Ysbryd, the knowledge and wisdom."

"I have?"

"Yes. By meditating. By being open. Now you might begin to realise that the visions you have are simply that. Visions of past, present, or future. You can see along the timeline. You can enter a past life to find out what lessons you've learned. You are connected to universal wisdom. Look, you've experienced déjà vu. That's your unconscious mind recalling your future timeline."

"Nain, I'm an eighteen-year-old woman from Wales. It feels like I'm weird. Different. Like I don't need other people. As if I'm happy on my own, with you and taid, or with the dogs, or the livestock or gazing at the moon and stars. Am I ever going to feel like I belong anywhere other than here, at Bryn Gosol?"

Gwen chuckled.

"You've witnessed two past lives cariad tlws. You've loved and been loved by a Roman Legate, a leader of men, a forceful personality, and another man, a determined, honourable, high-ranking King's man. You've loved and been loved by two children and two dogs. Certainly, you will feel a sense of belonging in this life. You already fit but you'll extend that circle by creating your own family, and your own close-knit group of dear friends. People who love you unconditionally, as taid and I do."

Seren left the comfort of her chair to hug her beloved nain.

"Nain. Even if I do the *love spell,* I'm not going to meet a Legate or a King's man in Llanrhos of all places. But thank you. I love you to the moon and back."

Gwen stifled a sob. Seren was undoubtedly the best thing that had ever happened to her and Tomos. Her living at Bryn Gosol Farm had worked out well for them all as Gwen had known it would.

The questions multiplied as Seren returned to her seat. The two of them carried on despite Seren saying she had absorbed enough!

"And what about being a gwrach gwyn? How do you know I'm a gwrach gwyn? I haven't got a broomstick. I don't want a cat – black or white! And there aren't any warts on my nose … yet!"

Seren jumped up to stare in the mirror and checked for wart-like symptoms. Her nain laughed.

"It seems to me that being a gwrach gwyn brings with it great responsibility, nain. I've seen the people who need guidance. Those who come to you. Sometimes in such emotional pain."

"Yes. It does bring with it an obligation to be straight with people, but you can shoulder those duties Seren. You're a strong woman. When the time is right though, you'll need a resilient partner to share your life with. One who's open-minded. I see you with a man who stands in a field of stars."

"A scarecrow?"

Seren and her nain giggled together.

"Please will you explain to me about being a gwrach gwyn? That sounds easier to understand than ethereal spirits and gods."

"A gwrach gwyn ... hmmm ... where do I begin? Right, let me start with the Goddess Luna. Her story is an important legend and you're already obsessed with the moon.

The moon transforms itself every month, from new, to crescent, to gibbous to full and back again. The Moon Goddess, Luna, with her siblings, Sol the Sun God, and Eos the Dawn Goddess dominate the sky. That infinite inky blue blackness of empty space. Luna can light up that space by pulling the moon across it with her chariot. She is the guide who illuminates the darkness, the one who throws light on illusions. She represents wisdom, intuition, and psychic powers. Appearing in dreams, daydreams, by using our inner voice, Luna gives answers to questions that puzzle mortals. That's why, after we've slept, sometimes things become clearer, or we suddenly have an insight which puts us on the right track.

There were temples to Goddess Luna, in Ancient Rome on Aventine Hill and the Palatine Hill. If you ever visit Rome, go to both hills, but you won't see either temple as they were destroyed in the Great Fire. Luna is the Goddess of gwrachod gwyn."

"What does a gwrach gwyn do nain? What will *I* do as a gwrach gwyn?"

"You've already begun by honouring the cycles of the moon Seren. The new moon is significant because you can use spells at that time to invoke fresh beginnings. Know that the waxing moon shows the beginning of events and waning times of the moon help you to banish unwanted negative energies. The full moon is most important because you can release and overcome obstacles. This is the most appropriate time to honour, petition or invoke the Goddess Luna. Tonight, this night of the full moon, is known as the esbat. A time of spiritual gathering when healing magic is performed."

Her nain paused momentarily, then continued.

"You will read tarot cards. I will give you a set. Treasure it."

Gwen watched Seren carefully.

"You can use your psychic powers to see events Seren. Like the Goddess Luna you will illuminate the darkness. Your sixth sense will alert you to incidents before they occur."

Gwen's eyes shone as she reached for a book she sometimes kept in a golden oak coloured monk's bench.

"When the time comes Seren, I will give you my nain's ancient grimoire. This book includes instructions on how to perform spells, charms, create amulets, invoke Ysbryd. It also includes Divine revelations. Guide people who need direction and advice. Always work for their, and your higher good. Remember that your own wellbeing is of utmost importance. Put yourself first. And make sure you invoke your guardians."

"Remember to tell me how to summon guardians nain won't you?"

"I will. Another time darling girl."

Gwen paused momentarily, then said:

"All around us there are lots of things we can't see, or touch, or hear Seren. We can't see invisible waves like sound waves, radio waves, wi-fi waves. We can't see a person's voice, or touch it, but we can hear it. We can't see a smell. We can't see gravity but it's there. Air is transparent. We can't see or feel it. Light is invisible. The trillions of stars in the sky at night, aren't usually visible to us, but they're there. We can't see, touch, smell or hear time, but we can see processes occurring over time. You need to believe. And be positive. Positive thoughts, words and deeds bring good things back to you."
"Nain, this is all a lot to absorb. People are going to think I'm a weirdo. I know it. Will I be able to live a normal life?"

"What do you view as a *normal* life? Are your taid and I *normal*?"

"Yes. I mean me. Having a job. Going on holiday. Buying a house. Having a partner. Having a family. Will my mind be able to differentiate between this *spiritual* life and a *normal* life?"

"But Seren, taid and I do that. We run the farm. I help people alongside that. I don't broadcast my abilities. I absorb them into my daily life. No-one knows about the wand though, that might be going a bit far! People will find you cariad tlws. People in need will seek you out. Be positive. You'll emit an aura."

"Aura. *I'll* emit an *aura*? How? What's that?"

"You've seen auras around angels in pictures. Remember? The most versatile Italian artist, Raphael depicted angels with a golden glow around them. Your taid has shown you images from Rome. You've seen the photograph he has of the Transfiguration. An aura is a unique electromagnetic field of light, an energy which surrounds your whole body and radiates from you. The aura emits different colours depending upon your feelings and level of spirituality. Gwrachod gwyn can see a person's aura. Subconsciously most people can feel others' aura even if they are unaware of its existence and colour. You've met people that you're drawn to?"

"Yes nain, I have, and I don't know why I'm drawn to them."

"And you've come across people who instantly repel you for some unknown reason?"

"Gosh, yes. That's happened too."

"It's their aura which is sending out messages about them."

"Can you see my aura?"

"Yes."

"What colour is it?"

"Indigo."

"What does that mean nain?"

"You've already described yourself cariad tlws. Drawn to animals and nature. Intuitive about people and situations. You can predict others' behaviour and are aware of events that have yet to occur. You want to make a difference in the work you do. Does that sound like you?"

"Yes" replied Seren without looking at her nain. "That's me. You understand me."

"I do darling girl. You have the characteristics of a person with an indigo-coloured aura. Look. You're eighteen-years-old. It's a significant time of life. You've waited to become a woman and now you're legally classed as one. The waiting period, that void when you're waiting for something to happen is known as a liminal space. The time between what is happening now and what may happen next. It can be the physical space of moving from one room in the farm to another, or the emotional space between having an examination and waiting for the results, or the metaphorical space when you're in limbo as you wait for a decision to be made and you don't know whether to go this way or that. Liminal spaces can be challenging to navigate because of the uncertainty of what will happen next.

You now need to navigate moving to be a young woman. An eighteen-year-old woman. Eighteen. It's a specific age milestone along the soul's journey. This is an age in a person's life when pivotal moments occur. This is the time that you begin to spread your wings Seren. You must decide what you are going to do next. We've spoken for a long time. Let's go and join taid in the kitchen and have some food. I'm famished."

"Nain. Please will you read my tea leaves at some point? Help me out here. I'm astonished. I'm afraid. I've gone from being a loner to a person who can access past lives, tell the past, present, and future, possibly call up guardians, and help people. I know you can do that but you're wise. And old. I'm neither."

"Thanks" smiled Gwen. "Yes. Sometime soon I'll read your tea leaves. Tonight, let's go and make a fuss of taid. It's important to show him how much we love him. We can do that by spending time with him."

As they entered the kitchen, Tomos was reading at the oak table, a freshly brewed cup of tea in a large blue beaker to his left. The smell of warm bread and a piquant aroma of stout-filled sailors' stew gravy floated around the room. Tomos stood, kissed his beloved wife, hugged Seren and went to stir the food.

"Make sure you stir clockwise Tomos, to bring good things in."

"I will. Sit down you two natterers. I'll make you both a drink. Have you had a good chat? No doubt she's told you about *protection*?" Taid chuckled to himself.

"Taid. My mind has been impressed by listening to nain. How am I going to face life?"

"We'll be right beside you cariad tlws. We'll always be beside you" he replied sagaciously, "in life or Ysbryd. You're well-equipped to deal with the good and bad which will come your way."

As they did every night, the three of them sat around the oak table, laughing, and chatting about the day's events, eating food, and drinking cups of tea. Tonight was no exception except that spring water sat outside on the windowsill, bathing in the light of the full moon and Seren knew she was a gwrach gwyn with an aura, in liminal space. *Waiting for something to happen.*

Chapter 5 – Space

There are moments we wish we could relive.

Exactly 2.1 miles away from Llanrhos lived the close-knit Thomson family; Jessie, Aila and Madoc. Although the two children and their mother Jessie had walked the Vardre, knew the legend of the Devil's Tree, seen Bryn Gosol Farm and visited Llanrhos parish church, they were completely unaware of the existence of Gwen, Tomos or Seren. Neither would they have known about the secret underground passageway, tarot card and tealeaf readings or past life regressions. Certainly not!

By the time he was nine Madoc had travelled to the nationless North Pole where the celestial North Star sits motionless in the sky and all lines of longitude meet. With its freezing temperature, he saw one sunrise, at the March equinox and one sunset at the September equinox. Madoc preferred to be there in winter, for twenty four hours of darkness appealed to him. He knew that the North Pole was warmer than the South Pole as he had visited both, many times, but that it would be unwise to pack shorts for either trip. The Atacama Desert in Chile was next on his list so that he could observe the birth of planets and stars, closely followed by a short trip to Tuscany where he could watch Jupiter's sunspots and catch glimpses of the moon's craters.

This miracle of instantaneous world travel and unending knowledge arrived at Madoc's home early one Saturday morning. A teleportation machine was placed in the corner of his mother's living room in the form of a black box sitting on the tea-stained black and white coffee table. '*Ironic*' thought Madoc. What he wanted most of all was to visit the moon via a wormhole and today his dream would come true. Courtesy of Radio Rentals who had delivered a state of the art black and white television to his mother's home in Conwy for two pounds a month. Cheap if you considered how far it encouraged Madoc to travel every day, in his imagination.

Madoc could just about remember when Jessie invited him to watch on video what half a billion other people had observed, the translunar injection of Apollo 11 as the rocket blasted off from Cape Kennedy into outer space. Jessie cried with relief and Madoc cheered when the voice of Commander Neil Armstrong said: "*Houston, Tranquility Base here. The Eagle has landed.*" Both watched eagerly as Armstrong planted his foot onto the lunar surface and proclaimed: "*That's one small step for a man, one giant leap for mankind*". This was Madoc's first encounter with the timeless images of outer space. He was captivated.

As they sat comfortably together on a gold-coloured sofa, Jessie taught Madoc that space was a vast store of negative energy and mass was positive energy spread throughout space. She said that the universe added up to nothing and everything was all about energy. Madoc wanted to feel the energy of nothingness. To float in space. But he couldn't, so the next best thing was to watch the event unfold before him through the miracle of invisible patterns of electricity and magnetism. These waves, Jessie explained, raced through the air at the speed of light 300,000 km per second sending picture and sound signals. Jessie taught Madoc that the waves couldn't be seen, felt, or heard, but they were there. Just believe Madoc, she urged. This was tricky for a boy with an enquiring, imaginative, problem-solving mind. He wondered how those waves were captured if they couldn't be seen, touched, or heard. '*Maybe they'd been programmed, just like the lunar landing*' he thought '*because there couldn't possibly be a guide*

*for the rocket when it landed on the moon. Or maybe it was the
Gods helping out.'*

The first love of Madoc's life was *stargazing*, brought about by
his single-mother's infectious enthusiasm for astronomy. Out
of her teacher's salary she had saved up enough money to buy
him a telescope and red torch for his birthday so that he could
observe the delicious, intoxicating night sky. Not that Madoc
knew the bizarre woozy feeling of intoxication except, one
Christmas when he'd sipped too much of Jessie's sweet sherry
in the kitchen. Madoc had retched so violently that sherry
whooshed out of his nose, and his face turned a delicate shade
of green. His older sister Aila cleaned him up and gave him
gallons of coffee, so that his mother wouldn't know. She
helped him a lot, his scholarly sister. She was always finding
him in scrapes.

"Why a red torch mum?" questioned Madoc.

"When it's dark, the pupils in your eyes get bigger to let in as
much light as possible. That's known as dilation. If you use an
ordinary torch, your pupils will contract. That means they'll
get smaller, and it takes a long time for them to dilate again. A
torch with a red light will allow just enough glow to be able to
see the stars, and keep your eyes dilated."

She thought of everything his mum. Madoc was delighted. He
and Aila would be able to use the torch and telescope that very
day as they were taking a birthday trip to Aberdeen to visit his
grandfather.

Every school holiday Jessie, Aila and Madoc journeyed to the
granite city. One could be forgiven for thinking that travelling
by car for eight hours between Conwy and Aberdeen would be

a torturously long journey. Admittedly it was time-consuming, but the three Thomsons, mother, daughter, and son entertained each other along the way, no persecution inflicted. Except once, to an unfortunate pheasant who decided to cross the road just at the wrong time. Aila didn't know who squawked the loudest, Jessie or the pheasant. Distraught, Jessie stopped the car. Madoc picked up the least blood-stained feather and tucked it into his pocket for safekeeping. The remains were buried by the side of the road at a privately attended funeral. Pity the pheasant didn't know the Highway Code. On their trip, the little family would out-sing each other (*terribly*), play *I Spy*, ask no more than twenty one questions, spot the car, use word associations, and add sentences to each other's stories. They're an inventive lot the Thomson Clan.

According to their grandfather, who was known as *The Ghillie*, (because he was a fishing guide), they were descended from Tomaidh Mor, grandson of William Mackintosh, who took his followers to settle in Glenshee. How Madoc's grandfather ended up working as an angler in the eclectic area of Footdee no-one can remember, but Madoc was delighted that he lived in the unique community. Number 12 Curlew Cottage, The Ghillie's three-bedroomed brightly coloured home faced inwards with its back to the ocean to protect the inhabitants from fierce storms. From the back bedroom window, Madoc and Aila watched many a savage tempest on their visits.

Known as the Silver City, historic Aberdeen offered the children many hidden gems to discover. Madoc and Aila wobbled on cobbled streets, charged around the 15th Century crenellated Cathedral known as St. Machar's, marvelled at the stunning Marischal College, took bicycles along the beachfront Promenade, tramped around Tyrebagger Forest with its pixies and faeries and photographed waterfalls and ponds from the bridge in Johnston Gardens. The pictures they would develop at Curlew Cottage later. The most bewitching jewel of all was the golden sandy beach where dolphins leapt at the harbour mouth and seals invaded the sand.

Worshipped by his grandchildren, The Gillie taught Madoc and Aila how to develop photographs at home from the camera film. In the scullery he had a makeshift development room.

"Don't take the film out of the camera yet Aila. Just hold your horses."

Aila smiled at her grandfather.

"See this development tank here?"

"Yes. Do I take the film out now?" asked an impatient Aila.

"No, not yet lassie" responded her grandfather. "Madoc, have you got the three measuring jugs?"

"Yes grandad, they're here on the side." Madoc had placed the containers on a worn wooden bench.

"Get the opaque, plastic bottles from the bench Madoc and bring them over here to me."

"Got them grandad" replied Madoc as he passed three cloudy bottles to Aila who handed them, one by one, to her grandad.

"Count the number of pegs Madoc that are on our little washing line."

"There's twelve, grandad."

"Grand. Just enough for our film then. Wonder if you've managed to capture any pixies or faeries in the park?" In the dim light The Ghillie's lovat eyes gleamed.

"That would be fantastic wouldn't it Aila?" exclaimed Madoc.

"It would" and the insides of her tummy felt tickly.

"Right. We need scissors and a thermometer. Who's got those?"

"I have" replied Aila seriously, as if she were preparing for an operation in a hospital theatre. Funnily enough, this was excellent training because her future self was a doctor.

"Right. Here we go" exclaimed grandad. "All ready?"

"Ready" shouted Madoc and Aila together as they looked at each other in excitement.

"Madoc. Remove the film from the canister by **only** touching the sides of the film. Careful now."

Madoc's tongue was clasped between his teeth until he shouted, "done grandad."

"Aila, cut off the extra film at the beginning of the roll while Madoc precisely holds the film."

"Done grandad."

"Damn I forgot the film reel."

"It's here grandad" replied Aila passing him the reel which was on the wooden bench.

"Well, that's grand. Aila, you hold the reel, Madoc you feed the film into the reel. Good. Place the film and reel into the developer tank. Between the two of you, fill the measuring jugs and dilute the developer, fixer and stop bath with water. Make sure the water temperature is 68°F."

"It's a bit difficult for me to see the temperature grandad" stated Madoc.

"Pass it to me wee one and I'll check it. There it is, see where the red line stops. It shows 68. So the temperature is right."

"Now what do we do?" asked Madoc.

"Take it in turns but it's got to be in this order. Pour the developer, the stop bath and fixer into the developer tank. Count to 120 and then remove the film carefully. Wash it under the tap at the Belfast sink there" ordered grandad "we'll leave the negatives to dry and come back later to check on the pixies and faeries."

Madoc and Aila giggled and were optimistic that the pixies and faeries would appear.

An intense, courageous, and affectionate man, The Ghillie instilled in his grandchildren a passion for the sea and a curiosity for the stars. He took them out on his boat, The Seashell leaving Aberdeen Harbour to follow exciting adventures on the wild and dramatic North Sea. The Ghillie taught Madoc the three 'B's: how to avoid *backlash* when casting so that the line did not tangle, how to *bail* which was tossing bait chunks and a baited hook into the water to trigger a feeding frenzy, and the point at which a fishing line would break, known as *breaking strength.*

The Ghillie and Madoc would sail up the rugged coastline to catch cod, pollock and coalfish. Sometimes Aila would join them. Around Cruden Bay, The Ghillie would point out the puffins on the rugged cliff edge and Slains Castle, where Bram Stoker was purported to have conceived the story of Dracula. Madoc and The Ghillie would fish for mackerel, sea trout, sea bass and take their catch to sell at Aberdeen Harbour. His grandfather would always have a few spare fish to take back to his unconventionally painted red and blue cottage. It was here that Madoc learned how to fillet a fish!

When they could bear the cold wind and steely sea, Madoc and Aila would spend their days joining locals swimming, paddle-boarding, and surfing. Occasionally, if he was feeling wicked, their Uncle Doug would lock them in the freezing cold fish warehouse close to the harbour wall. He thought it was hilarious. Madoc and Aila thought it was funny at first, until their hands turned blue. This wasn't the best part of their holiday.

The AAS, otherwise known as the Aberdeen Astronomical Society, held stargazing evenings on the fourth Tuesday of each month. Madoc, Aila and The Ghillie were delighted to attend the *Beginners' Guide To Stargazing* while Jessie enjoyed an evening out with friends.

"C'mon grandad, we'll be late."

"Don't worry Madoc, I've arranged for the speaker to wait for us."

The Gillie hadn't but he knew that saying it would ease Madoc's anxiety. They arrived at the brick-built building with five minutes to spare and sat at the back of the hall.

"The Big Dipper is one of the most familiar sights in the Northern Hemisphere's night skies."

The speaker showed an image of seven stars.

"It looks like a square pan, grandad, not a big dipper."

"I suppose it looks like whatever your eyes choose it to represent" replied his sagacious grandfather.

"The Big Dipper is visible all year round to observers north of latitude 41°."

"I find the Big Dipper first grandad when I'm looking at the night sky. From that I can place other stars" whispered Aila.

"This makes it an invaluable key to unlocking the night sky."

Grandad smiled and leaned over to Aila. "You just said that Aila. You could be the speaker."

Aila laughed and the speaker glared at her.

"Stars are born within clouds of dust and scattered throughout the galaxies."

"Could we make stars out of dust grandad?"

"Not tonight, Madoc. We'll stargaze instead and eat chips on the cliff top."

"Stars are fuelled by the nuclear fusion of hydrogen to form helium deep in their interiors" pointed out the speaker.

"We just need to create nuclear fusion grandad" insisted Madoc.

"We do. But let's leave it for tonight because we'll use your telescope and torch to see all the different stars. If we're lucky we might even get to see the Aurora Borealis" grandad promised.

"What's that grandad? A boat?" queried Madoc.

"No" whispered grandad. "Ask the speaker when she's finished."

"Will do" replied Madoc who waited thirty minutes for his opportunity to pose a question.

"Please will you explain the Aurora Borealis?" requested Madoc importantly.

"Certainly. An aurora is a natural colourful light display."

"Oh. So, someone turns on lights in the sky? Like at Christmas on a tree?" questioned Aila.

"Not exactly. Ions which continuously stream from the sun's surface are called the solar wind."

"Wind on the sun?"

"Shush Madoc."

"When a solar wind approaches from the Sun it meets the Earth's magnetic field. Ions of the solar wind collide with atoms of oxygen and nitrogen from the Earth's atmosphere. The energy released during these collisions causes colours that shimmer and change shape in the sky around the North and South Poles. Oxygen molecules at altitudes of 150 miles will glow green. Oxygen and nitrogen molecules at lower altitudes can glow blue, yellow or red. An aurora can only be seen at night."

"Wow" exclaimed Madoc. "I definitely want to see that. An aura can have green, blue, yellow, or red colours?"

"Yes and if solar flares and coronal mass ejections are created, this causes sudden extra bursts of energy in the solar wind."

"Does that mean that sometimes the colours and shapes are more intense?"

"Yes young man at the back. That's exactly what happens."

"Please may we see one tonight?" requested Madoc.

"You can't order them, like a pizza" retorted the speaker.

"One day Madoc, we'll see the Aurora Borealis together. One day," promised his grandfather.

That night, on the way home they stood on the clifftops searching the sky for the Big Dipper. The Ghillie pointed out Ursa Major, which was made up of stars from the Big Dipper, and the brightest star, which is Polaris, known as the North Star. They ate chips with their fingers.

"Look for two stars at the front end of the Dipper's bowl. These are pointer stars. Merak is at the closed side and Dubhe is at the open side. Draw an imaginary line from Merak to Dubhe and the first easy to spot star is Polaris."

Madoc and Aila took it in turns to stare at the North Star through the telescope.

"Ok. Look at Polaris and see if you can work out the W shape of Cassiopeia, the mythical queen of ancient Ethiopia. The mortal Queen is supposed to have upset the Sea God Poseidon by saying that she and her daughter Andromeda were more beautiful than his daughters. This infuriated the Sea God so he caused the lands of Ethiopia to flood. Andromeda's parents chained their daughter to the sea as a sacrifice to appease Poseidon, but she was rescued by a Greek hero, Perseus and they were married. Poseidon could not allow Queen Cassiopeia to go unpunished. He sat her on her throne, placed her in the sky, where her throne hangs upside down for half of the year as a torture. What's the moral of this story Aila?"

"Not to be vain I think grandad."

"Nor speak badly about other people grandad" added Madoc.

"Both correct. Well done."

For the following few evenings The Ghillie spent hours with the children teaching them about the stars. On the day they were leaving a white ferret popped its head out of The Ghillie's jacket pocket.

"Madoc shush. Here. Take the ferret home and look after him for me."

"Oh wow grandad. He's brilliant. My very own ferret. I'll call him Freddie after Freddie Mercury."

"Whatever you do, don't tell your mother ... yet."

"I won't."

"And Aila."

"Yes grandad."

"Here are the photographs we developed. Look after them bonnie lass. Have a close look because I think we've captured some pixies and faeries on them."

"Oh wow" exclaimed Aila and when she looked, there were little shadows on the photographs which may just have been y Tylwyth Teg.

For the eight hours' journey home, the white ferret snuggled inside Madoc's jacket. Snug as a bug in a rug.

In the weeks that followed Jessie forgave The Ghillie. When the news arrived that The Seashell had capsized off the coast of Aberdeen, around Cruden Bay, and that his body was unlikely to ever be recovered, the ferret was looked upon as The Ghillie's spirit. A guardian angel for Madoc, like a shadow, it never left his side. He hid his tears, but with a lump in his throat and a pain in his heart, Madoc wondered if Poseidon had snatched his beautiful grandad and made a star out of him. Sadly, Madoc, Aila and The Ghillie never did see the Aurora Borealis together.

In the future, Madoc would thank his lucky stars for two things. One would be his family; the other would be his fascination with the night sky which would lead him through the dimensions of time and into the arms of a magnificent soul. But not just yet, because first, Madoc had to grow up.

2009

Chapter 6 – A Man's Man

Can photographs portray lives lived?

Still living with her, Jessie's worry about Madoc finding a job
when he left school was lessened when he was offered a
contract to play football at Wrexham AFC. Exciting times as
the team had finished third in Division Three in the English
Football League. This meant training hard with very few
moments of leisure. When Madoc returned home battered and
bruised each day, with youthful intensity he believed that his
destiny was set. His football career would be meteoric. From
Wrexham he would prove his worth with the goal of playing as
a defender for his beloved Manchester United like other proud
Scotsmen Arthur Albiston, Gordon McQueen, Martin Buchan
and Darren Fletcher. If only United's Manager, Alex Ferguson,
would notice him.

Football training at the club was brutal. Well, more ferocious
than PE had been at school. Firstly, because PE only happened
once a week and secondly because Madoc would sometimes
mitch school. His mother never knew he played truant! There
was not any opportunity to skip football training because of the
manager. Affectionately known as *The G'vnr,* he was an angry
Yorkshire man whose wrinkled facial features were usually set
in a red-flushed menacing scowl. All the footballers bathed in
his angry breath. Young and old. Experienced and
inexperienced. It didn't matter who they were, because that
was how The G'vnr had won promotion for the team; the
players were propelled by his whirlwind personality.

One of the most exhausting, but exhilarating parts of training was the five-a-side football, where even the goalkeepers would play outfield and leave the goal nets unattended. Madoc had to be quick at defending especially because he was a boy playing against men and was easily pushed off the ball.

"Look over your shoulder Madoc before coming for the ball. Watch who's around you" barked The G'vnr.

If he saw something he didn't like, The G'vnr would snap orders too. There was never any doubt about his passion for the game.

"Don't pull out of the bloody tackle, Madoc. Concentrate lad" he would scream.

"Madoc, go and work in the gym to develop your strength and stamina" The G'vnr advised.

Madoc didn't know how to develop either until one of the trainers at the club advised him to do single leg box jumps, use the rowing machine and push barbells, increasing the weight weekly. Playing football for a living was not a golden opportunity he was prepared to lose. He knew how lucky he was. The training suggestions plus swimming and walking up the Vardre worked for Madoc who dedicated himself to becoming the best footballer he could be. By September he was match fit.

Each Friday the team sheet would be pinned outside the dressing room for Saturday's fixture. Madoc would search the single white piece of paper, praying to see his name as a defender in the first team, but he stayed with the reserves. The disappointment choked him, not because he was a brat and expected to walk into the first team, but because he so desperately wanted to live out the dream of being an established professional footballer. Madoc never made a fuss, he worked harder, became tougher, more focused on his ambition. A devoted student of the game.

It's awe inspiring to play in front of a football crowd, especially a troop of more than twenty people. On numerous occasions Madoc had been to Old Trafford to watch Manchester United play, where the ground was besieged by seventy-thousand supporters each game. Today was no different. Madoc observed the coiled skein of red and white football scarves waved by thousands of supporters on Warwick Road as they chanted the names of current and past footballers. His spine tingled. *'One day'* he thought *'they'll be singing my name on the terraces.'* He had gone to the night match specifically to watch defenders Rio Ferdinand and Gary Neville who were his favourite players. Unlike the other fans, Madoc made notes on the positions that Ferdinand and Neville placed themselves in, and the tackles they made which created space for their team-mates. Ferdinand was majestic and made defending the art of cool. Madoc had become a keen scholar of the beautiful game.

The shock arrived the following week when Madoc's name appeared on the first eleven team sheet. As a reserve. Still, it was a start. His first match for the Wrexham first team. Jessie and Aila were given tickets for the game and sat with the other players' friends and family waiting in heightened anticipation. Fifteen minutes into the second half, mother and sister waved enthusiastically to Madoc as he stripped off his tracksuit and entered the pitch. Phew. Finally. His debut.

"I'm so nervous mum. He's got to have a good game to be chosen again."

"I know Aila. I feel as though a million Mazarine butterflies are fluttering against every one of my internal organs."

Aila laughed.

"You do know he's well-prepared mum don't you and that preparation is everything?"

"That's what Madoc keeps telling me" replied Jessie.

"Wow mum, did you see that cross Madoc just made? Brilliant."

Both clapped vigorously. Hard enough to sound like seventy thousand Manchester United fans. Or so they hoped. Madoc looked at the crowd. Although he didn't see his family, he did see stands full of fans. *'Next match'* thought Madoc *'they'll sing my name.'* His prophecy came true. And they sang it the next match and the match after that. Man of the Match was presented to him on his fourth game. Madoc was riding high. He had a brilliant season, until the Ides of March.

It was a home game. Madoc was an established defender in the first team. The opposition were tough and quick. As he ran for the ball, the sprightly winger he was marking suddenly changed direction, quickly trying to do the same Madoc felt his leg judder, followed by a searing pain in his knee. His brain registered a popping sound. Almost immediately Madoc fell to the ground. The referee stopped the match to allow the doctor to run onto the pitch and attend to Madoc who couldn't move his leg. The red football shirt was pulled over his face so that Madoc could hide his tears of frustration. Damn. It felt like a bad injury. He was stretchered off the pitch.

In the large first-aid room, equipped with a doctor's bed, an oak table and a black leather swivel chair Madoc received the news he was dreading.

"Your knee feels unstable, and you've got swelling around your right knee joint lad. It might be a bad injury and that your ACL has gone."

"ACL? Do you mean my cruciate ligament?"

"Yes lad. They'll do a scan on it at the hospital. Don't worry lad. You're fit. You'll come back from this."

Madoc cried until Jessie and Aila joined him in the first aid room.

"The doc says that I need a scan mum, that's all. No need to worry about me."

But Jessie did worry. She knew that this could be a career-threatening injury.

Five hours later, in the Accident and Emergency department of the Wrexham Maelor Hospital, the registrar decided that Madoc needed painkillers and crutches. No scan necessary.

"There's tenderness, a little bit of swelling and I can feel a clicking sensation when I move your knee. Rest the leg until the swelling goes down Madoc, you'll be fine. Make sure you do plenty of walking using the crutches. In a few weeks it'll settle down."

"That's great news doc. What happens now? Will I have a scan?"

"I'll give you a prescription for painkillers, the nurse will get some crutches for you. No scan necessary."

"No scan? But the doctor at the club said I'd have a scan."

"No scan. It's not necessary Madoc" replied the registrar firmly.

"Whatever you say doc, I'm in your hands."

This welcome news buoyed Madoc. If it's possible when using crutches, Madoc *almost* skipped out of the hospital accompanied by a relieved Jessie and a slightly concerned Aila who whispered to her mother:

"I thought they'd do a scan mum just to be sure."

"They know best love."

"Yes, but I'm training to be a doctor mum and really, Madoc should've had a scan."

"Look at him, he's delighted it's nothing too serious. He's fine del.[10] If the registrar had thought he needed one, he would've had a scan."

"Perhaps you're right mum. Maybe I'm being over-protective of my little brother."

It was spring, bringing with it hope, freshness and new beginnings. Madoc had rested his bulbous knee for a couple of weeks by lying on his bed. But spring fever hadn't embraced Madoc. Rarely leaving his room. He kept the bedroom door

---

[10] Dear.

shut and Jessie worried that he was becoming so morose that he would be unreachable, he reassured her that he was "fine mum, don't fuss". But he wasn't. He was discouraged. Jessie left food outside his room. He ate scraps of it. His mother became so desperate with the situation that she asked Aila to intervene.

"Madoc, please will you let me in?" Aila requested.

"The door's not locked Aila you only need to turn the handle to come in" he said impatiently.

"You look like a scarecrow" exclaimed Aila. "Look at your hair all long and tatty, it's not been washed for two weeks by the look of it. You're as pale as a white sheet Madoc. Your face is skinny, and all that black stubble looks gross. You need a shave. You can't stay like this, in your bedroom all the time. You need to get that leg moving. And when was the last time you brushed your teeth?"

She was a whirlwind, his sister.

"I've been doing the exercises the doctor from the club gave to me Aila. There's no improvement. I've been walking around the bedroom using my crutches. The painkillers aren't making any difference. I've done what I've been asked to do. Nothing's working."

"You're a strong man Madoc. You can get through this. You need to be outside in the fresh air. Go swimming. Take your car up to the Vardre, have a little walk, take some photographs. You enjoy the view. Come downstairs. Eat with mum and me. I've brought some home-made soup."

"Not that horrible green sludge you make?"

"Yes" she affirmed. "My green sludge. C'mon."

"I'll be down in ten minutes Aila. I need a shower. And a shave. And to brush my teeth." After a pause he added "And thanks."

As she closed the door, tears welled in his sister's lovat eyes. She couldn't bear to see Madoc so downhearted.

The days turned into weeks, and Madoc's rehabilitation regime was not working. In desperation the club's doctor rang the Accident and Emergency department at Wrexham Maelor Hospital and spoke with a former colleague. The scan took place the very next day.

"The cartilage in the right knee is badly damaged."

"Will I play football again?" he asked cautiously.

"I'll ask the Consultant Orthopaedic Surgeon to see you Madoc. She'll be able to give you more information once she's had a good look at the scan" deflected the doctor.

Madoc waited. And waited. And waited. Two hours later the Consultant arrived looking dishevelled and tired.

"Right Madoc" said an exhausted Mrs Short "we can patch you up, no problem, but I'll have to operate on you."

"How long will it take to recover?"

"Probably somewhere between three and six months to return to football match fitness. You'll have to undergo intense physiotherapy after your operation."

"I'll do it" replied a resolute Madoc, who would have to get used to playing the waiting game instead of the game of football. "Thanks Doctor."

When Madoc arrived home, he angrily told his mother: "They should've done a bloody scan in the first place." The G'vnr's influence was rubbing off!

The week following Madoc's operation he rested then doggedly began to build up his rehabilitation regime. Initially it was challenging for him to visit the training ground and see his teammates carrying on footballing life without him. He needed a distraction and surprisingly, it was The G'vnr who had the answer.

"The lads tell me that you're an excellent photographer Madoc. Whilst you're recovering, I was wondering if you would take photos of the team training and visit the ex-players to take their photographs? We could have a montage around the ground and around the training centre. Something to motivate the lads. What do you think?"

'*Bloody hell*' thought Madoc. "That'd be great. Thanks, G'vnr. I'll start tomorrow."

The G'vnr smiled. He knew how to motivate people did that wily old Yorkshireman and he had heard that sadness engulfed Madoc.

On Thursday morning, spontaneously Madoc turned up at the training ground and snapped the players using his Nikon D70 camera with a zoom lens, without them even noticing he was there. Unobtrusively he deftly moved around the pitch taking the most unusual action shots of the players either as individuals or a few men at a time. So that he didn't have to wait for the results, he set up his own dark room at home, just as The Ghillie had taught him.

The next thing on his mind was to interview the ex-players and take photographs of them in a range of informal settings. He decided upon street photography where the pictures were taken in public places. Madoc arranged to meet the players in their favourite location which could be a café, a park, a sports club, with family, at work. The purpose was to show the ex-players in their new daily routine. This could act as a reminder to the current players that there was life after football.

Thanks to a golden setting sun, green and yellow woven hills and white foam tangled waves at Conwy Harbour, Madoc realised that alongside the sports photography, he could extend his repertoire and take travel photographs around the town. Well, there was plenty of scope in the stunning fortified settlement. He captured images of visitors paddleboarding and kayaking, busy townsfolk undertaking jobs, sights such as colourful fishing boats bobbing around the harbour, Welsh customs such as wearing the black Welsh costume, and sights like the imposing 13th Century military castle and the smallest house in the country which sat sedately by the quayside. His versatile trusted camera needed a wide-angle, fixed and zoom lens.

When the images were unveiled around the Club, it was as if the eyes of the world were watching Madoc. He could sense the expectation around him.

"Bloody hell lad, those are fantastic. Bloody brilliant. I'm lost for bloody words. You're a bloody professional" voiced The G'vnr.

Praise indeed.

"My grandad taught me everything I know about photography" was Madoc's equable reply.

"When are you coming back to training then?" his teammates asked "or are you Sir Don McCullin now? Will you photograph my wedding mate? I'm getting married next month?"

"I'm due back next Monday. See you all then and yes, I'll photograph your wedding."

In the months of Madoc's rehabilitation, he realised a delicate gift had been bestowed upon him. Perhaps by his grandad. He was expertly and deftly able to capture a millisecond of time in an image. And life is like a series of photograph shots, some are blurry, others are sharp, and the rest are simply exquisite moments sprinkled throughout time.

2023

Chapter 7 – Two Moons and a Star

Does twenty-twenty vision give us perfect sight?

Out of the classic, (antique might be a more appropriate word), maroon Jaguar car he heaved a Sony A7IV camera, telescope and stand preparing to capture, in all her splendour, the Full Moon. There was less light pollution on the Vardre than in Conwy town. Madoc's enjoyment of green hills and rocky mountains sprang from his desire to feel free, untethered, at one with nature. Whether allowed or not, he planned to wild camp here as the night sky shoved daylight away, because he couldn't yet devote himself exclusively to his first love which, as you know, was stargazing. Tonight, he wanted to concentrate on the Moon, Orion's Nebula, and the Andromeda Galaxy. Other celestial bodies in the veiled sky would be overshadowed. They were the main attraction since he wished to capture a marvellous image, brilliant enough to win an award.

Having strived to achieve his Gold Duke of Edinburgh Award at school and spent time in the magical empty ribbon of steppe and low mountain ranges in Chilean Patagonia, Madoc knew a little about how to live in the wilderness. Although tonight the freezing Vardre could not quite be compared with the wild and stunning backwoods of Chile, under this Wolf Moon it did present its own challenges. Not the howling hungry wolves of winter, but people. Visitors. Sightseers. Annoying humans. They rose and appeared out of the blackness, like spirits.

'There's no solitude anywhere' Madoc sighed. 'At least they'll be gone when it goes dark' he consoled himself.

As the strained frayed border between afternoon and evening gently unravelled, Madoc set up a small camp with his waterproof tent. He dug a modest fire pit, encircled it with stones, gathered dry twigs, dry leaves, dry grass, needles, dry bark, and the firewood he had bought in Conwy to prepare a fire. From his backpack Madoc withdrew provisions of boil-in-the-bag fish soup, jacket potatoes and beans. His sister Aila had included two apple bakes for his feast, lightly wrapped in foil to warm over the campfire when he was ready for his evening meal. An hour later, he rolled the potatoes in tin foil and threw them into the fire pit to roast. The soup was heated in five minutes and the bread he ate on a needs-must basis. The sweet apple bakes he *wolfed* in a trice. In his mind, he had eaten an epicurean meal. Well, not exactly, but the food tasted exquisite now that he was sitting uninterrupted, on a calm evening, on the Vardre, overlooking the elemental blackness of the Irish Sea. He rubbed his cold hands in anticipation of the evening's entertainment. Lunar juice.

A clear, lapis lazuli night sky of unfathomable depths flowed gently above him. In his thirty-four years Madoc had discovered many passions. Playing football for Wrexham, beating his mates at snooker and pool, watching Manchester United whenever he could, as well as photography. The latter enabled him to stargaze and tonight, as the first Full Moon of the year climbed alluringly in all her magnificence, Madoc wished to admire this siren's potted silvery sparkle by taking stunning photographs of her. He was determined to take a uniquely professional shot to enter a national competition. Expertly he set up his stand, telescope, and Sony A7IV camera. As he spent an hour preparing for a particular view he had in mind, the moon hung tantalisingly between the Vardre's two delicately uneven humps.

A wonder at proficiency and staging, the moment had arrived for Madoc. His camera clicked and whirred. Suddenly he stopped.

"Excuse me. Do you think you're the most important person in the world?" he shouted into the thin night air.

"Me?" replied an incredulous, female voice.

"Well, I don't see anyone else around here Missy" he bawled.

"I suppose to myself, yes, I *am* the most important person in the world. Why? Do you think you are too because we can't both be?"

"Listen Calamity Jane. You've just walked into my camera shot."

"Oh, have I? It's dark here you know, or hadn't you noticed?" the sassy voice retorted.

"Of course I've noticed. I'm trying to get a shot of the moon, in the dark" responded a furious, sarcastic Madoc.

"Hope you've got a strong aim Mister otherwise you'll miss from there. It's a long way away y'know. According to NASA it's an average of 238,855 miles from Earth, which is about 30 Earths away. That's too long to take a shot. It's a very long way. You can't catch a bus and you're not Cupid."

"Can't catch a bus! Not Cupid! You cheeky madam. I know how far away the moon is from Earth. I'M TRYING TO TAKE A PHOTOGRAPH OF IT AND YOU'VE JUST RUINED MY PICTURE" he bawled. "It's an hour-long exposure." Madoc stated that fact as if Seren would understand its importance to him.

"Sorry" she replied unrepentantly.

"And I know you don't mean that" barked Madoc.

"See you then Prince Charming. My Knight in Shining Armour" was the sarcastic response as Seren walked away.

"Hey Missy. What are you doing on the Vardre alone at this time of night?"

"Why? You going to take me home on your trusty white steed?" she questioned defiantly. "Or shoot an arrow from your quiver?"

"No I'm bloody not."

"Nice shot. See you around Mister" was the brazen retort.

With that the woman walked away, out of Madoc's sight. Thank goodness.

'And you look daft in that stupid bloody duvet coat' he thought. 'Cheeky madam.'

After about ten minutes he felt very guilty for letting the bolshy madam walk away, alone, on the Vardre.

'Damn. Should've offered to escort her home. Now she'll be on my conscience. And she's disappeared into the night. Bloody hell.'

During the late night and early morning Madoc snapped and clicked away, taking photograph upon photograph, using hour long exposures. He was using deep space photography to capture the brightest external spiral galaxy closest to Earth, at 2.5 million light years away, the Andromeda Galaxy. As well as aiming for a unique picture of the Wolf Moon, he was snapping photographs of two million years old Orion's Nebula. He thought he had managed to achieve the shots he wanted which satisfied him.

At daybreak he planned to take images of the sun rising between the Vardre's mounds. Now time for a doze. He zipped himself into the sleeping bag, settled into a comfortable position, and grabbed some rest before his camerawork bonanza began again. As he entered the unique state of consciousness which processed his past, present and future, images of the moon, stars and a woman silhouetted against the night sky invaded his dreams.

"What the bloody hell …" Alarm flared inside his stomach as Madoc felt something wet and warm lick his cheek. His eyes opened to see a close-up of two soggy black nostrils.

"Hello dog" he said in surprise to an affable medium-sized black cocker spaniel. "Where have you come from?" Madoc stroked its soft fur.

"Erm, hello Mister."

"Bloody hell" a shocked Madoc replied. "I didn't know dogs could speak."

"I don't like to boast but my dogs are amazingly talented. Especially Moon" replied Seren without pausing to think.

"Obviously, it's me speaking, not Moon. I'm the woman outside your tent" she added unnecessarily.

The dog, introduced as Moon, cheekily licked Madoc's cheek again.

"Please will you ask Moon to back out of my tent so that I can wriggle out of my sleeping bag?"

"I won't need to. He'll be back with me in a moment" said Seren.

Moon decided to pinch a piece of bread from Madoc's rucksack before returning to his mistress.

Hastily pulling on a pair of Levi jeans and a yellow Adidas sweatshirt, Madoc crawled out of his tent to stand in front of a five-feet six-inch fizz ball named Seren. But he didn't know her name because they hadn't been introduced.

"You!" he said.

"Just stopped by to say I'm sorry about disturbing your photo shoot last night" explained Seren.

Madoc was taken aback.

"Apology accepted. Thank you. I'm sorry for being bad mannered. I should've offered to walk you back down the Vardre."

"No problem" responded Seren as she turned away.

It was too early in the morning for him to think sensibly before the amusing fizz ball had marched on. An opportunity missed. He could have invited her to share breakfast with him instead, after a few moments he shouted after her:

"Your dog's called Moon?"

She spun around.

"Yes. This one's Moon and that one" she said pointing to another black spaniel "she's called Star."

With that, she turned and left without a backward glance.

"I was a bit sharp" he shouted.

She raised her arm in acknowledgement, still she didn't look back but thought 'when he's not growling, he's quite appealing' Seren chuckled at her own pun. 'And his green eyes are gorgeous. Bet he's happily married with about fifteen kids.'

'*She's out early*' ruminated Madoc as he gathered his sensibilities, and prepared porridge, eggs and one slice of hot buttered toast slathered with Conwy honey. The other slice had been pinched by that scamp, Moon.

Ten minutes later the sun was sassily sneaking a glimpse of the Vardre when Madoc set up his camera and stand. '*More stunning shots,*' he thought. '*Competition, here we come. At least that crazy woman won't come back and disturb me. Who calls their dogs Moon and Star?*' he wondered, then conceded '*brilliant names. She's an intriguing woman. Wonder who she is? Her amber eyes flecked with copper were mesmerising.*'

In the distance Seren's russet coloured hair shone in the low
sunlight as she walked along the side of Deganwy Castle ruins.
Madoc looked down to Conwy town framed against the white-
topped waves of a glittering sea, the shadowy green mountains
of Carneddau, Tal-y-Fan and Conwy to the left, and the
magnificent Great Orme to the right. He silently rebuked
himself for not asking her out, he had noticed the woman
wasn't wearing a ring. He manoeuvred himself back to the
photography task and decided that he'd better focus on getting
spectacular shots of the sunrise. Forget women, he decided,
they weren't his forte.

In the early morning sunshine, as she crossed the Vardre, Seren
was certain that she had judged the wild camper harshly. He
had waited for the correct timing, and she'd spoiled his
photographs. Silently she chastised herself for being lost in
thought last night and interrupting him. Her mind re-ran the
previous evening's events and her arrival at Bryn Gosol where
Gwen had been waiting anxiously for her return.

"Oh Seren cariad tlws, you're here, safe. I was beginning to
worry about you."

"Sorry nain. The time ran away with me and before I knew it,
the Wolf Moon was rising on the Vardre. I intended to be here
earlier for our tealeaf reading. This is a first for me and I'm
excited that we're doing it. Thank you nain. I'll go and put on
the kettle for a panad".[11]

Seren undid her navy puffer coat, hung it in the boot room,
walked into the kitchen, sniffed the aroma of freshly baked
Welsh cakes on the griddle, and sighed. It was always so heart-
warming here at Bryn Gosol. As she walked down the hallway

---

[11] Cup of tea.

towards the kitchen, simultaneously Gwen arrived from the front living room.

"Grab the old brown teapot Seren. You know the one I call Niwbwrch[12] that my nain hen[13] passed on to me? I think it's in the top cupboard out of harm's way. It should be next to the willow patterned cup and saucer which we'll also use."

"Ok nain. Please may I help you make the panad?"

"Of course cariad tlws."

Seren observed the tealeaf reading brew of her beloved nain, the gwrach gwyn. Gwen placed three heaped teaspoons of loose tea into the brown teapot, Niwbwrch, poured boiling water over the leaves and left the combination to stew for ten minutes. The two ladies busied themselves in the kitchen and chatted about taid.

"Right Seren, the tea should be ready now. Let's take Niwbwrch, the cup and saucer into the back dining room."

Her nain looked at her closely and instructed "be brave Seren, the Roman soldier won't disturb us as we read the tealeaves. You know that."

Seren tittered, inhaled deeply, and carried the tray into the back dining room. She removed a clear quartz crystal from the antique, black Welsh dresser and held it tightly in her hand. *For protection*! Her nain rolled a pink candle in lavender essential oil, then lit it. When nain stirred the tealeaves, Seren observed that they were swirled in a clockwise direction "to

---

[12] Town in Anglesey but used as a pet name for the teapot.
[13] Great Grandmother.

bring in good things" until a froth appeared on top of the liquid "because this brings in money" her nain imparted. Seren poured the tea and waited for it to cool.

"Remember Seren, don't add any milk and take three gulps. Turn the cup around three times and place it upside down onto the saucer."

Seren followed the instructions carefully.

Gwen lifted the teacup and her shrewd piercing eyes scrutinized the tealeaves in the cup.

"Well, cariad tlws, I see the shape of a ceffyl[14] with a male rider."

"Oh what does a man on a horse mean?"

"It's a lover coming to you. I see a tall man."

"Great. But not a giant?"

"No. Not a giant! See these raised triangle shapes around the cup?"

"Yes. Those shapes are very clear."

"They represent mountains. This man likes the outdoors."

"That sounds promising, because so do I."

"See these dots above him, they represent stars."

---

[14] Horse.

"Is he an astronaut?"

Gwen shook her head and laughed.

"There's a crescent moon about the marchogwr ceffyl.[15] That signifies success, and no, he's not an astronaut!"

"Pity, but good at the same time."

"The man has a bar across his shoulders."

"A gymnast?"

"It means he's carrying a load on his shoulders, possibly equipment."

"A hiker?"

"Possibly a hiker. Yes."

"Here, this shape, of an anchor, depicts stability and boats."

"A fisherman or a sailor?"

"Wait Seren" advised her grandmother.

"I'm getting carried away. Romance hasn't gone too well for me y'know nain. I'm in need of your powerful magic."

Gwen laughed.

"This shape here represents a ring."

---

[15] Horse rider.

"A lifeguard?"

"A lifeguard? Where have you got that from?"

"A rubber ring that you throw into the water to save someone, or that you learn to swim with" insisted Seren.

"No! Now you're being silly" Gwen chastised.

"He's going to ring me? On the telephone?"

"I know that you're teasing me Seren. You know what I mean. A ring that you'll wear on your finger darling girl."

Seren was flabbergasted. Astonished.

"Nain I hate to tell you this but you're way off the mark. There's no-one in my life that I'm remotely interested in. No-one's going to give me a ring."

"There are tealeaves here" and Gwen pointed to shapes which represented an eagle and a bull "which are puzzling. Why would an eagle and bull show up in your tealeaves?"

"I've got it. It's Titus. The Roman Legate. He had tattoos of an eagle and a bull."

"Goodness. Oh yes, you said he did. Perhaps it's that then, pointing to a past life. Perhaps unresolved issues?" Gwen's eyes opened wide in surprise.

"Furthermore, see these shapes that look like three columns with a triangle on top?" persisted Gwen.

"Yes. They're easy to understand. The shapes represent temples" replied Seren.

"Yes temples. You're right."

"The last shape is a plane to show a journey, and can you see there Seren? The initials T and M. Perhaps you're going to Rome to see Titus" chuckled Gwen.

"Very funny nain. You know that there weren't aeroplanes in Ancient Roman times and that Titus exists in one of my past lives. There aren't any Legates in Conwy."

"A tall man, with the initials T and M, who loves the outdoors, is going to give you a ring to wear. And you're going to visit Rome."

"Nain, sadly there is no man in my life, outdoorsy or indoorsy. I'm not even in *any* kind of relationship. There's absolutely no chance I'll receive a ring. No man I've ever met, and I'm twenty-seven now remember, no man I've ever met has been worth the effort. I don't even have any holidays booked, and there are no plans to visit Rome!" stated a baffled Seren. "In the mathematical law of probability, is it likely that this time you're wrong?"

"We'll see darling girl. Be alert to coincidences. To synchronicities. Make a note of your daydreams and sleeping dreams. Keep your eyes open for the unexpected and send out positive energy. Manifest what you want. The Universe will respond to your expectations by giving you what you ask for. Beware. Only ask for good things Seren. Bear in mind the lemniscate, the sign of infinity, the sideways number eight, as it represents what goes around comes around."

"I will nain. Tomorrow, I wanted to go up the Vardre very early in the morning. I've made an idiot of myself with a wild camper up there and I was hoping to apologise. I'll take the dogs with me. Do you mind if we eat breakfast a little later?"

"Not at all. Taid and I could do with a lie-in bed at our time of life. Especially, taid, he's been tired lately."

"Great. Thanks nain for doing my tealeaves. One day, please will you teach me how to read them?"

"Of course."

"Well, speak of someone and they're sure to appear. Here's taid, back with the dogs already. We're in the back dining room Tomos" shouted Gwen as she blew out the pink candle.

Noisy chatter, barking and scuffling emanated from the long hallway. A black cocker spaniel bowled into the back dining room, skidding on the stone tiled floor, followed closely by another. The two excited dogs bounded around until they were dizzy. As she watched them fondly, Seren's head was in a whirl. She felt impatient to walk the Vardre in the morning, to see the wild camper again and at least apologise for being thoughtless.

Both dogs nestled their noses on her knees, with soulful eyes they stared up at her affectionately. It felt as if they were enveloping her in a loving embrace. Their warmth restored Seren's hope. Perhaps the world was shifting? Possibly even in her favour? She hardly dared to believe that her nain would be right, she might meet someone she could love and respect who would feel the same way about her. She'd been heart-achingly lonely for a very long time and despite her grandmother's prognostications, harboured an irrational belief that she would always be alone. Surely twenty-seven was ancient to be without a partner. The only men she could manage to attract were in past lives.

Curious to understand how the mind works, Seren had been listening on YouTube to Sadhguru, a spiritual leader. He believed that the mind could cause people problems if they did not take control of their consciousness. He said that everything was referred to as *body*: physical, mental, energy, etheric and bliss but that meditation helped people to unlock the etheric part of their bodies for astral travel. This enabled the soul, the *vital energy* known as *prana,* to leave the physical body and visit different dimensions but required mastery of the mind. Most people would view astral travel as an *out-of-body experience.* For some this might be looking down at themselves from above, or a sensation of experiencing a separation from their body, or an awareness of events they wouldn't have seen from their usual perspective.

Sitting in the blue velvet chair, beside the wood-burning stove, Seren lit the diffuser with thyme essential oil. Both dogs lovingly at feet, she closed her eyes and meditated whilst nain and taid were in the kitchen. Holding a clear quartz crystal to her third eye, Seren breathed in deeply to the count of ten seconds, held her breath for ten seconds then exhaled for ten seconds. Within minutes, she entered a unique state of meditation, on the edge of wakefulness and sleep. Taking charge of her etheric body, her *soul* left her physical body for an *out-of-body* experience ready to travel along her timeline. She planned to return to the Vardre, on the Ides of March where the Legate was in battle with the mighty Ordovices and Ceres was anxious about the fate of her soulmate. This is what Seren experienced.

Standing on the spongy damp grass beneath the coiled branches of the Devil's Tree, Ceres shuddered and tightly clutched the amber handle of her pugio. She could hear the shrieks and yells of battle on the Vardre. The rancid smell of burning blood, flesh, hair, and sinew, the vile stench of death illuminated her senses. This was not the time to cry, it was an occasion to fight. She ran along the narrow lanes where contorted crack willow trees mixed with holly bushes to guide her way along the dirt track. Shivering with terror, heart bursting with fear, for the screams rising from the battle in the Ordovices village were inhumane, she carried on. As Ceres approached the settlement, her running slowed to a quick walk. Taking cover between the thick, fissured trunks of oak trees she dropped close to the evergreen gorse bushes. The coconut perfumed yellow flowers signified hope, regardless of the terrifying events unfolding in front of her.

Ceres knew that Titus had planned to take a group of eighty men into battle. With nerves of steel, she observed the night sky irradiate as legionaries shot burning arrows from their bows and fired balls of bubbling tar from onagers towards their enemy. Men with blue-painted faces screeched in scorched pain, blistered women howled, charred children shrieked and bawled, gutted homes smouldered. The Roman soldiers, led by Titus, were merciless. Illuminated by the blood-red blazing tar balls spitting through the night sky, a young woman fled deftly from the village towards the oak trees. Ceres watched the female crouch and hide behind gorse bushes. As the insatiable spectre of death visited those who lay bleeding with the village ablaze around them, in tight formation, the Roman army quelled the fiercely resistant Ordovices tribe.

The legionaries rounded up screaming and stomping women and disorientated, frightened children to take back to camp as slaves. Lives stolen. The fearful woman hiding in the bushes watched. Ceres sprang forward, held her pugio to the woman's throat, and grabbed her hair tightly.

"I'll slit your throat if you move" yelled Ceres. "Who are you?"

"I am Princess Teranica, wife of Chief Eigion, leader of the Ordovices" she stated bravely.

In the burning glow of the thin night air Ceres heard warmonger Titus bark orders to the legionaries, telling them to surrender any wounded male Ordovices to their fate, by slaying them. The chaotic, pitiless melee continued. Adrenalin coursed through her body, Ceres dragged her female captive by the hair, through gorse bushes, into the smouldering settlement and threw her to the ground in front of the Legate.

"This woman, Titus, has told me that she is Princess Teranica, wife of the Ordovices tribe leader, Chief Eigion. She was trying to escape."

"Ceres" he exclaimed in surprise, looking first at her, then at her captive. Titus smiled to himself. "I see you have used your pugio well."

"Yes. I was trained by a master. What will you do with the woman?"

"My soldiers will hold her captive and take her to Rome. She will be dishonoured, face the humiliation of being paraded through the streets because of her status, then killed. We will celebrate this success for Caesar in Rome at a ceremony called the Triumph."

Standing among the insidious filth of war, Ceres shuddered. She had observed that Titus had a brutal temperament but was more scandalized to witness her own ruthlessness. Her cruelty towards another woman, knowing she had condemned her to a fate worse than death, where she would be subjected to predatory Roman behaviour, was appalling.

With horror, as Seren watched this past life, she contemplated what lessons would her soul learn from this?

Chapter 8 – A Blind Date?

Life makes us the people we are.

"She's an older model."

"What, Kate Moss? I've got a blind date with Kate? Gareth mate, you've pulled a blinder there" exclaimed Madoc. "Thought she was married to Tom Brady? She'd be perfect for me."

"No you numpty. I don't mean the supermodel. And anyway, she *isn't* married to Tom Brady."

"Well I'm not going to another *grab a granny* night with you Gareth. The last time you arranged a blind date, that woman turned out to be a bossy, control freak who wouldn't let go. She was very needy. You know I'm a free spirit."

"By older model I mean she's not a spring chicken."

"What I infer from that is she's got chicken legs, like that one from Wrexham you landed me with."

"Nope. You've got it all wrong Madoc."

"She comes with a good reference this one."

"A reference from her guardian who will have a skewed view, or who probably wants to get rid of her?"

"Nope. She works with Haf at the Quay Hotel. Something to do with holistic therapies. You know, meditating and yoga. All the stuff that you do."

"I don't do yoga or meditating. I'm not bendy and can't let go of my thoughts long enough to contemplate anything other than what's happening right now. Have you got the wrong bloke?" chided Madoc.

"You're the archetypal outdoor man. Women love that."

"Look Gareth just because I walk up the Vardre now and again doesn't mean I'm Bear Grylls."

"You've been to Patagonia, Madoc. I thought that was a clothing brand, not a place. Look at me, it's a good thing that Haf loves me because I'm hardly Tom Brady am I?"

"A bit hefty mate, that's all. You're overweight because Haf's such a good cook so it's her fault really" Madoc concluded crisply.

"I'll drink to that" agreed Gareth good-naturedly, as he lifted his pint of Stella lager.

"I'll join you because I'm nervous as hell. Cheers mate. How is it you always persuade me to do what I *really* don't want to do?" admonished Madoc.

"Because I'm charming. Haf and her friend are due any minute. I can't remember her bloody name. Down your pint mate and I'll get another round in."

"Gareth. You know I'm rubbish with women. I don't know what to talk to them about. When I get tongue-tied and start blabbering, step in mate. Rescue me" pleaded Madoc.

"I usually do yer muppet. We've been mates forever and I always bail you out" Gareth chided.

"I thought you said they'd be here for eight o'clock."

"Probably seen you through the window and dumped you before the two of you have even met" Gareth said with relish at his mate's discomfort. "Haf won't let you down. You know that."

The two women did arrive unexpectedly late. Haf peered cautiously around the door of the Mulberry pub in Conwy and managed to catch sight of Gareth.

"They're here" whispered Haf, who didn't know why she was being quiet as Gareth and Madoc were across the room.

"Look cool" instructed Haf. "Follow me. I'm heading for the fireplace."

"I've got my head down so that I can't see him. I'm extending the length of time until disappointment engulfs me. I'll follow you. Lead on" replied her companion, staring down at Haf's purple high heeled shoes. She followed her friend, trying obediently to *look cool*, not quite knowing how to do so whilst her eyes were unable to gaze above ankle height.

The two women approached the two men. Upon meeting, Haf kissed Gareth on the cheek, then turned directly to Madoc, whose eyes were gaping into the fire rather than in her direction.

"Madoc" Haf said quietly.

Madoc stood up from his seat, and turned, all in one movement which caused him to stumble backwards into the leather armchair. When he landed the chair made an unpleasant squeaking noise. Nonplussed, the second attempt he made at standing was successful. The only casualty was his pride. He met the eyes of Haf and then her friend. Madoc squawked "I know you" and shook his head in disbelief.

"And I know you" Seren replied, smiling. "You're Madoc. Great to put a name to a face."

"Likewise, Seren" agreed Madoc.

"Shouldn't that be a face to a name?" questioned a bemused Haf.

"No" Madoc and Seren responded in unison, tittering at their interconnection.

"You two know each other?" questioned a befuddled Gareth.

"No" Seren and Madoc responded in harmony "but we do" and they both laughed.

"We'll get the drinks. Come on Haf, let's leave them to it" instructed Gareth as he pulled Haf to the bar.

"Did you know they knew each other?" a baffled Haf asked.

"No. They don't. I'm sure they don't" responded Gareth who really had no idea.

"They just said they did" countered Haf patiently.

"Let's leave them to it. Keep watch though because I've promised Madoc if he's looks lost for words, we'll intervene" said Gareth as though he and Haf were Superman and Superwoman.

"Good idea. He's useless at chatting up women. It could all turn sour in the blink of an eye" replied Haf, laughing.

But it didn't.

"Look at those two. They've not stopped chatting and laughing all evening" said a delighted Gareth.

"I know. Great isn't it? I knew she'd like him. What should we do? The pub's about to close. I'll go and tell them we're going home."

"Good idea Haf. You tell 'em" smirked Gareth.

Madoc and Seren were sitting comfortably around the fire.

"Excuse me you two. Gareth and I are leaving now. Do you want to come with us or shall I see you tomorrow Seren?" asked Haf pointedly.

Seren cast her eyes away from Madoc, towards Haf and beamed.

"Let's see each other tomorrow Haf. Thank you for bringing me and introducing me to Madoc" replied a bold-as-brass Seren.

Madoc excused himself and strode over to Gareth.

"You've pulled a master stroke Gareth. Thankfully she's not as tall as Kate Moss otherwise I'd have to go on tiptoes to kiss her. Anyway, forget what I said about the supermodel. Thanks mate. See you tomorrow?" babbled Madoc.

"Anytime Madoc" answered a delighted Gareth.

Unlike his unchivalrous behaviour the first night they met on the Vardre, Madoc insisted he walk with Seren to Llanrhos, back to Bryn Gosol Farm. She didn't invite him in to meet her nain and taid as she wished to speak to her grandmother. Instead, she arranged to meet him the following afternoon to walk up the Vardre.

"How did your blind date go Seren?" questioned taid who was sitting at the oak table in the kitchen. "Was it as awful as you expected it to be?"

"It was great" replied Seren as she kissed his head.

Her taid was shocked. Never had she enjoyed a date before. She was a fussy one his cariad tlws.

"Where's nain?" Seren wished to discuss her astral experience with her grandmother.

"She's sitting in the back dining room. Pop your head round the door, she's dying to know how the date went" suggested taid but Seren had other things on her mind which needed clarification first.

In the back dining room ylang ylang essential oil was burning and her grandmother sat by the inglenook fireplace, staring into the flames.

"Nain. You're burning ylang ylang. I thought that was to eliminate fear and anxiety? Funny that you should be burning that tonight. Are you ok?"

"Yes cariad tlws. I'm fine. How did the blind date go?"

"Taid just asked me the same thing. It was splendid. We got on very well thank you. We are seeing each other tomorrow and having a picnic at the top of the Vardre."

"Magnificent news. What troubles you then?"

"Anyone would think you were a white witch" replied Seren in a gently mocking manner.

Gwen smiled.

"Tell me what's on your mind" prodded Gwen.

Seren told Gwen about her astral travel revelations.

"So you see nain, I knew that Titus was a fierce fighting man but I didn't realise how ruthless *I* was in a past life. Do you know what lesson my soul will learn from last night's revelations?" she implored.

"You were upset by your behaviour, Seren? Your callousness? It was a time of war which brings great tragedy. Unspeakable misery. In those circumstances, I would view it differently cariad tlws. You recognise that you were cruel and now you are remorseful. Surely that's a lesson? You cannot be dispassionate when you understand human suffering. Isn't that an epic journey you've travelled, and a lesson learned? Take time to think about what you know Seren. Astral journeys aren't always sunshine and roses darling girl. Undertake them wisely."

"I know that now nain" sighed Seren. "Thank you for listening to me. Goodnight."

"Sleep well Seren. It sounds as though your sunshine and roses may happen tomorrow when you go up the Vardre."

The following morning dawned very brightly for Seren. She was excited to see Madoc and changed her clothes at least three times, before settling on Levi jeans and a green cashmere polo-neck jumper. She wondered if green suited her. It did. Leaving Bryn Gosol, she turned right and traipsed over the field that led to a narrow, overgrown lane which only locals knew about. She climbed the steep stile, dodged the soggy marshland, avoided stepping on some early blooming yellow-eyed, bright blue forget-me-nots before arriving, almost mud-free, at the bottom of the Vardre. Madoc was already waiting for her.

"You look lovely" he complimented.

"Thank you. So do you" she replied appreciatively.

As they approached the top of the Vardre, with Madoc panting for breath he said:

"I don't know about Puss in Boots, I'm more like Puffin' Boots carrying this picnic."

Seren laughed.

"Do you need me to lug anything? Are you ok?"

"Don't worry about me, I'm like a camel … but I never get the hump" was his straight reply, at which Seren exploded with laughter. Ice firmly broken.

When he was a young lad, Madoc informed Seren, he and his sister Aila explored Aberdeen town, paddle-boarded in the freezing cold industrial grey North Sea, took photographs of the night sky then developed them under the tutelage of his grandfather, The Ghillie, and fished from his grandfather's boat, The Seashell.

"The Ghillie's boat was called *The Seashell*?" questioned Seren, her voice rising.

"That's right. Why?" responded Madoc.

Seren lifted her hair, to reveal a seashell tattoo on the back of her neck.

"You're kidding me!!" Madoc exclaimed. "I don't believe this."

"Don't you like tattoos on women?" asked Seren briskly.

"Yes, yes I like them" reassured Madoc. "It's that you have a seashell tattoo and The Ghillie's boat was named The Seashell. What a coincidence. Do you have any others?"

"Where do I begin?" she teased.

"Anywhere you like" suggested Madoc saucily.

Seren rolled up the left sleeve of her green cashmere polo-neck jumper to show a seven-sided star on her inner wrist.

"What does the heptagram represent?"

"I'm a little embarrassed to tell you because this is where you'll bow out and decide not to see me again. You're probably going to think I'm weird."

Madoc was perturbed by this statement and wondered what on earth Seren would reveal about herself. '*If she is weird*', he thought, '*I'm running down the Vardre never to be seen again. Fancy her or not.*'

"Go on" he persuaded. And waited for the blow.

"I have another one on my right wrist" Seren responded and exposed the tattoo of a full moon, flanked either side by a crescent moon.

He raised his eyebrows and said: "Ok now tell me what they represent."

Seren took an unnecessarily long and deep inhale of breath.

"The star is a faery star. It's to signify the faery world."

She looked at Madoc who hadn't started to run. Yet.

"And the other tattoo?" he questioned brazenly.

Seren looked at Madoc shyly and blushed.

"The triple moon represents the Goddess."

"Which Goddess? The Moon Goddess?" an intrigued Madoc pushed for answers.

"This tattoo represents intuition and psychic insight" unveiled Seren.

"Why do you have those tattoos then? What's important about them?"

"Before I answer those questions, first, do you have any tattoos?"

He laughed and said: "well dodged."

Seren smiled.

"I'll show you when we stop to eat our picnic" he promised.

"Nice change of subject Madoc" laughed Seren. "What have you brought for us to eat?"

"Spam sandwiches, lemon curd tarts and ginger beer."

"Oh all totally disgusting" winced Seren.

"Thanks. That's given me a lot of confidence in my choice of food Missy" he teased.

"Really? What have you brought?" persevered Seren.

"A variety of sandwiches: chicken, roast beef, cheese, egg, and tuna. Two vanilla cake slices as a reward for hiking up here and a flask of coffee. I hope the sandwiches aren't stale because I made them last night as soon as I got home."

"Even if they are stale, I'll use my manners and eat them without complaint. I'm vegetarian so I'll go for the cheese and egg please" replied Seren.

"You're quite charming" responded Madoc, amused.

They ate their picnic on the flat lush top of the Vardre overlooking picturesque Conwy Harbour and the unruly Irish Sea. Perfection even if the wind was a little blowy. When they had finished eating Seren prompted Madoc to show his tattoos. He lifted the leg of his Levi jeans to reveal the mark of Julius Caesar's elite Legio X Equestris on his left calf. Dumbfounded, it was an age before Seren spoke.

"Do you have any others?" she probed quietly.

"Yes. Two more here." Madoc removed his jumper and rolled the sleeves of his white t-shirt to reveal tattoos of a bull and eagle on his shoulders. Seren choked. She'd seen them before. In another life.

2023

Chapter 9 – Goodnight Darling

Spiritual people are tested.

It was unsophisticated, she knew, but Seren practically ran all
way the home from the bottom of the Vardre after her second
date with Madoc. Splashing in the mud on the marshland, she
traipsed through the damp field, clambered over the rickety
wooden stile, ran down the narrow, overgrown lane, and turned
left to Bryn Gosol Farm. Full of excitement.
'Wait until nain and taid hear all about this' she thought
incredulously as she sprinted home. 'They will not believe
what's just happened to me.'

The gate to Bryn Gosol Farm was open which stopped Seren
dead in her tracks. An ambulance was parked outside the
farmhouse, with its back doors open. She spotted a stretcher
being carried out of the house. A red cotton blanket covered a
patient. Seren's heart skipped plenty of beats, not just one.
Running down the driveway felt like jumping into thick, black,
melted tar. Breathlessly she arrived at the farmhouse. It took
all her might not to cry.

"Seren, it's taid. He's very poorly cariad tlws. He's had a
heart-attack. The ambulance driver is going to put on the blue
light to get him to Abergele Hospital as quickly as possible"
bumbled a flustered Gwen.

A sudden, unexpected, ugly thought leapt into Seren's mind:
'*what if he doesn't make it?*' She leant over the stretcher and
kissed the top of taid's head, as she'd done a million times
before, but this was the first time she'd kissed him on a
stretcher. He felt clammy and was pale as a glass of freshly

squeezed cow's milk. A putrid grey hue. His eyes remained shut tight. He didn't even flinch.

"Please don't let this be the last time I see him alive" begged Seren of the paramedics.

"We're doing everything we can" was the reassuring response.

"Taid. I hope you can hear me. I love you so much. Please hold on" implored Seren.

In the daylight hours, from Saint Hilary's church yard an owl screeched again and again and again. Seren and Gwen knew owls to be harbingers of death. They looked at each other in horror as the ambulance sped away.

Awkwardly, Seren gathered belongings which she thought her grandfather might need in the hospital and quickly placed them in an old blue holdall. She bustled her shaky grandmother into her white Mini Cooper car and sped to the hospital as fast as legal speed limits would allow. A few may have been exceeded. Once parked, directly outside the Accident and Emergency Unit, encumbered by bags, car keys and a bundle of regrets, Seren accompanied her shrunken grandmother to Reception.

"We're here to see my grandfather Tomos Williams said a shaky Seren.

The Receptionist screwed up her grey eyes and checked the computer to find Tomos's whereabouts.

'She probably needs glasses' thought Seren.

A puzzled look appeared on the Receptionist's finely red-veined face.

"I probably need glasses as I can't find his name here. Just a minute. Let me check on another screen" she said before trotting off to view a different computer.

Seren nearly said "neigh. You can't find him?" but decided against it under the circumstances. Instead she placed her arm gently around her grandmother's sunken shoulders and said the most stupid thing that people in challenging situations seem to always say: "don't worry, it'll be all right." Absurd because Seren and her grandmother knew it wouldn't be all right.

"Aahh. Here he is" reported the Receptionist as if she had found Tomos inside the computer. "I'll just take you to waiting room number 12. A doctor will be with you shortly."

Seren bought her grandmother an insipid, lukewarm cup of tea from the nearby vending machine to drink while they waited.

"What is it about hospitals, that you seem to spend a lifetime waiting but not much happens in between?" quizzed Seren.

"The doctors are arguing about whose turn it is to tell the relatives that someone has died" stated her grandmother straightforwardly.

"Nain!" exclaimed Seren. "Please don't say that."

"Seren, you know he has cariad tlws. They're gathering his belongings and will ask us to go and see his body. Prepare yourself."

Gwen began to cry.

"We've been together since I was eighteen Seren. I don't want to carry on without Tomos. He was my soulmate. We did everything together. We were happy with each other. Most people spend a lifetime searching for the kind of joy which we shared. We were sprinkled with moon dust. I'm thankful for Tomos and the life we've had together."

Her tough grandmother's pitiful expression horrified Seren. She moved to hug her nain more tightly than she had ever done and as she did so, felt her grandmother begin to wither away. Powerless, in silence they sat together for an eternity. In reality it was forty-five minutes before a grim-faced doctor came to tell them the news that Tomos had passed "despite their best efforts". That ounce of glimmering hope that Seren held onto was extinguished.

Gwen and Seren were taken from room 12 into a bright white side room where Tomos lay under a pale blue cotton blanket. Alone. Gwen stroked his ashen face and kissed his purple lips, Seren planted a kiss on the top of his head wishing he would spring into life, but instead she bade him goodbye. His clothes, watch and wedding ring had been placed into a plain white plastic carrier bag. Seren picked up the bag, along with his blue holdall, held her grandmother's trembling arm and the two of them walked away carrying a lifetime of happy memories.

Ffarwel cariad nosda, Na'i dy garu di am byth. X

Farewell darling, goodnight, I will love you forever. x

Chapter 10 – The Story Of My Life, Begins and Ends With You

Can we physically move to moments in time?

When his mobile 'phone rang, showing Seren's number, Madoc answered warily.

"Hello."

"Madoc?"

"Yes" he replied guardedly.

"It's Seren."

"Oh. Yes?" his voice didn't sound welcoming.

"Do you have time to speak?"

"I have a few minutes free, yes" he still didn't sound friendly.

"I wanted to apologise for not contacting you sooner."

"Oh, it's no problem. I've been busy and hadn't noticed." But he had.

"When I got back to the farm after our picnic last Sunday, my taid was being taken away in an ambulance."

"I'm sorry to hear that Seren. How is he?" Madoc's tone changed to one of concern.

"Well, that's the reason I've not been in touch. He died in the hospital on the same day."

"Bloody hell Seren. I'm so sorry to hear that." Madoc slapped the side of his head because he had assumed Seren wasn't interested in him and that's why she hadn't telephoned.

"Thank you." She sighed. "Look, it's the funeral next week and I know we said we'd catch up with each other soon, but please may I leave it until after my taid has been buried? My nain needs me and I've lots of organising to do."

"No problem." He was relieved that Seren still wanted to see him at some point. "Is there anything I can do to help with the arrangements, or around the farm, or get some groceries?" he burbled.

On the other end of the 'phone, Seren smiled.

"No thank you, we're fine. But is it ok if I ring you sometime soon?"

"Absolutely." He sounded delighted.

"Great. I'll see you before long then."

"You will. And Seren?"

"Yes."

"I really *am* sorry to hear about your taid. I could tell how much you love your grandparents from the way you were speaking about them when we met on the Vardre. I feel as though I know them intimately."

Seren smiled.

"Thanks Madoc. I do go on about them, don't I? I'll ring you soon. Bye" and with that she ended the 'phone call before she wept.

The days following taid's death felt as if their lives had been scrambled by a tornado, whipping Seren into a frenzy of activity and sending her nain into hiding. Day after day, nain sat in the front living room, by the inglenook fire, staring into the twirling flames watching the wood charring, scorching, and cracking. As the wood discharged heat energy, in synchrony, nain's energy was released too. She wilted. Seren ensured that the farmworkers carried on with their routine jobs and hired four extra staff to cover the chores of nain and taid. She queued up at Conwy Register Office, which was based in Llandudno to record taid's death.

"Right I'll need his: birth certificate, Council Tax bill, driving licence, marriage certificate, NHS medical card, passport, proof of address (eg utility bill)" reeled off the Registrar as if this was a routine list. Which it was. For him but not for Seren.

She answered endless personal questions about taid's name, date of birth, address, occupation until finally the Registrar had enough information and said:

"Ok here's a green form. It's a Certificate for Burial or Cremation and it gives permission for burial or an application for cremation. I'm also going to give you a Certificate of Registration of Death. This is known as form BD8. You might need to complete this and return it if your taid was getting a State Pension or benefits. It's got a pre-paid envelope then you'll know where to send it."

Seren sighed, loudly.

"Is there anything else I can help you with?" queried the Registrar in a perfunctory manner.

"Is that it? Have we finished?" enquired Seren, blood thumping around her brain, cheeks flushed.

"Done. Over in a jiffy. All done and dusted."

'Ashes to ashes. Dust to dust' thought Seren.

It was traumatic and Seren was glad she had told nain to stay at home. Her taid's life registered as over and it had taken less than an hour. She left the building, walked along Penrhyn Crescent, and headed towards the park. Seren breathed in the kelpy sea air so deeply it bounced off the bottom of her lungs. She imagined she'd heard her name being shouted and had a shock when a hand grabbed her arm. As she turned, Madoc was holding on to her.

"Madoc" exclaimed a startled Seren. "How lovely to see you."

"Talk about being difficult to attract! I've been shouting you, but the sound of my voice must've been blown away by this blustery wind. Fancy a coffee?"

"That was my intention. Yes please. I've just registered my taid's death and need a hot drink."

Madoc noticed how pale she looked.

"I don't know what to say Seren except how sorry I am for you and your nain."

He appeared awkward. Seren smiled.

"This is the way, Madoc. People die. People are born. In between we live a little in our liminal space. It's called the circle of life."

Madoc stared at Seren.

"You see the time between being born and then dying as liminal space?" asked Madoc.

"I do, because life, that *inbetweeny* bit, is challenging to navigate!"

'She's delightful, if a little weird' thought Madoc.

"Here, these are for you" said Madoc as he passed a red envelope to Seren. "I was going to post them to you. I didn't expect to bump into you in Llandudno of all places."

"Serendipity" was her response as she opened the envelope.

It contained three photographs; Bryn Gosol farmhouse, a close-up of the refulgent Moon and a panoramic view from the Vardre which comprised Conwy, the Irish Sea and three mountain ranges.

"Oh Madoc, they're exquisite. I shall treasure them. You took these?"

"Yes. For you."

He bent closer to her, to look over her shoulder and removed one photograph from her clutch.

"You see this panoramic view from the Vardre? We live in this picture. We live in that moment. You, your nain and taid are somewhere in that photograph."

She turned to her right, where Madoc was bending at her shoulder, she could feel his breath. Boldly, Seren kissed his cheek.

He was embarrassed and jumped back.

"What would you like to drink? Which type of coffee? Let's get a takeaway so that we can walk and talk" he suggested.

"Café latte for me please. No sugar."

The air felt chillier than usual as they walked across the park, along the elegant Victorian esplanade towards the Great Orme, drinking takeaway café latte in green cardboard cups. Madoc pointed out his home, a yellow-painted three-story Victorian period property which overlooked the curmudgeonly ceaseless wash of the Irish Sea. Seren said his house looked "stunning". She pulled her duvet coat closer around her. Madoc thought she looked graceful! Today, they didn't have time to ride the famous Great Orme tram or cable car to enjoy elevated views of Snowdonia and the Irish Sea, Seren needed to return to Bryn Gosol and her nain.

"Here's my car. Thank you for a lovely time. I needed that" Seren said quietly as they approached a side road.
Madoc bent down and kissed her cheek.

"Keep in touch Seren. Let me know if you need anything."

"I will."

Seren fumbled for her car keys, dropped them on the floor, picked them up and one of her red gloves fell.

'What a bumbling idiot he must think I am' she thought.

If only they knew the symbolic significance of giving a single glove, for it indicated fidelity and loyalty for hundreds of years.

Madoc laughed, picked up the glove and kissed her cheek again. This time she blushed as her heart swelled.

'What a delight she is' thought Madoc.

They waved goodbye to each other. On the way home, as she drove the six minutes journey from Llandudno to Llanrhos she thought about Madoc, her taid and her nain. A tiny piece of the humungous sadness which engulfed her had been pushed away by Madoc. '*After all*' Seren thought '*love is at the centre of the circle of life, bringing with it immense joy and enormous sadness in equal measure. Love always ends in tears, but the liminal space can be amazing.*'

And that's how it was.

Nain and Seren woke early on the day of taid's funeral, each ate a light breakfast of one boiled egg and soldiers before taking a walk around the farmland.

"This will be yours Seren when I move into the spirit world and join taid. Tomos and I talked about you inheriting the farmhouse and the farmland when we died, but I want you to have it now. It's time for you to take over cariad tlws. Prepare yourself as I'm not planning to wait long before I join Tomos. The future without him is so empty and dark. I cannot envision life without him beside me. I am achingly, achingly lonely for him."

Seren merely cried because she knew how lonely life can be. Her nain held Seren tightly against her gentle, olive skin, her penetrating black eyes peered into Seren's soul as she said:

"You have always been protected by taid and me. Before I die, I will show you how to invoke your guardians. Remember? Taid teased you about having protection?"

They both laughed.

"Yes. I remember nain. Let's give taid a good send off today. One that he deserves."

And they did.

The hearse arrived at Saint Hilary's Church carrying taid's coffin surrounded by daffodils, yellow roses, and a photograph of him standing proudly with Gwen outside Bryn Gosol Farmhouse. At the lychgate, The Arch Deacon of Saint Asaph's Diocese began the first part of taid's burial service as the farmworkers formed a guard of honour along the yew tree walk on that sunlit morning. There was standing room only inside the little church. It appeared the whole community of Llanrhos and Conwy turned out to pay tribute to the Church Warden, farmer and decent man that was Tomos Williams. The Farm Manager, James, read Psalm 23, *The Lord is My Shepherd.* It was appropriate for taid, a righteous man who had spent his life walking through the valleys and in green pastures, whose soul would be reincarnated. Indomitable Gwen was like a shadow, frail, delicate, grief ridden, shrinking into herself. When the Welsh choir sang *Men of Harlech* and *All*

Things Bright and Beautiful, Seren understood that her
grandmother's heart had broken as she held her trembling hand.

Sprinkles of spectral light streamed through the stained-glass
windows and onto the pulpit when Seren stood nervously
waiting to say the eulogy. She looked around at the mourners.
Madoc standing tall at the back of the church, next to the large
carved stone set in a niche in the wall, acknowledging Ancient
Roman rule, smiled at her. She began:

"Tomos Williams, my taid, bought Bryn Gosol Farmhouse fifty
years ago with my nain, Gwen. Together they built up the farm
and created a warm, loving, vibrant community for the workers,
many of whom are here today. When I was twelve years old, I
went to live with them at Bryn Gosol, where they offered me
kindness, love, and stability. My nain and taid were the most
amazing grandparents, and the most wonderful people, that
anyone could ever meet.

My taid had a life well-lived, with love and honour in plentiful
supply. Now he is farming in the sublime, celestial green
pastures of heaven and the real pleasure is knowing that his
energy lives on.

Ffarwel cariad nosda, Na'i dy garu di am byth.

Farewell darling, goodnight, I will love you forever."

Taid's body was interred in the peaceful churchyard of Saint
Hilary's, as the crow flies, directly facing Bryn Gosol Farm.

That night as Gwen slept, she felt that Tomos had travelled on
an astral plane, to gently stroke her cheek and tenderly kiss her

goodnight. She lay wrapped in Tomos's loving arms all night. Although this might not fit with received wisdom, it *was* real.

Chapter 11 – Guardians

How can we explain transcendent experiences?

Scientists like Physicist Sean Carroll may explain *consciousness* as "emerging from the collective behaviour of particles and atoms". Mystics such as Sadhguru might describe it as a *"dimension of intelligence which is free from memory, boundless in its nature"*. Seren tried to rationalise consciousness. Loss of her taid had brought to the forefront a range of emotions which she was struggling to fathom.

'Why do we love some people and not others. And what is love? What is sorrow? What creates our feelings? Where do those emotions exist in our body?' She was driving herself dotty.

Seren found it challenging to define, and demanding to believe, that everything was driven by a person's chemistry and biology as most people purported. She was convinced that there must be a spirit, a deity, that exists outside of the chemical and biological, perhaps with powers greater than those of ordinary humans. A dictionary definition led her to consider that an etheric body might be the answer *'a spirit which interacts with humans positively or negatively, to carry us to new levels of consciousness beyond the ordinary day-to-day existence'*.

Deciding to be open-minded was an excellent choice, as her nain was about to blow Seren's mind.

"Cariad tlws there are a few things we need to discuss."

At college, or work, if someone had said those words, she would have been concerned that a chastisement was on its way, but not with her nain. Seren knew that expressions of the utmost importance were going to be delivered.

"I'll make us a panad nain, cut some cheesecake and bring them into the front sitting room."

Stoic Gwen moved slowly to the front sitting room where the fire in the inglenook fireplace smouldered. The tall frame of the worn brown leather wing-backed chair made her delicate body appear tiny. A gold velvet cushion softly propped Gwen's aged spine.

"Here we are nain. Cheesecake freshly baked this morning and a refreshing panad."

Seren poured tea into a blue China cup, cut a thick slice of cheesecake, and handed both to her nain before sitting beside the fire in her favourite faded pink flowery chair. She curled her legs beneath her bottom.

"There are three things we need to discuss cariad tlws which are important to me."

"This sounds serious nain."

"It is serious. I have taken advice from Eleri Holmes, she's a Partner who works at Neville and Mason Solicitors. You know the firm? Based on The Square in Conwy?"

"Yes, everyone knows about Neville and Mason. They're famous in Conwy. Is something wrong nain?"

"Yes and no. Taid and I have put in our Will that you will be the sole beneficiary, receiving Bryn Gosol Farmhouse and farmland when we die. I'm not dead yet though."

"I'd noticed that nain" replied Seren with a twinkle in her eye.

"But I soon will be!"

"Nain, you can't say that" responded an indignant Seren.

"I can say what I like. It's my life! This young woman, Eleri, very efficient she is, she's given me advice."

"About what?"

"Before he died, taid and I discussed you owning the farm and us building a bungalow on the land for ourselves to move into. Leaving the farmhouse and land to you. But taid died before we could begin our plan, and I want you to have it all while I'm still alive. You're running it. I'm not. You manage the farmworkers. I don't. It should be yours. Never mind waiting until I die. Miss Holmes, Eleri, has said that I can give you the farmhouse and the farmland now. Something called a" she paused to look at a scrap of paper, "Deed of Gift. There you are. The farm is yours, but we need to see Eleri Holmes to go through the paperwork to make it official and I want to do that tomorrow. We have an appointment at 10.30 a.m. Don't joke with Eleri Holmes, Seren. She's very" nain searched for appropriate words "shrewd, and sensible."

Nain was still a woman of action despite her devastating loss.

"Are you sure about this nain? You know I could throw you out onto the streets, don't you?" teased Seren.

"I am sure. Definitely. This farmhouse and the land should be yours. That's the first thing I wanted to say. Second thing, when are you going to bring your young man here for me to meet? You've been dating a few weeks and I need to give him a reading before I die."

"Nain. Thank you about the farm. You know I'll treasure it. As for Madoc, I don't want to scare him away with magical talk. You know that some people can be a bit ..." Seren was lost for words.

"A bit one-dimensional? Madoc has got to know sooner or later that he's involved with a gwrach gwyn" said her grandmother sternly, eyes lambent. "It's not something you can, or should, hide."

"I know but how do I approach that? By the way Madoc, you're dating a white witch. I really like him nain. I don't want him running in the opposite direction."

"Don't be ridiculous Seren. He's not going to run away."

"He might walk quickly then."

"I would like to meet him. Tomorrow night. He can have his cards read by me" retorted nain insistently.

There was no arguing with her unshakeable nain.

"Lastly. At your age, you need to know about protection."

"Nain!" exclaimed Seren.

"I'm going to teach you how to invoke your guardians for protection. I promised you that I would teach you ages ago, and I haven't. We'll do it now. I could be dead by the end of the week."

"Good grief nain. Stop speaking like that. You won't be dead by the end of the week! On second thoughts, you might be if we have to do all that wiggling and jiggling we did last time you got out your wand."

Nain laughed.

"We'll stay sitting for this. Save my weary bones. I'll use my wand but I'm going to sit here in my lovely chair. Are you ready Seren?"

"No. I need to text Madoc that he's going to be vetted by you tomorrow. Give me a minute please because my 'phone is in my handbag."

Seren popped to the boot room to text Madoc:

'Are you free to meet my nain tomorrow evening?'

Within two minutes his response was:

'Yes great'

'Oh bloody hell' thought Seren 'that's the end of us then.'

Seren returned to the front sitting room, added some logs to the fire, and sat opposite Gwen in readiness.

"Ready cariad tlws?"

"Ready as I'll ever be" responded Seren "here we go?"

Her nain nodded affirmation, leant across to Seren and passed her an amethyst to hold. Gwen patted the top of Seren's hand as she held the crystal, for reassurance.

"Light one of the white candles on the side table cariad tlws before we begin to meditate."

Seren did as instructed. The cosy room suddenly fizzled with energy.

"Come and sit here, in your favourite place beside the fire. Place your feet flat on the floor to ground yourself. Now, close your eyes and inhale deeply to the count of five, hold to the count of five and release to the count of five. Keep doing that. Release anything in your energy that may be blocking you from the presence of your guardians."

Seren did as instructed. Gwen looked at her sweet face. Unassuming Seren had no notion that she looked like a Roman Goddess. But doesn't every grandmother think that of their granddaughter?

"In your mind, call for the guardians of your highest good, tell them you can receive them. Call upon your ancestral spirit guides."

Seren concentrated on breathing deeply, clearing her mind, and calling upon her guardians. Gwen waited for a few minutes.

"Envision yourself in a circle of golden white light" instructed Gwen.

Seren smiled and continued breathing deeply.

"Let this power surround you and be at peace" said Gwen softly.

Seren was imagining herself to be surrounded by a circle of golden white light while entering a peaceful state of meditation.

"Continue to control your breathing, envision that circle of golden white light around you. Empty your mind."

Seren breathed deeply.

"We have guardian angels, spirit guides, and guides who come into this life with us. They are always looking to direct us on the path for our highest good. Invite your guides and angels to join you" instructed nain.

The air in the room sparkled.

"I can feel a heat at the back of my neck nain, and a tingling sensation around my head and hands" said Seren, surprised.

"Open your third eye and heart chakra to meet and embrace your spirit guides" directed Gwen.

"The tingling sensation is coming through very strongly nain."

Although Seren couldn't see her, Gwen beamed.

"This is the moment where you imagine yourself in a gorgeous place cariad tlws, such as a garden, beach, mountain, the countryside, on a river, wherever you feel the happiest and most comfortable."

"I'm imagining being on the Vardre watching the gentle undulating waves in the distance" responded Seren.

"Breathe gently. Call to mind a memory of a person. Your guides will show you an image or you may see or hear words. You might imagine a feather, or sense a smell such as baking, cigarettes, flowers, perfume. You will know that the guardian has come to you because you will have thoughts and impressions about them."

There was a long silence. The air sizzled with energy.

"I feel as though taid is in the room with us and I can smell his cigarettes. The lady from my vision, the woman who was with Titus is here too. The Roman soldiers called her Ceres. She has long flaming-red hair, a straight nose, a rosebud mouth and is wearing a lurid green dress."

"Good. You will instinctively recognise a feeling of being loved and protected" reassured nain.

"I feel peaceful. Very calm" responded Seren.

"When you meditate this is a way of meeting your guardians," said Gwen.

"I feel as though I'm in a bubble. Taid is stroking my face, and Ceres is giving me a hug. I don't want to be anywhere else."

"It's a unique energy that you're feeling cariad tlws. Embrace it."

There was a long pause, and they could both feel the energy in the room fizzle.

"Let's finish now Seren. Thank your guardians for being with you. It's important that you close the golden white light. Pull the golden white light up from the floor cariad tlws and breathe gently. When you're ready open your eyes."

It was a long time that both women remained silent. The energy in the room became serene.

Gwen wafted into the kitchen as Seren sat peacefully in her favourite chair beside the fire. She brought Seren a glass of water along with a chocolate biscuit to ground her. "It's important to have a biscuit or some chocolate, and a glass of water. It's very emotionally draining to meditate and meet your guardians" advised Gwen.

"Wow nain that felt amazing. Really comforting. Thank you. Now I know how to call in my protection squad."

"Good, I feel peaceful myself now that you know how to do this. Once you have invoked your guardians Seren, you will start to notice familiar names appearing to you for example on billboards, car number plates, on vans, in shops. In some of the strangest and unexpected places really. You'll see."

"At least I now know to look out for them. To be open and aware of what is happening around me."

"Excellent Seren. You will find that meaningful songs will play on the radio."

"That's peculiar because I heard Luke Evans singing Calon Lân, taid's favourite hymn when I turned on the radio this morning."

"See, the person you thought of reminded you of them. When you switch on the tv or radio or when you're out shopping, or travelling somewhere, or as you sit, they'll remind you that they are still around you" advised Gwen.

Both women sat in silence for a few more minutes.

"The guardians will always make themselves known to you, but you must be open to this. Our guardians are guides that are with us all the time. You must get to know your guardians and see who they are. You will have a gut instinct that they are with you or trying to pass on a message to you."

Seren pondered for an age until Gwen said:

"You know when you think sometimes '*I'll go this way*' and a voice inside you takes you in a different direction? That's your inner voice. Your guide trying to protect you."

"I've experienced that and when I've ignored my inner voice I've always ended up in trouble. Now I know better and will take time to listen" vowed a perceptive Seren!

"When people are born, they are born with a guardian angel" stated Gwen earnestly.

"I always thought that was folklore nain" confessed Seren.

"Hmmm. Don't believe everything that's repeated to you. Make your own mind up cariad tlws based upon what you see, hear, think, feel, and intuitively *know*. Your gut instinct, that inner voice, your intuition, your sixth sense is usually correct."

"I will do that nain."

"There you are. I've taught you about protection. One other thing. Numbers are important. We will talk about numerology at some point cariad tlws but tomorrow we will see Miss Holmes and I'll meet Madoc. That's enough enjoyment for me today."

Nain clapped her thin, purple-veined hands in excitement. There was ample life in the old girl yet. Seren went to bed with a piece of paper full of wishes which she placed under her pillow, a head full of guardians and a puzzlement about numerology. She always had something extra up her sleeve did nain.

In less than twelve hours they were in the impressive offices of Neville and Mason Solicitors with the efficient, if a little intimidating, Miss Eleri Holmes. A woman of few words, blonde hair tied in a ponytail, she wore all black, her only stab at colour was an eye-catching, unique, hand-crafted pearl and coral necklace. Eleri greeted Gwen and Seren by immediately offering them tea which was served to them by her assistant.

"Your grandmother wishes to give you Bryn Gosol Farmhouse and seven acres of land, Seren. Do you understand that?"

"Yes Miss Holmes" replied Seren as if she were addressing her teacher!

"We don't need a Will for this and your grandmother, Gwen Williams, wishes to know that everything will go to you before her death."

"That's correct Miss Holmes" approved Gwen.

Miss Holmes half-smiled at Gwen and nodded.

"Your grandmother can transfer property this way through a formal legal document known as a Deed of Gift. This means that ownership of Bryn Gosol Farmhouse and the seven acres of land transfers to you without payment from you. She wants you to know that this is done out of the love she and her husband, Tomos Williams, your grandfather, have, or had, for you."

"Thank you nain" said Seren, graciously accepting the generous gift.

Silence in the office was punctured by teacups being raised and placed on saucers.

"On the Deed of Gift, your grandmother will be known as the Donor and you because you're receiving the farm and land Seren will be known as the Donee. Any questions so far from either of you?" asked Miss Holmes professionally.

"No" responded Seren and Gwen in unison.

"The Deed of Gift must be witnessed by disinterested parties. That means they cannot have an interest in the transfer of property. We have two Administrators who work her at Neville and Mason, would you like them to witness this document?" asked Miss Holmes.

"Yes please" agreed Gwen.

"What does giving Bryn Gosol Farmhouse and land mean legally to my nain? Where does she stand in all of this?" probed Seren.

"Good question. Gwen as the Donor retains no right or interest in the farmhouse or the land" responded Miss Holmes.

"Are there any problems that you envisage Miss Holmes?" questioned Gwen.

"There might be one problem Gwen that I can foresee and forgive me for saying this" replied Miss Holmes gently. "If you die within seven years of Gifting Bryn Gosol Farmhouse and the land to Seren, and the gift is valued at more than the Inheritance Tax threshold, then you will need to pay Inheritance Tax Seren on the value of the Gift" replied Miss Holmes.

"Worry about that if it happens Seren" advised her grandmother. "What do we do now Miss Holmes?"

"Are there any more questions?"

"No thank you" replied Gwen.

"Not that I can think of" agreed Seren.

"Good. I'll call in the two witnesses and we can sign the Deed of Gift."

What a twenty-four-hours! Within a day Seren had learned about guardians and had been Gifted Bryn Gosol Farmhouse and its land. But the day was not over yet. Madoc needed to be appraised of important news.

"Seren today there will be a New Moon. Make your intentions to the universe. Write your list by the time the Full Moon comes in" instructed her nain.

"I will" responded Seren absent-mindedly. She was more focused on the upcoming introduction of Madoc to her nain and was unsure whether to be in high spirits or not. Eventually, she decided high because if it all ended tomorrow, she may as well make the best of things tonight.

From the kitchen window she saw Madoc's strapping frame striding down the lane, towards the front door before time allowed for a check in the mirror. Madoc saved any embarrassment about Seren's appearance by forcefully thrusting a bouquet of twelve Angel Cheeks pink peonies into her hands. Nothing could dissuade her from his appeal. Smelling freshly baked bread and hearing broth bubbling heightened his appetite as he hadn't eaten since lunchtime. They embraced at the front door before Seren instructed him to:

"Take off your coat, I'll put it in the boot room, wait for me here."

Madoc waited obediently for Seren's return. Almost immediately Moon and Star greeted him with licks, sniffs, and paw shakes while Madoc rubbed their silky black fur.

"My nain is in the back dining room." Seren shivered. "This room gives me the creeps" she disclosed "but my nain loves its energy. Come and meet her but be prepared. She's extraordinary" warned Seren.

Madoc's eyebrows almost shot up to his receding hair line. He wondered what to expect. As Seren opened the oak door, Gwen was sitting in the light of a pink candle rolled in orange essential oil at the aged, wobbly oak table with heat from the log fire to warm her guest. She had laid out her tarot cards in preparation for Madoc. On the antique, black Welsh dresser with ornate carvings Madoc spotted a collection of crystals, candles, and incense diffusers.

'Bloody hell nain' thought Seren. 'What an introduction.'

Unsurprisingly, Madoc was taken aback but dealt with the surreal situation with aplomb.

"Don't stand up Mrs Williams" he instructed as he bent to kiss the wizened cheek and passed her a pink jewel box containing Prestat chocolates and truffles.

"Thank you, Madoc. It's lovely to meet you. Call me nain. Seren has told me very little about you. She wanted you to be a surprise to me!"

'*Bit strange*' thought Madoc.

"You probably think that's a bit strange" said Gwen.

Madoc's lovat eyes almost popped out of his head.

"But I like to make up my own mind about people" continued Gwen.

"Well, nain I hope I pass muster" responded Madoc awkwardly.

"You may think this somewhat bizarre Madoc, but do you mind if I read your tarot cards?"

"Err" he looked helplessly at Seren who nodded. "I've never had my tarot cards read before. I think my sister Aila has had them done at some point, but that's a woman's thing, isn't it?" he gibbered. "I don't know what to expect."

"There are many men who have their cards read Madoc. People are more open these days to the spiritual side of life. Sit here opposite me cariad tlws."

Madoc obeyed nain. Seren sat on a brown leather chair and observed.

"I see you've brought with you a tall, muscular Roman soldier" stated nain. "He's your guardian."

Madoc turned around to see if there was anyone else in the room, was almost going to say "eh?" but decided saying nothing was probably better. His heart was beginning to beat quickly.

"Yes" continued nain "his leather arming doublet lies on his linen undershirt and the finest woven red tunic is over his shoulders. He's wearing a thick leather skirt and leather open-toed sandals."

"Oh" was all Madoc could say but wondered 'what the hell is a Roman soldier doing acting as my protector'.

"He has tattoos of a bull and eagle on his shoulders and the mark of Julius Caesar's fearful Legio X Equestris on his left calf."

'*Hang on. These two are poking fun at me*' Madoc thought but had the good grace to stay quiet out of respect for Seren and her nain, who both appeared to be taking this very seriously.

"Who's Jessie?" asked nain.

"My mother." Madoc braced himself.

"She's handing you yellow roses. She's in the spirit world."

"She is" responded Madoc sadly.

"She watches over you Madoc. She placed you in Seren's path. She's telling me you have a problem with your right knee. That you had an operation on it, but it wasn't dealt with quickly enough."

"That's right" replied a shocked Madoc. He hadn't told Seren about that.

"You were a footballer" announced nain.

'Ha' thought Madoc. I have told Seren about that part of my life, that's how nain knows. 'Now she's fishing.'

"Yes" replied Madoc. I'm a retired professional footballer. I played for Wrexham all my career. The knee injury held me back from moving up into the Premiership."

Nain listened and replied, "I'm seeing curlews around you".

Madoc stayed motionless.

"Curlews are important. They're linked to the house your grandfather lived in. There was a lot of trouble about the house when he died because he hadn't left a Will."

Now the hairs were rising on the back of Madoc's neck. He hadn't told Seren about the Will either.

"The house went to a distant relative when your grandfather wanted you and your sister to have it. He told your mother that, but there was nothing in writing."

Madoc remained stock-still.

"See this?" nain held up a card depicting the image of a man fishing under a moonlit sky. "That's your grandfather. He also watches over you. I see that Chester is important in your career."

'Bloody hell' thought Madoc. 'I've not told Seren about my work in Chester.'

"Rome will be important. Are you interested in archaeology? You're doing something with an archaeological dig" stated nain.

"I've never been to Rome and whilst I'm interested in archaeology, I'm unlikely to ever be involved with a dig" responded Madoc, delighted that nain wasn't right about *everything*.

"You'll see. Rome will be important to you" was her calm reply.

"The Goddess Minerva, she's significant too."

"I don't know why" countered Madoc "as I've never heard of her."

"You'll see" said nain sagaciously.

And he would. Soon enough. But nain hadn't quite finished with him.

"I see you standing in a field of stars" stated nain.

Seren sat up straight and recalled when she'd laughed with her nain about a scarecrow in a field of stars. Madoc too sat bolt upright and replied:

"My mother and I did the pilgrimage to Santiago De Compostela before she died. Compostela means field of stars" said Madoc quietly. "I also stand on the Vardre at night taking deep sky astro-photographs which means I do stand in a field surrounded by stars."

Nain ploughed on.

"Your sister."

"Yes?" responded a startled Madoc.

"She's expecting a baby."

"She is. How did you know that? She's only told her husband and me" he exclaimed incredulously.

"The baby will be fine. Your sister will be fine. Don't worry about her working too hard" was nain's reply. "Is there anything you want to ask me Madoc?"

"Err no. No thanks. That was err my first experience and I err found it fascinating" was his polite riposte.

"Shall we eat?" suggested Seren hoping that she would see Madoc again despite her nain's introduction to *witchy* life.

That evening Seren wrote her intentions to the universe. 'If it's for his and my highest good, please may I continue seeing Madoc romantically' she asked. 'When the time comes, let him accept without question that I am from a long line of gwrachod gwyn. Thank you x'

Chapter 12 – Chester

Deva Victrix

It was three days following Madoc's visit to Bryn Gosol, and he hadn't been in touch with Seren other than to send her a brief text message thanking her for an *interesting* evening.

'*What does that mean*?' she fretted and wondered whether events that night had fractured their relationship.

Madoc had been intrigued by nain and found his reading amusing at best, until he received an email from the Historical Society which he re-read three times. On the fourth reading he opted to text Seren:

'Are you free for a walk tonight? We could meet at Conwy Harbourside at 6. X'

'*See you there x*' was Seren's response. She had kissed too many frogs with warts to play too hard to get.

It was six minutes door to door from Bryn Gosol to the harbourside. Seren left the farm at 6 pm exactly. No point being on time if he was going to dump her, she believed. Madoc left home early so that he would be in good time and watched Seren drive her white Mini over the bridge and past Conwy Castle. He walked past the *Smallest House* in Wales to meet her. She looked harassed as she strode towards him. Madoc bent to kiss her. Relieved, she kissed him back and gave him an extra-long hug, which she hoped he wouldn't mind.

"Sorry I've not been in touch Seren. I've been putting together a portfolio of images and can't get my mind to work properly to decide which photos to use. I've even begun to annoy myself about it, so there would be no point seeing you if I'm distracted. Although you are good company" he added gently.

"You weren't put off by having your cards read by my nain then?" she had to ask and put herself out of misery.

"It's not something I would choose to have done. It was unnerving. That's partly why I asked you to meet me."

"Oh no. Here it is' thought Seren 'I'm being dumped.'

"Listen to this" continued Madoc. "It's an email I received today:

Hi Madoc

We have been impressed by your cutting-edge photographs which are currently showcased at the Puxley galleries in London and Chester.

Please would you be kind enough to contact me, at your earliest convenience, to discuss working on a project in Chester to photograph an archaeological dig?

Best wishes,

Eleanor

"Which bit are you surprised by?" asked a confused Seren.

"What do you mean which *bit* am I surprised by?" replied a bewildered Madoc.

"Am I missing something here? That's what you do isn't it? Take photographs? Why is that such an important piece of communication? I don't understand" retorted a bemused Seren.

Madoc took a deep breath and exhaled loudly.

"I have never worked for the Historical Society before and they're asking me to be involved with an archaeological dig. Three days ago, your nain said I'd be involved in an archaeological dig. I received this email today. How did she know?" he demanded.

"Oh that? But she told you other things that she couldn't have known about you" responded Seren calmly.

"I know, but she has informed me of something about my future that she couldn't possibly have established through anyone else. Unless" he said running his fingers through his cropped black hair "unless she knows someone at the Historical Society."

There. He'd found an answer which satisfied him.

"She's *old* Madoc but she's not involved with the Historical Society. I promise you."

"This is a bit difficult for me to comprehend Seren. I'm a very open-minded man. I look into the night sky to observe the stars and know that there is so much that we don't realise, but this" he said and thrust a printout of the email in her direction "this means that your nain can see into the past, present, *and* future. No-one can do that. It means that there are numerous dimensions of time which most people aren't aware of, and I'm finding it tricky to buy into that."

"My nain *can* see the past, present and future Madoc" replied Seren quietly.

"What?" exclaimed Madoc.

He had a delightful habit of raising his eyebrows so high that they nearly entered a different dimension of time on their own.

"She's a gwrach gwyn."

"A bloody white witch?" stated a flabbergasted Madoc.

"Yes" responded Seren. "She really is, but white witches work for the highest good Madoc."

"That means you're one too" he said accusingly. Sardonically.

"Yes" answered Seren. "I *am*."

Madoc didn't run a mile. Silence hung in the night air like a gentle, golden caul entangling disbelief in its web. He had time to run away but didn't, instead he breathed deeply, looked out to sea, looked up at the stars, stared at Seren and held her tightly. Eventually, what he said was:

"How amazing. I'm seeing a gwrach gwyn. Incredible."
It was then, at that moment, Seren realised he cared about her deeply. She let out a long sigh of relief because the main hurdle had been jumped.

***

Not many weeks after that astonishing revelation Madoc invited Seren to join him on a visit to Fortress Diva, or Chester as it is now known. His aim was to wander around the city, which was originally settled by the Romans in the first century AD, and along the River Dee to see at first-hand a range of Roman ruins and plan his photoshoot. He had accepted the invitation from the Historical Society to photograph an archaeological excavation but wished to dig a little deeper (forgive the pun) into the heart of the area.

The Jaguar car boot was crammed with all kinds of photographic related paraphernalia, including a bag for different types of lenses plus a tripod for still shots. As Seren helped Madoc unpack the equipment, she volunteered to carry the tripod and camera bag so that he would be unencumbered as he took photographs. He appreciated the sentiment behind the offer and accepted, better to take photographs unfettered by his kit. The warmth of the sun put the pair in high spirits. Before their visit, they had heard rumours about a secret sand-stone pillar in, of all places, Pret A Manger on Northgate Street, which they were keen to investigate for the price of two café lattes.

"Is it true" Madoc asked of Cody the Chief Barista, "that in the basement of this building there are sand-stone pillars?"

"Yes mate. They're remnants from some important Ancient Roman building where the money was held to pay the soldiers. I think it was called the Principia."

It wasn't challenging to spot that he was a professional photographer, but Madoc felt the need to say:

"I'm a professional photographer working on an excavation with the Historical Society. Any chance you'd let me have a quick look Cody so that I can take some photos?"

"Well we don't do it usually otherwise we'd be taking tours all day instead of selling coffee."

Madoc looked pleadingly at Cody.

"Seeing as we're quiet, I'll take you to look in the basement and leave you to wander around for as long as you need, but you must buy drinks from here."

"Thanks Cody. I appreciate that" replied Madoc with great warmth.

Madoc spent an hour taking photographs of the aisle columns of the headquarters of the Roman legions, with Cody happy to accommodate his presence in the basement. Seren enjoyed speculating about the lives of the Romans depicted in a mural on the wall of the Principia building, imagining what it might be like to live during Roman occupation. When Madoc had finished, he thanked Cody for his kindness, saying the café latte was "the best ever" and the pair left to begin an elevated walk of Chester around the two miles of the city's raised Roman Walls.

"Let's start at the East Gate Clock Seren" suggested Madoc as he looked at a city guide map. "There is a story that the clock tower is haunted by a Roman soldier who's on guard," he said.

"Poor man. I wonder why his spirit is still here?" replied Seren.

They climbed the worn stone steps to the city Walls.

"Gosh, it's quite high up isn't. Look Madoc you can see the Welsh mountains in the distance" an excited Seren declared in her delicate Welsh accent.

"Yes. The Roman Walls are forty feet high. I think they were reconstructed with sandstone by the Legio XX at the end of the first Century."

"Isn't that the tattoo you've got on your calf? Legio XX?"

"You've obviously not looked closely enough Seren" teased Madoc. "It's the elite Legio X that I have" he said raising his eyebrows to infer ominiscity.

"Why? What does it signify and what inspired you to have that tattoo?" questioned Seren.

"It's Julius Caesar's first Legion, known as the Tenth Legion. He raised it in Spain and the soldiers served with Caesar during his Gallic and Civil Wars. The men were his most loyal soldiers and fought the hardest. He hand-picked those he wished to join the Tenth Legion and considered them his personal bodyguards. I have much admiration for Caesar. I've read about his exploits and leadership. Listen, I'm embarrassed to tell you this, but I have lucid dreams about Romans fighting in Gaul and me being Caesar's best lieutenant. I've never been to Rome so no idea where the dreams come from except perhaps eating too much cheese and pickles late at night or too much reading before bedtime!"

"Odd that you're interested in Ancient Rome and at some point, not now, you'll need to explain to me about lucid dreams" responded Seren.

"One day I will. What's perplexing is that an artist friend of mine painted me as a member of the Roman Senate reporting to Julius Caesar. Doubly weird is your nain saying that a Roman soldier was my guardian."

"Yes, *you* might think that's a little peculiar. Coincidences can be put down to anything, but I always think there's a reason for these things."

"Are you interested in Ancient Rome Seren?"

"I could say yes, but I've not thought about it. I'm a gwrach gwyn so perhaps I was a Seer in a previous life, who knows? I don't know much about Ancient or modern Rome, and I've never visited the place. Neither did I study Classics at school. I suppose if you're captivated by Caesar and his battles, I'd better learn some ancient history!" retorted Seren.

"Let's walk along the Walls Seren, I'll take some aerial shots of the city, then we'll stop at the Roman Gardens and have our picnic" suggested Madoc. Seren wandered the whole walls and returned to Madoc who was delighted with the images he had taken whilst she had explored.

"Did you know that there are fragments from the Roman fortress Deva in the Roman Gardens?" said Seren.

"Yes, I'd read about that somewhere. There's a mosaic that I'm interested to see which offers a cipher for history. It's not the original one, but a reproduction of The Four Seasons which was laid in the Roman Bath House. I've heard it's superb. I'd like to take some shots of it and will need to use the tripod."

They both stared at the map.

"It's there Madoc." Seren indicated a point on the map which located the Roman Gardens. "We come down from the Wall at Pepper Street and the Roman Gardens are on the right."

"Let's head to it" instructed Madoc "and then we can walk back towards the Roman Amphitheatre."

Madoc led, stopping to take photographs along the way.

"The Gardens showcase a few relics from places such as the Roman Baths and the Legion's Headquarters" he stated knowledgeably. "I'll take some snaps of those as we pass by."

Seren had never seen Madoc so animated as he marched on ahead taking photographs of time-worn columns and damaged carved facias from the Roman Headquarters. She criss-crossed the area, and wandered along a tree-lined avenue, searching for the Four Seasons mosaic, waiting patiently for him. Eventually he arrived.

"Is that it Madoc, down the two steps? That huge colourful circle surrounded by little shrubs?" asked Seren doubtfully. "I hope it is because I've set up your tripod, just in case."
"Oh you're right Seren. Yes, that's it. Thanks. Let's sit close by as it's quiet here and so that no-one nicks my stand."

Madoc looked like an excited little boy, his photographer's eye capturing in freeze-frame the intricacies of the shapely mosaic design. Once he had finished taking images, he unpacked the food which Seren had prepared for he had made the last picnic.

"Right let's see what you've created Missy and I hope it's not all that green leafy stuff you like."

"I've packed a treat. Loads of sandwiches, eggs from the farm, beef from the farm, tuna and a pork pie from Marks and Spencer! In that cake tin you'll find nain's home-made scones for us and a flask of coffee. Will that do?" she challenged good-naturedly.

"Absolutely. Fit for a Roman Legionary to eat before battle" he quipped.

"Or a Legate" Seren responded quickly, and then blushed.

"A Legate? What do you know about a Legate if you've not studied Ancient Rome?" quizzed Madoc.

"Not much really" she admitted.

"But something?" he queried.

"Yes, a bit" she replied, reluctantly.

"Your reticence is making this intriguing. Go on" he urged.

"It's daft." Seren was embarrassed.

"Seren, this whole thing is crazy so whatever you say to me, is not going to make my head explode, is it? If I can accept that you're a gwrach gwyn, I can cope with anything."

Seren confessed.

"I keep having this vision, I can't call it a dream because dreams are random, and this isn't random. My vision is of a Legate called Titus who lives on the Vardre and he, err, he has a relationship with a woman called Ceres. Titus has three tattoos, a bull and an eagle on his arms and the mark of the, what did you call it, the mark of the Legio X on his calf. Don't look at me like that Madoc" said Seren, pulling her face.

"Like what?"

"Incredulously, that's what."

"Well, it's a bit far-fetched isn't it that a Roman Legate with my tattoos is in your *visions*. It's clear that you're dreaming of me! Sweet."

"Maybe, maybe not."

"What do you mean?" questioned Madoc.

"I dreamt of Titus, the Legate, way before I met you."

"So, you had a premonition about me?"

"No. That's not it. It was in another life. In another life you were Titus and I was Ceres."

"NO!" he exclaimed in shock. "Tell me about the *visions* then. What do you mean *another life?* What was I like as Titus?"

Now Madoc *was* intrigued.

"You were the leader of Roman legionaries, with a silver-grey mastiff Cane Corso called Hercules and you planned to, then attacked a tribe of Ordovices."

"Yep. That sounds like me. Intriguing. Tell me more. Who was Ceres?"

"She lived at Bryn Gosol Farm, but it wasn't a farm as we know it, it was a Roman Villa which was used as a farm. Ceres and Titus were, hmmm, err, in love with each other. When Titus went to battle on the Vardre against the Ordovices, his right knee was injured."

"NO!" exclaimed Madoc in shock. Again. "My right knee was injured playing football, which meant that I stayed for my whole career at Wrexham. Not quite agile and bendy enough to become a footballer for Manchester United but at least I stayed with Wrexham's first team for sixteen years. Even had a testimonial" revealed Madoc proudly.

Seren's sharp amber eyes were drawn to the thirty-four-year-old ex-footballer. She smiled at him warmly.

"You are adorable." Seren lent over and kissed Madoc firmly on the mouth despite that he was eating a pork pie of all things. "Yeuch. I am a vegetarian you know?" she shouted.

"I didn't know you were going to kiss me. Give me a warning in future!"

They both laughed.

"Carry on with this *vision* then" he prompted.

"This bit is somewhat traumatic. A lot traumatic. Hideous actually."

"Excellent. I love a bit of hideous" he teased "and trauma."

"Let's hear what you think of me after this."

"Great." Madoc folded his arms, extended, and crossed his legs. "I can't wait."

"Titus is injured in a battle with the Ordovices, which he wins and destroys their village plus, listen to this."

"I *am* listening" Madoc smiled.

"Takes women and children hostage to be used as slaves."

"Gruesome. I'm not quite liking him so much now. He was all right when he was a handsome Legate, but a mass-murderer isn't so appealing."

"Wait. It gets worse."

"Worse than that? How?"

"Me. Well Ceres. Who's me. Like Titus is you. In a past life. I was just as horrible as you were!"

"Not possible" he teased.

"It is. I grabbed a princess by the hair, dragged her through a hawthorn bush, and threatened to cut her throat with a pugio."

"What's that?"

"A dagger with an amber handle. Well, mine had an amber handle because Titus had it made for me. And an amber ring. With the inscription TM, a tiny eagle and SPQR inside. Amber is for protection you know?"

"I'm beginning to learn a lot. Carry on. Did you slit her throat?" Madoc asked, agog.

"No. But I handed her to Titus knowing that she would have a fate worse than death. By losing her freedom and being taken to Rome, dishonoured, and humiliated by being paraded through the streets and then killed. She would have been better off if I *had* slit her throat."

"Yes I agree. You were a bad 'un Ceres" smiled Madoc.

"The vision isn't over though" confessed Seren. "Last night I had another one."

"There's more? You were *worse* than that and you want to tell me about it? Shame on you." Madoc laughed.

"Because Ceres had captured the wife of the Ordovices leader, she was in incredible danger of revenge attacks. Titus arranged for his legionaries to create a tunnel between Bryn Gosol Farmhouse and Saint Hilary's Church. Obviously, the church wasn't there at the time, but churches were built over pagan sites of worship. It became an underground tunnel to the Temple of Mithras. Ceres could use it to hide, or escape the Ordovices, if necessary."

"Hang on. I've heard about the Temple of Mithras. It was a secret place of worship."

"You're right. And to make matters worse for me, because I feel guilty about what Ceres did in a past life, there really *is* a secret underground tunnel between Bryn Gosol Farmhouse and Saint Hilary's with a Temple underneath the church."

"NO!" exclaimed Madoc. "How do you know?" he interrogated.

"Because nain, taid and I use it all the time."

"NO! Bloody hell Seren. Your family really *is* weird. I love it. Are you going to show me the tunnel?" replied Madoc enthusiastically.

"I'll speak to my nain first."

"What happened to Titus and Ceres?"

"I don't know. That part of their lives hasn't appeared to me yet."

"Bloody intriguing you are Seren."

"Thanks. I like to think so."

"And past lives. How do you access them? Through dreams?"

"No, I've told you that dreams are too random" Seren insisted "it's through past life regression. My nain helps me with them."

"Oh I've gotta get me one of those" stated a delighted Madoc "to see myself as a Legate."

"It doesn't work like that Madoc. When you do past life regression you can end up in any past life."

"We must do it Seren. This is bloody marvellous" Madoc said excitedly. "On second thoughts, it's not mind control, is it? You're nain won't take over my body, will she?"

"I'll ask my nain to take us both through a past life regression, at the same time."

His initial response was:

"Bloody brilliant."

Then:

"Possibly."

Finally:

"Not sure. Come on, let's finish our picnic and have a whistle stop tour of Chester's Roman history. There can't feasibly be any more surprises to be sprung on me can there?"

"Not that I can think of" was Seren's non-committal reply.

Madoc kissed Seren full on the lips then smiled.

"You're adorable" he said.

"Hey, you can't pinch my word" she responded. "What are we looking for next?"

"The Amphitheatre" was Madoc's reply. "It's not far."

Chester had been ear-marked by the Ancient Romans as the capital of Britain. It was difficult to imagine that the city's

crumbly oval Roman Amphitheatre would have been the largest
amphitheatre in Ancient Britain, but there remained evidence of
at least two tiers to it. Much like the gigantic Colosseum in
Rome it was used for entertainment, where spectators would
have accessed their seats by vaulted stairways but possibly not
to view gladiatorial fights or watch the legionaries practise their
military manoeuvres.

Most amphitheatres have shrines outside the arena, in Chester,
to the left of the north entrance was an altar said to be dedicated
to Invidia, the Goddess of jealousy and vengeance. Seren
found it difficult to reconcile why Invidia would be erected in
the Amphitheatre unless it was to avert the *evil eye* as the
Ancient Romans performed rituals and magic for the Gods.
They also called upon Seers, Prophetesses and the most
important group of women in Rome, the Vestal Virgins whose
role it was to keep alight the eternal flame in Rome's Forum.

Madoc was enthralled and took photographs from various
angles, Seren wandered quietly among the ruins and found her
way to Saint John The Baptist Church, constructed out of the
red bricks from the Amphitheatre. She was surprised to see a
plaque commemorating the marriage of Llywelyn the Great to
Joan, daughter of King John of all things. A connection to
Conwy and the Vardre. '*What an astonishing coincidence*' she
thought. But coincidences don't exist in Seren's world.

After a long while, when Madoc had finished taking
photographs, they made their way through the City Gates,
underneath the clock and towards the Racecourse.

"Did you know Seren that the River Dee led to a major port in
Ancient Roman times?"

"No."

"The area, this part where the racecourse is built was a harbour for the garrison of Deva. I think that some of the anchor stones have been preserved and we might be able to see them."

"Oh no. Look, the racecourse is shut Madoc."

"Damn." He was disappointed. "I was planning to take some important images around here. Not to worry, we'll walk beside the River Dee. There's a nice pub called The Ship Inn where we can stop for a drink. Have you been there before?"

"Never."

They ambled along the paved promenade known as 'The Groves' admiring the stunning river-bank homes which were stacked along the gentle, green slopes on the right-hand side of the swirling river. Madoc couldn't help but stop to take photographs of black-tailed godwits, which Seren had never heard of, along with harassed lapwings but his favourite was the declining population of curlew which he pointed out, as the birds waded in the rills of current on the River Dee. Their long, down-curved bills made an unusual bubbling noise as they called to each other. *'Curlews. A link to The Ghillie'*, thought Madoc. *'Curlews. A link to taid'*, thought Seren. Neither person voiced their thoughts. A common blue butterfly, which she recognised was male by its violet-blue upper-wings with grey-beige undersides, landed on Seren's arm. It flew away too quickly, as Madoc was changing lenses he missed a photo-opportunity. Some say that butterflies are the souls of departed loved ones. If that is true, resolute Seren decided, it was taid saying hello.

Madoc stopped by the river to watch paddleboarders, which reminded him of happy holidays with The Ghillie in Aberdeen which he talked about to Seren. A river cruise would take too long as time was pressing so they walked across the medieval Old Dee Bridge with its variable span of the four arches, to the trendy Ship Inn. The bar man, Gareth Williams, had a Welsh accent, and as Seren chatted away to him in Welsh it turned out he was from Newborough, near the Warren and Ynys Llanddwyn where her nain was born! Even more outlandish, he was Aunty Maggie's (her nain's sister's) grandson! Fancy that.

Gareth asked Seren and Madoc whether they had seen the Roman shrine to the Goddess Minerva from the rear windows of the Ship Inn. They confessed that they hadn't even known Minerva's shrine existed in Chester. Seren was thrilled. She knew all about the Goddess Minerva. Once they had finished their drinks, she persuaded Madoc that they needed to take the two-minute walk along Edgar's Field, for closer inspection.

"I can see you can't wait to tell me about the Goddess Minerva, Seren. Go on" prodded Madoc.

"She was the most important Roman Goddess. The Goddess of wisdom, the arts, and healing. Later she was recognised as the Goddess of war. Her image, depicting her carrying an owl and a spear, is found on coins of different Roman emperors. There is an important temple at the Forum in Rome dedicated to her."

"Interesting."

"The Quinquatras festival in Rome is held in her honour."

"What's that?" queried Madoc.

"It's a festival which begins five days after the Ides of March."

"Now I know about the Ides of March because that's when Julius Caesar was assassinated" stated Madoc proudly.

"Correct Sir. The festival starts on 19th March and lasts until 23rd March."

"What's the, what did you call it? Quinquatras festival for?"

"I think it's to celebrate Minerva's birthday and acknowledge the Roman army. There was a performance called the Salii where young men danced in full armour, and there were gladiatorial games to honour Minerva. On 23rd March there was a ritual of purification of the signal trumpets known as Tubilustrium."

"You certainly *do* know about Minerva" said Madoc impressed by Seren's awareness. "She looks bedraggled and raggedy now though, doesn't she?" he said, taking photographs from different perspectives and with various lights. "Not much to look at sadly."

Madoc and Seren returned to the Ship Inn for their evening meal to celebrate a stimulating day. They sat by the back window, in a cosy, white-washed room which reminded them a little of Bryn Gosol Farmhouse. Madoc was looking forward to working in Chester on the archaeological dig so ordered a Beef Feather Blade meal to celebrate. He wasn't quite sure what it was, but as Gareth had recommended it, thought he had better take a chance. Seren chose the less exotic and safer option, Vegan moussaka.

"I've got a great collection of photographs from today Seren and in my mind's eye have been able to see a million different ways to represent the Roman architecture we've visited. It's all about timing you know, with photography. I'll be able to put together a portfolio that might be used in the Grosvenor Museum."

"Will the museum have an area for photographs?"

"Yes they will be able to create a small exhibition of today's work. So great job all round and a lovely day out."

"Do you want to see if the Grosvenor Museum is still open?" queried Seren.

"If you don't mind. That would be great. I could have a rummage around the displays."

They arrived at the museum half-an-hour before closing time. Phew. Just made it and Madoc asked permission to take photographs of various artefacts such as crockery and jewellery. Authorisation was granted. As Seren and Madoc wandered among the glass cabinets, they came upon a skeleton standing alone, sentry like, displayed in one cabinet, another smaller cabinet held a criss-crossed, handcrafted, leather open-toed sandal. Seren speculated whether the sandal had belonged to the skeleton and what his life had been like.

"The poor skeleton" she said. "I feel so sorry for him, with his ramrod bleached bones. He was once a proud and noble soldier of Rome based here in Diva. I wonder if he is the Roman soldier in folklore who fell in love with a tribal girl, which led to Diva being attacked by her tribesmen? His bones are in that glass case, but his soul is still here too. He needs to be sent to the other side, to go into the light. I sense the kernel of his spirit still here, in Chester. He died in a lot of pain."

Seren was silent for a few minutes with her eyes closed. Madoc watched her and thought '*you are a funny little thing*'. As they walked away, he asked Seren what she had been doing.

"The skeleton's soul has been trapped for 2,000 years. I opened the light on the earth plane to send his spirit where he should be. Home."

"I'm sure you will have freed the Roman soldier and despatched him to a better place" smiled Madoc. He was quietly looking forward to the next few months with Seren, which would turn out to be more adventurous than even he could have envisioned.

2023

Chapter 13 –The Magic of Telescopes

Looking through time

It was April, a lovely bright Saturday evening and Madoc
turned up at Bryn Gosol Farmhouse to have dinner with Seren
and nain. He knocked on the door unaware that if Gwen didn't
like him, when he left, she would have thrown salt outside the
front door, followed by a spit. Thankfully, Madoc would not
experience that humiliation, for now at least. He had brought
his telescope to show nain the stars. As a gift for her, he also
had with him sustainably caught, plump, amber-coloured meaty
Conwy mussels. A seasonal treat caught from a small fishing
boat known as a dory by fishermen who carefully scoured the
Conwy sea floor using a rake. How was he to know she
wouldn't eat them? *'They would do for the farmworkers' lunch
tomorrow'* thought nain.

For Seren he had brought a small box, wrapped in plain brown
paper, and tied with string. It wasn't an empty box! That
would be unkind. Opening it revealed home-made scallop-
seashell-shaped shortbread Aberffraw biscuits. These were the
third version as the first had been too crumbly (he used too
much butter) and the second had burned (he forgot to set the
timer). Seren was touched by his thoughtfulness and delighted
he had agreed to spend the evening with her and nain,
especially after his first encounter which he said had been a
little weird.

"Do you know why I brought Aberffraw biscuits Seren?" he
asked shyly.

"Yes, because they reminded you of the seashell tattoo on my neck."

He took that as an excuse to kiss the back of her neck, which made Seren giggle. Nain noticed, said nothing, but inwardly smiled.

Much to Seren's chagrin they sat in the eerie back dining room for their meal. The energy in the room sizzled but no Roman soldier appeared. Madoc enjoyed laverbread alongside home-produced lamb broth and dumplings flavoured with rosemary, thyme, mint and parsley from nain's herb garden. Although she wouldn't eat the meat, Seren ate the potatoes and vegetables. Her nain said "r'wyt ti'n hogan fach ryfedd"[16] which was coincidental as at the Museum Madoc had *almost* said the same "you are a funny little girl". Madoc found enough room to eat a highly calorific baked Welsh cake cheesecake followed by just one, he insisted, Aberffraw biscuit. The assignment in Chester had proved to be frenetic and Madoc hadn't had time to recuperate. Tonight was a real treat especially having a home-cooked meal.

"Nain have you ever walked the Camino Way?" asked Madoc unexpectedly.

"No. Tomos and I spent most of our days working on the farm. Our break was every August on The Warren in Abersoch where we would take Seren for two or three days. The place we stayed, Curlew Cottage, had a narrow path opposite which led to the sea. The three of us would walk down that sandy trail, sit on the charming beach at night when it was quiet, and stare at the moon and stars whilst the waves lapped against the shore. It was magical. Happy days."

---

[16] You are a funny little girl.

Madoc jolted at the name of the cottage which nain had unwittingly revealed. Coincidence? Serendipity? Who knew? "It's funny that you told me about the field of stars nain when you read my tarot cards because, as you now know, my mother and I did the pilgrimage to Santiago De Compostela before she died. *Sant Iago* means Saint James and *Compostela* means field of stars. It was a time of reflection for us both."

Madoc paused to take a sip of his Stella lager.

"I researched the Camino Way recently. According to various websites there was a pagan trail which followed the Milky Way because its furthest star could be seen in Finisterre. With your interest in the mystical, you may like to know that Finisterre was once believed to be the End of the World. The legend is that the veil between this world and the spirit world thinned at night-time. To counteract any potential ill will, pagan prayers and offerings would be made to appease the Gods."
Madoc had another swig of his bubbly golden drink.

"There's also a folktale that the Romans used a route along the Camino Way known as the Janus Path. They started their walk at the Temple of Venus in Rome and headed for the Cape of Finisterre. Roman legionaries would watch the horizon slice the sun as it unravelled on the horizon where the mythical altar, Ara Solis, was located."

Madoc paused for breath.

"People of different faiths and beliefs are guided along the Way by a web of routes marked by scallop-shaped-seashells like Seren's tattoo. The lines of the shell represent the different routes pilgrims can take. If people walk the last one hundred kilometres of the Way, to the Cathedral of Santiago, they receive a certificate. As you meet people along the Way and chat, there's an unwritten rule that you don't ask anyone their reason for walking. I've never spoken about the trip with my mother."

"Is that because people undertake the walk for very personal reasons?" asked nain.

"Yes. It's a spiritual journey of self-discovery for many" replied Madoc.

"The Camino Way sounds like an interesting walk. I would like to tackle that, but I couldn't walk a hundred miles."

"You don't have to do it in one day nain" joked Madoc. "You're allowed to take your time. Seren and I could take you one day soon."

"I'd love that. Thank you, Madoc."

"Now Seren, you promised that you would tell me my number in numerology and what that means" said Madoc.

"Oh I did yes. I worked out that you're a number five and I've written down what that implies. Just wait and I'll get my notebook which is in the kitchen."

Seren ran along the hallway to the kitchen just in case the Roman soldier decided to make an appearance. He didn't. When she returned, Seren sat opposite Madoc and read:

"A number five makes quick decisions around business. They prefer to set their own boundaries because they are not good at taking orders. They are fond of travelling, like making changes, love challenges and problem-solving. Does that sound like you?"

"I suppose it does. Remind me later to tell you about going travelling. Now what about you nain?"

"Oh I don't know much about numerology. What would my number be Seren?"

"Nain you are a number eleven. It indicates that you're deeply intuitive, highly psychic, a healer and comforter. In fact, part of the angelic realm on a higher vibration."

"Nain, you're on the angelic realm. Fantastic. Seren, are you the same number?" grilled Madoc good-naturedly.

"Me? I'm not a number eleven. In fact, I'm number seven. They are usually spiritual people who don't belong to the material world. They are always searching for the deeper meaning of life. They are healers, clairvoyants, therapists and are interested in the quantum way of life. I think that numbers are important for example, 1, 2 and 3, like nain, have links to the angelic realm. Everything that happens in life is connected by numbers."

"Give me a brief overview Seren about numerology" suggested Madoc.

"It's thousands of years old where people believe that there is a powerful relationship between numbers and the divine energy which influences our lives."

"How have you calculated my number Seren and what might I use it for?" asked Madoc.

"It's the total of each number in your birth date reduced to a single digit. For example," Seren wrote a number to demonstrate, 11 11 1969 "watch what I do to turn that number into a life path number:

The day is 11 so 1+1 = 2
The month is 11 so 1+1 = 2
The year is 1969 so 1+9+6+9 = 25 and 2+5 = 7
Add the final numbers together:
2+2+7 = 11

If the final numbers are 11, 22 or 33 they are Master numbers so are never reduced. A master number indicates the highest energy and those who have a master number, like nain, are old souls with high energy. They are associated with success and the spiritual realm.

In this example the figure that I'm left with, 11, denotes that soul's purpose in life. If the number had been, say 13 I would add 1+3 to make 4 and the life path number would be four. When I calculated your life path number it showed you would be a leader and my number showed I would be a therapist or seer. Now I've told you a tiny bit about numerology, can you explain to nain and me about lucid dreams?"

"Hmm you've put me on the spot a bit there. Let me think. Excuse me if I get this a little wrong but here goes. People often wake up and can remember a dream, or parts of a dream that they've had whilst they've been sleeping. But they don't have any influence over their dream as it's happening, and they can't control what they dream about. A lucid dream means being aware that you're dreaming and influencing that dream. It's a little like directing a film, only it occurs in your mind.

You can decide who is in your film, what happens, where it takes place and how it ends. It's about managing the dream.

I keep a journal at the side of my bed and write down my dreams as soon as I wake. I think it helps me to understand myself a little better. Creative people are often lucid dreamers. They might write a song, or a score of music or the plot of a book or solve a problem during their sleeping hours. It's a powerful way of thinking without limits. I often dream that I'm a Roman soldier fighting in Gaul with Julius Caesar and Marc-Antony."

"That's not like an out-of-body experience, is it?" asked nain. "I keep having those and I visit taid."

Seren and Madoc looked at the stoic lady, who so wanted to leave this life and be in the next one with taid. What happened next surprised Seren because Madoc left his seat, walked round the table, and gave nain a kiss on the cheek. One tiny teardrop sneaked out from behind her eyelid as she said kindly:

"Thank you, Madoc. You're a good man."

Keen to make a fuss of nain, Madoc asked if she would like to look at the stars through his telescope, to which nain was delighted to answer "yes". Grabbing a jumper, coat, and scarf for nain, as her skin was thin and her blood thinner, Seren thanked Madoc in the hallway as he left the house.

Out of the boot of his Jaguar car he lugged his travel tripod, high viewing capacity telescope and began to set up this paraphernalia in the garden. Thankfully the tripod could be adjusted to accommodate nain's small size. He also placed his beloved camera around his neck to take photographs of nain,

Seren, the moon and stars, not forgetting the dogs Moon and Star.

Rural Bryn Gosol farm was the perfect place for night sky observation, away from the light pollution of Conwy. Seren brought a heavy oak chair from the kitchen for nain to sit on and a green velvet cushion on which to rest her gnarled back. Once seated, Madoc adjusted the tripod to nain's height. He questioned her carefully to find out what she could see through the 120x magnification focal eyepiece and modified the power to manage the brightness.

"Right nain. Can you see the moon?" asked Madoc.

"Yes but I could already see that without a telescope" was her response. Madoc laughed.

"No I mean, if you can see the moon through the telescope, I can direct you to the different planets and stars. We can use the moon as a reference point."

"I see" she chuckled at her own silliness. "Yes I can see the moon Madoc."

"Ok. See the first very bright planet below the moon?"

"Yes I can."

"That's Jupiter. Named after the King of the Ancient Roman Gods. It's unlikely to be able to support life and is twice as massive as all the other planets combined. Jupiter's Great Red Spot is really a giant storm that has raged for hundreds of years. See the bright planet below it?"

"Yes cariad tlws I can."

"That's Venus. The planet of love. It's Earth's closest planetary neighbour and is a rocky planet. It's often called Earth's twin because it's similar in size and density."

"Oh, I say. That's very clear Madoc isn't it?"

"Above the moon, to the right, can you see what looks like a sideways W?"

"You might have to move the telescope Madoc, I'm not sure what I'm looking at. You find it cariad tlws and then I'll have a look."

Madoc helped nain to find the sideways W.

"That is known as Cassiopeia. My grandad, The Ghillie, taught me about it one night in Aberdeen. I remember very clearly the time I spent with him. Cassiopeia is the remnant of a massive star that exploded about three hundred years ago."

Seren watched Madoc as he spent time, extending patience, demonstrating care and gentleness when dealing with her nain, as they observed the night sky together. Intermittently he would take photographs of the old lady, staring through the telescope into a cosmos of infinity. Madoc appreciated that one photograph captured a moment. If all the pictures taken throughout nain's life could be strung together, it might portray a snapshot of her experience. The dim light of the past could be witnessed through the spectrum of colours generated by a prism of images.

For her part, nain knew that somewhere out there, on a different plane, were the souls of The Ghillie, Jessie and Tomos. Their energy might have crumbled in this dimension, but the vast universe that she could see through Madoc's telescope, was gathering more energy as it grew and there were several dimensions of time. Wise nain knew that we all travel along the time dimension at various rates which is why she was able to view the past, present, and future, because for her, time and space were flexible and intertwined. Nain wondered if everyone knew that because *she* understood that she and taid would be together in a different life.

"Well I never" said nain "what a marvellous contraption that telescope is. I've been able to see the wonders of the night sky close-up and understood where many different planets and stars are placed for the first time in my life. Amazing. Simply superb Madoc."

Nain was delighted and clapped her hands.

"I'm feeling the cold now Madoc. I'm going to go inside and leave you two young ones to it. Thank you cariad tlws, I've enjoyed myself. I'm going to the front sitting room. Seren, come and have a look through the telescope. It's magical" and with that, nain shuffled inside.

"Thanks Madoc. You are very kind to nain. I appreciate that. Now, let me see what marvels the night sky has to offer" said Seren excitedly.

The pair stayed outside for another hour at least. As Madoc packed away his night-sky equipment, Seren went indoors, made panad and took a tray into the front sitting room where nain was ensconced in her favourite chair.

"Have you enjoyed yourself tonight nain?"

"Very much cariad tlws. It's been great and taid was beside me all the time."

Seren smiled at her nain and kissed her cheek. He's around us nain, I know that. Do you think he'd like Madoc?"

"He'd think he was just right for you darling girl. Just right."

Not long afterwards Madoc joined them.

"It's chilly out there now. Thanks for this warm drink, I need it and to stand by that roaring blaze" he exclaimed as he turned his back to the log burning fire.

"Seren tells me that you wanted to try a past life regression Madoc. Is that right?"

"I'm very sceptical about this nain. Who would do the past life regression for me and what if I have a traumatic experience like drowning, or being imprisoned and going to the guillotine, or being in a fight to the death? Will I die?"

"I'll do it with you Madoc. I won't put you in a position where you'll die. Would you like to try?" nain encouraged.

"What do I have to do?" he asked warily. "I'm very worried about this" he confessed.

Nain laughed a sweet, tinkling sound. "Sit down by the fire and cover yourself in this blanket." She handed Madoc a teal cashmere cover.

"I recognise that you'll be a little concerned" stated nain "but there's nothing to fear Madoc. I'll be with you. You'll still hear my voice and feel sensations. I'm going to use my hawkstaff and when we start, I'll stomp it on the floor *to put energy into the ground* and when we're finished, I'll stomp it on the floor again and say *the deal is sealed* by banging onto the ground.

"Your what?" asked a startled Madoc.

"My hawkstaff. Look here it is" said nain as she showed the driftwood. "Tomos made it into a hawk's head on this long pole. I placed a blue appetite crystal in the hawk's eye socket as this stone helps me connect with angels, the spirit world and astral travel. Think of it Madoc, a little like Gandolf's staff. It amplifies my magic."

Madoc looked askance!

"Just breathe deeply through your nose and exhale through your mouth to calm your anxiety" stated nain, eyes twinkling.

"Have you meditated before Madoc?" asked nain.

"No" he replied.

"Right well I'll try and help you to meditate. It's a case of breathing deeply and calming your mind. Make yourself comfortable. You're in control, you can stop at any time. I'll guide you. I'm going to stomp hawkstaff *now*" said nain and banged her hawkstaff on the ground "to put energy into the ground. Choose a spot on the ceiling and focus upon it. Breathe deeply to the count of five, hold your breath to the count of five, breathe out to the count of five. I'll go from ten to one. As I say each number blink your eyes."

Gwen carried on in this way for quite some time.

"Close your eyes Madoc and concentrate. Can you see the steps?" asked nain.

"Nope" replied Madoc.

Gwen tried again.

"Choose a spot on the ceiling and focus upon it. Breathe deeply to the count of five, hold your breath to the count of five, breathe out to the count of five. I'll go from ten to one. As I say each number blink your eyes. When I get to one, close your eyes Madoc" she instructed.

Madoc listened intently, sighed and tried as hard as he could to empty his mind, but thoughts came in repeatedly.

"Can you see the steps?" queried nain.

"Nope" said a discouraged Madoc.

"Choose a spot on the ceiling and focus upon it. Breathe deeply to the count of five, hold your breath to the count of five, breathe out to the count of five. I'll go from ten to one. As I say each number blink your eyes. When I get to one, close your eyes Madoc" she instructed.

Madoc listened intently, sighed and tried as hard as he could to empty his mind, but thoughts came in continually.

"Can you see the steps?"

"No I can't nain and I'm finding this frustrating because I cannot clear my mind. It's too full of ideas, images, imaginings."

"Never mind Madoc. I'm going to stomp hawkstaff *now*" said nain and banged her hawkstaff on the ground "the deal is sealed. I'll count back from ten to zero. When I say zero your eyes will open. Open your eyes. We can try another time. Maybe we've all exhausted ourselves tonight trying to absorb infinity." Nain laughed. "It's not a problem cariad tlws. Now is not your time to meditate. It'll come with practice."

"I'm sorry nain. I couldn't get past my own notions."

Madoc pushed the cashmere blanket away from him and for many moments there was silence in the front sitting room until Seren said: "Madoc, you asked me to remind you about travelling."

"Ah yes, travelling. My assignment with the Historical Society in Chester has been going well" he announced buoyantly.

"That's great to hear. Was it useful to visit Chester beforehand to gauge a little of the Ancient Roman connection with the city?" asked Seren.

"Yes Seren, it was great as it gave me a clear understanding of the layout of the place plus your musings made me view things differently. Take for example the skeleton in the Grosvenor Museum. I would never have considered that he had a life before he ended up on display in a glass cabinet. He might have had a wife and children. He may have left his parents in

Italy, never to see them again. His death could have been traumatic. So many endless stories to tell from one man's bones. Now, Eleanor from the Historical Society has invited me to undertake another assignment for the organisation."

"That's fantastic Madoc. Well done" congratulated nain.

"Yes. I'm proud of you" said Seren. "Where is it next time? York? Manchester?"

"No. Neither of those places. There's a huge archaeological dig taking place on the site where Julius Caesar may have been assassinated. It's a place which is now called Largo di Torre Argentina."

"I didn't think Julius Caesar was assassinated in Argentina" said a puzzled nain.

Madoc smiled.

"Pompey the Great who was hailed a God, organised an enormous building scheme in his own honour in Rome. We know it as the Largo di Torre Argentina but back in Ancient Roman times it was known as the Campus Martius which means Field of Mars. The newly discovered site has gardens, temples, porticos, meeting rooms and the curved Theatre of Pompey which was large enough to seat about forty thousand people. Well, that area is way below street level and is inaccessible to tourists. It's being excavated. It's currently a cat sanctuary and will remain as such but will also become a new visitor site."

"I see. That sounds like an interesting job for you Madoc. Cats are very important. They are viewed as the souls of the dead who cannot leave a place" said nain.

"Apparently, temples, the possible place of Julius Caesar's assassination, statutes and various artefacts have been uncovered and the Historical Society want me to document the findings through images. I'll also be taking photographs to use on the visitor information panels. I'm so thrilled."

"Wow Madoc, that's fabulous news. Well done" praised Seren again.

"I'll be there for two weeks in June" he stated baldly.

"Oh. You'll be away that long?" Seren was dismayed for herself, not for Madoc.

"Yes. I hope you'll be able to get two weeks off work Seren as I'd like you to come with me. If you'd like to?" he asked nervously.

"Nain will you be ok if I leave you for two weeks?" asked Seren gently.

"I'll be amazing on my own cariad tlws. What a fabulous opportunity for you both" said nain generously. "I can spend the time researching our walk along the Camino Way" she said boldly "or I could even book myself a tour and go alone. Yes, I just might do that."

"Wow nain, that'd be brilliant and in that case Madoc, when do we leave?" squealed an excited Seren.

"Thursday 1st June" he replied as he hugged her then kissed nain on the top of her head. "We'll fly from Manchester Airport."

The three glanced at each other and burst out laughing.

Serendipity had brought them together and was giving them the opportunity to live a different life. The next remarkable few months would bring them great joy and uncomfortable truths in equal measure because that's the circle of life.

2023

Chapter 14 – Roman Holiday

What is the direction of time?

Nain had insisted on giving Seren a street map of Rome, and sixteen sheets of self-adhesive tiny circle stickers in assorted colours. She had bought them from the Spar shop on the corner of the High Street in Conwy in preparation for the *big trip*. A lovely woman in there, whose father was Italian, had helped her. Seren didn't know who was more excited, her or nain.

"You and Madoc could make a list of the places you would both like to visit Seren. Put a sticker on the map to indicate each location, and when you've done that, you can allocate discrete days for trips in the same area." Her black eyes glittered. Logical nain would live this holiday vicariously.

A few days later the oak table in the kitchen was strewn with scraps of paper, coloured stickers and an unfolded A3 map of Rome as Seren and Madoc eagerly decided together upon sites of interest to visit. When in Rome they could use their mobile 'phones but seeing their plans materialise in front of them in Conwy was more exciting. Nain glanced at the two of them occasionally as she made chicken pies with all butter pastry, and a special leek and potato pie for Seren. She was inwardly priming herself for the silence which would descend on the farmhouse when Seren and Madoc were in Rome. Although, she consoled herself, it wouldn't be too quiet, she had sole responsibility for Moon and Star. The two lively dogs would keep her occupied and the farmworkers would be milling around.

On the first day of June, they both said goodbye to nain at Bryn
Gosol Farmhouse when Madoc collected Seren in his antique
Jaguar car to drive them to Manchester Airport. He hoped the
car would survive the journey. Madoc whispered something to
nain as he hugged her farewell. In reply she gave him a kiss on
the cheek and said *"yes"*. Seren hung out of the car window,
waving goodbye long after the old lady had closed the
farmhouse door. She hoped her nain would survive their
absence.

Buoyed by the successful exhibition of his photographs in
London and Chester, Madoc was determined the composition
and creation of images would make an excellent impression of
Rome. This could be the beginning of a long link for him with
the Historical Society. He had been delighted when Eleanor
booked a two-bedroomed self-contained apartment in the centre
of Rome for the stay. It was close enough to stroll to and from
the site of the Forum and the Largo di Torre Argentina to take
pictures for his magazine commission.

Madoc parked in the long-stay car park at Manchester Airport.
As they both unpacked their luggage from the gasping elderly
car, Madoc looked at confident, well-dressed Seren beside him,
and felt heightened anticipation for a significantly memorable
trip. She kissed him and said "that's the first leg successfully
navigated. All roads lead to Rome." An hour queue at the
check-in desk and a one-and-a-half-hour queue getting through
Security at Manchester Airport proved stressful as passengers
argued with each other in frustration. Struggling with staff
shortages, following layoffs during Covid, Airport staff dealt
slowly with slews of people. When their flight to Rome was
delayed by five hours Seren wondered if Madoc might blow his
top, but apart from the occasional tut, sigh and shuffling of feet
at others' poor behaviour, he remained calm given the

circumstances. Although Seren enjoyed people watching, she ended up experiencing dizziness and a terrific headache caused by absorbing too much negative energy. '*Not a great start*', she thought.

Exhausted and weary they arrived by midnight at Rome Fiumicino Airport, so late that their transfer taxi had left them high and dry. A one-hour weaving Uber ride later they arrived in the complex centre of the Eternal City which still thronged with locals and tourists even in the early morning hours. The Uber driver stopped 250 yards away from their self-catering apartment on Rome's main thoroughfare, at the northern part of Via del Corso. As this area was pedestrianised, they had to walk the final section, Seren's dizziness and headache intensified so much she thought her head might explode. As Madoc opened the door to the surprisingly modern stark white apartment in an old Roman palazzo, a welcome blast of cold air-conditioning stroked Seren's burning cheeks. In the kitchen she poured herself a glass of water, walked to the outside terrace furnished with chairs and sofas, plonked herself on the rattan furniture, and fell asleep.

Roused from her slumber by the smell of freshly brewed Italian Lavazza coffee wafting upstairs, by the time Seren awoke, Madoc had visited a local panetteria where he bought fresh pane di Segale and focaccia. He had also prepared a welcome, hearty breakfast of oats, Greek yogurt, fruit, scrambled eggs accompanied by Italian bread. A perfect start as Seren couldn't even remember climbing into bed.

"Shall we have a leisurely day?" suggested Madoc. "We could walk from here to the Spanish Steps and up to the Villa Borghese Gardens."

"I'd love that" was all Seren said.

Their apartment was perfectly located, just seven minutes' walk through the delightful Piazza di Spagna, past the fountain of a sinking boat decorated with bees and suns before arriving at the sweeping Spanish Steps.

"It's worth walking 135 steps to see the Chiesa della Trinità dei Monti. What a stunning church" said Seren, panting slightly as surveyed the two white bell towers either side of the Gothic white building.

"Look at that view Seren, behind you, over Rome. How spectacular. If we walk along this elevated path above the city, past the Villa Medici, it leads to the Borghese park. We should have an interesting vantage point looking down on the various areas of the city along the way. There are pieces of Ancient Roman artefacts embedded in the walls of the Villa Medici. Can you see?"

"Yes. There they are" pointed out Seren as she stood beside a red granite vase. "The view over the fountain towards St. Peter's Basilica is unbelievable. Spectacular."

Madoc stopped to take photographs as they walked past the palace, down bosky lanes to the terrace at Pincio Hill and into Borghese central park. In the Villa Borghese gallery Seren spotted a marble sculpture of Proserpina crafted by the Italian sculptor and architect, Bernini.

"Look Madoc. There's Proserpina."

"Who? Is that someone you know?"

Seren laughed.

"Maybe I do, but don't know it yet" she replied.

"What?" was all Madoc could say.

"This is Proserpina. She was the Goddess Ceres' daughter who was abducted by Pluto. When he took her to live in the Underworld with him, Ceres searched for her. Proserpina made a pact that she would stay with Pluto for six months of the year, if she could be with her mother for the other six months. Pluto allowed her to do that.

I was interested in Ceres because that's the name of the woman the Legate Titus fell in love with in one of my past lives."

"It would be amusing if I turned out to be Titus and fell in love with Ceres" replied Madoc. "That means Proserpina might have been my daughter. Oh, now this feels a little awkward, being here, seeing this tiny woman being held roughly by Pluto. A woman who could be my daughter in another life. Look Seren you can see the tears on her face. This detail is astonishing."

"She wouldn't be your daughter Madoc! You need to try past life regression again to see whether you were indeed Titus! Proserpina is the daughter of Goddess Ceres and the God Jupiter. This is interesting, in my guidebook it says that Ceres is supposed to have been able to switch between life and death, and helped the energy of new spirits move to another dimension. If someone's death was untimely, and their anguished spirit remained in the wrong dimension, they would haunt the living and could be exorcised only when their death was reasonably due."

"Bloody hell. That's what you did to the skeleton's spirit in Chester. You sent him off to the correct dimension."

They both laughed and Seren brought Madoc's attention back to Proserpina.

"If you look even closer you can see the finger marks on her arms where Pluto is holding her tightly. This God is very muscular. His wild hair and thick beard, I suppose, depict his strength and virility."

"Better grow me a beard then if you think that shows manliness" laughed Madoc.

"It's a shocking statue, isn't it?" asked Seren.

"If you consider them to be real people, then yes, it is" agreed Madoc.

As they moved around the gallery another sculpture, started by Bernini but finished by his student Finelli caught their interest.

"Here's the God Apollo chasing Daphne a nymph because he's struck by her beauty. He falls in love with her. As a nymph, Daphne was not allowed to love men, so his attention was unwelcome" explained Madoc.

"Why is her arm like the branch of a tree?" asked Seren.

"She prayed to her father, Peneus to stop her being beautiful. Her father turned her into a tree."

"Has her hair turned into leaves?" questioned Seren as she looked at the figures from an altered perspective.

"Yes and look, her feet have turned to roots."

"If you stare at the statues from various angles, the composition changes. It's fantastic isn't it?" said Seren as she moved around the figures. "Is that the kind of thing that you see when you take photographs?"

"I try to interpret what I perceive in various ways, so yes. I suppose that both statues here are a metamorphosis of unrequited love. The two Gods are running off with women who don't want their attention."

"And the laurel leaf is a sacred symbol of Apollo. Triumphant Roman generals wore them to signify victory, physical and spiritual cleansing" added Seren.

A few hours later Madoc and Seren walked along a tree-lined footpath towards the Ancient Roman Temple of Asclepius, Greek God of medicine and healing.

"According to this guidebook the Senate ordered the temple to be built after consulting the Sibylline Books" explained Madoc. "A plague hit Rome and a delegation was sent to Greece to obtain a statue of Asclepius to ward off illness."

"Sibylline Books? That's something to do with Seers, Sibyls and Prophetesses, isn't it?" queried Seren.

"I've no idea? Why? What do you know?" enquired Madoc.

"I've read about Sibyls or Seers or Soothsayers or Prophetesses in Ancient Rome. A Sibyl was a Prophetess whose predictions were collated in the Sibylline books. Supposedly there were nine or three books, depending on whose version you read, and kept in the Temple of Jupiter on Capitoline Hill. The books could only be consulted by the Roman Emperor in emergencies, and he decided whether the Senate should know about a prophecy or not. The Sibylline books were supposedly lost in a fire" explained Seren.

"What? A Sibyl was like your nain? Able to see past, present, and future?" exclaimed Madoc.

"Gosh. Yes. Exactly like my nain" stated a surprised Seren. "I never put the two together. My nain. A Sibyl."

"Seren. Don't you realise that you too could have been a Sibyl in a previous life? I don't want to state the obvious here but you're a gwrach gwyn like your nain."

Seren sucked in a deep breath.

"We need to visit the Temple of Jupiter perhaps there are clues about the Sybilline Books. This feels weird because of the connection to Seers. Why would we discuss Sibyls on our first day in Rome?"

"No idea but being involved with you is definitely remarkable" exclaimed Madoc.

"I hope remarkable means good" retorted Seren.

"Absolutely." Madoc kissed Seren. "Now let's test your muscles by hiring a rowing boat. I'll relax, you row," laughed Madoc.

***

Thanks to Madoc's innate ability to understand directions, the following day, after breakfast they headed straight to Rome's Civic Museums, at Capitoline Hill in search of Jupiter. Armed with his A71V Sony camera, bag of equipment and Seren carrying the tripod, Madoc was keen to view the tailing blocks from the Capitoline Temple of Jupiter, an excavation he had read about in the Historical Society's magazine. The Museums would offer solace from the searing heat and sustenance for imaginative minds. They clambered the steep, seemingly never-ending steps to the Museum. You had to be fit to tour Rome.

"Oh look, you can see the Ancient Roman Forum, from here" exclaimed Seren but Madoc was too busy taking photographs to hear.

They wandered around the Capitoline Museums for five hours absorbing the ancient masonry on the ground-floor courtyard, sculptural collection on the first floor and the picture gallery on the second floor. At one-point Seren lost Madoc when she strayed down a long passageway with windows overlooking the Forum. As she entered one of the rooms on the first floor, she felt dark presentiment overwhelm her in the face of the statue of the Goddess Fortuna who had power to control Destiny. It was as though Seren instinctively knew that Fortuna was inconsistent with justice and delighted in mischief. The forceful, tense atmosphere, in a room full of tourists, overwhelmed Seren. She left quickly, in search of Madoc.

"There you are Seren. I've been looking for you all over and this is a massive place teeming with people." He sounded as though he had been anxious about her whereabouts. "We've been in the Museums for ages, let's take a break. Trying to take photographs around so many people is almost impossible" he complained. "The café, Terrazza Caffarelli is on the second floor with fabulous views over the city. Let's rest for a while."

Seren agreed immediately because sustenance was needed, but she held Madoc's hand tightly in case they were unfortunate and encountered Fortuna on the way.

"Did you manage to get all the photographs you wanted?" asked Seren when they were eating.

"After much faffing and exercising patience with people who walked in front of my camera, then yes, and more besides. Despite the aggravation I've had a great time. This is a fantastic place. I can't wait to see the Forum. Let's head there next."

"I know from personal experience how you behave when someone gets in the way of a good picture" stated Seren.

Madoc and Seren had read that the Roman Forum was at the heart of Ancient Rome, its public focal point offering multi-purpose activities such as shopping, social gatherings, public speeches, criminal trials, and religious ceremonies. Many monumental symbols in stone and marble were erected to commemorate the Gods, emperors, and military victories. Whilst most had been destroyed by earthquakes, age, fire, and the weather, some were still intact.

"Let's head to the Temple of Saturn first. I wonder if he is connected to Goddess Ceres as he was the God of agriculture and wealth?" asked Seren.

"Possibly" replied Madoc. "The Romans brought food offerings to the temple and Saturn was also supposed to protect their earnings. The Temple became a kind of bank" responded Madoc "and reserves of gold and silver were stored here. At one point, it housed the state archives."

"It's quite emotive being here, isn't it? I have a sense of peace and tranquility even though we are among so many other people. See that flock of birds Madoc" she pointed above him, "they're in the shape of an arrow which shows an important journey or moving forward with a situation. It's a good omen. I feel that I've brought offerings here before and that I was dancing. My mood was happy and light. I'm going to leave one of my little bags that nain taught me how to create."

"You're a funny little thing. What's in the bags?"

"Things I've collected. Seashells from Conwy beach, an assortment of crystals from the Great Orme mines, a little fairy perched on a crescent moon, feathers, and tiny white candles."

"I'm sure there's a reason for each of those items Seren. Go on, place your little bag on the pediment if you can" urged Madoc.

"It's leaving a little piece of me, here in Rome in the hope that I'll return one day."

"Oh, you'll return. Never fear" was Madoc's response. "Have you got any more bags?"

"Of course. Lots. I wonder what the Security Man thought at Manchester Airport when he saw my collection of little bags? Probably deemed I was silly."

Madoc kissed Seren. "Charming more like. Come on. I'd like to see Caesar's Acropolis. It's straight ahead" he said and led the way. They walked through the Forum in the scorching heat.

"Here it is. The Temple was dedicated to Caesar and some people say that it is the site of Caesar's cremation, but there are differing accounts about what happened to Caesar's body" explained Madoc.

"Imagine Madoc, that we've walked in the same places as Caesar. That he lived and reigned here two thousand years ago. It's incredible."

"Why are you crying Seren?" asked Madoc.

"I have an overwhelming sensation of loss, sadness. Like I've lost a mentor who had an important impact on my life. I sense an aura of fear for the future, anxiety for my husband in a past life. I warned him but he didn't heed me."

"Who did you warn?"

"Julius Caesar. I have the impression that I warned him. His death was needless. Do you have a sensation of anything here?" she asked Madoc quietly.

"I know exactly what you mean. I have a sense that I participated in fighting and witnessed carnage here. When I was lucid-dreaming I saw Marc-Antony addressing an enraged and angry mob who were incensed by Caesar's murder. Marc-Antony spoke to the Roman people, telling them that Caesar had fed and clothed them all, and he was killed for the sake of an idea but there would still need to be an Emperor. Why couldn't it be Caesar? It's a heart-rending place, isn't it? I wonder if I'll get the same emotion when I'm taking photographs in the Largo di Torre Argentina because there is a claim that Caesar was killed near there and not here."

"I didn't know that Madoc. As a mark of respect, I'm going to throw one of my little bags onto this rock inside the Temple."

"Go on Seren. Do just that. Nobody's watching."

"Done. Where next?" asked Seren and sighed.

"We're heading for the Temple of Jupiter. Very little of it remains" said Madoc as he strode off with Seren in pursuit "so don't be too disappointed."

"That could be it Madoc, over there" said Seren.

In front of them was a high platform, with a single wide staircase which led to a three-column deep porch, fronted by six columns. The Temple of Jupiter had three interior rooms to honour three deities: Jupiter, Juno, and Minerva.

"This was a temple fit for the Gods Seren. It must have towered over the city to solidify its importance as a cultural, religious, and civic centre. It would have been a powerful building to signify a formidable leadership. Not a bit like the statue we saw of Minerva in Chester."

"Did you notice any of the fragments from this Temple when we were in the Capitoline Museums?"

"Yes I did. As you said Madoc, there is very little left of it now. I read that there was once a large terracotta statue of

Jupiter driving a four-horse chariot, known as a quadriga, possibly on the roof."

"How on earth was that hoisted up there, onto the roof? Does make you wonder, doesn't it? This Temple began life as a pagan Temple, not a Christian one. Must have been an impressive building once. I wonder if it was a repository of some kind, as it held the Sibylline Books and wasn't just a temple? Wonder where they were kept?"

"To think that the Sibyls have been here and one of them may have been my nain or me in a different dimension of time. I read somewhere that the Temple was also a meeting place for the Senate, and the location of pageantry. It feels as though we are peeling back layers of time, doesn't it?"

"Leave one of your little bags here Seren, so that we've paid our respects to the Gods."

"We've seen plenty now, let's call it a day Madoc. This heat is unbearable. We can carry on exploring tomorrow before you start work the following day because then I'll have to sightsee on my own."

They both agreed that this was turning out to be an interesting break from Conwy. Madoc even admitted that he had butterflies when he visited the Forum which settled their excursion for the morning, the Campitelli area and possibly the Forum, again.

***

Another blistering day. Clambering the Gemonian Stairs, also known as the *mourning stairs,* Seren was dizzy and uneasy.

She sensed the ominous presence of many souls, some of whom had been thrown off the steep cliff known as the Tarpeian Rock, which overlooked the Roman Forum. The souls' crimes were thought to be treason, murder and fleeing from slavery.

"Did you know Seren that people who were considered criminals were hurled off the tall cliff? That would've been a grim death" conceded Madoc.

Seren agreed but was quiet. "I feel nonplussed here Madoc, please could we go and look at the Temple of Vesta? I really don't like it here."

Concerned when he saw how pale and anxious she looked Madoc agreed immediately.

"I'm sorry, I forget that you are affected by negative energy. Let's go" he said, marching off towards the Temple of Vesta.

They approached the circular-shaped Temple, dedicated to the Goddess Vesta whose main responsibilities were to care for the home and family. Seren stroked one of the Temple's sensuous columns and said:

"This is made from marble, which was, and still is, expensive material. The Ancient Romans must have valued Goddess Vesta. Look how tall the pillars are."

"The architecture is like that of early Roman homes. This Temple housed Vesta's holy fire."

"My nain told me a beautiful myth about the holy fire of the Temple of Vesta, Madoc. The flame came from Troy. Aeneas, who lived in Troy fought the Greeks and was supposedly the last man standing. He had a vision that his dead wife told him he had to leave Troy and become the founder of a city where the Tiber flowed. Aeneas took a flame from the burning city of Troy and carried it to the Tiber. Along the way he had numerous adventures, one of which was meeting and falling in love with Dido, but he abandoned her to follow his Destiny. Dido committed suicide by throwing herself on a burning pyre because she couldn't live without him. Finally, Aeneas settled here, and this is where the eternal flame was kept as a symbol of safety and prosperity. It's the reason why Rome is known as the Eternal City and why the flame was never allowed to go out."

"If Aeneas was the founding father, how do Romulus and Remus fit in? I thought they were the legendary founders of Rome?"

"Rome is full of contradictions isn't it and we rely on others' accounts to try and inform the past. Weren't the Vestal Virgins around before Romulus and Remus? Their role was to keep the flame alive. I think they kept Divine secrets too."

"That was their responsibility, was it? I didn't know that. It says in the guidebook that the Vestal palace had fifty rooms and was three-storeys high."

"Just a tad bigger than your three-storey house then Madoc" teased Seren.

"The palace was built around a double sized swimming pool. Nice life if you can get it" retorted Madoc.

"Perhaps the Vestal Virgins might have thought it was a nice life, although women of means in Ancient Rome did have a degree of independence. They could own property and have money, but they had to take a back seat when it came to attending social events like gladiatorial battles whereas the Vestal Virgins were so highly thought of, they had front row seats."

"Let's go then and see the House of the Vestal Virgins, it's just behind the Temple of Vesta" suggested Madoc.

"The House has a series of statues of Vestal Virgins along one of the walkways" said Seren referring to her guidebook. "Did you know that the women were chosen around the age of eight years old and had to serve for thirty years, remaining chaste all that time. If they didn't, they were buried alive. They made bread for feast days, especially on 1st March which was the Roman New Year. Their other jobs were keeping the flame alive at Vesta's shrine, preparing ritual food, and attending Vestalia which means Vesta's feast days between 7th and 15th June. My birthday falls on 12th June within Vestalia!"

"I'd better make a note of your birthday then Seren. You'll never forgive me if I forget!" declared Madoc.

"I wonder if that's why I feel an affinity with the Vestal Virgins because my birthday is during their feast days. I feel that the Vestal Virgins were very important to Julius Caesar. If he wanted something to be agreed, he would pass it to them first."

"That's a peculiar thing to say Seren. How would you know what was important to Julius Caesar?"

"Madoc. I've no idea but what I do know is that I'm hungry. Shall we head for the Trattoria Restaurant that we saw earlier near the Largo di Torre Argentina?"

"Good idea. I've seen enough for today and I'm getting hangry" agreed Madoc.

"Hangry?" queried Seren.

"It's when you become angry because you're hungry" laughed Madoc. "We can walk past the Trevi Fountain on the way.

"Can't wait to see it" responded Seren.

Twenty minutes later Seren was shocked that there was no space at all to stand close to the beautiful Trevi Fountain, set in an unassuming intersection of three streets, because the area teemed with people gripping cameras of various sizes and quality. The sound of police whistles reverberated off buildings as tourists were shrieked at for sitting on the travertine marble perimeter wall. The Fountain, designed by Nicola Salvi, was built on the fascia of a palace wall.

"Did you know that the aqueduct which supplied the Fountain, is the original Roman aqueduct?" asked Madoc.

"No" responded Seren. "It's a delicious design, Neptune with his tritons rising from the rasping sea to depict water as life giving."

"This might interest you Seren. I read that Salvi was fed up with the complaints of a barber while the Trevi Fountain was being constructed. He created a sculpted vase, shaped like the Ace of Cups on a tarot card to spoil the barber's view when the

Fountain was completed. I'm sure that you know tarot originated in Italy?"

"Yes, I know about the origin of tarot as my nain told me. She has an original set of Tarocchi cards passed down through generations of her family. The Ace of Cups represents new beginnings, and is auspicious for personal relationships, because it links to love, our emotions, and unexpected, wonderful opportunities" explained Seren. "Perhaps it was propitious for the barber?"

"Maybe. Let's make it lucky for us and we can take a selfie beside it. There's no way I'll be able to set up the tripod here" suggested Madoc.

"We can come back another evening" replied Seren.

"Consider it a date Miss Williams."

"I will Mr Thomson."

It goes without saying that the *Trattoria* was a typically Italian restaurant on Via della Mercedes. Madoc and Seren chose to sit outside in the courtyard, under a poppy red umbrella on a balmy June evening, both selecting pasta dishes followed by home-made tiramisu.

"This restaurant seems familiar even though I've never been here before" stated Seren.

"That's odd. I was just thinking the same thing."

"For some reason I sense that there is a bull and an eagle on the floor of the restaurant. Go in Madoc and have a peep around will you please?"

"I don't think I'd have to peep if there was a bull and an eagle here! They'd certainly stand out wouldn't they Seren?"

She laughed as he walked through the front entrance and into the main restaurant. He was gone for at least fifteen minutes only to return without evidence of creatures.

"Never mind. Perhaps I'm wrong" conceded Seren. "Did you find out where the toilets are?" she whispered.

"No" Madoc whispered back and smiled.

"I'll pop to the loo. I won't be long." Famous last words.

Twenty minutes later, Seren returned looking flushed and excited.

"Where have you been? I thought you'd climbed out through the back window to avoid paying. I was debating doing a runner" confessed Madoc.

"You wouldn't do that. I know you too well Madoc Thomson. Listen, you're not going to believe this" said Seren tantalisingly.

"I believe anything you tell me" replied Madoc seriously, "except that you've won the Lottery."

"There's a bull AND an eagle in that building!"

"You're taunting me. I didn't see any evidence of them."

"That's because you probably didn't go *downstairs.*"

"Why would I go downstairs?" he asked in puzzlement.

"That's where the toilets are. On the floor downstairs is an extraordinarily vivid mosaic with subtle nuances of colour which a creative genius like you would appreciate. Go to the toilet and have a look."

It was years since Madoc had been summoned to '*go to the toilet*' by anyone except his mother Jessie. He laughed.

"Ok, I'll go an inspect this mosaic."

"You'll be astounded" promised Seren.

And he was. Upon his return he almost exploded.

"How is it possible that you sensed about the bull and eagle mosaic without ever having been here before? And how can anything so expressive as that mosaic be conveyed through a few pieces of exquisitely cut glass, shells, coral, and marble? Extraordinary. I took some photos with my 'phone camera."

"Let's pay the bill and walk back to the apartment" suggested Seren. "We can ponder things."

"I'll leave a tip. The service and food were both excellent."

It took an hour for them to criss-cross their way through the exhilarating streets of Rome back to their apartment. On the way, they debated whether it was an irrational belief that Destiny was weaving her mysterious spell around their souls, with relics from the past propelling them into the future.

2023

Chapter 15 – The Ace of Cups

New Beginnings

Madoc Thomson would always remember the evening in June when he photographed the Crescent Moon, in conjunction with Venus because he settled his mind on something that had been puzzling him. He remembered saying:

"For the first time in two thousand years, there's a union with the Moon and Venus and I'd like to take some night-time photographs of this event tonight Seren, if the sky is clear."

"The Crescent Moon in conjunction with Venus in astrological terms means a combination of beauty, harmony, love, unification, and passion in a relationship. The Crescent Moon holds potential for the future. It's a magical time for love affairs new and old."

With that, Seren kissed Madoc full on the mouth.

"Love like that" she laughed.

Madoc shook his head and asked: "what are you planning to do today when I'm at work?"

"I'll amble around, head for the Pantheon. Write to nain. Send some postcards" responded Seren.

"I'll finish in the early evening so I'll ring you when I'm ready and we can arrange to meet."

"Ok. Enjoy excavating."

"I will. You know I will."

"I'm sure you'll get lost in your own world of chiaroscuro depicting the past."

"What a great word. I'll use that today" promised Madoc.

Seren walked with Madoc as far as the Largo di Torre Argentina where she waved him goodbye. He was like an excited little boy as he left to join the team of the Historical Society who were starting their excavation that morning. Madoc's role was to record moments of the dig. Seren wandered around looking down at the enormous site which was way below street level and full of stray cats. *'Those cats'* she thought *'are the souls of the traitors who assassinated Julius Caesar doomed not to leave the perimeter of the Square.'*

In Ancient Rome the site was known as the Field of Mars and when Pompey the Great returned from conquering Turkey and Syria he ordered a huge building complex to be undertaken in the area now referred to as Largo di Torre Argentina but known then as the Campus Martius. The buildings included an enormous theatre dedicated to Pompey the Great, called the Theatre of Pompey. Modern apartments had been built on the curved site of the former Theatre of Pompey *'which was a shame'* Seren thought. As well as the theatre, there was a huge garden complex, with a covered arcade where creative work was displayed. In the middle of the archaeological spot was a large sunken area and Seren could see ruins which were supposedly four temples. It was a little like looking down at a smaller version of the Forum. There were few tourists around, which surprised Seren but would please Madoc. She strained to make out the Curia di Pompeo. This was the place that some meetings of the Roman Senate were supposed to have taken place. It was possible that Julius Caesar met his fate here on the Ides of March. Despite the heat of the day, Seren shivered.

Although it was only a few minutes' walk to the Pantheon, Seren stopped for a leisurely, heavily roasted espresso and propped up the unassuming bar Pascucci with the locals. It was interesting to try and decipher their loud and lively conversations, but none of the citizens loitered for long in the café. She had forgotten her hat so browsed in a few of the local shops for a parasol to help shade against the blazing sun. A purple parasol caught her eye, but she jettisoned the idea of buying it because she would rather spend her money on treats for other people, but regretted that decision later in the day as her skin burned red.

A detour past the Trevi Fountain Seren felt was a must, after all, she had most of the morning to herself. The crowds were thinner today, and she was able to stand close to the water. She had read about the Ancient Roman practice of tossing a coin into a river or ocean to ensure that the Gods who ruled the water granted safe passage. Seren also appreciated the folklore associated with throwing coins in the Trevi Fountain: one coin guaranteed a return to Rome, the second coin ensured meeting the love of your life and having a romance and the third coin meant your wedding bells would ring. She stood with her back to the Fountain, and with her right hand tossed three coins over her left shoulder. '*Here's wishing*' she thought and wished hard.

The Ace of Cups story had intrigued and surprised her. Seren strolled around the perimeter of the Trevi Fountain to have a better look at the depiction of the life-giving vase. '*Why did Salvi choose the Ace of Cups?*' she contemplated. An odd selection as it's not in keeping with the rest of the architectural design. Puzzled, and without answers, Seren made her way to the Pantheon where she had to queue for an hour to gain access. She followed a group of tourists who were being led by a guide and listened.

"The Pantheon is the only totally preserved Roman temple. It has been maintained because it changed from a Pagan temple to a Christian church. The Pantheon has only one form of light. If you look above you, the oculus in the middle of the dome is open to the elements, which allows the sunlight to flow through, and all the other aspects of weather stream through too. It is possibly the only unsupported dome of its size in the world." The guide hardly stopped to take a breath. "Here is Raphael's tomb. He was an esteemed artist" pointed out the guide, possibly unnecessarily. "He died on his 37th birthday. I'll translate the Latin epitaph which reads:

'Here lies that famous Raphael,
By whom great Mother Nature feared to
Be conquered while he lived,
And when he was dying
Feared herself to die.'

Please will you donate five Euros for the tour?" requested the guide. "You're free to wander around the Pantheon now."

Seren smiled to herself at the cheek of the guide asking for five Euros, hardly value for money, but she paid all the same. Madoc would have refused but it was worth having a whistle-stop tour of the Pantheon and the solitary browse afterwards was enjoyable. She had remembered her nain and taid discussing Raphael's work and made a vow to see his depiction of the Transformation in the Vatican Museums. There was so much to tell nain. She couldn't wait. On the way back to their apartment, Seren lost her way several times and tutted at herself. Madoc would have rolled his eyes in despair. Lost, three times she walked around the same Square, eventually arriving at her destination, tired, skin burning, face red. Seren took a cool shower, headed for the shaded terrace, and slept until Madoc gently shook her awake.

"Hello cariad tlws" he greeted her. "You didn't answer your 'phone so I assumed something was wrong. Now I know what it is. Your face is as red as a beetroot. You need a parasol or a hat" he recommended as he stared at her crimson face and freckled nose. "You also need to wear total sunblock" he advised.

"You're right. I don't feel too well this evening. I'm thirsty and cold."

"Looking at you I'd say a touch of sunstroke. Let's stay in and I'll cook us something light" he suggested.

That evening, they savoured being alone together, and didn't leave the apartment.

***

The day of the *revelation* brought with it a repeat of yesterday's weather; identical blue sky and burning sun, but Seren was better prepared. At least she wore sunblock, a white cotton dress to reflect the glaring sun, and was going shopping on the way to work with Madoc for a hat or parasol. They made their way along quiet streets, past the Largo di Torre Argentina and headed to a little milliner's shop that Madoc had spotted the day before. He bought Seren a wide-brimmed white hat which shaded her face and neck. An excellent choice as she looked

230

chic. They arranged to meet for a late lunch in the Terrazza Caffarelli at the Forum and kissed each other goodbye.

The main entrance to the Roman Forum was near the Piazza Venezia. Normally hectic, today again it was peculiarly quiet. Seren was thankful for small mercies as she found it difficult to cope with too much energy created by people around her. She made her way to the House of the Vestal Virgins, wishing to know more about these rare women who were chosen to be full-time religious officials. Rest was offered to Seren in the shape of a marble bench opposite a statute of a Vestal Virgin. She referred to her guidebook and read the section about Vestal Virgins again.

'The Vestals were chosen from female Roman children around the age of eight and entered the House of Vesta for thirty years as Priestesses. Vestals had to remain celibate, if they did not, they were buried alive. Their duties were to ensure the fire of Vesta stayed alight, otherwise lore said that Rome would crumble. The Vestals prepared and attended rituals and were guardians of many sacred documents, Divine prophecies, and Wills. They were powerful and influential, and as such extraordinary rights and privileges were afforded to them, the main one was close links to the Emperor. They had the power to free prisoners or slaves, were given ring-side seats at public games and theatrical events, were escorted wherever they went, could make a Will, and pass on property to other women. The Vestals were also well-paid. Once their period of duty was over, it was considered an honour for a Roman man to marry a Vestal Virgin.'

As she swigged from a green bottle of San Pellegrino sparkling water Seren watched two middle-aged women who were wearing the distinctive white headdress and long white gowns

of Vestal Virgins. '*Surely the order doesn't exist anymore?*'
she speculated. Enthralled, Seren laid down her guidebook and
observed proceedings. These Vestals were formulating a ritual
and without knowing why, Seren knew exactly what they
would do! They were preparing wheat to make it edible for
Vestalia, and once finished, lit white candles. Astonishingly,
one of the Vestal Virgins approached her.

"Good afternoon. I see you're taking an interest in our ritual,
but I haven't seen you here before. What is your name?"

"Me?" said Seren looking around to see that she was the only
person within earshot.

"Yes."

"Seren."

"You are English?"

"No. Welsh. From Conwy in Wales."

"Seren. Did you know that you emit a golden aura?"

"I know that everyone emits their own colour of aura. People
are repelled by some auras and drawn to others. Yours too is
golden white and I think that's unusual, isn't it? My nain, I
mean my grandmother has told me that this aura indicates
ethereal wisdom, intuition, and positivity. My aura used to be
indigo, so I must have cultivated deeper wisdom since my nain
last told me the colour of my aura."

"You're an interesting woman. Why are you here?"

Seren remembered her nain's words about her aura '*people will seek you out*'. Nain was right. This woman had sought her out.

"Why am I in the Forum? My partner Madoc is working on an archaeological dig at Largo di Torre Argentina and I'm here on holiday. I decided to return to the Forum to absorb some of the energy from the House of the Vestal Virgins. Apologies, I haven't asked your name."

"It's Bella. What do you mean about energy?"

"Hello" replied Seren, offering her hand to the Vestal. "I know that the universe is made up of energy that we can't see, feel, or touch and we must accept its presence without necessarily being able to prove it existence. There's an ethereal spirit known as our soul. When it's created, the soul goes on a journey, in different physical bodies, throughout time, until it has learned all life lessons, and becomes a God or Goddess. A deity perhaps with powers greater than those of ordinary humans. Some people have the gift, the power of retrieving different dimensions of time, to view the soul's journey, to help themselves or others. At least, that's what I believe."

Bella smiled brightly and asked: "May I sit with you?"

"Of course, here" Seren patted the bench "please sit."

"Have you been in Rome long?"

"Not very long, this is my first visit, but I've spent enough time in the city to realise that I have the strong sensation that the place is familiar to me. That I've been here before. In another life."

"Another life? That's interesting" responded Bella. "What do you know about other lives?"

"My nain, my grandmother, taught me how to meditate. I meditate to enter different dimensions of time to see the other lives I have lived and understand the lessons I need to learn." Incongruous as it may seem, this explanation was accepted without question by Bella.

"I understand. I also believe that different dimensions of time can be accessed and that our soul goes on a long, and sometimes painful, pitiful journey but along that voyage of discovery the soul can also experience unrestrained bliss" stated Bella.

"My nain is a gwrach gwyn. She's a white witch and so am I. We work for others' highest good."

"Do you have ancestral connections to Rome?" questioned Bella.

"I'm not sure. My nain has a set of original Tarocchi cards and an ancient grimoire both of which have been passed down through the ages. Tarocchi cards originated in Italy so there's a possibility that we have connections to Rome. Also visions of a past life with a Roman Legate, Titus and his partner Ceres repeatedly appear to me."

"I see. Did you know that the Goddess Ceres is the sister of the Goddess Vesta?" questioned Bella.

"No" exclaimed Seren. I didn't know that."

"Have you heard of Sibyls?"

"I've read about Sibyls, Seers, Soothsayers and Augers in Ancient Rome. A Sibyl was a Prophetess whose divinations were collated in the Sibylline books. Supposedly there were nine or three books, depending on whose version you read, which were kept in the Temple of Jupiter here in the Forum. The books could only be consulted by the Emperor who might pass on the information to the Roman Senate but only in emergencies. They were lost in a fire" explained Seren.

"Yes, Sibyls were Prophetesses, *some* were Vestal Virgins. The Sibylline books held Divine secrets. The Sibyls and Vestals wrote the divinations which were shown to them in visions, not unlike the ones you have told me about with Titus and Ceres. As you are aware, certain people can move between the various dimensions of time. Past, present, future. Only the Emperor was ever told about the prophecies, and he could choose to share them with his Senators. There were many secrets kept in Ancient Roman culture."

"The other day when I was in the Forum, I had a vision that I warned Julius Caesar about the traitors. His death was needless" revealed Seren.

"That is thought-provoking to hear Seren. The Sibylline books were kept in the Temple of Jupiter. Not all of them were destroyed" revealed Bella. "When Julius Caesar was murdered a Sibyl fled the city, with three books for safe keeping. Among the chaos that followed, it was difficult to know who could be trusted which is why they were placed in the hands of a Sibyl with a golden white aura around her."

Bella stared keenly at Seren and then said:

"You understand what we are practising here today in the Temple of Vesta don't you?"

"Yes, you're preparing for Vestalia. My perception is that I've participated in this ritual in the past. Is there going to be a ceremony here in the Forum?"

"That's remarkable that you perceive yourself in this ritual" responded the Vestal. "We will have a private rite here every evening between the 7th and 15th June to celebrate Vestalia."

"It's my birthday on the 12th June. Would I be able to see the ceremony if I lean over the wall to the Forum on that day?"

"Join us if you like. Come and practise with us now."

"Would I be able to bring my partner, Madoc?"

"Now?" asked Bella looking around.

"No. On the 12th June."

"Certainly. It's a private event but you will both be welcome to be here. Why not practise with us now?"

"Really? This is phenomenal. Thanks, Bella."

In her white garb Seren didn't look out of place as she helped the two Vestal Virgins prepare their service. She arranged to join them on her birthday and couldn't wait to tell Madoc about her incredible afternoon.

***

"We'd better buy you another white dress then for the occasion" suggested a stunned Madoc when Seren told him about her encounter with the Vestal Virgins. He did shake his head once or twice in astonishment.

"Really? Oh this is so exciting Madoc. Isn't it amazing that Bella said there were still some Sibylline Books in existence? All those prophecies made two thousand years ago. Wonder what they were? And I'm curious about who has the books now. Moon dust they are. And for me to join in the ritual! In the Forum! On my birthday! I'm going to predict it will be a perfect evening."

"I do hope so Seren" responded Madoc seriously.

Outside in the balmy evening air, Madoc listened to an excited Seren. Her verve for life and gentle acceptance of the incredible, amused and intrigued him. She inspired him. She was like sunshine through a window. The copper flecks in her amber eyes sparkled when she recounted the tale of the Vestal Virgins. Delightful. That's what she was. In one word. Delightful. Madoc steered Seren towards Via di Monserrato, a cobbled street lined with an array of authentic Italian shops. He was determined she would wear a stunning white dress for her evening with the Vestals.

As they meandered, they passed an antique shop stuffed to the rafters with paraphernalia covered in layers of dust. A musty cigar odour emanated from within. In the window Madoc spied a gold ring with a huge amber stone. He marched inside before Seren even knew what was happening. Behind the counter, plumes of white cigar smoke emanated from the pursed mouth of a short man who was scratching his shiny bald head. He was a shrewd manager of money. He could smell it. His beady eyes never left Madoc's face.

"Please could you tell me the provenance of the amber ring in the window?" asked Madoc, much to Seren's surprise.

'I didn't see an amber ring' she thought. 'In the window?'

"Sì" replied the owner, as he retrieved the ring from the shop window, took it out of a crimson leather box and passed it to Madoc. "Are you Welsh?"

"Yes. From Conwy, North Wales. How did you guess? Most people ask if we're English. I'm Madoc, this is Seren. What's your name?"

"Gabriele. I thought I recognised the accent as my wife is from Wales. Anglesey."

"Small world. We live near Anglesey. Do you know about the history of the ring?"

"Yes. It's about two thousand years old and the amber stone is from Wales."

"No. That can't be true."

"Yes. It's true.

"There are dark marks in the amber. Is that a fault with the stone Gabriele?"

"No Madoc. There are shadows in the stone that are meant to be there. They represent the ghosts of life, the amber is brightness, the spirit of life."

"Try it on Seren" suggested Madoc.

Startled and embarrassed, Seren placed the ring on the third finger of her right hand.

"Does it fit?" asked Madoc.

"Yes. Perfectly" replied Seren.

"How much is it?" asked Madoc, not one to beat about the bush where finance was concerned.

"Fifteen thousand Euros Madoc."

Madoc gulped. He would not part with his hard-earned money easily. Even though he was well-paid and had inherited money from his mother Jessie, he would be hard-pressed to let it go on a trinket.

"The ring is special Madoc" explained Gabriele. "It has a solid gold band. The amber stone has been authenticated that it *is* from Wales *and* it *is* two thousand years old. Not many people own a ring that old do they? It's been in my family for an age and now is the time to sell it."

Madoc thought it unlikely that many people would have a ring of that period, so had to agree.

"I was offered twice as much for the ring Madoc by someone else. I chose not to sell it. I didn't get the right sense of him.

He didn't have the right aura. He wasn't the right person to buy the ring. I don't need to sell it. I will only sell it to the right person. Do you understand what a lemniscate is Madoc?"

"No" replied Madoc truthfully.

"It's a sideways number eight. It signifies what goes around comes around. The right person will buy this ring."

With that the Gabriele tucked the amber ring back into its leather box and closed the lid with a bang.

"Thank you for showing us the ring Gabriele" said Madoc politely. "Let's go Seren" and with that, they left the dusty antique shop.

Seren was astonished that Gabriele had mentioned the lemniscate as her nain had said exactly the same thing to her. She was doubly astonished to have seen an amber ring as it was furthest from her mind. Memories of her visions about Titus and Ceres flooded back. She needed to be alone and told Madoc that she wished to buy some fridge magnets for the farmworkers and t-shirts for their friends Haf and Gareth. Madoc also needed to be alone and encouraged Seren to pop into some nearby shops. She told him she had spotted a beautiful necklace, a world within a world, for nain and a small statue of a lion. Madoc knew Seren would be absorbed for some time. He walked back into the antique shop as Gabriele knew he would. Madoc bargained him down to twelve thousand Euros for the amber ring.

"What changed your mind Madoc?" asked Gabriele.

"The inscription of TM, a tiny eagle and SPQR on the inside of the ring" responded Madoc. "What goes around, comes around. That ring is priceless to me."

***

On the evening of 12th June, the night when Seren was joining the two Vestal Virgins for the Vestalia ritual the Moon was full, the sky adorned with stars and Madoc's sonorous voice reverberated around the apartment.

"You're as giddy as a kipper Seren. Come on. We'll be late" chided Madoc.

"You do realise that a Full Moon makes everyone dizzy, don't you? It indicates that changeable situations will reach their peak" countered Seren.

"We need to be at the Forum for seven thirty on the dot. That's what the invitation states, here, very clearly" he pointed to the perfectly hand-crafted cream parchment.

"Does it say *on the dot* as that would be a strange detail to include?" queried Seren.

"*I* said on the dot. Not the invitation" retorted Madoc.

"You're a bit tetchy tonight, aren't you?"

"Seren, tonight you get to participate in a once-in-a-lifetime opportunity. A private ritual with two Vestal Virgins in the Forum and I get to photograph it. Life doesn't get much better does it?" he explained. "And I don't like to be late."

"Neither do I, but how do I look Madoc? I'm anxious."

Seren looked indisputably elegant in a silk satin Guinevere styled maxi dress with criss-cross white leather sandals.

"Like a classy lassie, as The Ghillie would say."

"Thank you, Madoc," she hugged and kissed him "you look so very handsome. Please will you fasten my necklace for me?" she asked and passed him her amber necklace.

"Ok" he said, a little embarrassed.

"Perfect. I hope I can make it in these sandals."

"I could always carry you home" suggested Madoc. "Come on. We'll be late. The Uber driver is waiting for us."

"Damn I didn't know he was already here" said Seren applying her coral lipstick without a mirror.

Their taxi whizzed through the streets of Rome. Seren wished the driver would slow down so that she could see the night version of the city, but he didn't. They arrived at Piazza Venezia, the main entrance to the Roman Forum where Bella was waiting for them. She wasn't difficult to spot as she too was wearing an all-white long satin gown, a white satin veil, known as a suffibulum held in place with a brooch, over which was placed a circle of white fragranced jasmine flowers around her head.

"Come on Seren and Madoc. Where is your photography equipment?" Bella asked, looking at Madoc.

"Bloody hell, it's in the Uber."

Madoc ran after the car gesticulating for the driver to stop, which he did, at a red light. When the driver's door was yanked open, the driver yelped, then realised that he recognised his assailant who simply wanted to retrieve his bag from the back seat. Relieved, the driver passed the camera bag to Madoc and drove off at Roman speed. Swiftly.

'What a twit I am' thought Madoc. 'I nearly ruined tonight with my forgetfulness. That was a close shave. The most important thing was in that bag.'

"Come on Madoc" shouted Seren "we need to get started."

They walked together to the Temple of Vesta where the other Vestal Virgin, Aria was waiting for them. She passed Seren a small bouquet, placed on her head a crown of perfumed jasmine flowers and fastened the crown with a seashell shaped gold brooch.

"The jasmine represents beauty, innocence, purity, inspiration, and resilience. It is a Divine gift to you."

"Thank you Aria" said Seren with grace.

The smell of jasmine filled the air. Bella passed Seren a large white candle held in the richly decorated golden shape of a dolphin. Madoc took photographs of the sequence of events which followed under a clear Full Moon in Rome. With shame he recalled the evening he first met Seren on the Vardre under a Full Moon when he had shouted at her.

In the Forum, he captured images as the three women purified the Temple of Vesta and built a lustrous fire in a golden cauldron. The wispy blue smoke coiled around them as they lit six white candles to honour the Goddess Vesta, all recorded by Madoc. Each woman held a golden olla, containing ingredients to make bread, which they offered in a ritual as Madoc snapped the unfurling events.

When the ritual ended, a radiant Seren walked serenely to Madoc.

"We are going to meet again. Bella and Aria have said that I can join in the ceremony next year. That's incredible, isn't it? They want you to place the images you've taken into the Historical Society's magazine as well as on the Forum's advertising material. This is the first time it's ever been captured on camera."

"Wow Seren. That's fantastic. What a coup. Well done." He kissed Seren gently and grabbed her hand.

"Come on" he instructed "let's get to the Temple of Saturn while we can. I'd like to take photographs of it in the moonlight" he explained. "This is our unique opportunity to capture the Forum in the dark."

Madoc trained his camera on Seren as she stood in front of the Temple. They moved under an arch and peered out at the night sky. Madoc held Seren in his arms and said:

"Would you like to get engaged?" and passed her an open crimson box which held a gold ring with an amber stone.

Madoc had taken Seren by surprise and she hadn't registered the ring.

"Good grief" she replied, "we've not been going out very long."

The moment wasn't quite lost or spoiled, because when she noticed the amber ring, Seren took it gently out of its box and cupped it. Madoc switched on the torch of his 'phone so that Seren could read the inscriptions TM, SPQR and see the little imprint of an eagle. She cried and passed him the ring which he placed on the third finger of her left hand.

"I'm assuming that's *yes?*" he asked.

"Yes. Of course, yes. My nain predicted this. She said that I would travel to Rome and be given a ring. I can't believe it's happened. Does she know?"

"Yes. Of course she knows. I asked her permission before we left for our trip."

"I take it she gave her blessing?"

"She did."

"Madoc, does this amber ring mean that Titus and Ceres really existed in another life?"

"It looks like your visions were real Seren, doesn't it? Here's the physical proof which I left in the bloody taxi. That's why I had to run after it like a twit. My camera equipment I could replace, but the ring is unique. Come on, I've organised for a horse-drawn carriage to take us to Piazza Navona."

"I didn't realise you were so romantic" exclaimed Seren wobbly with excitement.

It was fitting that a horse-drawn carriage took them from the Forum, it reminded Seren of Jupiter's horse-drawn chariot on top of his Temple. She thought about the flock of birds she'd seen in the shape of an arrow. This was a sign of moving forward in their romance and thankfully a good omen. Piazza Navona, which was once the oval site for Ancient Roman athletics, was abuzz with tourists. In Ancient Rome, the stadium had been named after Emperor Domitian and held thirty thousand spectators. Now built upon, a pedestrianised area encircled by Baroque mansions and a palace, three extravagant fountains were placed in the oval: the Fountain of the Four Rivers, Fonta del Nettuno and Fontana del Moro. The dramatic church of Sant'Agnese took pride of place.

Madoc and Seren, both on an emotional high wandered among other tourists in the busy town square and chose to eat in a glamorous restaurant down one of the side roads. Across a candlelit table Madoc asked:

"Where would you like to get married Seren?"

"In Rome if possible. Could we have a handfasting ceremony here?"

"You're full of surprises. What on Earth is that?"

"It's a Pagan ritual and involves our hands being tied together with ribbons. Vows are exchanged as our hands are intertwined and bound together. We would need to find someone to officiate and a venue. It doesn't have to be a huge, grand affair and our family and friends could tie different coloured ribbons around our hands."

"What do the various colours represent?"

"Blue indicates loyalty, green signifies growth and abundance, orange is for energy, purple embodies wealth, red denotes passion, white symbolises purity and new beginnings and yellow is for joy."

"It's going to be difficult to choose colours then by the sound of that list. Can we have them all?"

"I'm sure we'll decide upon colours. I can't wait to get home and tell nain all about Rome, participating in the ritual with the Vestal Virgins and our engagement. Obviously not in that order as the key thing is us getting engaged. It's wonderful."

"It's been a life-changing two weeks Seren. Thanks for sharing this time with me."

Madoc's feelings for Seren were tender and deep; as for her feelings, she loved and respected him. They had become equal partners, soulmates enjoying a special, compassionate, enduring kind of love, until their dying day.

Madoc had solved a puzzle and was rewarded with the prize of his life. This was the day that Madoc Thomson would always remember.

Chapter 16 – The Great Escape

Some people come out of adversity stronger.

There were no misconceptions about nain. She had been born in Anglesey, moved to Conwy with her husband Tomos, was a Seer who experienced Divine revelations and the keeper of a mysterious ancient grimoire. One evening after their engagement, Madoc had asked Seren whether she had ever seen her nain's spell book. She had to admit that she hadn't seen it at close quarters.

"Does she use it for past life regressions, or when she reads tarot cards for people or when she concocts potions?" questioned Madoc.

"I've never held it. I've only glimpsed it once and heard her mention it" admitted Seren.

"Where does she keep it?" insisted Madoc.

"Under lock and key. I heard taid tell her that the key to her grimoire was in her special place."

"Where's that?" persisted Madoc.

"Probably in a private area. I don't know Madoc. Ask her."

"You ask her. She'll think I'm being nosey."

"Why do you want to know where it is? Why are you interested in it suddenly? You *are* being nosey."

"Is it not strange that in Rome the Sibyl, Bella talked to you about the Sibylline books, that three books were missing and that you and your nain could have been Sibyls in a previous dimension of time?"

"No it's not strange. Bella saw my golden aura. I saw hers. We clicked. I was asked to participate in a ritual. Your conjecture is that nain's ancient grimoire could be one of the Sibylline books? Preposterous! All I know is that nain said I'd inherit her book when she died."

"The mystery could be solved if you asked nain about her ancient grimoire. It'd seem odd coming from me."

"But it *is* coming from you. You're the one who's suspicious about her spell book."

"I'm not suspicious. I am convinced it's a Sibylline book."

"That's bonkers."

"No more crazy than you saying that you've lived different lives."

"I thought that you believed me. Especially when you bought my engagement ring. Surely that was concrete proof that lives exist in numerous dimensions?"

"I need more convincing than a serendipitous event like seeing an amber ring in a jeweller's shop in Rome with the inscription TM SPQR and engraved with a tiny eagle. And visions from *your* past life regression. *I* couldn't do a past life regression so how do I know they exist? By the way TM are my initials but backwards."

"To settle this argument, I'll ask nain to give us a past life regression together. See if that works for you and unravels the mysteries of your mind. I'm not sure we've got until forever to unscramble what goes on in your head! And I know TM are your initials backwards. I'm not a *total moron* Thomson Madoc."

"You make me smile when you're angry Seren Williams."

"And also. You've had visions about fighting in Gaul, but you call that lucid dreaming. Here's nain. I'll ask her."

"What's all the kerfuffle about you two? What are you debating?"

"Nain, is it possible for you to do a joint past life regression on Madoc and me? Is there the likelihood that it would work? And do you need your ancient grimoire to do a past life regression?"

"Goodness that's a lot of questions. I can certainly try a joint past life regression, but I've never done one before. The ancient grimoire is under lock and key until I die, then it is entrusted to your safe keeping."

"Please may I see it nain?"

"I'll see. Let me think about it. We can do the past life regression tomorrow and kill two birds with one stone" replied nain.

"See I told you it was dangerous to do past life regression. Nain's thinking of killing us" teased Madoc.

"Stop taunting me Madoc Thomson. I meant that I could do past life regression AND show you the secret tunnel to the Temple of Mithras. You've not seen it yet Madoc. You're in for a treat" said nain.

***

Twenty-four hours later, as he was led down the dimly lit, secret tunnel, Madoc was ruing agreeing to do a past life regression. It wasn't usual to be underground heading to goodness knows where with two Sibyls carrying candles, blankets, and a gawk-eyed hawkstaff, possibly never to return. He shook his head and hoped three things. One that he was being unusually melodramatic, two, that his mate Gareth didn't find out about this experience otherwise he'd never hear the end of it and three, that he could undergo a past life regression this time round.

The damp, musty underground tunnel finally widened to reveal part of the hidden Temple of Mithras. Madoc was astounded by what he saw. He marvelled that Roman legionaries had secretly worshipped here. With his finger he traced the dim carvings on the wooden pilings of Mithras slaughtering a bull and dining with Sol, the Sun God. Seren led him down worn stone steps to the central nave as shadows in the northern alcove bounced and sprang nimbly.

Soothing in manner, Gwen instructed Seren to lie in the nave on the right-hand side of Madoc. She wrapped them both in her red and black Welsh plaid, handstitched tapestry blanket so that they would remain warm throughout the ritual. It would be an understatement to say that Madoc was nervous as his eyes constantly focused on the frayed shadows of the nave in case there was a sharp knife and human sacrifices were the order of the day. Not that he would admit it, but fastening upon nain's hawkstaff, with its shiny blue appetite crystal eye, which shimmered menacingly in the orange candlelight, freaked out Madoc. Noticing his jittery jumpiness nain said:

"Remember Madoc, this hawkstaff is a little like a staff used by wizards or witches that you might have seen at the cinema. It acts as an amplifier of magic. I'll use mine by stomping it on the floor to begin and I'll say: '*to put energy into the ground*' and when we've finished, I'll say '*the deal is sealed*' then I'll bang my hawkstaff on the ground."

Madoc cleared his throat so that a little squeaking sound, like that of a trapped mouse, wouldn't pop out of his mouth.

"It might help if you hold hands" suggested nain, noticing Madoc's uneasiness.

Seren placed her left hand into Madoc's right hand and gave it a little squeeze for reassurance.

"Don't be fearful my cariad tlws. I'll be with you" said Seren.

Nain smiled.

"Ok you two. You'll still hear my voice and feel sensations. To begin with, breathe deeply through your nose and exhale through your mouth. We will meditate before doing the past life regression. Make yourselves comfortable now that you're lying on the nave. You're in control, you can stop at any time. I'll guide you. I'm going to stomp hawkstaff *now*" said nain and banged her hawkstaff on the ground "to put energy into the ground. Choose a spot on the ceiling and focus upon it. Breathe deeply to the count of five, hold your breath to the count of five, breathe out to the count of five. I'll go from ten to one. As I say each number blink your eyes."

Gwen carried on in this way until she felt that Seren and Madoc had both reached a state of introspection.

"Close your eyes. Can you see the steps?" asked nain.

"Yes" replied Seren.

"No" replied Madoc.

"Keep your eyes closed. Breathe deeply to the count of five, hold your breath to the count of five, breathe out to the count of five. I'll go from ten to one." Gwen carried on. Seren waited patiently in contemplation.

"Can you see the steps?" asked nain.

"Yes" responded Seren.

"Yes" responded Madoc.

Gwen felt a frisson of relief.

"As I count up to ten, walk up the steps, slowly" instructed Gwen.

Madoc and Seren listened intently.

"Can you see two chairs?"

"Yes" they replied in unison.

"This is your safe space. You can always return to a chair."

There was a brief pause whilst nain considered the enormity of what the three of them were about to undertake.

"There are several doors before you. Choose one door which is drawing you to it. Tell me the year on that door."

"It's 53BCE" they both responded in unison.

"Good. Now open the door and walk through it into a past life. Tell me what you see, hear, and feel" instructed Gwen.

There was silence. Gwen touched Madoc's arm.

"How old are you?" queried Gwen.

"I'm twenty-four years old."

Gwen touched Seren's arm.

"How old are you?" queried Gwen.

"I'm eighteen years old."

"What is your name?" she gently touched Madoc's arm.

"Titus."

"What is your name?" she gently touched Seren's arm.

"Ceres."

"Good" responded Gwen aquiver. "Take it in turns to tell me what's happening. Titus, you start first."

"My scouts have informed me that the Ordovices wish to seek revenge for the attack on their village some months ago. Ceres is in grave danger as they know she captured Princess Teranica, wife of Chief Eigion, leader of the Ordovices. I am on my way to her homestead, with members of my legion. There are eighty of my legionaries, led by a centurion, to remove her and her grandparents away from harm" he said resolutely. "My men will fight to the death."

Seren, as Ceres, took up the story:

"From the kitchen window I can see Titus and his men marching towards the farmhouse, their shot bows, arrows, spears, and shields glinting in the golden sunrays. My grandparents, Anwen, my nain and Dafydd, my taid are with me. Dafydd is holding a trident and spear as he realises danger is afoot. I am clasping my pugio."

There was a long pause and a deep breath from Seren.

"Titus has burst into the kitchen and is shouting orders. He is in full command of the situation."

"I am directing Ceres, Anwen and Dafydd to escape through the tunnel to the Temple of Mithras" added Madoc.

"Was the tunnel already there?" asked Gwen.

"Yes. I foresaw that this might happen. For weeks my men have been creating a secret underground channel from the homestead, and building a Temple dedicated to Mithras where my soldiers can worship. There is a covert entry and escape point on the other side of the Temple. We sent the farmworkers away while it was being constructed and some of my legionaries helped on the farm in their absence."

"What is your plan for Ceres, Anwen and Dafydd?" probed Gwen.

"My Optio, Marcus is waiting on the other side of the Temple. He will lead the family to our ship in Deganwy. The Tenth Legion, under my command, has been called to Gaul by Julius Caesar. The ship is prepared and ready to leave. We will stop at Deva Victrix on our way. There will be a garrison built here in Cambria so that the Roman army can continue its battles."

In a meditative state, a strange event occurred, Seren turned to Madoc and said:

"Titus. I am not leaving here without you."

"I'll meet you on the ship Ceres. It's important that you leave now. Look, the Ordovices are already on your land."

"My taid Dafydd insists that he will fight with you Titus and has passed a large golden key to my nain Anwen. He's told her it's the key to his heart. She is sobbing. Anwen will come with me" said Ceres.

There was a pause then she continued. "Two legionaries helped us down the steep stone stairs. A spear just missed me and pierced through the throat of one of your men. His blood is all over me. He died, instead of me. He died because of me."

'He could be the Roman soldier who haunts Seren' thought Gwen. 'He might blame her for his death.'

"The Ordovices were close. Battle was raging around the homestead. What did you do?" asked Gwen of Ceres.

"Anwen and I ran along the tunnel, bouncing off the muddy walls, slipping on the moist floor, all the time in darkness. My nain was gasping for breath. By the time we arrived at the Temple of Mithras we could hear the squawks and squeals of battle, the smell of burning wood and acrid smoke began to fill the passageway. Barely able to breathe we scrambled to the Temple."

Madoc took up the story.

"Dafydd stood beside me, outside the homestead and was pierced in the heart by a spear. He choked on blood which spewed from his open chest and purple lips. He died like a true legionary. He battled to the end."

On hearing this, the pain in Gwen's chest almost brought her to bend double as she immediately recalled the recent death of her own beloved Tomos.

"The key. The key to Dafydd's heart? What happened to the key?" Gwen asked anxiously.

"Anwen rummaged around in the nave of the Temple. She used the key to open a gold box which was hidden under a stone floor tile engraved with the Ace of Cups. She checked that the ancient grimoire was there, locked the gold box and placed it with the key deep into her clothing, next to her heart. She told me to tell no-one about the book."

Gwen sighed. "What was happening in the homestead?"

"The Ordovices had surrounded the farm and were pelting it
with tar fireballs. It set alight as did the outbuildings. I lost
twenty soldiers that day, including Dafydd. We battled all day
and all night. Thankfully there was no moon to light the
battleground so my men could move under cover of darkness.
It was freezing cold, and we had limited supplies. At one point,
I thought I had failed my warriors, but they marched on in tight
formation. They threw javelins, drew their gladii, and fought
hand battles, man-to-man. The acme arrived when I sent my
horse-riding soldiers, my cavalry, into the incursion. We
defeated the Ordovices. Again! On horseback I rode to
Deganwy. To my ship and Ceres."

"What happened once Anwen had the ancient book? What did
you do?" probed Gwen of Seren.

"We carried on past the Temple. In the distance we could hear
Marcus shouting my name and we followed the sound. He had
a raeda waiting for us."

"What's that?" asked Gwen of Seren.

"It's a wooden carriage, with wooden benches which is drawn
by four horses. Marcus and two of his most trusted men
escorted us to Deganwy. We joined the naves gallicae there.
In the distance we could see the black smoke beyond the
Vardre and knew that our home was lost. I was terrified that
Titus would have passed on to another life."

"What are naves gallicae?" asked Gwen.

"Roman transport ships" reported Titus. "I joined Ceres and Anwen on the lead ship. We sailed along the turbulent North Wales coast into the calmer waters of the River Deva to Deva Victrix where we left Anwen with her cousin."

"What happened next?" prodded Gwen of Seren.

"Anwen reassured me she would be well-cared for by her cousin. The pitiful black eyes of this esoteric lady looked deep into my soul and her wrinkled hand clutched at the key taid had given her. The key to his heart. With pools of tears welling from deep within her nain pressed the golden key into my hand, together with her gold box holding the ancient grimoire which she had rescued from the Temple of Mithras. '*Guard these with your life*', she instructed. '*May we meet again cariad tlws, in this lifetime.*' Titus told Anwen that I would become his wife. Anwen clasped his hand and said he was an admirable man. She and I hugged on the quayside until it was time to depart. It was poignant, dreadful, and thrilling in equal measure as we left to begin a new life together, in war as a married couple. We didn't know how long our lives would last."

"We sailed that evening under cover of darkness" explained Madoc. From there we travelled to Gaul to join Julius Caesar. Word had reached me that the new leader of the Gauls, Vercingetorix, had led an attack on Cenabum, a Roman settlement, and killed the entire Roman population. Julius Caesar's elite Legio Ten platoon, led by me, was called upon to join Caesar.

"A frightening adventure sailing into the unfathomable unknown depths of a new life" replied Gwen tenderly. "It's time to find the chairs Seren and Madoc, go back to the chairs."

After a few moments Seren exclaimed: "I've found a chair."

"I've found one too" responded Madoc.

"Good." Gwen was relieved. "Sit on them. I'm going to stomp hawkstaff *now*" said Gwen and banged her hawkstaff on the ground "the deal is sealed. I'll count back from ten to zero. When I say zero your eyes will open. You will return to your current life."

Both Seren and Madoc were pallid as they began to re-emerge from their meditative state. Bone cold, despite the warm blanket, both shivered.

"How are you feeling you two?" quizzed Gwen. "Is there something you have learned about yourselves during that past life regression?"

"Nain, I learned that the Roman soldier who has terrorised me so much over the years is likely to blame me for his death. When we return to the farmhouse, I should release his essence to the light on the earth plane and send his spirit where he should have been two thousand years ago. And I ought to apologise to him first. I also learned that I loved Titus so much that I left everything behind to be with him."

"And I've learned that I'm a leader of men and that I would defend Ceres and her family to the death. Now I'm thirsty and eager to eat something sweet" replied Madoc.

"Ah" responded Gwen "good thing I've brought a flask of coffee and some home-made chocolate biscuits with me, isn't it?"

Madoc smiled and calculated that a past life regression was invigorating and illuminating. He thought that he might even chat about this in the pub with his mate Gareth who wouldn't believe a word of it.

The three of them, nain, Seren and Madoc had learned that the ancient grimoire was on its travels guarded, under pain of death, by a Legate named Titus, with a legion at his disposal, and his wife Ceres. Perhaps Madoc had obtained the information he had been seeking, that nain's ancient grimoire may be a Sibylline book full of Divine prophecies.

2023

Chapter 17 – Gaul

Walking with Caesar.

"Nain I'm going into Conwy to meet Madoc for a coffee. Do you want anything whilst I'm out?" asked Seren.

"As we are going to Rome for your handfasting ceremony next month, please will you see if there are any walking shoes that you think are appropriate for me in Strollers shop on Castle Street? Save me having to traipse around looking for suitable footwear. I fancy a nice pair of those Doc Marten shoes or boots in dark red or shiny black. They look so comfy."

"Size four nain?" asked Seren not a bit surprised that her nain would wear something unusual for a woman of her age.

"Yes, or size five so that I can wear thick socks" replied nain.

"Rome will still be warm in October. Are you sure you'll need thick socks? I could get you some Doc Marten shoes with those slipper socks so no-one can see you're wearing socks."

"Whatever you think is proper for our trip cariad tlws. But I did fancy sandals or boots. I plan on having a mooch around on my own in Rome. I'm not tagging along with you two, or your friends Gareth and Haf. You'll be on honeymoon" responded nain.

"Madoc and I are going to visit Florence and Venice whilst we're on honeymoon. You'll have plenty of time to explore Rome on your own. I know how excited you are." Seren couldn't believe how her nain's zest for life had been spiced.

"I really am. I can't wait. Thank you for buying me the guidebook to Rome. Today I'm going to put stickers on the map to show all the places I would like to visit. I'll need to stay for a month, not two weeks!"

"You can stay as long as you like nain. This is the first time you've travelled outside of Wales so make the most of it. You'll enjoy being in Italy" replied Seren. "And you really don't need a map. You can use the map on your mobile 'phone. It'll even show *you* moving on the map, so you don't get lost like I did. It's a little like the Marauder's map in the Harry Potter books you used to read to me. I don't know why I didn't use it when we were in Rome!"

"You've shown me how to use the map on the 'phone. I've been practising handling it around the farm. It's marvellous but it's not the same as having an overview and planning out where I'd like to go and seeing with my own eyes the little stickers and holding the map in my hand. Folding and unfolding it. I wish Tomos was here. He'd be so excited about travelling abroad to exotic lands."

Seren laughed and kissed Gwen on the top of her head.

"You're going to Rome nain. Not Patagonia! It's only three hours flight away. I'll see you later. Is it ok if Madoc and I join you for dinner but please don't tell me it's lobscouse *again*."

"There's plenty of food. I'll make Welsh rarebit for you. Madoc and I can have cawl, with plenty of vegetables so you can help yourself to the extra ones. Oh. Please will you buy some vanilla slices from Popty's Bakery. They're the best vanilla slices I've ever tasted. Even better than my own" said nain, and that was quite a statement.

"I will nain. You can come with me to Conwy if you like" suggested Seren.

"Oh no cariad tlws. I don't enjoy shopping. I've got plenty to do here at the farm" replied Gwen, unfolding her worn map of Rome for at least the one hundredth time.

"Ok I'll see you later. Good thing I'm going in the car because of the gigantic shopping list you've given me" teased Seren.

Before she left Bryn Gosol Farmhouse, Seren had cut some Mexican sunflowers and deep red dahlias from nain's garden which had been grown from seed. She had separated the flowers into two bunches. Seren drove to Saint Hilary's Church, parked her little white Mini on the road, and walked along the yew tree path. She placed the Mexican sunflowers on taid's grave and the red dahlias on the grave of Madoc's mother Jessie. As she stood before each headstone, she asked taid and Jessie to give their blessing to her forthcoming handfasting ceremony with Madoc. It was hard not to cry knowing that they would both be there in Ysbryd but wouldn't be able to physically wrap their arms around her and Madoc to reassure them that all would be fine.

"Everything moves in circles" she thought as she left the church "and the circle for taid and Jessie, in this life, is complete."

Whizzing through the country lanes in her little white Mini car, Seren crossed the Conwy Bridge, past Conwy Castle and into the harbour area. She parked the car near the estuary and walked briskly to Pen y Bryn Café where Madoc was already waiting. He stood and kissed her cheek.

"I've been dying to see you" he admitted.

"Me too with you" she said, a little perplexed. "Why have you been dying to see me? Is something wrong?"

"You always fear the worst. Let's order food and then I'll tell you my *good* news."

"Oh lovely. Good news is always welcome. I'll have a cheese and Branston pickle sandwich on granary bread please and a café latte. What are you having?"

"I'll go for the same. Don't go anywhere, I'll just order at the counter" commanded Madoc.

"The café is about ten feet wide Madoc. You'll easily spot me if I try to escape!" retorted Seren.

Madoc had barely returned to his seat, when Seren demanded:

"Right. Tell me your news."

"Look at this" said Madoc, passing a cream coloured A5 envelope to Seren. Cautiously she opened it and pulled out a piece of cream coloured card inscribed with gold writing.

"Oh goodness" she shouted. Everyone in the café looked at her. "Sorry" she said and whispered to Madoc "you've won first prize in the national photography competition. Oh Madoc. I'm delighted for you. Well done. Which picture did you enter?"

"This one" he said, pulling out his mobile phone to show Seren a night-time image of her nain, sitting and staring through a telescope, into the magpie feather blue sky with a Crescent Moon, and the planets Jupiter and Venus in conjunction.

Seren gasped and began to cry. "You've entitled it '*Time Without Age*'. Oh Madoc. You really are adorable."

"Thank you. I'll accept that my gorgeous fiancée" acquiesced Madoc.

"What does this mean for your career?" she asked.

"It means my profile will be highlighted in the photography world and that I've already been offered another three commissions with the Historical Society."

"Fabulous. Where?"

"Pompeii, followed by a trip to Patagonian Chile and then Devil's Throat at Iguazú Falls!"

"No! Really?"

"Yes. Really."

"I can't believe this. I've just said to nain she's not going to Patagonia and here you are. Off to exotic places!"

"I've bought you a little present, as a thank you for being such a supportive partner."

Seren clapped her hands in delighted anticipation. Madoc passed her a small parcel, wrapped in brown paper, and tied with cream coloured string. Seren untied the string and tore at the brown paper packaging. She couldn't even begin to imagine what Madoc had bought.

"What's this wrapped in a purple velvet bag?" Seren untied the bag. "Oh. Moon Tarot Cards? Why? It's thoughtful, but why? Thank you so much" and with that she leaned over and kissed him.

"Well … I've been thinking about this. If I'm travelling around the world on photography assignments, I'd like you to accompany me. I don't want you to stay at home whilst I'm away. I would like an adventurous life that we can enjoy together. Why don't you give up your job and dedicate yourself to divination? You've got James who can run the farm. Your nain is an independent woman who's been given a second wind. Once she's been to Rome, she might want to travel to see us further afield. You could work as and when you can. Work the hours to suit you. What do you think? You could even have a base here for when we're home."

"What do I think? That my life is magical. That a Divine wobbly path on the Vardre, led me to you. That's what I think."

Seren stood up and kissed Madoc full on the lips much to the shock of the other patrons in the café, but Seren and the usually reserved Madoc didn't care.

"There's one other thing I'd like though Seren," said Madoc.

"What's that?"

"Your nain to do another past life regression on us both. I'm curious to know what happened to Titus and Ceres because these dreams I have about the Legate feel real. I want to find out if my lucid dreams link with a past life. It'd solve a mystery for me."

"I'm sure she'd be delighted to offer that service" responded Seren impishly. "In fact, she could do it tonight after dinner. There are some errands I need to do in Conwy before we go home. Nain wants some Doc Marten boots, sandals, or shoes for her trip to Rome."

Madoc's eyebrows lifted almost to the back of his head.

"and some vanilla slices from Popty's Bakery."

"I'll have to leave plenty of space for those vanilla slices. They're the best. Buy an extra one for me" instructed Madoc.

Nain got her cherry red Doc Marten Clarissa style sandals and six vanilla slices from Popty's Bakery. What she hadn't bargained for was what would be revealed through the past life regression with Seren and Madoc that evening when they reverted to their lives in 52BCE. The following narrative is the beginning of what was unveiled to Gwen by Madoc about his life as Titus.

***

"For seven years Julius Caesar's legions had waged military campaigns with assorted tribes of Gauls. When an entire Roman population based in the town of Cenabum had been massacred under the leadership of Vercingetorix in 53BCE, my parents included, an incensed Julius Caesar recalled me, and my fearsome Legio Ten warriors from Cambria. The treacherous sea journey, with its threatening murky waves and enormous swell proved torturously long and slow. One of the younger soldiers, Corvus Corax demonstrated incredible bravery during the journey when he jumped into the raging sea to save one of the legionaries who had fallen overboard. Despite his youth, I have already made him one of my trusted Centurions and presented him with my special gladius, forged in Segontium.

During the journey some of my warriors suffered seasickness and diarrhoea making them weaker than they would be normally. The men were exhausted. Ceres offered marvellous support, creating medicinal potions from her nain's ancient grimoire to help quell the men's queasy stomachs. She poached ginger root, added a few pinches of cumin, and made sure my warriors drank plenty of boiled water. They grew to admire my calm and supportive wife and became protective of her.

In January 52BCE when we arrived in Gaul, it was winter. Our skin reddened because of the low temperatures. Alongside my men, Ceres waded through piercing blizzards. Frosty snowflakes blurred our vision and soaked our clothes. We slept under sopping blankets and were blighted by icy winds until the etiolated bones in our bodies lost any feeling. In a forest I organised my men. Ceres, helped by some of the legionaries, conjured food for us all by foraging among the trees and shrubs, using the ancient grimoire to work out which plants were safe to eat. We had nettles, parsley, chervil, flatweed and mushrooms in a broth, simmered escargot with chestnuts and dandelions accompanied by rotten blackberries stewed into juice. The men lopped trees to create temporary shelters, created fires to light the way and dry our blankets and clothes.

We warmed our aching bones and slept soundly for the first time in weeks. My wife was stoic throughout.

Once we had received sustenance, and were rested, I met with Julius Caesar who had, on hearing the news about the attack on Romans in Cenabum, dashed to the area. We agreed that my Legio Ten legionaries would surround the town, which we did, and recaptured it easily from the Gauls because of our surprise, silent night-time attack. We slaughtered every man, woman and child then burned Cenabum to the ground. We marched on, knowing that Vercingetorix was a pitiless leader of his men, but also aware that Caesar was a master tactician and equally callous. Vercingetorix had ignited the unstoppable inferno which was Julius Caesar.

Enigmatic Vercingetorix had ordered the destruction of every farm and unfortified town in the region so that they could not be captured and used by our legions. The heavily reinforced hillside town of Avaricum was surrounded by river and marshland. The Gauls believed that Caesar would not be able to defeat the tribes within this rich city. Buoyed by our success in Cenabum, my Roman legion continued onwards. Around the bottom of Avaricum's protected walls a multitude of Roman workmen and slaves, brought by other legions, created enormous ramps to bridge the moat around the city. Artillery soldiers were placed at the bottom of the ramps, alongside huge makeshift towers. My soldiers were able to climb the battlements, over the walls and enter the city.

Our unexpected arrival caused terror within Avaricum, and people fled their homes screaming in panic. If anyone left the city, they were eradicated by the artillery soldiers. If they stayed inside the city walls, they were massacred by my Legio Ten warriors. We were there to avenge the death of Romans in

Cenabum. We showed no mercy. The Gauls were taller than us, with longer swords, but my men were brutal, sadistic even, and each legionary fought with the strength of ten men. In close combat, despite the height advantage of the Gauls, my legionaries demonstrated no compassion. We killed anyone who stood in our way, men, women, and children. We stormed the city of Avaricum, sending a frightful message to the Gauls and used it as a base for our next attack. That was where I left Ceres, safe in the knowledge she would be protected by the legionaries around her.

By the time we landed in Gaul, the legionaries and I had realised that Ceres was a prophetess. With the abilities of an Augur, she could interpret the behaviour of birds and was able to indicate whether their conduct showed approval for our actions. Ceres said that the number of birds that she saw was important, for example a bird on its own indicated a need for solitude, thoughtfulness, and introspection. If birds were fighting one another that indicated battles ahead. If a bird flew into a place or person, it revealed an important message was on its way. She read birds' flight patterns. Heading south denoted passion and motivation, spiral patterns suggested forthcoming demise. If my legionaries heard a hooting owl, they became fearful as this was associated with death.

One of my Centurions, young Corvus Corax too demonstrated some skills as an Augur. He became known as Magpie because of his name from the raven family, and in honour of this, had an image of two magpies tattooed on his neck. Wherever he went tidings of magpies followed and he was able to comprehend their actions in relation to our battles. The Magpie said that at times the birds symbolised bravery and offered protection, but on other occasions acted as a warning about who to trust. He and Ceres became firm friends. It was she

who had predicted our safe passage from Cambria to Gaul.
Ceres also had visions. She told me beforehand about the
Roman defeat at Cenabum, that my legionaries would be
glorious in the battle of Avaricum. When we met, I informed
Julius Caesar about my wife's extraordinary divination
abilities. He was intrigued and, when they were introduced,
charmed by her.

Ceres and Caesar had much in common. They both believed
strongly in the Divine, its influence on life and the power of the
Gods. As Romans we all worship Gods, particularly the Sun
God, Sol and the Moon Goddess, Luna. There's a delightful
story which Ceres told Caesar, about the doomed love affair
between Sol and Luna. Usually, the sun and the moon can only
pass each other, and are destined to meet rarely, but when they
do join, it causes an eclipse where the world stands in shadow.
Sol's legacy to Luna is that she gives birth to stars that light the
night sky. The Gods communicate their intentions through the
conduct of birds, and visions. Only a skilled Augur could
interpret the Gods' intentions. Ceres was a remarkable Augur.
Not only that, but she had visions of the future which helped
inform the actions of my Legio Ten warriors. She became an
invaluable asset to me professionally and personally.

It was Ceres who cautioned Caesar that his troops would
struggle to defeat General Vercingetorix and the tribes in
Gergovia. She warned that disparate, small groups of vicious
soldiers would undertake terror attacks on us, like invisible
spirits, and they would win future battles. Caesar chose to
ignore her prognostications. Sadly, Ceres was proved right.
On a steep cliffside, Vercingetorix used his warriors to
subjugate supply lines leading to the starvation of Roman
legionaries. In the heat of battle, with the spirit of death riding
alongside, other legions were overcome by the Gallic army.

Only my Legio Ten legionaries heard Caesar's celestial trumpet order to retreat. We maintained our battle formation and not one of my men died that day but across other legions numerous legionaries perished. All the warriors of Legio Fourteen were annihilated. We Romans weren't always as successful in conflicts as we presumed to portray.

Buoyed by his victory, and a force to be reckoned with, Vercingetorix and his huge confederation army waited for battle at the hilltop fortified settlement of Alesia. Caesar ordered my Legio Ten legionaries to attack. This was the first time that I was anxious about leaving Ceres in a temporary camp close to the hilltop city of Avaricum. She was living in a wooden house, built hastily by my legionaries as Ceres was about to give birth to our first child. An added apprehension of mine was that wily Vercingetorix had defeated Roman legions too many times for comfort. We faced danger, the prospect of defeat and as I kissed Ceres goodbye, we both sensed sinister foreshadowing."

Chapter 18 – The Battles for Alesia

Mi hai cambiato la vita
R'wyt ti wedi newid fy bmwyd[17]

"He was a charismatic leader Vercingetorix, who had trained
with the Roman army and could anticipate Caesar's tactics. In
Alesia the Gauls created a trench around the fortified town to
stall our advance. Vercingetorix also sent out small groups of
Gauls who soundlessly attacked marching Roman legionaries
as they trooped towards the fort. The united army evaporated
into the night like ghoulish spectres. I suppose I could call
them Gaulish spirits! The Gauls were easily a match for us
Romans.

Julius Caesar, Marc-Antony, Gaius, and I met to discuss how
long the Gauls' food supply would last as Vercingetorix had
approximately 100,000 people in the fort. We were aware that
we had to prepare the legionaries for a prolonged battle, that
this was a confrontation we could not afford to lose. To repeat
history, with a crushing defeat of the Romans by the Gauls was
unthinkable. The legionaries would lose confidence in our
guidance, we would be recalled to Rome by the Senate and face
public humiliation or exile from Rome. We couldn't
underestimate that we had enemies in Rome who would revel
in our failure. We considered this to be the battle of, and for,
the future of Rome. We needed to win at all costs.

Good use was made of our skilled engineers and expert
builders. The four of us agreed a strategy to encircle the fort of
Alesia. With a high wall and wide ditch our tactics caused a
blockade so that nothing could go into or come out of the town.
Our approach was to starve the Gauls. Although during

---

[17] You have changed my life.

construction we had small battles with Gaul guerrillas, they were only partially successful in delaying us. Word came to Caesar that reinforcements had been called by Vercingetorix, so Caesar ordered a second wall to be built to keep out any support for the confederate army. Our Roman soldiers were placed between the two walls. When the old, infirm, women and children, were sent out of the gates of Alesia by Vercingetorix, who likely thought we would offer them food, we had no nourishment to share, as our own legionaries were starving. We had to leave the Gauls to starve to death. For the first time in battle, I thought about the lives of these people, my own wife, and our unborn child.

The elite Legio Ten had the most challenging battle when part of the Roman defence line was breached at Alesia. On his stallion, Caesar rode alongside me at the front of the battle. At the height of the clash Caesar and I got off our horses and, together with the Legio Ten warriors, fought side by side in hand-to-hand combat. Watching red-cloaked Caesar and me on the front line, leading with such disgusting ferocity, galvanised my soldiers. That day, the Magpie proved his weight in salt. As I fought with the Gauls, three men surrounded me, splaying their long swords, attempting to hack me to death. They caught my right leg at the knee. With bone splintered, tendons severed, blood jetting out of my arteries, my leg hung by sinews.

On witnessing this, Magpie intervened quickly, expertly picked me up on his steed and delivered me to Caesar's personal physician, Antistius. He poured acid vinegar onto my leg to clean the wound and gave me powdered scopolamine which acted like a spell and deadened the pain. My life hung in the balance, and I asked the Magpie to kiss Ceres and our baby and tell them I loved them both with all my being. As I felt my essence slipping away, I witnessed a vision of Ceres and our unborn baby. She wove a golden white light around me and the baby, as their lives too were dissipating. I fell into a deep slumber."

Seren adopted the narrative from the perspective of Ceres.

"Knowing nothing of Titus's life-threatening injuries, whilst in labour I experienced dreadful, exotic visions of him dying, wrapped in his blood-red paludamentum.[18]

Four days alone at home in an improvised wooden shack with barely enough food to eat, painful labour pains contributed to my physical and mental exhaustion. As was customary, and in line with the Goddess of all things feminine, Juno Luciana's will, I kept my hair loose. Had I been able to do so, I would have rubbed my swollen stomach with warm oil, eaten oregano with verbena root and made a drink from sow's dung to relieve my labour pains and encourage the safe passage of the baby. But those items were not available to me. A bracelet of white cowrie shells promised a successful birth consequently I wore it as a magical amulet. At my lararium in the cabin, I had also pressed a white cowrie shell into a small, lit white candle, with the slit pointing outwards to increase its powers of enchantment. I had primed myself for the birth as well as possible. Titus always said that preparation was everything.

Mustering all my strength, I managed to trudge the steep hill and entered a fortified building which had been turned into a makeshift maternity unit within the improvised settlement near Avaricum. Once there, I collapsed with enervation. In labour, I was aware that sometimes babies become stuck because of a mother's irregular shaped pelvis, or the baby might be in a

---

[18] Cloak or cape fastened at one shoulder.

breech position and may not be able to pass through the birth canal. Unknown to me, my baby lay in an occiput posterior position, otherwise known as a back-to-back location in the womb. The baby couldn't move easily through my pelvis. Although my first pregnancy, I sensed that this would be a particularly challenging and dangerous birth. I called upon the Goddess Juno Luciana to help me with my labour and delivery. I begged for help. In agony, I beseeched the Goddess. I promised not to have another child if only this one arrived safe and well and if my husband could hold the live baby.

There was one experienced woman acting as midwife in the building that day, Martia who usually managed a farm and had knowledge of helping sheep and cows deliver their offspring. She placed me into a birthing chair in a mortared rubble-faced room alongside two other seated women who were also in the latter stages of childbirth. Martia sat in front of me and examined my cervix. It was almost fully dilated. She believed that my baby would be delivered soon.

One of the other women was also suffering debilitating labour pains. She was ready to deliver her baby. Martia worked tirelessly to help her concentrate on pushing and resting, pushing, and resting. Within an hour, the baby arrived easily. Mother and baby survived and a tired Martia turned her attention to a third woman who was squirming in the chair next to me. Macabre screams emanated from the woman when Martia inserted a knife to cut the foetus loose from its mother. Those cries will stay with me until my dying day. Within minutes, the mother and baby experienced a bloody and painful death, witnessed by me. I was appalled and petrified.

Weak from pushing the baby, the contractions stopped. Horrified looks passed between the midwife and me. Martia said that she would need to cut open my stomach and pull out the baby if it were to have any chance of existence. I knew that a caesarean section was performed to pull a live baby out of a dying woman. An intoxicating drug, Martia encouraged me to drink milk of the poppy, but my chances of survival, she warned me, were slim. I asked Martia to tell Titus and the baby I loved them. As I closed my eyes, and floated above myself, I looked down at Titus holding a delightful, healthy baby. I was willing to die for my little family."

Chapter 19 – An Apparition

alea iacta est, the die is cast.

Seren continued the narrative from the perspective of Ceres.

"Martia sent a note by carrier pigeon to the garrison at Alesia to let Titus know our baby had arrived safely. She told him that I was close to death. Having haemorrhaged heavily, I was unconscious when the baby was delivered and still very weak two days later. It was Magpie who received the message on behalf of Titus. Himself having lost much blood the Legate was battling to survive.

As was customary, Martia needed to know if Titus, as head of the household, wished the baby to live. When Magpie ran into the ersatz maternity building on the side of a steep hill, he believed that time was running out for Titus and Ceres.

"Martia" shouted Magpie.

"I'm here" she responded. "Who are you?"

"Corvus Corax, Primus Pilus of Legio Ten. My Legate, Titus Marius is the husband of Ceres who gave birth three days ago. You wrote to the Legate to inform him of the baby's safe arrival. How is Ceres? I need to take both to Titus."

"Ceres is unwell and feeble, but you may speak to her, she's here."

"Oh, thank you Martia and Goddess Juno Luciana for saving them both" shouted Magpie in relief.

My eyes were closed but I heard everything. Footsteps meant that Martia had led Magpie to me. He knelt at the side of my bed and kissed my hand.

"Ceres" he whispered. "It is Magpie. I have seen eight magpies on my way here from Alesia. Remember the rhyme we used to sing together about magpies: *one for sorrow, two for joy, three for a girl and four for a boy, five for silver, six for gold, seven for a secret never to be told. Eight's a wish and nine's a kiss. Ten is a bird you must not miss.* My wish Ceres is that you are strong enough to travel so that I can take you and your baby to Titus. He is gravely ill. He needs you. He wishes to feel you and your baby close to him."

My eyes remained closed. Magpie rubbed my hand and I heard Martia bring the baby to him.

"Here's the baby Corvus Corax."

"Call me Magpie" he instructed.

"Hold the child, Magpie" instructed Martia as she passed the tiny bundle to the giant of a man with the intimidating Corvidae tattoo.

Never having clasped a child before, he questioned "How do I hold the baby?"

"Like this" answered Martia "you cup the baby against your breast."

Magpie copied her action.

"As I gaze into the divine face of my best friend's child my heart has swelled with love" he told Martia. "I feel incapacitated by grief. Titus may die without seeing this child."

I could feel Magpie's breath as he bent down against my ear and whispered:

"This baby needs its mother and father. Get better Ceres" he demanded, as if I could easily obey his orders.

Martia, who had been standing close to Magpie bustled away and returned with an unguent of honey and vinegar to disinfect my slashed stomach. The wound was held crudely by sutures.

"If she walks, she will lose blood Magpie" stated Martia firmly. "That is why she is so weak, she is haemorrhaging."

"I'll carry her to the carpentum. It is outside waiting for her."

I opened my eyes and looked at Magpie's anxious face and Martia's unwavering expression.

"Let me feed Ceres first" demanded Martia who rushed away, brought back a plate of food, and pushed lamb's liver into my mouth. She insisted I chewed then swallowed the burgundy mass to boost my iron and immune system. I retched. When she had finished shovelling the food into my mouth she turned to Magpie and instructed "mother and baby must be wrapped up warm Magpie. I'll gather some blankets for the journey."

"Where is Titus?" I asked Magpie.

"He's in a valetudinarium,[19] attended by Caesar's personal physician, Antistius. We need to get to him quickly" he responded.

"What happened? Did the Gauls win the battle of Alesia? Tell me Magpie" I demanded "is my husband alive?"

"He's alive Ceres, but only just. Facing starvation in Alesia, General Vercingetorix surrendered to a victorious Julius Caesar. He is now a prisoner of war and will be paraded in a Triumph in Rome to celebrate Caesar's success. The cost in human lives, on both sides of the war, has been inestimably high. Legio Ten has lost three of its warriors in the battle. Caesar fought alongside our legionaries, and Titus suffered a grave injury to his right leg. It was almost severed at the knee. We must hurry."

"Magpie, please take me home. I must go to the lararium first to ask the Gods to help Titus."

"I have brought you these, Ceres" replied Magpie as he handed me a bronze votive of a leg and another of a pregnant stomach. "We can place them on your shrine at home before we travel to Titus." I kissed him gently on the cheek.

Martia selected my raiment of thick sandals, an indigo silk dress to cover wide bandages around my pelvis, with a money zona looped around my waist and a navy cashmere cape to keep me warm. She remarked that my colourless face remained expressionless. Magpie collected some tan woollen blankets to wrap around me. He picked me up tenderly. My forlorn amber eyes must have reflected my melancholy and my long corn-ringed russet braids fell loosely over his arms. Martia carried

---

[19] Roman military hospital

the swaddled, crying baby. Magpie said he was fearful that his Legate may pass to the spirit world before the baby and I could be transported safely to Titus, so quickened his marching step.

It was late summer and warm weather meant that the four-wheeled carpentum, with its wooden roof and decorated interior offered comfort and protection from the sun. During the journey the crying baby latched on to me, and as I peered at the divine face, an intense love surged within me. I couldn't believe that Titus and I, with the help of the Gods, had created this tiny person. We quickly stopped at the shack. Magpie carried me to the altar and helped me place the bronze leg to represent Titus's leg and the belly to represent my pregnancy. We made offerings to the God Aesculapius and the Goddess Iaso asking for a speedy recovery for us both. We left within minutes knowing that recovery for Titus and me had been placed safely in the lap of the Gods.

As we passed stone milliaria marking the distance between towns, I tried to calculate how many miles away we were from Titus. We stopped only once at a roadside mansion. The three of us entered a two-storey square tabernae for a brief rest, use of the latrine and to eat. On the long marble counter were pitchers of warm punch mixed with fresh mint, ginger, and honey. Magpie enjoyed helping himself to the refreshing drink. At a table in the shaded open courtyard, we were served a generous portion of fish stew followed by fresh apples and blackberries. I'm ashamed to say that I picked at my food but felt heartened to watch Magpie devour his. Already nourished, the baby slept.

We journeyed for three more hours, over bosky, mountainous terrain through alluvial forests and past wild meadows where violets attracted pearl-bordered and silver-washed fritillary butterflies. A lepidopterist's dream but Magpie and I agreed that they represented the souls of brave warriors waiting to cross into other dimensions and be reborn. At Sancerre we passed a Roman temple on the hillside and stopped briefly to pay homage and make offerings of fruit and cakes which Martia have given to us. Magpie gathered some small sticks, picked the herbs juniper and laurel then gathered red bergamot flowers and indigo plumes of buddleia. We created a small fire on the raised altar to smoulder the herbs. The essence of frankincense, which Magpie carried with him, juniper and laurel rose to the sky to give thanks to the Gods for the safe arrival of the baby. I made a garland out of the red and indigo flowers and placed it at the side of the altar. We moved on in haste to reach the fort before sundown.

We entered the town of Alesia just as the ragged seam of orange sunrays worked loose on the horizon and illuminated the large leather tent housing the valetudinarium. This was where emergency medical care was offered and where lay Titus. Magpie carried the baby and held my arm to assist me, as I walked gingerly through the flapping front panels of the heavy leather cover and past the long support poles. The acrid smell of dried blood, mixed with vinegar hit my nostrils as I scanned the four beds where lay wounded officers. We stopped at the foot of a bed furthest away from the entrance. Pallid, sickly with a greedy spirit of death hovering around him Titus reclined motionless. Magpie passed the baby to me and made a small seat on the floor out of his brown woollen cloak. I knelt on it, at the side of Titus, and held on tightly to our baby. Discreetly Magpie quietly moved away.

"Titus" I whispered. "It's Ceres. I've brought our baby to you. Open your eyes my darling if you can hear me. Please open your eyes."

Titus breathed gently but his eyelids didn't flicker. I waited for an hour until Caesar's personal physician, Antistius joined me at the bedside.

"I've given him scopolamine otherwise known as burandanga, extract of deadly nightshade plants. He's been asleep for twenty-four hours already. When he wakes up his mouth will be dry, his pupils will be small, and he will feel drowsy. Be careful near his leg as I have placed highly porous cobwebs over the top of his injury to knit together his damaged nerves and disconnected skin. The thread nerves will be used by the body as guides for the nerves and skin to grow along. I'm hoping that he will not remember much as Titus has undergone extensive surgery to save his right leg."

"Isn't that *devil's breath* you've given him? Will he survive?"

"Some people call it that because a dose can kill a man. I'm optimistic that Titus will recover. Speak to him Ceres. Tell him about his baby. You'll pierce his brain with your words."

"The hungry baby began to cry. I sat on the bed and rocked the child from side to side. The sound of the baby and the gentle rocking motion must have stimulated Titus because his eyelids lifted. Antistius elevated Titus's head slightly and gave him a sip of ice-cold water, at which he gasped. It took him a few minutes before he realised that I was with him."

"Ceres? Is this a vision? Are you really here?" he asked uncertainly.

"Yes my darling. It is Ceres and our baby."

Titus smiled and my heart skyrocketed. He held out his arms.
I moved towards him, still clutching the baby as he wrapped his
muscular arms around us both, nuzzled into my hair and
whispered, "I love you both to the core of my soul".

"We have a daughter Titus. Hold her. Look into her face. Do
you want to keep her? As head of our household, it is your
decision to make."

Titus clung to us both as if he would never let us loose.

"I thought I had lost you both" he answered, "I saw the two of
you when I was unconscious."

Without embarrassment, for the first time in his adult life, a
little stream of tears trickled from his lovat eyes. He warmly
embraced me. He kissed our daughter, then said:

"Of course we will keep her. She will not be discarded. I will
guard you both and protect you with my life as long as I live"
he declared passionately.

I recounted to Titus the trauma of delivery, how our little girl
and I had battled to survive, and the role Magpie had played in
bringing us together.

"What name would you like to give her Titus" I asked gently.

He was silent for an age before he said, "Alesia, after the
valiant battles we have both fought and Amber in recognition
of your birthplace, your ring and the pugio which saved your
life. I name our daughter Alesia Amber. Welcome to our first-
born child. May she be betrothed to a worthy man when the
time comes."

I clung to my husband, silently wept whilst simultaneously offering thanks to the Gods for the honourable man that Destiny had placed in my path. When I glanced around the tent, our true friend Magpie was observing us from a distance. Nothing can keep any good man down.

* * *

For the following three years we fell into army life in Gaul. Titus worked with Marc Antony and Gaius as a senior military campaigner for Julius Caesar whose conquering military campaigns had brought him immense wealth and the accolade of his warriors. Titus's injured leg meant that day-to-day armed combat would be too challenging for him. Magpie was promoted to the role of Legate of Titus's elite Legio Ten. I spent time with Alesia and was also employed by the senior Centurions as a Prophetess advising them by using and making notes in the ancient grimoire and watching the heavens for signs and symbols. On the muddy banks of a thorny river in the northern territories, our routine existence was Divinely brought to an abrupt halt in January 49BCE when we attempted to return to Rome.

"Caesar you have secured military command over Gaul, something that the Senate did not believe possible. You're an ambitious and determined fighting man, we now need to return to Rome" advised Titus.

"We all desire to walk the streets of our city, among our compatriots and enjoy peace for a while" advocated Gaius, which turned out to be an ironic statement.

Caesar told them that a month earlier the Senate in Rome, led by Pompey the Great, had warned him not to return to his homeland because his military operations throughout Gaul had not been sanctioned by them. He was incensed because his legionaries had captured more land, murdered more people, and brought more riches than any other military leader, including Pompey. But Pompey had his own problems, the Senate had voted for him and Caesar to give up command of their legions. Both refused.

"Marc Antony is in Rome. He says there are those in the Roman Senate who long for me to relinquish command of my army because of my supposed crimes against humanity" he bellowed to Titus and Gaius. "Where is the dignity in that?"

Despite the Senate's warnings that Caesar should not take his army into Rome, the trio decided to return with Magpie leading battle-hardened Legio Ten, me as Prophetess, and toddler Alesia. We all stopped on the banks of the Rubicon, a river which divided the northern territory and Italy, when Titus asked:

"Are you sure you wish to do this Caesar? If we enter Rome with the legionaries, it will be seen as an act of treason. It may provoke unrest in our city." Titus was concerned as Caesar had been known to flout even the Gods.

"Ceres, what do the Gods say?" probed a hesitant Caesar knowing that the next step would be immutable.

I banged the hawkstaff which Titus had made for me in Alesia, looked to the heavens for signs and consulted the ancient grimoire. Heralding success, there was an impressive hoary wolf with yellow eyes sitting on swards by the river. I told Caesar that whatever direction he chose, his men would be victorious for a while, but that much blood would be shed. He

wavered again. On the opposite bank of the Rubicon an
ethereal apparition appeared in front of us, surrounded by a
golden white glow, wearing vividly coloured silk robes of blue,
green, and orange hues, in one hand holding the Ace of Cups,
signalling prosperity ahead and in the other a trumpet used to
denote the beginning and end of battles. We were startled.
This stunning, captivating vision with flowing golden curls
sounded the trumpet to signify that we should cross the river.

"The Gods have spoken Caesar" I said.

"alea iacta est"[20] he shouted as he crossed the Rubicon, leading
us all into northern Italy.

Caesar was right. The die had been cast and what happened
next had irrevocable consequences for us all."

---

[20] The die is cast.

Chapter 20 – Seven For A Secret Never To Be Told

Only Gods and Goddesses can explain the mystery of time dimensions.

"We moved slowly through northern Italy on our way to Rome. By the time we reached the city, Pompey the Great was overseas, fighting in the East for territory. Some Roman citizens perceived dictatorial Pompey to be the head of an anti-Caesar campaign, others were supportive of Caesar. He was no less autocratic but still, some chose to join forces with us in northern Italy," said Titus. "Rome was awash with riches plundered from other countries but a civil war bitterly divided Romans and their Italian neighbours. There were exigent questions to be answered by the Senate about how the riches could, or should be shared and, if all Italians belonged to Rome, should they be considered Romans?

When we reached Rome, Ceres and I set up home in a newly constructed magnificent villa. We enjoyed choosing the layout and décor for our home environment. We had a specially designed multi-coloured mosaic of an eagle, to represent the Roman Empire and the bull as a permanent reminder of the indomitability of my Legio Ten. The mosaic took pride of place in our ground floor atrium. The large, cool rooms provided respite for Ceres who occasionally found the summer heat unbearable. She felt safe in the villa, away from Roman military confrontations and the pitiful unassuaged misery of the poorest Roman citizens.

There was a large public space, and four magnificent temples close to our villa which ran alongside the Tiber. It's where Ceres often visited the white marble Temple of Venus, where the Goddess represented the power of love through human resilience. She found the sweet smell of jasmine in the gardens to be calming and the sound of flowing water through the fountains that this area offered were an oasis away from the conflict and morbid possibilities of crowds in other parts of Rome. As a Senator, within minutes I could easily reach the white marble Curia di Pompeo where the Senate met, opposite the Theatre of Pompey. Our meeting place in the Forum had burned down a few years earlier.

The plan was to get involved with chariot racing which offered entertainment to vast crowds in the city. Magpie and I had quickly bought four horses; Castor an Arabian horse, Pollux we brought in from Andalusia, Callisto from Hispania, and Ganymede a North African horse. It took an age for the beasts to be transported to Rome. We employed a brave Hispanic slave, Feliciano to race our four-horse chariot. He turned into quite a celebrity because he was handsome, with flashing black eyes, a broad, toothy smile, muscular frame, and carefree attitude.

Feliciano won many races at the Circus Maximus and quickly became an agitator, a high-ranking driver within the red team. We enjoyed watching him manipulate the six sharp turns at the Circus Maximus with skill and audacity. We trained the horses well, and Feliciano placed complete faith in the Goddess Vesta, always making offerings to her of honey, wine, and pomegranates at the sensuous Temple of Vesta in the Forum. The crowds too loved to cheer our winsome charioteer and despite being a slave, he caught the eye of many Roman ladies. Ceres was thankful that only single women could attend the chariot racing. She disliked the carnage at the Circus Maximus especially when the charioteers fell, were run over by other chariots, or trampled to death by thundering horses.

A girl from a small village, Ceres was shocked when Magpie warned her to keep her belongings close as there were many pickpockets around Rome who would easily steal from her, especially if she chose to visit or walk past the markets. She found it difficult to believe that fellow-countrymen would filch from each other, after all that we had been through, but there was civil unrest in the city, and we needed to be guarded. Magpie and I were equally protective of my wife as venomous people surrounded us in Rome. *'Beware even your friends'* we would tell her. We didn't realise the ugly truth in this advice or how anxious she felt in some areas of our city.

Despite the poisonous atmosphere I was euphoric to be back and eager to install Ceres in my beloved Rome" revealed Titus. "Once the in-fighting ceased, I believed that Rome would become a fabulous place to live because Caesar planned to introduce many reforms including aid to the poor and a cure for pestilence. Warfare for ten years in foreign lands meant I had missed living in the city. Ceres was pregnant again. Wishing her to be settled and comfortable in Rome, Caesar gave permission for Antistius to act as her physician. Caesar had been gravely affected by the fate of Julia, his treasured daughter, who was Pompey's wife. She had died during childbirth a few years earlier. Caesar was aware that Ceres had almost danced with the spirits herself during her first pregnancy.

Knowledgeable about Sibyls around the ancient world, Caesar was grateful for the prophecies presented by Ceres during the Gallic wars. When in Rome, he introduced her to two Prophetesses, Cassinia and Albunea, who were known locally as the Cumaean Sibyl and the Tiburtine Sibyl. There used to be nine known Sibyls based in different parts of the Empire. Now there were only two, until Caesar encouraged Ceres to join them as his Sibyl and participate in divination rituals. He referred to Ceres as his Cambrian Sibyl."

Ceres interjected at this point.

"Titus took pleasure in taking me on tours of the city. Everywhere I looked there were remarkable examples of ingenuity and breath-taking feats of engineering. We visited the enormous entertainment stadium, Circus Maximus which held over two hundred thousand people. Chariot races took place there, religious parades, ceremonies and the spoils of war would be on display during Caesar's Triumph ceremonies. Dignitaries and citizens enjoyed the races. The purse was high for those who won, and free food was available for all. Titus and Magpie trained our horses and entered the races with our slave Feliciano as their charioteer now that their fighting days had come to an end. I was anxious about their involvement as chariot racing was a bloody sport which led to premature deaths of many charioteers. When we settled in Rome, I had hoped that Titus and Magpie would eschew carnage after their years of fighting but perhaps the thrill of it coursed through their veins.

The colossal amphitheatre sited near the effigy of the Sun God Sol emitted an energy of desperation. I rarely visited the area, but Titus and Magpie enjoyed their ringside seats in the box with Caesar and Marc Antony watching battles or animal hunts. I was overwhelmed on first sight of the bustling area of the Forum, a government and public space filled with temples, hundreds of steps leading to them, many honorary columns with bronze statues on top depicting Godlike figures, impeccably painted reliefs in blues, greens, and yellows, porticoes, and shops. I had never witnessed such decadence. Occasionally I enjoyed standing in front of the rostra among other Senators' wives listening to members of the Senate, including the influential author and politician Cicero debating policy or proposing laws. At the back of the burned Senate building another Temple of Venus stood. She was Caesar's preferred Goddess as he believed he was descended from her. To him Venus represented desire and the mixing and mingling of life cycles.

In the Forum, one of my ideal places to visit was the Temple of Vesta where the eternal flame burned brightly, representing the life of the city, attended by stunningly scintillating Vestal Virgins. The temple had an open roof to emit the smoke of the flame. Occasionally the fire was almost extinguished, sometimes due to the rain, other times because a Vestal lacked concentration. If the latter happened the offending Vestal would be whipped even though, alongside Senators' wives, and Prophetesses these were the most important women in the city. These women lived in the House of Vestal Virgins which was also in the Forum. The world of women would become my second home in the city.

The Vestals' white marble home was breath-taking, sited along a tree lined ostium. Offering a glorious array of colours in spring, magnificent pink and red camellias, surrounded by white, purple, red, orange, and yellow azaleas which filled the area with vibrant hues and fragrant perfumes. It was calming to breathe the sweet-smelling aromas. The main entrance hall of the House was inlaid with tessellated bright squares which revealed finely woven mosaics of eagles, magpies, dolphins, and horses. The flooring provided a feast for the eyes. Offering access to any of the ground floor rooms, which had underfloor heating, was the atrium, decorated in the middle with a shallow, white marble sunken pool and an enchanting golden dolphin fountain. The sound of running water was soothing. A small alcove was used to house the tablinum where important documents were stored. The maids worked in the side rooms of the culina and the bakery where food and drinks were prepared. Although the Vestals could use the Temple of Vesta whenever they wished, they also had a lararium where offerings of flowers, bread and wine were made to the Gods. They tended their own vegetable and herb gardens, the result of which were also used as gifts for the Gods. We often sat outside on marble benches in the open courtyard. In the blazing heat of the summer months, we swam in one of the two pools or sheltered under a shaded portico waited upon by maids.

It was at the House of the Vestals that Cassinia and Albunea, the Sibyls, showed me two books which belonged to them. Inscribed on the front of each book was an image of the Ace of Cups. The two women used their books to transcribe Divine revelations, spells, and instructions on how to invoke spirits. They called them their Sibylline Books and were identical to the one given to me for safekeeping by my nain.

Sometimes I would meet Cassinia and Albunea at the House of the Vestal Virgins and, under Caesar's direction, in secret we would discuss the prophecies with the Vestals. When we had finished, for protection, we placed our Sibylline Books in a sacred vault in the most important of all temples, the Temple of Jupiter. The three Sibyls each held a key to the crypt. Our prophecies were discussed further with Caesar who was the Dictator of Rome either at his palace atop Palatine Hill or at the House of the Vestals. Only Caesar could decide if the Senate needed to be made aware of the foresights during times of crisis in Rome or across his Empire.

Cassinia revealed information from her Sibylline Book about the Temple of Seti I at Abydos in Egypt. She said that there was a portal at the Temple to points in the universe where people could move along different timelines. Caesar was enthusiastic to hear this intelligence. I was shocked when Albunea divulged an exposé from her Sibylline Book that a ruler of the Roman world would soon be beheaded in Egypt and the country would be led by a Queen.

We debated oneiromancy with Caesar which he found interesting. We all followed the practice of interpreting dreams as messages sent to the soul by the Gods. One of my visions had been about Rome sharing its realm with Constantinople because the Empire had become too big, another was that only one God would be honoured in Rome. Choosing not to share immediately any information about a recent vision, in which Julius Caesar was repeatedly stabbed on the Ides of March and afterwards the sky lit up with a bright stream of stars, I thought this a revelation too far. But the vision had unsettled me, it was so vivid and about our friend. Not long afterwards, I discussed the matter with Titus, after all, he was a Senator, although I knew I was breaking the Sibylline rules by revealing this to him. I hoped he would be able to avert disaster for our ally and leader. He advised me to add this prophecy to my Sibylline Book as I would have the opportunity to discuss it personally with Caesar. I decided to wait until our next rite.

Not long afterwards, the two Sibyls invited me to perform a divination ritual with them at the Temple of Jupiter. It certainly was not the shocking, frenzied Bacchanalian event which we had heard whispered about in the city. Individually beforehand we had to cleanse our body, mind and soul and undertook a purification ritual where we fasted and took a hot bath. At the Temple we meditated together, the other Sibyls rhythmically chanted as I played the tibia. The altar in the Temple was positioned in an open area, where we sprinkled vervain for purification. Upon the altar we laid out herbs of lavender and sage, added bread, and poured violet wine as an offering to Jupiter. We burned white candles and inhaled the spiralling peppermint incense smoke from a golden cauldron, ingested laurel leaves, and held rosemary herbs to ward off evil spirits. We lay down and on our third eye placed belladonna leaves, soaked in fat to incubate our thoughts and encourage astral travel. Those few actions were enough to enable us to enter a trance, opening a space in our unconscious mind, encouraging free thinking. Our visions channelled us to witness the most astonishing things revealed by spirits.

We prophesised that a woman named Matilda from Tuscany would lead her troops into Rome, that a king would begin a new religion away from Roman impediment, and a star shower would soon burn in the daylight to signify the death and deification of a great leader. These prognostications were added to the Sibylline Books. We took the books to the House of the Vestal Virgins where we had a meal with the Vestals and Caesar. Over dinner, we discussed our revelations which were more profound and far-reaching than Caesar could ever have anticipated. I was heavily pregnant and felt labour pains so left the dinner early escorted home by courteous and thoughtful Caesar and his Praetorian Guard who served as his personal bodyguards. That evening I had already revealed to Caesar my vision about him being attacked and when we were near home, in a whispered voice I begged him to beware the Ides of March."

Titus took over the narrative from Ceres.

"Magpie was the first to discover Ceres in labour and ran to find me at the equestrian training ground. Alesia, with her God-given gift for learning, was taken by Magpie to her private tutor for reading and writing lessons. Magpie then ran for the physician Antistius. When I arrived home, the smell of frankincense, which burned in a golden cauldron on a golden stand, permeated every room. I found an agitated Ceres, remembering her earlier delivery trauma, sitting astride a birthing chair planted on the mosaic floor. Her hair was loose, she had been eating cinnamon and was drinking sow's dung to help with labour pains. I rubbed her bulging and lively stomach with warm olive oil, prepared verbena root seasoned with oregano and lit a white candle adorned with a cowrie shell to encourage safe passage to our baby. Attractive to me even as Ceres screamed in pain, I continued to rub her stomach and tried to mop the blood as it seeped out of her perspiring body.

Exactly when Antistius arrived with a midwife I was not aware, but thankful for his support especially when he gave Ceres milk of the poppy. Her agony receded, but still she shrieked as she pushed. To me the delivery seemed to be over in a short while, but I don't suppose time was fleeting to Ceres. A baby girl, covered in blood and slime was wrapped in a white cotton towel and handed to me by the midwife. Ceres was still in pain as I showed her our baby daughter. Perplexed, Antistius looked at me and said that a second baby was about to enter the world. Shocked, Ceres and I stared at each other, and despite the astonishment, we received delivery of another blood-soaked, screaming daughter. Antistius presented the second healthy baby girl to me and asked if I wanted both babies to live. I told him that the girls had arrived to join our family through the generosity of the Gods and that they should endure. They were our good fortune and we named them Sabine and Fausta. On Ceres' womanly features, the midwife applied fenugreek as an anti-inflammatory remedy and oregano to fight any infection. She smeared Ceres' body with cinnamon to warm her. I held Ceres in my arms, stroked her sodden tangled russet hair, kissed the luscious mouth of the mother of my three beautiful daughters and thanked the Gods for Divinely placing her in my path."

Ceres took up the narrative.

"Within a year of being introduced to Cassinia and Albunea, we learned that Pompey the Great had been murdered by Egyptians whom Pompey considered to be friends. Shortly afterwards, when Caesar arrived in Egypt, he was distraught when Pompey's head, preserved in salt, was presented to him in a basket. The two had once been allies and Pompey had been his son-in-law. This led Caesar to successfully support Queen Cleopatra VII in her quest for the throne of Egypt. Further evidence for me about the accuracy of the Sibyls' prophecies which made me anxious for Caesar's future especially when ours was inextricably linked with his success.

For a while, life ran reasonably smoothly thank the Gods, after settling in Rome, until something emotionally grim occurred in December 46 BCE.

Having left the three girls with Titus I headed for the Temple of Saturn as we three Sibyls were planning to prepare a ritual for Saturnalia. This was the most important rite in the year for us because it was, after all, decreed in the Sibylline Books that the Romans celebrate Saturnalia. In its imposing position overlooking the Forum, there was to be a public banquet around the Temple. In the late afternoon darkness, I carried my golden cauldron with its burning flame of fat to light the way. I climbed the marble steps and entered the Temple by passing one of the six enormous granite columns at the front of the building. My footsteps echoed on the play of blue squares and green circles on the marble floor which bedazzled me. The golden cauldron illuminated teasing shadows on the blue walls where the engraved yellow stars appeared to frolic in the waxy light. I shivered with excitement as this was going to be an evening to remember. The beginning of Saturnalia.

Before Cassinia or Albunea had arrived, Lucretia, Vestalis Maxima approached me at the altar. She made me jump as I hadn't been expecting to see the head of the Vestal Virgins. She said:

"Ceres. I have witnessed your charioteer in a compromising position with a woman."

"He is unmarried Lucretia. Was it with another slave?" I asked.

"No" she replied bluntly.

"A man?" I probed.

"No" Lucretia responded vigorously.

"Was it with a Roman woman?" I questioned.

"Yes" she replied brusquely.

"Is she a married woman?" I enquired.

"No" Lucretia replied candidly. "She is a single Roman woman. I don't know what to do about it."

"Do you have to do something?" I asked confounded.

"Yes. I think I do" she responded despondently.

At that moment, Cassinia and Albunea bustled into the Temple.

"If there's any doubt in your mind, Lucretia" I whispered "do nothing, say nothing. Persuade your mind that you've not witnessed it" I advised.

In a low trembling voice Lucretia pleaded "ask Titus to order Feliciano to stop this romance, otherwise there may be dire consequences."

I promised to speak to my husband.

But.

One kiss is all it takes."

Chapter 21 – Slave To Love

Time takes its toll.

Titus intercepted to chronicle events.

"On 17th December Saturnalia began, bringing with it revelry and holidays for all, including slaves who were given temporary respite from servitude. All formal business and social conventions stopped so that all those in Rome could party together. Even slaves could be waited on by their masters.

As Ceres had already left for the Temple of Saturn, Magpie helped me with Alesia, Sabine, and Fausta. Thinking that it was their holiday too, the girls' three pet rabbits had found their way out of their cage. They were madly hopping around our courtyard accompanied by the delighted shrieks and yells of the children. Magpie and I quickly fixed the latch on the hutch door and safely returned the naughty bunnies to their cage. To celebrate Saturnalia, the five of us made wreathes together using holly the girls had picked from the bushes in our courtyard, followed by time spent cleaning the blood from their scratched arms with fenugreek and oregano. The girls were creating offerings to take to the Temple of Saturn. Alesia filled each girl's basket with fruit and vegetables including cavolo nero, radicchio, scorzonera, topinambur, pomegranates, and quince. They would leave the baskets outside the Temple. Sabine and Fausta collected orange rosehips and yellow winter jasmine flowers to place on the altar.

The five of us fashioned candles out of beeswax collected from a nearby apiary. The three excited children were keen to carry the candles, but much to their disappointment, I insisted the candles remained unlit until we arrived at the Temple. Even with Magpie's help, managing three spirited little girls was more of a match for me than working with my legionaries. At least the soldiers obeyed orders!

There was a kerfuffle in the villa about the clothes the girls would wear but I should have guessed as much. They were miniature versions of their mother asking: *'Is this dress ok? Does this dress look better? I like the orange dress, but I thought the green dress was lovely too. May I wear mother's necklace, as it matches this outfit, and she won't mind? Am I allowed to wear my shoes instead of boots? Please may I wear my hair down for a change? Must I wear socks? Do I have to wear my cloak?'*

I wondered how many questions could be fired at me all at once! When I finally took command, things ran like clockwork. I responded: *'Alesia the orange silk dress suits you as it brings out the colour of your warm auburn hair. Sabine the bright yellow satin dress enhances your delightful freckles. Fausta the green velvet dress complements your stunning green eyes. Nobody can wear mother's jewellery except her and make sure you all wear your gold lunula pendants for protection against the evil eye. Boots tonight, not shoes. Hair worn up, not down. Cloaks for each of you as it's cold and the air is thin.'*

Ever the diplomat, Magpie agreed that I had managed that melee very well except the girls insisted on asking how old they would need to be to wear a different necklace instead of their crescent moon! I didn't really have a credible answer for that, except *'as old as mother'* to which they replied: *'do we really have to wait **that** long?'*

Having spent the afternoon with the three of them, Magpie and I were in awe of the patience and good humour always demonstrated by Ceres when she managed them, day after day. Being with *one* of the girls was exhausting but being with *three* all at once was completely draining! Although it was all worth it when the girls wrapped their arms around Magpie and me, kissed both of us on the cheek and thanked us for a fun afternoon. They laughed heartily when Magpie appeared wearing a floor-length red silk synthesis with a green velvet belt and at me, wearing a satin cobalt blue floor-length synthesis tied at the waist by a yellow satin belt. They were used to seeing us in our short white togas, not in colourful long gowns. '*Daddy and Pica. You look handsome,*' said Alesia eventually. Enough to make our hearts melt. It was sweet to hear the children's favourite name for Magpie.

Afraid we might miss the beginning of the Saturnalia ritual at the Temple of Saturn, we scurried out of the villa as time that day had passed quickly. Time, I now know, is the relentless devourer of all things. On an evening of rare occultations in the night sky, Magpie and I proudly walked through the narrow alleyways of our multicultural metropolis escorting Alesia, Sabine, and Fausta to the Temple of Saturn to observe their mother perform the first ceremony of the holiday period. From time to time we stopped and pointed out the bright planets of Jupiter, Saturn, Mars and the rarely observed stars that streamed light in their path. I shivered with excitement as this was going to be an evening to remember."

Ceres grasped a pause in the tale and took over the story from Titus.

"As Cassinia, Albunea and I concluded our ritual, many children presented flowers to lay upon the altar. Outside the

Temple of Saturn, Roman citizens watched as Caesar, during a rare visit to Rome, untied the woollen bindings from around the feet of the statue of Saturn, an indication that the festivities had begun. Romans, and slaves, were unfettered for three days. The crowd cheered wildly. Almost immediately soaring music led to rousing dancing around the Forum where food and wine flowed freely, and moral bondage slowly unwound.

One kiss is all it takes.

I managed to speak to Titus alone as Magpie danced with others in a group which surrounded our three little girls.

Titus, tonight I have been approached by Lucretia. She has asked if you will order Feliciano to stop a romance he is having with a woman.

Titus looked askance."

"Ceres" he replied "I have no business in Feliciano's romances. He is our successful charioteer. You've seen how women are with him, even knowing him to be a slave. They crave his attention. He has lots of girlfriends. A winner on the racetrack. It makes him notorious and generally people find that alluring. He's a single man. It's not as if he's married or in a serious relationship, is it?"

"Titus, I know the effect Feliciano has on women. I have witnessed it myself. But this is a Roman woman. Lucretia is not one for idle gossip."

"Ceres. I have the utmost respect for Lucretia. She is trustworthy but I cannot base advice on something that is unknown to me. That I cannot validate. Life is black or white for me. There is no grey area."

"Titus. Lucretia said if you don't intervene, there may be dire consequences."

"For whom? You? Me? Lucretia? Feliciano? The Unknown woman?"

"I don't know."

"Exactly. You don't know and I'm not going to speak to Feliciano without concrete proof of wrongdoing. And you say you have none."

"Titus. I don't have any proof. I don't know who the woman might be that Lucretia is concerned for, but Lucretia is my friend, and I would like to help her. Why don't you speak to her? I have a foreboding that this will not end well."

"I'm sorry Ceres. Dire consequences or not. I cannot get involved. In the next few days Feliciano is competing in numerous chariot events. I am not going to stop him or interfere in his romances. We have been successful on our red team. The stakes are high for the next chariot races. The blue, white, and green teams are strong. We aim to win. And you don't have any proof Ceres of misconduct. Look, I'm used to dealing with situations where many lives are at stake. This is not life and death, is it? I'm sorry, but no. Saturnalia is a time of games, partying, and laughter Ceres. During this time, we are all equal so Feliciano can date whomever he likes. All bets are off. People wear masks to hide their identity. Anything can happen during Saturnalia. Look let's enjoy ourselves. And

Ceres, how catastrophic can be the consequences of a romance?"

"With that, the matter had to close.
For now, at least.

For my family, and I include Magpie in that declaration, it was important that I shook off my presentiment. I looked around the Forum at the candles burning to light the way and listened to the area reverberate with laughter as people bustled around, mingling with each other. The sky was clear, the planets shone brightly, the atmosphere was blithe and optimistic. Titus, Magpie, and I danced with the children in the Forum, I played the tibia whilst Magpie sang. Some of the Vestals joined us, dancing, singing, eating, and drinking. Lucretia appeared to have returned to her normal sanguine self. Later Feliciano joined us, danced with all the ladies, and still the atmosphere remained buoyant. The men were in optimistic mode looking forward to the forthcoming chariot races.

The first child to yawn was Fausta, followed quickly by Sabine so Titus and I agreed we would need to take the girls home to bed. Determined Alesia insisted she stay for a little while longer and asked if Pica could take her home. Magpie agreed. He planned to return to the festivities later, having been reacquainted with an intriguing lady, Kemsit, Queen Cleopatra's Lady In Waiting who had recently visited the stables when Magpie was working with Feliciano. The Vestals, out of their usual 'white uniform' appeared to be enjoying having fun, their typically serious life cast off for a short while. Three of the younger Vestals were listening to a tale told by Feliciano, which seemed to be uproariously amusing. By this time, Lucretia had moved to another area of the Forum. Her eagle eye, blind to tonight's events. But my eyes weren't unsighted. I observed the way Feliciano leaned in closely to Diana, an eighteen-year-old Vestal Virgin, how he paid attention to her movements and how she returned his smile and laughed with him. They both looked happy and carefree. It's easy to spot love but difficult to stop. Even if you wanted to.

Over the next two days, festivities continued apace. Life in the villa was chaotic, the three children were busy making Sigillaria to present at the end of celebrations. The girls used warm wax and fashioned their favourite animals to give as gifts to their friends. The figurines created by Fausta and Sabine defied description. Blobs of wax appeared in every niche of their playroom and most of the floor under the haphazard supervision of Alesia.

During the festivities we took the children to visit the area around the Forum to buy a gift made of gold for Magpie. Many craftsmen had set up temporary workshops along the cramped labyrinthine alleyways. We headed for the goldsmith area where sweating jewellers curved over their workbenches, heated gold metal mixed with alloys to create intricately designed pieces of jewellery using anvils, hammers, files, and blowpipes. Sometimes the goldsmiths added precious jewels to their work. The children requested our favourite goldsmith make a unique item for Pica. The jeweller twisted threads of glinting gold to create a ring with a filigree pattern and added an iridescent moonstone which Alesia chose, to shine a bright light on his pathway. Unbeknown to the three girls, we had asked the same jeweller to make a delicate gold Sigillaria for each of them, a butterfly for Sabine, an owl for Fausta and sunflower for Alesia.

Once inside the busy Forum we bumped into Iris, Diana, and Valeria, three of the younger Vestals who were enjoying their

short-lived freedom. They were happy to take our three
children back to the jewellery area to help choose a suitable gift
of gold for their father. In high anticipation and excitement, the
Vestals told me they would attend the chariot races, after they
had participated in the Saturnalia procession through the city
which ended at the Circus Maximus. The Vestals were pleased
to hear that Alesia was being considered by the Pontifex
Maximus to join their number when she reached eight years
old. As the freeborn daughter of a Roman Legate, she would
receive ten years of education, followed by ten years of
attending the eternal flame and the final ten years she would
become a teacher of other Vestals. In this role she would be
considered 'married to the Goddess Vesta' and would have to
remain celibate for thirty years. Vestal Virgins were revered in
Rome and had many privileges. Once they retired, they
became wealthy women and were free to marry whomever they
wished. I was unsure about this lifestyle for our daughter, but
Titus thought it a great honour that out of all the young girls in
Rome, our daughter may be chosen to be one of six new Vestal
Virgins.

Titus and Magpie had already left us to meet with Feliciano at
Circus Maximus, walk the racecourse, and check on our horses
before the chariot race. Feliciano was unaware that his last
duty as our slave was to compete in the chariot races. Titus had
planned to enrol Feliciano onto the Roman Census, declaring
him a freedman as soon as Saturnalia ended.

The last day of festivities, the day of Sigillaria, it was as if
nitrous oxide had pervaded Rome. An air of perpetual
anticipation wafted around, as Roman citizens and slaves were
exposed to an overwhelming, circulating atmosphere of
lightness. In brightly coloured costumes, the children and I
paraded through the streets alongside the Vestals at the front of

the procession to honour our Gods. Alesia, Fausta, and Sabine, dressed in garishly coloured outfits, each carried small golden statues to show respect to our three most important Gods, Jupiter, Juno, and Minerva. Enthusiastic dancers and mesmerising musicians with their alluring harmonies whipped the crowds into a frenzy. Some charioteers walked in the middle of the cavalcade amidst screams, shouts, and cheers from lively spectators. It took thirty minutes to arrive at our destination Circus Maximus where over two hundred thousand people waited in heightened anticipation of gory, valiantly fought chariot races and Caesar's Triumph parade.

Titus and Magpie had gone on ahead to the stables to prepare the horses. As men and only single women were allowed to watch the chariot races, the three children and I observed the Triumph of Caesar as the Gallic rebel Vercingetorix, the screaming half-sister of Queen Cleopatra, Arsinoë IV and the wretched Princess Teranica, wife of Chief Eigion, leader of the Ordovices were led into the Circus Maximus, presumably to their death. With a shudder I realised that Princess Teranica should have been murdered by me on the Vardre. That would have been a more dignified end for her instead of the torture and humiliation she had faced, which would now be followed by a gory lingering death. The children and I wandered the carnival streets of Rome until the sky became crepuscular and the alleyways turned raucous. The heavy weight of responsibility bore down on me, and I loathed myself for what I had done. It was very late in the evening when a lugubrious Titus returned home."

Titus spoke.

"As the red team, we were racing a quadriga. In the starting blocks Feliciano managed the four stallions as if he were

Jupiter preparing to skim across the sky in his chariot. Caesar dropped a white silk cloth to signify that the race had begun, our formidable, sinewy horses burst out and ran as if their lives depended upon the outcome. Feliciano was an experienced and gifted rider with the strength of two men and agility of mind to counteract any potent racing strategy adopted by his three opponents. Turning any one of the six bends was tricky and at the final curve our chariot's wheels touched with the wheels of the blue chariot, dust and sparks sprayed the track. The blue chariot overturned, and the driver was thrown to his death under the hooves of his own horses. An aggressive opponent, Feliciano remained focused on being the first to successfully cross the finishing line to cheers and roars from the vociferous and appreciative crowd. It was sweet success for the red team and the bitter losing white, blue, and green teams jealously coveted our charioteer. Feliciano had already won enough sesterces to buy his own freedom, he didn't need me to set him free, but that was my intention so that he could keep his coins and use them for his future life.

In the twilight Magpie and I walked with Feliciano to the stables. He was obviously delighted with his win that day and when we told him he would no longer be a slave, he cried, overwhelmed with happiness and gratitude. He said it was the happiest day of his life. As we each brushed down a horse in different sections within the stables I heard Diana, the young Vestal Virgin quietly speaking with Feliciano. Both were unaware of my proximity. Diana warmly congratulated Feliciano on his win. Enthusiastically he told her that he was a freedman. Diana was quiet whilst Feliciano revealed that he would wait for her to complete her role as a Vestal Virgin, in the meantime he would create a home for them and continue working as a charioteer in Rome. He promised to visit her at the Temple of Vesta and in return, she pledged to watch him in the chariot races. She was anxious that he must wait eighteen years for her to be free. Feliciano promised that he would remain true to her until she was released from her vows. He said that he knew he could not hold her, that their love was immortal, and they would be together eventually. I was embarrassed to have witnessed their spoken intimacy, but they weren't physically close to each other. I think their love was that strange inestimable elemental mix, a triumvirate of intellectual, spiritual, and emotional essence, not yet based on physical intimacy. Ethereal Diana blew Feliciano a kiss and left the stables as quickly as she had arrived.

I apprised Ceres of this because Magpie had been informed that three Vigiles from the night watch of Rome arrived at the stables and dragged Feliciano away. My enquiries revealed that Feliciano clambered the Gemonian Stairs, was whipped then thrown to his death from the Tarpeian Rock. His crime? Daring to fraternise with a Vestal Virgin. The Pontifex Maximus had already dealt with Diana. As it was law that her blood could not be spilled, she was taken to a murky, underground vault, given a little bread and water, and left to perish. She was placed in purgatory until the spirits rescued her. There was nothing we could do to help. Magpie and I tried. We vigorously pursued every avenue of hope in the short passage of time knowing that Caesar favoured exercising clemency for Romans. That night Caesar could not be found. He was entertaining Queen Cleopatra.

Perhaps I challenged the Gods when I asked how catastrophic can be the consequences of a romance? I should have listened to Ceres when she beseeched my help. I should have known that her presentiment did not augur well. I could have advised Feliciano to stop his love affair.

I held Ceres as we both wept for two young people whose lives were cruelly and viciously snuffed out because they dared to love each other at the wrong time in their lives.

One kiss is all it takes.

Fifteen months later, on the Ides of March in 44 BCE, the gossip among Romans had still been the love affair between a Vestal Virgin, a slave, and their slaying. People did not name Feliciano and Diana. Everyone seemed to forget that they were humans with emotions. People just like us but who had endured torture then were murdered by their own people, and for what? I asked myself in which society did Romans turn against each other? Tormented by conflicting sentiments, it made me reconsider allowing Alesia to join the Vestal Virgins. Foul guilt gnawed mercilessly at my intestines. Despite all the atrocities I had witnessed and engaged in, for the first time in my life, I despised being Roman. The city was awash with avarice, simmering insecurity, and malevolence. Was this what I had fought for in foreign lands?

During a private visit to our villa early that morning, Caesar discussed his plans with Marc Antony, Magpie, and me. He had decided to place me as General in Cambria from the following day and said that a war ship was already available for me in the port of Ostia. To avenge the murder of Crassus at Carrhae, Caesar intended to go to war in the Parthian Empire the following day and would take four war ships with him which were also docked in Ostia and ready to set sail. He wished Marc Antony to remain in Rome and lead the Empire during his absence. Magpie would help but remain as Legate of the elite Legio Ten. These matters of importance to Caesar would be presented to the Senate at the Curia di Pompeo that evening. Caesar requested the vocal support of us, his loyal

Senators, because he believed there were other Senators who plotted against him, motivated by his proposed reforms for resettling the poor and his plans to overhaul Roman governance. Some Senators had privately expressed concern to Marc Antony that Caesar appeared to have the ultimate power of a king.

Whilst he was at the villa, Ceres gently reminded Caesar of the Sibylline Prophecy, to beware the Ides of March, but he seemed preoccupied and more focused on the forthcoming war where he envisioned his next glorious battle. The prospect of combat and victory in another foreign country thrilled him. "Don't worry Ceres" he said confidently "There will not be any conflict until tomorrow. By then, the Ides of March will have passed."

That day twizzled with activity. In the afternoon, Caesar walked with Marc Antony, Magpie, and me around the gardens of his home on the Palatine where we planned the Parthian attack. Once Caesar left us, Marc Antony, Magpie, and I colluded before the full Senators' conference that evening when six hundred men would be delegates. We decided upon a strategy where we would each persuade small groups of Senators that Caesar's reforms were in the best interests of all Roman citizens. As Caesar had been given leadership of the Empire for ten years, we would urge the Senators to follow him as his route so far had been triumphant.

In the late afternoon I returned home to prepare for the evening's events by changing into my toga, edged in purple silk which denoted that I was a member of the Senate. Once I was ready, Alesia, Fausta, and Sabine scrambled to sit on my knees. Their favourite story, about a man and lady meeting on the Vardre in Cambria on a moonlit evening was recounted to them by me, much to their amusement. I informed Ceres that we would leave the following morning and return to Cambria, she was happy about this change of residence. She used this brief time when the children were being entertained by me to visit the Temple of Venus in the Curia di Pompeo. She pledged offerings of thanks but also asked for help because she had been feeling anxious all day about Caesar.

Magpie called at the villa before the Senators' meeting so that he could play magic tricks on the girls. An hour later Caesar and Marc Antony arrived, closely followed by Ceres. Caesar put his arms out to Ceres and laughingly said 'look, it's the Ides of March Ceres and I'm still here'. She told him that the day was not yet over and advised him again to '*beware the Ides of March*'. He hugged Ceres and told her not to worry so much about him. She thanked him for my promotion. When we were ready to leave the villa, Caesar led the way. Marc Antony, Magpie, and I followed him to the Curia di Pompeo as a glorious orange sky heralded the fall of dusk.

Once inside the Curia di Pompeo I was with Caesar and Cassius where we discussed the prophecies from the Sibylline Books which had been divulged at the most recent Senate meeting. As he moved around the room, Marc Antony, Magpie, and I reminded Caesar that his oratory skills would need to persuade some of the Senators to his way of thinking. The Curia di Pompeo was bursting, the atmosphere one of heightened tension. Loquaciously six hundred cosmopolitan men bobbed around in a sea of white and purple cloth. Moving into the large main room, we briefly lost sight of Caesar as we individually engaged in dialogue with small groups of men, and Caesar mingled with one larger group.

We were all unaware of the horror about to unfold.

Without warning there was a commotion on the rostra. Shrieks and yells reverberated around the semi-circular room. Magpie and Marc-Antony lunged towards a group of approximately thirty Senators whose ceremonial white togas were splattered with blobs and sprays of deep red hues. Pushing my way through the hysterical crowd I saw the intensely wretched image of a blood-soaked growing stain on a Senator's cloak wrapped around a man's body on the floor. The gown covered his face. I bent and lifted the drenched, bloodied shroud to witness dead eyes staring at me. Julius Caesar had raised his arm so that the white toga masked his face from the ignominy of a life's end brought about by grubby, weak men whom he had considered friends.

Here was the collateral damage of jealousy. Enraged, when I looked up, white-robed Senators were running in all directions yelling that Caesar had been murdered. Calmly Marc Antony grasped instantly that Ceres would be in danger because of her warnings to Caesar. He advised me to find Magpie and send him to alert Ceres. My eyes scanned the room, as I pushed my way through throngs of garrulous men, Magpie approached me. Stumbling for breath I instructed him to seize Ceres and my girls and escort them to the port of Ostia where a warship would be waiting. There were enough oarsmen on standby for the war Caesar had planned the following day who were available to power the vessel. Marc Antony and I, together with Caesar's Praetorian Guard brought about calm in the Curia. As we regained order within the auditorium, one of Caesar's murderers, Cassius, ran away from the Curia di Pompeo area. Unbeknown to me, he was heading for the elegant Temple of Jupiter to retrieve the Sibylline Books. They held the prophecies he was anxious should not be exposed."

Ceres commandeered the story.

"Shockingly, Magpie burst into the villa where I was about to put the children to bed. He told me the divination had come true about the Ides of March and instructed me to grab the three girls. 'We are not safe in the city now Ceres' he said. 'The Senators know about your foresight. You're in grave danger and Titus wants me to take you to the port where you will board a ship tonight bound for Cambria.' I replied by telling Magpie that I needed to retrieve the Sibylline Books and take them with me for safekeeping. Some of the murderers would be sure to steal them to find out the remaining undisclosed prophecies. The Sibylline Books could not be kept in Rome, or contents known by the Senators.

Magpie swept Alesia and Fausta into his muscular arms. With one arm I grabbed Sabine, with the other I put the key to the crypt of the Temple of Jupiter into my pocket, seized my pugio and darted from our villa. It would be the last time I saw our home. Chaos ran amok along the moonlit, fetid narrow alleyways while we pushed our way through disbelieving, thronging crowds who were openly discussing Caesar's assassination. Some were hysterical. We arrived at the Temple of Jupiter. The iridescent full moon hung low in the sky, casting petrifying obscure shadows on the building. In my anxiety I slipped on the steps almost dropping Sabine. As we entered the Temple we touched the dark walls along the three rooms for guidance, not daring to light a candle and alert anyone to our presence. When we reached the altar, with one hand I felt around the crypt for the Ace of Cups insignia, fumbled with the key, opened the door of the sepulchre, and pulled out the three Sibylline Books. I gave one each to my three girls for safekeeping.

The five of us, like silent black cats, crept out of the Temple but encountered Senator Cassius on the steps. He confronted us, grabbed Sabine by the hair, tugged her from my arm and threatened to kill her if I didn't give him the Sibylline Books. Deftly, I drew my amber-handled pugio and forcefully stabbed him in the shoulder. He dropped Sabine and fell to the floor. Magpie kicked him in his hoary face rendering him unconscious. Good. I spat on him, and grabbed brave Sabine who had held onto one of the Sibylline Books as if she would die rather than let it go. She was her mother's daughter.

Magpie led us through the thronging, chaotic streets of Rome to the stables near the Campus Martius. Expertly he saddled two of our horses, Castor and Pollux. He placed us on the beasts and rode with the four of us to the port at Ostia. The children and I were now the keepers of the prophecies held in the Sibylline Books. In hushed trepidation I pondered our future, away from a weary Rome, and beseeched the Gods for the safe arrival of Titus."

Titus resumed the narrative.

"At the Curia, Marc Antony spoke to the stunned and confused Senators. He explained that Caesar had been murdered by a group of their own. He ordered Caesar's Praetorian Guard to enlist the help of the Vigiles and force people to return home. There would be no-one allowed on the streets for the next twenty-four hours otherwise retribution would be swift and severe. Once a terrorised semblance of order had been restored in the Curia, Marc Antony persuaded me to stick with Caesar's wishes to become General of Cambria. He organised papers for my departure and insisted I leave within the hour. Despairing about the loss of a beloved friend, inspirational leader, and his vision, I walked despondently through the now

eerily hushed and still dark alleyways of my birthplace. It felt
as though millions of eyes observed me, although I saw not one
soul. At the stables, I saddled Callisto. The forceful stallion
galloped to the port as I prayed to the Gods that my family and
beloved friend Magpie would be safely at the quayside of
Ostia.

The six of us met on the wharf, at the side of the naves longae
bound for Cambria and ready to cast off. I hugged Magpie as if
I would never see him again and thanked him from my soul for
delivering my precious cargo safely. Beneath the full moon we
vowed under no circumstances to forget our friendship. We
would love each other as if we were brothers until our dying
day. Ceres sobbed uncontrollably at leaving Magpie but most
challenging was peeling the three little girls from his loving
arms. They were hysterical about leaving behind Pica, in
return, he too was wretched.

Magpie tried to give Ceres the gold moonstone ring that the
children had presented to him. She refused to accept it. He
wept for my wife, the three feisty children he cherished as his
own, for me, his beloved friend and for our great leader,
Caesar, who was no more.

Sabine, Fausta, Alesia, Ceres, and I stayed on the ship's deck.
We waved goodbye to Magpie who watched us until the vessel
was a dot on the horizon. Long after we had left him on the
dockside, the children claimed that Magpie's moonstone ring
shot dazzling rays across the Bay, to illuminate our journey.
Did Destiny intervene to create this tiny diaspora of souls, our
exodus from Rome barely noticeable to others?

We watched as the night sky set alight with trailing bright
golden white flashes of energy. These bright stars falling like

jewelled teardrops signified the death and deification of our great leader, Caesar, as he headed to a different time dimension. They heralded for the six of us, new beginnings on altered timelines."

2023

Chapter 22 – No-one In The World

Nulli Secundus.

Madoc heard nain's voice echo around his head.

"I'm going to stomp hawkstaff *now*." She banged her hawkstaff on the ground. "The deal is sealed. I'll count back from ten to zero. When I say zero your eyes will open. You will return to your current life."

"Madoc" he heard Seren say nervously, "are you ok?"

If it were possible, he'd swear the voices were swimming in the clear colourless plasma of his cerebral fluid.

"I'm as fine as a Dandy's bum fluff" responded Madoc.

"Are you drunk?" asked Seren.

"I feel weird. Very strange" answered Madoc uncertainly.

"As find as a Dandy's bum fluff? Who says that?" questioned Seren.

"Me?" replied Madoc tentatively.

"Here" said nain passing Madoc some home-baked lemon drizzle cake and a cup of scorching hot coffee from a flask she had brought to the underground Temple of Mithras. "Eat the cake, the sugar will do you good. Use the drink to slurp it down."

Madoc obeyed. The shadows bouncing off the Temple's damp walls created vivid images of Roman legionaries marching to battle.

"Are different timelines possible?" he asked of no-one and then redirected his question to nain. "Nain, are different timelines possible for us? Can we reach a higher dimension whilst we are living this life?"

Silence ricocheted around the cavernous room until the sound of Madoc gulping his coffee echoed and nain replied:

"There are many things in this life Madoc that the most sophisticated and erudite people cannot answer. The brain is a mystery to even the most intellectual neurologist or psychologist. In some instances, the wonders of the stars, planets, and galaxies have the most scholarly scientists stumped. I don't consider myself to be a gadfly, and numerous gifted people spend their lives trying to unravel obscurities which are thousands of years old, like timelines and time dimensions, but I believe that diverse timelines can be accessed. If we want the best life, we must aim for our higher self. We can learn lessons from past lives. My advice is to listen to your intuition, it's your soul's voice. It will not lead you too far away from the path you should be following. Aim for the stars Mr Stargazer."

Madoc smiled at Nain.

"Nain, I watched as the night sky set alight with spewing bright golden white flashes of energy. There were meteors which signified the death and deification of Caesar as he headed to a different dimension. I was his *friend*. My wife Ceres and I *knew* Caesar. I was the father to three children. Three little girls. My wife was a *Seer*. We had a dear friend called Magpie. The lessons I learned from my past life regression are manifold. I now know that it's possible to love people enough to be prepared to die for them, that not everyone can be trusted even when you think they are a friend, and that you nain, are a keeper of at least one Sibylline book" revealed Madoc.

"These are important lessons Madoc as you embark on the next chapter of your life. Your wife, and children if you have them, will be the bedrock of your existence" responded nain. "As for the Sibylline books, well only three of us know that secret. Welcome to the family Madoc."

He laughed.

"The woman in my past life, Ceres. She was my wife. Does it make sense that she could have been Seren in a different life because in this life Seren is a Seer?"

"Yes Madoc. You are piecing together your past life and realising that it is connected to this life. The Seer and The Stargazer!"

"Then who was Magpie? Could he be my mate Gareth? I can't imagine Gareth being a Roman Legate. He wouldn't even have a tattoo he's so squeamish. He loves deliberating theories at Bangor University and seeks the visceral pleasure of observing celestial objects in the night sky with Haf, Seren and me. He's scholarly, not brave as a lion."

"Scholarly doesn't necessarily imply cowardly Madoc. People can demonstrate courage in different ways. Gareth is probably amazing at amassing and assessing data to produce ground-breaking information. He ventures into the largely unexplored and secretive cosmos every day. That takes mettle. In this life you might not have encountered Magpie yet. Remember, you've only just met Seren so Magpie could be someone from your future life" advised nain.

"Ahh that's interesting, I hadn't thought about any of that," said a pensive Madoc.

"The *visions* or *dreams* that I've been having were really my past life. I've just witnessed that through my past life regression. How do I make my future life appear?" questioned Madoc.

"The same way. Through your dreams, daydreams, or visions. By channelling them through meditating. You can envision the life you wish to live. You can make your highest life happen by imagining it, being discerning with your time and proactive in your approach. Make a list of the things you wish to happen for yourself. We call this type of creativity, *manifestation*.

Your brain holds a complete collection of everything that has happened, is happening now and will happen in the future. Your past, present and future can be accessed through the internal, timeless library held in your brain. Meditate. Allow your mind to be still so that you can merge with the universal life force. Shift your focus to within yourself. You have free will Madoc. Ysbryd will not intervene unless you ask for help.

You should always ask Ysbryd for your and others' highest good, otherwise the consequences may be dire. Remember Madoc, what's meant for you will not miss you. That's known as Destiny."

"If I want to live in Rome for example, you're saying if I imagine it, write it down, ask Ysbryd for help, then that life will materialise?" queried Madoc.

"I'm saying that if you want to live in Rome, Ysbryd will place things in your path to help you along the way, but you must be on the lookout for those signs, be proactive, ask for what you wish. Believe. Meditate. Make conscious decisions" replied nain. "Never doubt that it will happen. And, be prepared for the consequences of your wishes."

Seren shivered.

"Does anyone mind if we go back to the farmhouse? Despite the blankets and candles, it's cold and damp down here" stated Seren.

Madoc gathered hawkstaff along with the heavy plaid blankets and carried them the length of the dimly lit tunnel. Nain and Seren followed with the left-over cake, brightly burning white candles, and a large blue flask. Madoc was the leader of a triumvirate. Had he realised it, Madoc would have smiled, but instead his mind was piecing together strategic manoeuvres in Gaul, enmity in Rome and the life he and Seren had once led.

***

With four weeks to go until their handfasting ceremony Seren was nervously waiting for Madoc in Bisgedi, a coffee shop in Llandudno. Madoc was already forty minutes late and Seren was beginning to think he'd changed his mind. She ordered her third café latte, despite knowing that her nerves would be caffeine jangled. '*What if,*' she pondered '*what if he's decided not to go ahead with it?*'

"I think she's been stood up" she overheard a pretty, young waitress whisper to another. Having never been in that position, they both laughed.

'*Mean things*' thought Seren '*pretty outside, ugly within*' and pretended to be engrossed in her mobile 'phone.

It was another ten minutes before she discerned Madoc running down the main street. His muscular frame burst into the busy café. He spotted Seren at a corner table near the window and strode over.

"You ok?" Seren questioned.

"Yes great" Madoc replied breathlessly.

Seren smiled. He was adorable.

"Did you do it?" she asked.

"Do what" he responded.

"Is this twenty-questions?" she queried.

"What do you mean?" he responded, oblivious to the irony.

Seren laughed.

"Did it go ok?" she asked him pointedly.

"Yes thanks" was his glib reply.

"*Madoc*" Seren insisted "I've been waiting for four hours. For three of those hours, I've been wandering around Llandudno.

I've even been up the Great Orme to the Copper Mine, read all about its Bronze Age history and had time to buy some malachite crystal from the shop. Did you know that malachite crystal represents the Goddess Venus and is linked with transformation, new beginnings, and dispelling with that which is no longer of use?"

Seren took one look at Madoc's face and knew that he did not want to know anything about crystal meanings.

"*Madoc are you listening?* For the past hour I've been sitting here looking like a sad git. Please tell me all about it. The suspense is killing me."

"Excuse me sir" interrupted one of the teenage waitresses "would you like something to eat or drink?"

Madoc turned around and looked at Seren who sighed.

"Sorry Seren. I am listening, just a little preoccupied. Would you like to stay here or go for a walk?" he asked.

"Get something to eat and drink here Madoc. You must be famished by now and I want to hear all about it."

"Please may I have a boiled egg sandwich on brown bread and a café latte?" replied Madoc as he sat down at the wooden table. His huge frame made the dark chairs appear tiny.

"Thank you" responded the waitress politely to Madoc. On her way back to the counter, Seren smiled when she heard the girl whisper to another waitress "he was worth waiting for."

"Why are you smiling?" enquired Madoc.

"Nothing. You are worth the wait" she acknowledged to him.

Puzzled, he shook his head and raised his eyebrows.

"Ok. Look at this" he demanded and pulled up the right leg of his Levi jeans.

"That's amazing. It's so realistic. Who'd have thought that a tattoo portrait of Julius Caesar could look as fantastic as that? It's detailed artwork on your leg."

Seren bent down to closely inspect the calf of Madoc's right leg and asked, "when does the cling film come off?"

"I've got to keep it wrapped overnight. Sean cleaned it with antibacterial soap. He said not to wash it straightaway nor dry it with a towel but afterwards I need to keep it well moisturised."

"Will it be *set* by the time we get to Rome?"

"Tattoos don't *set* Seren," laughed Madoc. "It'll be fine in Rome, I'll put sunscreen on it."

"What's Sean's new studio like? He's moved since he did my tattoos" stated Seren.

"Well, he's renamed the business. It's now called the Magpie Tattoo Studio and has a brilliant sign outside of, *wait for it*, two enormous black and white magpies. I thought the name was a bit surreal Seren because of our link to Corvus Corax. Magpie in our previous existence!"

"That is a coincidence" replied Seren "or a sign. Pardon the pun."

They both laughed and Madoc looked sideways at Seren.

"I didn't notice much about his studio Seren. To be honest I kept my beady eye on his work. I was more interested in whether he was doing a good job of Caesar."

"And he has" Seren replied soothingly. "Tell me what Sean has been up to since I last saw him."

"He's rebranded his business and raises money for the organisation, Blind Veterans UK. Sean was telling me that one of his friends works at their Centre of Wellbeing in Llandudno."

"How lovely. He's a kind lad. I've heard about the Centre. It's a great cause. I hope you gave a donation on our behalf."

"I did" reassured Madoc. "In fact, I've had a mad morning" he confessed.

"What? You did something madder than getting a tattoo of Julius Caesar?"

"Yes" Madoc admitted.

Seren leaned across the table.

"Great" she replied, "I can't wait to hear all about it. But tell me as you eat your sandwich, otherwise we'll be here all day."

"You know the place near Conwy Castle called Benarth Beach offices?" he continued.

"You mean the one that looks over Conwy Castle and the estuary?" she answered.

"That's the one. I've been there earlier today. When finished my tattoo, I had a quick visit before I came here."

"Why did you need to go there?" she asked quizzically.

"Let me finish my food and we'll have a trip over there and I'll show you why" he stated.

"You do mean the place near to where I go to for physiotherapy don't you?"

"That's the one. I'll drive. It's only five minutes away. I'll have finished eating in a short while."

Puzzled, Seren wondered what he'd had been up to. Twenty minutes later, as Madoc's classic maroon Jaguar car wheezed its way across the bridge at Conwy Castle, he guided it left into the lush countryside and she found out.

Madoc parked the Jaguar under an ancient yew tree. Seren got out of the car and turned her back to the glittery sea. She stared at the stone and flint building with its enormous windows overlooking the estuary and breathed in the briny air.

"Now are you going to tell me why we are here? The suspense is killing me."

"You won't die of curiosity Seren, you're not a cat! Be patient. There's something I'd like to show you. Come on."

"Am I on a mystery tour?" she joked.

"Yes. Prepare yourself. Be brave. I'm not taking you to learn of your grim fate under the spooky yew trees. We're going indoors" was Madoc's riposte.

They walked across the crunchy gravel path towards the delightful building. Madoc unlocked a treacle-coloured arched wooden door and pushed it open. It didn't creak eerily, it simply opened.

"It's just upstairs. Come on" he directed.

Seren followed him up a sun-filled wooden staircase. She peered out through the window on the half-landing which overlooked the Fairy Glen Forest sited at the back of the building. A bewitching place where myth collided with beguiling reality. At the top of the stairs, she sat on a green velvet wraparound chair, which offered a welcome resting place for those who might find the stairs a little too steep or for those who simply wished to contemplate. Seren did the latter. When she gathered her sensibilities, she stood up. Above the chair Seren was surprised to see the framed photograph depicting the panoramic view taken from the Vardre of Conwy, the Irish Sea and three mountain ranges. The picture which Madoc had snapped.

"Oh Madoc. We live in this picture."

"We do. Come on Seren" instructed Madoc perkily as he pushed open one of the three white doors on the voluminous landing.

As Seren walked inside the room a large, mesmerising portrait of Circe hung on the wall opposite the door. The image showed Circe's enchanted Ace of Cups placed at her lips, to fool warriors into supping her magic potion before she turned them into swine, lions, or wolves. She was a guileful one that Circe. At the sight of it, Seren laughed. The portrait was flanked on the left by a black and white image of a full moon proudly exhibiting the potted shadows and shades of her surface. On the right was a mystical illustration of a large tawny owl in flight against a backdrop of black trees. In the middle of the room sat a substantial oak table with two drawers. Perched either side were two wooden rattan chairs.

"Close your eyes" directed Madoc "and hold out your hands."

In complete trust, Seren did as ordered. She heard Madoc walk across the wooden floor, then felt a heavy weight across both her arms and Madoc's hands underneath hers to help support the heft.

"Open them now" instructed Madoc.

When she did, Hawkstaff, or rather its almost identical twin, gawked at her. The only difference between this and Nain's hawkstaff was its shimmering moonstone eye.

"I don't understand" said Seren. "What's going on?"

"Welcome to your new life."

"My new life?" probed Seren.

"Yes. This room is yours. I've arranged with Winifred that you can have this room for your tarot card readings and past life regressions whenever we're in Conwy. You can decorate it however you want. I've put up some of my photographs, which you don't have to keep on the walls if you don't want them" explained Madoc.

He was disconcerted by her silence. Tacitly he watched as she looked around the room.

"Nain helped me to choose the things that you might like in this room. Look" he pointed "I've brought your glittering moonstone and rose quartz crystals. You can add your malachite crystal to the set. See, I do listen! I collected shells from Conwy beach and here they are on this shelf. I've bought different coloured candles for you to burn, and incense sticks from that Cosy Home shop on The Square that you're always going into. The owner said your favourite candle was honeysuckle scented so I've got two of those. She even gave me some interior design tips about where to place items on these shelves. Nain made you some essential oils." Madoc selected certain tiny brown bottles with rubber stoppers and showed them to Seren. Needlessly, he read out each label "bergamot, geranium, lavender, rose, jasmine, ylang ylang. I've framed your poem and placed it on the wall here" he indicated a gold framed tapestry.

Seren gently touched the frame and whispered the words to an aged poem she had written about a witch:

"A witch's eyes are green and clear
Her heart is pure and dear
She knows what tomorrow will bring
And has answers for everything
In her small hands she deals her cards
And can reel off poetry by the bards
She sees beauty in Nature's life
And sweeps away negative strife
Her spells sparkle, she fills my heart with hope
And with a turn of her cloak, she vanishes into smoke"

When she stopped, Madoc looked around the room, uncertain what to express. Seren was silent. She looked fragile. Madoc plucked at the wordless air around them for something to say.

"We've talked about you starting your own business. Being your own boss. Working your own hours. You said you'd love to take up tarot reading as a job so that you could guide people, if only you had a place with the correct aura. I brought nain to look at the room. She felt that it had the precise energy for you to begin your craft. Nain approved of it. She even brought her wand. *I didn't know she had one.* She walked around the room, put up her right arm and did a spell. Truthfully, I couldn't believe my eyes. I certainly didn't know what to say. She had me stumped. I wondered if that was the magic spell, so that I never spoke again!"

Seren cried. Madoc hugged her.

"Oh Madoc. Thank you" was all she could muster. After a few moments Seren said "did she do this?" and she acted out nain's spell.

'By the power of the sky'
"Turn to the right" ordered Seren.
'By the power of the sea'
"Turn right again."
'By the power of the earth'
"Turn right again."
'By the power of the trees, cast my circle.'

Seren and Madoc laughed. Nain had infused them both with an effusive, wonderful, entrancing spirit. They loved it.

"Yes. Exactly that," laughed Madoc. "You're both bonkers and I love you both for it" was all he could say.

"Thank you. You *get* me. I will always love you for that, no matter what."

Seren assured him that the room was perfect for her new life. And this was only the beginning.

"Come on. We've got a handfasting to finalise" prompted Madoc who found it difficult to remove Seren from her Divinely found witchy space. "We're meeting Haf and Gareth in an hour."

'Gosh. I'd forgotten about our meeting' she thought. 'The rest of the day's plans have been totally usurped by this wonderful gesture from Madoc.'

Seren took a lingering look at her new room. Perfect. With its view over the Conwy estuary guarded by the Fairy Glen Forest at the back of the building, it was ideal.

"Here's the key Seren. Enjoy every moment of being here" wished Madoc. And she would.

They arrived at the Mulberry pub to meet Haf and Gareth with ten minutes to spare. It offered a little time to relax and for Seren and Madoc to discuss their wedding plans. Two lagers and two gin and tonics later, their effusive friends joined them.

"We've had confirmation from the Hotel de Russie about our transfer from Rome Fiumicino airport. There will be a car waiting for us" announced Gareth.

"It's a great location just between the Spanish Steps and Piazza del Popolo. I'm pleased that you two will be staying at the same hotel as us and nain" replied Madoc.

"Will nain be ok Seren? In Rome I mean? We can take her out for trips around the city when you're not there. It's not a problem for us" said Haf.

"That's a generous offer from you both Haf and Gareth, but nain will be fine on her own. She's practically memorised the map of Rome she bought. Nain knows how to use the map app on her 'phone. She's been practising around the farm and in Conwy!" responded Seren.

"Nain's a pragmatic woman. She's looking forward to having a solo adventure" divulged Madoc. "Please don't take responsibility for her when we're not around. I guarantee that whilst she's in Rome, people will seek her out to speak to her.

She's in her element listening to other people and nain will love exploring the Eternal City. I wouldn't be surprised if she stayed longer than two weeks" stated Madoc.

"She already knows a few Italian phrases" said Seren proudly.

"Wow. Nain's putting us to shame" responded Haf.

"Now is there anything that you need the two of us to do for you before the big day?" asked Gareth.

"No. We're sorted thanks. But I'll warn you that I'm wearing the Thomson clan outfit so bring your sunglasses," laughed Madoc.

"Will it be warm enough in October for a kilt Madoc?" queried Haf.

"Absolutely. It's not Conwy y'know. We *are* heading to the Mediterranean where the sun dazzles, and storm clouds don't gather as much as they do here," laughed Madoc.

"Seren is your outfit ready yet? Have you had another fitting of your dress with Mrs Taylor?" prodded Haf.

"I'm going tomorrow for the final sizing up! Come along if you like. Have you collected your outfit yet?" asked Seren.

"No. I could text Mrs Taylor and ask if she can see me just after your appointment" offered Haf.

"Perfect" agreed Seren. "We can meet up and go there together."

"What have you two been up to? We've not seen you for a while" asked Gareth changing the conversation away from wedding bells.

"We've been to Ancient Rome" disclosed Madoc.

"You've what? Ancient Rome? You mean you've watched a film about Ancient Rome?" asked a perplexed Haf.

"Nain did a joint past life regression on us a few weeks ago. We ended up in Ancient Rome. I was a Legate in Caesar's army, Seren was a Seer. We were married with three children" explained Madoc.

"Have you had too many lagers mate?" joked Gareth.

"Gareth you wouldn't believe it unless you'd had it done. It was amazing. A bit like watching a movie. A movie in your own mind. But then, if you think about it, everything is perceived by your own mind and body," revealed Madoc. "Life is never anyone else's view."

"It sounds like a fantastic odyssey" said Haf.

"At first, I was dubious. In fact, initially I couldn't clear my head of thoughts, so the meditation was a non-starter. When I began to trust nain, I found that I could relax. The quietness of my mind enabled me to participate in a past life regression. Then once my mind was quiet, I was able to have my mind blown! I'd recommend it to you both" stated Madoc.

Seren was astounded at Madoc's genuine enthusiasm.

"It had such a positive effect on me that I had this done today" revealed Madoc as he rolled up the leg of his Levi's to reveal his inventive tattoo of Julius Caesar.

"Bloody hell Madoc. That's quite a statement" conceded Gareth.

"That's not all we've done" revealed Seren. "I'm starting my own business. Madoc's organised for me to have a room at Benarth Beach offices, overlooking Conwy Castle and the estuary" she said proudly.

"Doing what?" asked a surprised Haf.

"Tarot card readings and past life regression."

Gareth spat out his lager and took a sidelong look at Madoc and Seren.

 "Well. You're certainly taking an alternative view on life, which I applaud" acknowledged Gareth. "We do have epistemic access to the recent past as memories. As a scientist, our confidence in those remembrances is constrained by evidence such as photographs and letters. I didn't realise that the source of our knowledge could be reminiscences from thousands of years ago. Or that past lives are real. Is it possible to look at our future lives?

That brings into question a matter of free will. As a scientist, I appreciate that it's not always possible to have evidence of something, which doesn't mean it's not true. Many events occur which are inexplicable. My experience tells me that not everything in the universe is clear or understandable. But where does free will come into our lives if those lives have already been lived?"

Gareth's enquiring mind had been detonated.

"Free will comes in because there are various paths we can take Gareth, and different lives we can live" answered Seren. "Choices we have made in the past should enable us to learn lessons so that we make better selections in our next life. We don't always opt for the beneficial though. Sometimes we are destructive and damage ourselves or others by our behaviour. We choose the lives we live. It's only when we make conscious choices about our life and discern what is for our highest possible good by asking Ysbryd to help us, that we get to live our *best* life. We must choose how to spend our time, and the people we wish to love.

I think we must surround ourselves with those who nourish us. If people don't bring out the best in you, then question their role in your life. You can choose to walk away otherwise you repeat the same circle. Past life regression can be exciting when it helps you to see mistakes, or helps you understand why you enjoy certain activities such as painting or writing, or when you feel a calling to be a nurse or a teacher for example. Past life regression unlocks those doors. Ultimately you decide upon the kind of person you want to be and the life you wish to live."

"Do you fancy giving it a go then Gareth?" asked Madoc.

"No way am I having a tattoo mate. I have a mystifying fear of needles," laughed Gareth.

"No yer numpty, I meant a past life regression and your tarot cards read. Seren can practise on you in her new room" replied Madoc.

"Oh. Let me think about it mate. Will my head be scrambled?" Gareth asked seriously.

"Lightly poached maybe" responded Seren jokily. "Gareth. What are you going to do with this wonderous life?"

"I'll have my cards read Seren" agreed Haf.

Gareth was pondering something. After a few moments he said, "there's an interesting young Italian bloke whose researching with me at the University. He's attracted to the occult. I'll bring him along to one of our stargazing sessions on the Vardre so that he can meet the three of you, but he might want to see you beforehand Seren."

"Thanks Gareth" replied Seren. "I'll look forward to meeting him but for now, I'm thrilled about meeting Haf tomorrow morning for our fittings."

***

After an early morning coffee at Pen y Bryn café in The Square, Seren and Haf walked through the town. They popped into Plas Mawr to have a look at some books on offer before peering through the window of the Storiel Gallery, where they admired the Segontium Sword, an Ancient Roman artefact recently discovered locally. It was the talk of the town, on loan from the Storiel Gallery in Bangor.

In no time at all they had arrived at a double-fronted cottage on Rosemary Lane with its gold star above the black front door. This was the base for workaholic Bertha who Haf said was a famous seamstress in North Wales. Luckily for Seren she had chosen to station herself in Conwy. Originally from Anglesey, Bertha had decided that she could make a successful business creating wedding outfits on the mainland coastline, which offered close links to Chester, Liverpool, and Manchester. She had been feverishly preparing for a fitting with Seren and Haf.

"Morning Seren. Morning Haf. Who's going first?" asked Bertha.

"Let Seren go first" suggested Haf "in case we run out of time. I can always come back another day" she said generously.

Voluptuous Bertha bustled to her workshop at the back of the ground floor cottage. In a room full of mirrors at the front of the cottage, Seren and Haf sat in large brown leather chairs and waited patiently.

"Seren, here's your dress" said Bertha as she opened the curtain to a large changing room. "Try it on" she instructed.

Once Bertha had buttoned the pearls at the back of the buttercup yellow silk dress Seren emerged from the changing room. The sleeveless body-hugging long dress with white embroidered thistles along the bottom accentuated Seren's curves. Bertha had also created for her a long cloak, identical in colour and pattern, which fastened with scalloped gold brooches on either shoulder. Haf gasped. The outfit was stunning and expertly created.

"The scallop represents the feminine form. I recently visited the Uffizi Gallery in Florence and saw Botticelli's painting of a fully-grown nude Venus emerging from a scallop shell. I took my influence for the brooches from this image. I hope you like it Seren as I know you live your life guided by Goddesses."

"It's unbelievable. I'm thrilled. Over the moon. It's better than I ever hoped. Thank you, Bertha. Thank you."

"Seren you'll look exquisite on your handfasting day. I'm so looking forward to it" said Haf.

"I'll wrap it in tissue paper Seren and if you like, I'll pack it for your trip so this will be the last time you'll see it until you unpack it for the big day" advised Bertha.

"Perfect. Thanks Bertha. I'm overjoyed. Now I can't wait to see what Haf's chosen for herself. Quick Haf, pop into the other changing room."

Bertha brought an orange-coloured trouser suit and a cream silk shirt for Haf to try. She was sure it would accentuate Haf's strawberry blonde hair and pretty eyes of green perfectly. The buttons on the shirt, wide-legged trousers and single-breasted jacket had adularescence moonstone fastenings which Seren had asked to be added to the outfit as the stone represented passion and true love.

"You look beautiful Haf. Really stunning" acknowledged Seren.

"Thank you cariad tlws" responded Haf. "I feel amazing."

"You'll both light up the Roman Forum with your bright colours and smiles" assured Bertha. "I can pack both outfits if you like, ready for you to collect any time before you leave for Rome."

Haf and Seren hugged each other. Enthused to be sharing a life-changing event.

"I've got Gwen booked in for tomorrow Seren. Please remind her. She wants her outfit to be a surprise for you, so you're not allowed in the shop when she's here tomorrow" ordered Bertha.

"I know. She's told me that it's a secret. She's been busily knitting herself a green and lilac cashmere pashmina for the day which means she's planning to wear something outlandish. I'll drop her off and collect her when you ring me, Bertha. Thanks again cariad tlws."

As she left Mrs Taylor's dressmaking shop, Seren felt delightful anticipation at the seeds of a new life being delicately sown.

Chapter 23 – Ciphers

Time is ticking?

The trip to Rome came soon enough and nain felt the need to do a spell before they left Bryn Gosol.

"Right everyone. Close your eyes" directed nain to her four co-travellers. "Imagine a white cord attached to you and your suitcase, so it stays safe with you. Wrap a gold line around yourself, your travel companions, the aeroplane, and the cars, to ensure a safe journey and protection from the God Mercury. Here's a little bag for each of you. It contains shungite crystal for protection and safe travel. It's especially good for travelling at altitude. It creates a safe shield around you. Let's enjoy our trip."

"Thanks nain" said a bemused Gareth. The others gave her a hug.

The wedding party of five travelled in a minibus from Conwy to Manchester Airport for their direct flight to Rome Fiumicino airport. Although enormous swathes of people queued in the Security area, this time they were transported through the zone without too much waiting. As she lingered in line Seren had images of a different life where she had been a migrant, queuing to leave her warring country to avoid hatred, bullets, and bloodshed. She clutched her passport, looked at nain and gave her a hug in case she too was experiencing similar haunting thoughts and feelings of desperation.

"We're embarking on a delicious adventure Seren" reassured nain.

"Are you nervous of flying nain?" Seren asked.

"I'm excited cariad tlws. It's only in our recent history that people have been able to get on an aeroplane and fly. Not many individuals get to look at the world from above. And I've never travelled at five hundred miles an hour, except when I used flying ointment, but that's a different story. I can't wait" responded an animated nain.

"One day" Seren promised "I'm going to tell Haf about your flying ointment."

"Good grief no" responded a startled nain.

"I heard that comment about flying ointment. I must hear more" stated Haf.

"Another time Haf" whispered Seren.

Once cleared by Security personnel, Madoc led his troop through the airport, straight to a café and commandeered a corner table. He organised food and drinks ably assisted by Gareth. '*Madoc can't help being in charge*' thought Seren fondly. When their boarding was announced on a nearby television screen Seren grabbed nain's arm and felt a little tremble.

"This is our escapade nain. Next stop Rome" she whispered.

"I know cariad tlws. I'm looking forward to seeing the Eternal City" replied nain. "I'm going to see Raphael's paintings around Rome, especially the Wedding Banquet depicting part of the legend of Psyche. It's at Villa Farnesina and I'm also keen to view Raphael's depiction of four of the Sibyls at the Chigi Chapel in the Church of Santa Maria della Pace."

"What's the story of Psyche?" enquired Haf as they boarded the aeroplane.

Once their flight was mid-air, and nain had enjoyed the rousing thrill of sitting in a vehicle which travelled at five hundred miles an hour, she recounted the fable of Psyche, the Goddess of the Soul and Cupid, God of Love:

"There are many versions of this allegory. The two lovers, Cupid and Psyche represent the masculine and feminine soulmates whose love is destined to be, but only if they prove their deep feelings for one another. The Goddess Ceres was willing to help Psyche but was forbidden by the Gods to offer support.

When Cupid abandoned her, Psyche was set four strident tests by the Goddess Venus, including entering Hades, to see if she had the willingness to do whatever it took to keep alive her love for Cupid. To become spiritual, Psyche had to conquer her dependence on Cupid. She needed to be aware of and accept the demons he hid within himself. Psyche rose to the challenges. In turn, before he could return to her, Cupid had to recognise the devil inside himself, and overcome the monster within.

Only after suffering and surmounting personal obstacles could Cupid and Psyche be rewarded with eternal love. Which they were, eventually. Never underestimate the power of love.

In paintings of Psyche, above her head flies a butterfly which is a symbol of the soul and transformation."

"That's certainly quite a story for a wedding party" said Seren.

"And the Sibyls?" queried Haf. "Who are they?"

Seren and nain laughed.

"We'll tell you during the holiday" promised Seren. And they did except, of course, the part about the Sibylline books. Nain and Seren agreed the ancient grimoires must remain a family secret.

There was a minibus waiting for them at Rome Fiumicino airport which transported the wedding group to the luxurious Hotel de Russie. Upon arrival at the hotel Nain, who had never travelled abroad (in this life) was overwhelmed by the courteous service and stunning surroundings.

"Wait until she sees her room Madoc" whispered Seren.

"I'm pleased we got a good deal on this hotel Seren because it's out of season, otherwise it would have cost us and an arm and a leg" admitted prudent Madoc.

"We've been very lucky Madoc to be able to stay at such a sumptuous place. Thanks for organising it" soothed Seren "and let's thank our lucky stars too."

"This is just the beginning Seren. We're going to have a fantastic time. I promise you that" pledged Madoc. "And the weather is set fair, so we might even get in a spot of stargazing."

On Friday afternoon, after two hectic and interesting days exploring Rome, handfasting day arrived. Seren, Haf and nain had agreed to meet Madoc and Gareth in the hotel's reception area after lunch wearing their wedding garb.

As Seren and Haf walked down the stairs to the lobby, in their bright yellow and orange outfits, all eyes turned to them. Seren's natural sparkle was accentuated by her yellow long fitted dress which clung to her curves. Haf's ageless orange trouser suit, enhanced her body. Onlookers agreed, both women looked equally stunning. In her lilac silk flowing dress, colour-matched Doc Marten boots and vibrant butterfly clips balanced in salted black hair, nain burst forward with flowers.

"Here Seren, Haf. Each of you must take a bouquet of pink roses and a pink rose buttonhole for your man."

"Oh nain, they're gorgeous flowers. How thoughtful. Where did you get these? Have you pinched them from the hotel garden?" laughed Seren.

"Of course not" responded nain in pretend indignation.

"There's a lovely flower kiosk down the cobbled path at the side of the Tiber. When I told Vincenzo, the owner, the story of our journey here from Wales, he created the bouquets for me and matched the buttonholes. He was very interested in hearing all about us. I've spent ages chatting to him over the past two days, mainly about gardening. We've even had an espresso or two together."

"Nain. You haven't?" queried Haf.

"I have and he's lovely."

Seren and Haf locked eyes and smiled.

"You dark horse nain" teased Seren.

"Oh it's not romantic. Nothing like that" replied nain shaking
her head but her black eyes glittered. "Come into the garden
you two. Madoc and Gareth are waiting for us there" she
instructed, but Seren could tell that nain was flustered.
The hotel garden smelled of jasmine and lavender flowers,
which lined the way along a short path. Nain led the two
women to the hotel's glorious floral arch entwined with
eucalyptus, pink roses, and purple hydrangeas. Madoc and
Gareth stepped forward in the Thomson clan traditional
Scottish dress which comprised navy jacket, a tie and kilt of
matching blue, red, black, and white hues, cream-coloured
socks, and black shoes. As she kissed Madoc, Seren spotted a
sporran, a kilt pin, and a sgian dubh.

"How on earth did you get a small dagger through security
Madoc?" she interrogated.

"It was in my suitcase which I checked in" revealed Madoc.

"We're a little early for the handfasting at the Forum though"
said Seren.

"I know" he replied, "we are being legally married first" and
with that, he produced a gift of a gold lunula pendant for Seren
as protection against the evil eye.

"I didn't realise we were getting married in Rome. Is it here in
the garden?" was all Seren could muster.

"No. We are going to the Caracalla Wedding Hall which has
an Ancient Roman church in the Caracalla gardens. The
service is legally binding. I thought it was important that we

did things properly Seren. The ceremony there only lasts about thirty minutes. The place is not far from the Forum. I've ordered two taxis to take us. Nain, Haf and Gareth will follow us. Come on otherwise we'll be late."

Seren hesitated.

"You do want to marry me, don't you?" asked an apprehensive Madoc.

"Of course" replied Seren breezily. "Just that I thought we were only having a handfasting ceremony. I'm a little taken aback that's all. Let's go."

Kindly, the taxi drivers drove unusually slowly through the streets of Rome which enabled the five of them to do a little more sightseeing, but heightened Madoc's nerves as he wished to be on time.

"You can never see enough of Rome" said nain to Haf and Gareth. The couple agreed and vowed to return. Like a tourist guide nain said "if you throw a coin into the Trevi Fountain it guarantees your return. I did it on our first day here" she confessed.

The taxis passed a verdant park ablaze with the autumnal colours of copper, saffron and pomegranate before arriving at the former church in the setting of the Caracalla Baths. An unenticing brown exterior, with its arched wooden door and windows on the first floor, was the first introduction to the Caracalla Wedding Hall. Seren felt a little disappointed until she stepped inside and appreciated its dizzyingly high wooden ceilings, stunningly colourful floor mosaics which, as Madoc would say, were a cipher of history, and its niches to place offerings to the Ancient Roman Gods.

Although the room could hold fifty guests, there were five red and gold velvet chairs placed at the front of the Ancient Roman church. Centred between two lit white candles in clear glass hurricanes on the large marble altar was an intricate and arresting circular floral display of yellow and orange roses, interspersed with dark green foliage. Captivated by nain's winsome ways, the flowers had been fashioned by Vincenzo, who had been intrigued to see the little bags she created. Nain showed him the little blue bag she had made for Seren to hold alongside her bouquet which contained a blue feather for air, a little blue candle for fire, a white shell for water and for earth a black jet crystal. The bag was tied with a little blue butterfly. For Madoc, nain had made a little blue bag which contained a moonstone tumble crystal and a tiny silver horseshoe. He discreetly placed the bag in his sporran.

"The circle of flowers represents eternity" stated nain "like a wedding ring".

"Oh no!" exclaimed Seren. "I don't have a wedding ring for Madoc."

"Don't worry Seren" reassured Gareth "I've got both wedding rings here in my sporran. We knew you were getting married today."

And that's what they did.

Nain, Gareth and Haf, witnessed Seren and Madoc legally become Mr and Mrs Thomson in the Ancient Roman church of Santa Maria in Tempulo. Afterwards the wedding party walked through the narrow alleyways to the Temple of Saturn for their Pagan handfasting ritual.

Upon entering the Forum, a middle-aged Italian lady, with a furrowed brow and a flustered air, approached Seren.

"Here" she said thrusting a silver coin in Seren's hand "it's lucky to meet a witch on your wedding day" and with that, she briskly marched away.

Madoc was flabbergasted. "Which one is the witch?" he asked a bemused and delighted Seren.

When she composed herself, Seren asked nain:

"Have you got the ribbons in your gorgeous green bag so that our hands can be tied together?"

"Of course, cariad tlws. I'm officiating aren't I, so I've come well prepared. This bag is like a Tardis. You won't believe what's in here" she said affectionately patting the only elegant handbag she had ever owned. It had been made especially for her by Minnie and Mabel, Conwy Saddlers of all things.

At twilight the Forum was quiet. Seren and Madoc stood between the two central columns at the Temple of Saturn in front of nain. Only a handful of tourists and locals watched as Haf and Gareth stood either side of the newlyweds. Nain passed eight silk ribbons of assorted colours for Haf and Gareth to hold. She had covertly organised with Bertha that individual ribbons would incorporate a singular gold pendant. Nain was about to begin the ritual when Seren shouted:

"WAIT."

"WAIT?" asked Madoc.

"WAIT?" cried nain.

"WAIT?" said Haf and Gareth in unison.

"Yes please. Wait as I need to throw my bouquet. We nearly forgot that tradition. One, two, three" shouted Seren as a posy of pink roses flew high into the air.

"IT'S MINE" shouted a young woman behind her. "THANK YOU BRIDE."

"YOU'RE WELCOME" yelled Seren. "Nain, now you may begin."

Which she did and what follows is their simple handfasting ritual.

"Seren and Madoc we have eight ribbons here today to perform the handfasting rite. As Haf or Gareth pass you a ribbon you might notice a tiny gold pendant which represents a stage of the moon's cycle. Obviously one ribbon does not have a gold pendant as it's not possible to see a new moon! The moon symbolises life's ebbs and flows, beginnings, and endings. Eternal love stays the same. It doesn't matter what life throws at you, like the moon, you'll wax and wane alongside each other."

The guests smiled.

"We have a green ribbon for prosperity, an orange one for kindness, yellow for joy, and silver for creativity. The next colours have been taken from the Thomson clan plaid. Blue for sincerity, black for strength, white for peace, and red for passion. We wish you both much happiness as you begin married life together. The ribbons are a symbol of being committed to each other, bound gently. This does not mean that you lose your independence, rather you are choosing to share, and possibly widen your freedom, respectfully with each other."

Seren responded with the lucky chant, "quando tu Gaius, ego Gaia"[21] to which Madoc replied "quando tu Gaia, ego Gaius".[22]

The pair had been practising tying a lemniscate into a knot but it's *not* easy in front of witnesses. The ribbons remained tied until the ceremony ended then Gareth and Haf had to unknot the knotty ribbons. This was perhaps symbolic of the gentle help they would offer throughout Seren and Madoc's married life.

The ritual over, nain had made five of her little bags for the wedding party to place at the Temple of Saturn. Once sited, Madoc and Seren pulled away to visit Caesar's Necropolis.

"I know this wasn't here when we lived in Ancient Roman times Madoc, but I thought it important that we place a little bag as a mark of respect for the great man" Seren said by way of explanation.

"What's in your little purple bag?" enquired Madoc.

---

[21] When-and where-you are Gaius, I then-and there-am Gaia.
[22] When-and where-you are Gaia, I then-and there-am Gaius.

"An amethyst crystal, a purple feather, a gold sun and a white moon charm."

"Explain to me what those items represent" he asked kindly.

"Well, amethyst is the most powerful and protective crystal, the purple feather represents nobility, lightness in your soul, trusting your instincts and a connection to Ysbryd. The gold sun indicates that everything revolved around Caesar, and the white moon symbolizes the power of transformation, the repeating cycle of life and death."

"You've put a lot of thought into creating that little bag Seren." Madoc kissed her. "It was fitting that Augustus, Caesar's nephew commemorated where Caesar was cremated. He should be immortalised as a God" said Madoc quietly. "Come on wife, your carriage awaits. Let's join the others."

Seren scanned her thoughtful husband who had an unshakeable belief in Caesar's greatness.

Romantic Madoc had arranged for two horse-drawn carriages to collect them outside the Forum. He had also booked a table at the *Trattoria*, which Seren and Madoc were convinced had been built around the villa from their life in Ancient Rome. In their opinion, the undimmed mosaic depicting the bull and eagle offered ample proof of their previous existence.

As they were walking through the Forum to leave, Gareth said sagely:

"Did you know Madoc that today the Orionid meteors will peak?"

"Yes. That's why I booked the wedding for today" replied Madoc.

"Are you going to stay out all night to watch them?" questioned Gareth.

"Yes. After our meal at the Trattoria, we are going back to the hotel to lie on our veranda with our feet facing southeast. That way we will see as much of the sky as possible" responded Madoc with a glint in his eye.

"Are you really?" queried Haf.

"Absolutely. We're stargazers! Can't miss a spectacle like the Orionid which lasts until dawn. They're one of the brightest and fastest meteor showers of the year. The burning shower of rock and debris flicker like glistening stars which leave glowing trains and appear to come from the constellation Orion. Listen, if we lie down here, now, because our eyes have already adjusted to the dark, and the moon is only a crescent shape so doesn't shed much light, we should be able to see some shooting stars. Come on" instructed Madoc who lay down where he was in the Forum.

The others followed his lead, even nain.

After a few minutes Haf shouted "I can see one just to the right of Orion."

Nain was delighted to see it, and many more that evening.

 "Even Mother Nature is celebrating today's events" she said.

They lay in the Forum for twenty minutes until they were asked politely to leave as the Portiere wished to lock up. They'd never been thrown out of such a spectacular place before. Luckily the horse-drawn carriage operators had waited patiently for their five customers and the *Trattoria* owner was expecting them when they arrived.

"Ah Mr and Mrs Madoc, your table is outside in the courtyard as you requested. It's away from the other customers so you have some privacy."

"Thank you, Ettore" responded Madoc with a smile.

The little group of friends chose the simple dish, lagane e cicciari infused with sage made with passion by Ettore's wife, followed by tirimasu with a topping of grated Roman dark chocolate. Bright, warm, earthy companionship passed effortlessly around the table alongside the champagne, wine and sparkling water.

"What have you seen in Rome nain that you've found most interesting so far?" asked Gareth.

She pondered for a while and responded, "I've visited Palazzo Barbarini, a luxurious Baroque palace and I was captivated by a painting of the Three Parcae, the Three Fates."

"I know the legend of the Three Fates" declared Gareth.

"Oh" said Haf "enlighten us then please."

"The Three Goddesses of Fate control life from birth to death. Supposedly even the Gods fear them. The first Fate, *Nona* uses a spinning wheel to spin the golden thread of life. She decides when souls are born. The second Fate, *Decima* measures with her rod the length of the thread of life for each soul. She decides upon the temptations and joys each soul will encounter during their life. The third Fate, *Morta* cuts the thread of life. She has the power to choose how and when a person dies. Perhaps you might call them the three witches" explained Gareth. "That's how they were depicted by Shakespeare. The Fates, or witches weave the golden skein of life, add or remove knots and unravel the skein at will."

"Some people portray witches, or the Fates, in a bad light" stated nain "but they aren't evil. Just because we can predict the ups and downs of life, our supernatural activities are feared by some. Our core, our soul, our Destiny if you will, speaks to all of us in many ways through dreams, daydreams, intuition, visions, voices. Witches choose to listen, that's the difference. If we all gave ourselves over to the three Fates, or Destiny if you like, to allow ourselves to see what Destiny has in store for us, we can receive personal freedom. Although we have freewill about the choices we make, we need to stop believing that we can control our own Destiny. I thought it was interesting to see a triumvirate of '*Fates*'. In witchy terms, when people see the number three repeatedly it indicates that they are experiencing a crucial time in their lives."

"What you're saying nain is that Destiny allows us to make choices about the thorny and smooth times, and ultimately, we live the life we choose. We can reach our highest good, our best life, if we listen to our inner voice?" asked Haf.

"And that the Fates, sometimes depicted as witches, are neither good nor bad? Do they offer nudges, or signs, or clues, to remind us that we might need to leave behind old habits or behaviours and embrace new challenges or turn a different corner to walk into a new life?" asked Seren.

"Look. The Gods are offering Nature's fireworks tonight. The comets are indicating a transitional time. Always listen to your inner voice and move forward into your best life" responded nain.

"Perhaps when Kipling wrote '*If you can meet with Triumph and Disaster and treat those two impostors just the same*' he was referring to Destiny, accepting our Fate with grace," said Gareth.

Prosaic Madoc raised his eyebrows. "Let's see what Destiny has in store for us," he said. "I'd like to propose a toast. Here's to those we love who can't physically be with us, and especially to Caesar. Without him, we wouldn't be here in Rome. Everyone is destined to be great. I count my blessings and thank my lucky stars for my family and friends, my fascination with the night sky which has led me through the dimensions of time and thank the Gods for placing Seren in my path, again!"

They all raised their glasses and cheered. The lively chatter, intoxicating music, avid dancing, infectious laughter, and scintillatingly twinkling comets continued until the early hours of the following day.

***

The trip to memorialised Rome was now a teeming collection of dazzling images, mainly snapped by Madoc and Gareth. The wedding party had been back in lush Conwy for three weeks and Seren's new job as a Seer had only just begun.

Although Seren's first professional Tarot reading was with her friend Haf, she paced ceaselessly to and from the large window of her room which overlooked the glary Conwy estuary. Tonight, she was also going to read Tarot cards for her first stranger. She felt surprisingly edgy. Without warning there was a gentle knock on the door, it opened and Haf burst into Seren's room.

"Hello. Welcome. Come in" was Seren's enthusiastic greeting. "What do you think of my room?" she asked as she hugged Haf.

"Let me see it" said Haf disentangling herself from Seren.

"Well. It's fabulous. Very *you*" replied Haf as she noticed the commanding hawkstaff propped in the corner of the room, the image of spellbinding Circe behind Seren and an engrossing array of crystals, incense sticks, tiny essential oil bottles, shells, crescent moons, various colours of feathers, a bubbling golden cauldron, a figurine of a Welsh dragon, a fairy dangling from a blue silk ribbon (not a real fairy), green, yellow, blue, white and pink candles, a large moonstone and a selection of Madoc's remarkable photographs suspended around the walls, taken on his world travels and his outer-world view of the cosmos.

"Wow. I love it Seren" said Haf enthusiastically.

Sitting on a shelf in her room, the golden cauldron emitted intoxicating sage incense swirls. Seren recalled the momentous evening when she spied a waxing gibbous moon shining through the window which illuminated a clique of women in the back sitting room of Bryn Gosol farm. How far she had travelled. She asked Ysbryd to guide her on the next part of her Destiny.

Seren motioned Haf to sit opposite her, as she did so Haf's strawberry blonde hair tumbled around her pixie face. Her green eyes cast apprehension.

"Choose twelve cards Haf then pass them to me."

After a swift examination of the cards, Seren looked up.

"You have a nain in the spirit world. It's your father's mother. She is offering you her ring, but your father currently wears it."

"Why would my nain offer me her ring when my father wears it?" questioned Haf.

"She must want you to have it Haf" replied Seren.

"We'll see" said Haf. "He's a hoarder. Not keen on giving up what he views as his own."

"You'll be the owner of your nain's ring soon enough" responded Seren.

"There's a wedding."

"Whose? Gareth and I don't have any plans to get married" divulged Haf "and I don't know anyone else who is planning on getting married."

"I see a wedding over water, there are rollercoasters and boats" revealed Seren.

"That sounds more like a holiday than a wedding" stated Haf.

"The chapel has purple and pink flowers at the side of it. The setting is spectacular" continued Seren. "There is a honeymoon where the pink flamingos wander freely."

"Oh. Where could that be?" contemplated Haf.

"You're changing jobs and getting a new uniform. You will be working with aesthetics and holistic acupuncture."

"I have been thinking about a change since you've started your own business. I miss you at work" said Haf.

"I see a property in the middle of a field. You're going to buy that home. You'll also buy a camper van."

"Well, that sounds exciting" responded Haf "but why on earth would I want a camper van?"

"You'll have two little boys who will be very different. As an adult, one will move to Australia" unveiled Seren. "Is there anything you would like to discuss with me Haf?"

"Goodness Seren. That's certainly given me hope and plenty to think about" enthused Haf. "Perhaps I will have an adventure? No, I don't want to discuss anything thank you. I'm going now cariad tlws as I've got a lot to absorb. I'm not sure I should tell Gareth about my reading."

"That's your choice Haf. Now for my next appointment. I'm a little apprehensive about meeting Gareth's friend from the university."

"Romeo's lovely" replied Haf.

"Is that his name? Romeo? I've booked him in as '*Gareth's friend*'."

They both laughed.

"That's part of his name. His full name is Gaius Romeo Cangini" revealed Haf. "But he prefers Romeo."

"I expect he does" said Seren with a lift of her eyebrow. She must have been taught that move by Madoc.

"Thanks for my reading Seren. It was uplifting. I'll see you at the weekend" promised Haf and with that she left.

Outside Seren's room, on the wide landing, the energetic genius quivered within Gaius Romeo Cangini. With ease he had ascended the wooden staircase and now perused the intricate detail held in the panoramic view which Madoc had taken from the Vardre incorporating Conwy, the Irish Sea and three Welsh mountain ranges.

Seren took a deep breath, opened the door to her room, offered her hand to the handsome, black-eyed Italian man and smiled warmly.

"We live in the picture" he said. His opaline smile lit up the landing.

'*Goodness*' she thought.

"I'm Gaius Romeo Cangini" he announced, "but everyone calls me Romeo."

Seren almost curtseyed but didn't.

"Welcome Romeo. Come in. I had you booked in as *'Gareth's friend'*. I hear you work with Gareth at Bangor University."

"I do Seren. Yes. It is good to meet you. I've heard a lot about you. You are famous already" he said.

"That's very kind of you to say Romeo, but no, I'm not famous. Please sit down."

Romeo perched on the edge of the wooden chair. He stared at three colourful sets of Tarot cards on the imposing oak table.

"I wanted to meet you because, although I'm a scientist and usually need proof of *everything,* since I was a small boy I've experienced visions, images, dreams. Sometimes an event will happen, and I've known beforehand that it will occur. It's unsettling" Romeo explained. "That's why I followed the physics route, to find answers to the unknown, but I haven't solved my own conundrum yet."

Seren sat opposite him, saw his blue aura, and absorbed his energy.

"Gosh. You're surrounded by birds. Magpies. How interesting" stated Seren.

"Yes, my ..." he began by way of explanation.

"Oh, please don't tell me. Let's see what the cards reveal. Here" said Seren as she gave a set of Tarot cards to Romeo. "Choose twelve cards and hand them to me" she directed.

Romeo expertly shuffled the Tarot cards then offered them to Seren.

"Here goes" he said, a little abashed.

"You're a stargazer" she said.

Romeo smiled.

"You have the choice of plenty of women, but you're waiting for your soulmate."

Romeo chuckled.

"Women are queuing down the street for you" Seren laughed too.

Romeo bowed his head and drew his fingers together.

"These women want you for the wrong reasons."

Romeo looked Seren straight in the eye. He leaned forward in his chair.

"You keep picking the wrong type of woman."

Romeo's rich, coal black eyes opened wider.

"To meet your soulmate, you must look away from bars, and clubs. You won't find her there."

He pursed his lips, sat back in the chair, ran his fingers through his thick mane and clasped his hands. Seren thought that his collar-length hair had the dark brown colouring of a nuummite crystal, with lustrous spectral colours of gold latticed with copper flashes.

"You need a woman who will be happy simply to sit and look at the stars with you."

Romeo shifted in the wooden chair.

"This soulmate of yours. She's not your usual type of woman. Initially you will connect with her emotionally, spiritually, and intellectually."

In silence, Romeo looked directly at Seren who continued unabated.

"This is strange" said Seren nonplussed.

"What is?" asked Romeo, slightly alarmed.

"This woman is already in your aura. You've already met her but when the cherry blossom falls, you will meet again."

Romeo leaned forward.

"This woman will always love you unconditionally. She will bring out the best in you. She will be good for you."

Seren paused. Romeo smiled brightly.

"I was going to ask you about my love life" he laughed. "Now I don't need to."

"You understand that our soul is immortal and repeatedly reborn?" questioned Seren.

"Yes" replied Romeo. "I know that it will be reincarnated in another until our lessons have been learned.

"And you're aware that our soul dominates our thoughts and must be attuned?"

"Absolutely. The soul is our inner voice. Nurture of the soul is important. I have studied Plato's work on Socrates" he confessed.

"You sound like my nain, and she would say …"

"Nain?" questioned Romeo.

"Yes nain, it's the Welsh word for grandmother."

"Ah. There are lots of Welsh words I need to understand" Romeo responded. "They're confusing."

"As my nain would say, 'Nurture of the soul is important and never underestimate the power of love'."

There was a long silence in the room as Romeo absorbed the positive energy and spied the paraphernalia which Seren had placed on shelves. He was drawn to a large wooden effigy which stood majestically in one corner of the room. It appeared to have an iridescent eye. Romeo decided not to ask any questions about hawkstaff. Instead, he queried:

"The photographs on the wall. You took them?"

"No. My husband Madoc is a professional photographer. He travels all over the world snapping images. Occasionally he works alongside archaeological excavations. That's his job. His hobby is stargazing. Perhaps you'd like to come with us one evening when we're next stargazing on the Vardre? In

November, the fast bright Leonids will be livening up the night sky" she said.

"I'd like that Seren. Thank you."

"I hope I wasn't too direct Romeo. With your reading I mean. I say what I see in the cards. The Ace of Cups which came out depicts new beginnings for you, and is auspicious for personal relationships, because it links to love, our emotions, and unexpected, wonderful opportunities. It's always an important sign" explained Seren.

"New beginnings? Good. And Seren, I do have a link with magpies. My grandfather played for Newcastle United" Romeo divulged.

"Fancy that" Seren exclaimed, not understanding the connection.

"I had this done in his honour."

Romeo pulled down the left side of the neck on his black polo neck jumper to reveal a tattoo of two magpies.

"*One for sorrow, two for joy*. I think that's how the song goes isn't it? Magpies are the emblem for Newcastle United, but I've always felt drawn to magpies."

Seren gasped and stared hard at Romeo.

"The visions you mentioned at the beginning of our tarot card reading, I think I might be able to help you understand those, Romeo."

"Do you think the mysterious essence of time links with my visions?" he replied. "The only way I can reconcile them is to believe that time is emergent."

"What does that mean? *Time is emergent*?" questioned Seren.

Romeo considered for a while how he would explain this to Seren, sighed, then said:

"Time is real in the sense that it emerges from events and processes. We can't see, hear, feel, smell, or touch time but it dominates our lives."

"Go on" she urged.

"We are living mortal lives. We think that time passes because we have allocated it to link with the moon phases. As I'm Italian, I will blame Julius Caesar for that. Time for us in this body, is finite. We witness ourselves and others getting older, but time for our souls is infinite. Time in the universe is eternal, but for us mortals time passes in the chunks that we have allocated to it, namely seconds, minutes, hours, days, months, seasons, years. Do you understand what I am saying?" Romeo asked, exasperated with himself. He placed his hands behind his head and continued "is it possible that as mortals we can experience different lives or different dimensions of time and that some people, people like you Seren, encounter events in the past, present, and future because for them, and I mean *you*, time is experienced in a different way? As a scientist, I'm trying to work out the mysteries of time and how that links to my life."

Her eyes refulgent, Seren asked "have you ever had a past life regression?"

Romeo gave a wry smile, took a deep breath, and replied, "so you think our time, our life, isn't ephemeral? *carpe diem!*"[23]

The End
(It's never the end.)

---

[23]Let's enjoy ourselves while we have the chance.

Acknowledgements

This is a fiction novel, but some of the places, historical events and historical references are real. The characters are imagined, except Julius Caesar whose life and battles have been dramatised for the purpose of this story. All other characters, events and locations are the product of the authors' imagination.

Ceris and I have worked tirelessly to create this narrative. We have carried out studies on Ancient Rome, witchcraft, physics, spirituality, and the night sky using thirty or more authors, whose books, websites, podcasts, films, and documentaries were invaluable for the historical, magical, scientific, and planetary research. Thank you to those authors.

Special heartfelt thanks extended to:

- *Martin Thomson* for his extensive knowledge of Caesar's battles, the night sky, creating the book cover and always demonstrating an unfailing belief in his wife.
- Inspirational *Nain and Taid Williams*. Whose lives were well-lived with love and honour. *Na'i dy garu di am byth.*
- Linguist and teacher *Angela Shafiq* who patiently, carefully, and repeatedly checked the manuscript.
- The current owner of Bryn Gosol Farm, *Jackie Hindmarsh* for allowing us to use its name in our work.
- Welsh grammar and translation expert *Lowri Thomas* for information about the use of Welsh.
- *Ysbryd*, for gentle guidance when crafting the narrative.

Finally, a toast to *Julius Caesar*, alea iacta est. But … is there no turning back?

If you enjoyed reading *The Seer and The Stargazer*, overleaf is an excerpt from *The Segontium Sword,* another book in this series.

THE SEGONTIUM SWORD

Prologue

The sweeping rain slanted in the freezing afternoon. The light was fading fast when Allan and Jim sighed simultaneously. They were exhausted, and disappointed. Cold seeped into their bones. For hours they had been metal detecting through a waterlogged field in Caerhun within the Conwy Valley, in the grounds of the ruined Ancient Roman Fort of Canovium.

"Even the sheep are sheltering" Jim said to Allan as his fingers, bitten blue by the raw wind, clutched a metal detector. "I know we are new to this Allan, as it's only the second time we have been here, but I think we should call it a day. There isn't anything to be found on this land."

Allan lifted his sodden parka hood, blue eyes glittering and objected.

"I have a funny sensation about this place Jim. I can feel its energy. The Roman Baths are to our right, the Temple of Mithras was found hidden under the riverbank to our left, I'm sure Roman legionaries would have made offerings around here. Let's keep trying for a little while longer. Rome wasn't built in a day."

Jim grimaced. Allan shoved his metal detector down onto the sopping earth for one last try. It began to ping loudly. A signal registered on his metal detector. Falling to the wet ground, both men grasped at the mud with their hands. A grubby, aged leather strap was exposed, followed by the top of a faded lapis lazuli embellished pot. Jim carefully tugged at the strap whilst Allan held the blue pot in place, careful not to damage it. Five minutes of gentle manoeuvring revealed a faded leather pouch inside the pot. Jim stared at Allan.

"Open it then" shouted Allan.

Hands shaking, Jim slowly unravelled the little bag to reveal a hoard of green, corroded Ancient Roman coins. He stared at Allan and whispered:

"Welcome to 2023 ancient coins. You are in one of the most beautiful and mysterious places on earth. Wonder who you once belonged to? See Allan, I told you that truth is stranger than fiction."

***

November 2023

Chapter 1 – Collective Subconscious

Our energy is interconnected.

"Nain, you're not going to believe this. I've conjured someone out of thin air!" shouted Seren as she burst into the kitchen of her grandmother's newly built bungalow, Bryn Gosol Bach.

"Well, that's novel!" laughed nain. "Even though you're a witch Seren, you can't magic someone to appear. Although there is something magnetic and enchanted about the collective subconscious" replied nain good-naturedly as she turned from a bubbling pot.

"What's collective subconscious?" asked Seren as she helped herself to a cup of nettle tea from the teapot which her nain had christened Niwbwrch.

"Have you ever thought of someone, and they've messaged you out of the blue, or remembered somebody you've not seen for a long time, and then met them unexpectedly?" enquired nain as she blended lavender pods and bee pollen together.

Seren answered, "Yes, of course. That happens to everyone doesn't it? But I don't mean someone messaged me and it was a surprise, or that I bumped into somebody I already know. What I mean is, I've just encountered a man that I've never met before *in this life* but who I think appeared in my *past life regression*. Remember Magpie?"

Nain said, "Now you *have* piqued my curiosity. You mean the Ancient Roman Centurion who was based at Canovium in the

Conwy Valley and had skills as an Augur? The one who became known as Magpie because of his name from the raven family, and who had an image of two magpies tattooed on his neck?"

"Yes. Him! Wait" demanded Seren, "before I say any more, please explain to me what you understand to be *collective subconscious.*"

Nain's obsidian eyes shone as they held Seren's attention. "It's simple really" she responded, "we can communicate with others telepathically which means we are all interconnected. We link across space and time, through different dimensions, because the energy within and around us collects our thoughts and feelings and transfers them as information to other people. But there are only certain individuals who are receptive to sending and receiving telepathic messages since their minds are open to a life of possibilities."

Nain stopped to stir her concoction in a clockwise direction, '*to bring in good things*' she would say. She added the contents to two cups of panad then placed the fingers of her right hand on her forehead, in between her closed eyes as if searching for something within her. After a few minutes she faced Seren.

"We all have the option to turn on our psychic abilities, but most people choose to ignore signs and symbols. Sometimes this is because they can't believe what they are seeing, or feeling, or hearing, or dreaming. Have you ever felt as if someone is around you, but they can't be seen?" nain asked.

"Yes. Doesn't everyone have that sensation?"

"They do, but most explain it away as *'just being a daft feeling, or just imagining things'* and even though what they are experiencing might not fit with received wisdom, it is real."

"So, you believe that because Magpie appeared in the past life regression Madoc and I had with you in the Temple of Mithras, he has now materialised for he sensed this as a psychic message from Madoc and me?"

"Yes" nain replied. "When your minds stepped back to Ancient Roman life in 52BCE your thoughts would have attuned to Magpie, in this life. He could have intuitively sensed your existence in this time dimension. Serendipity and so-called *coincidences* may have led him here, to Conwy. Destiny has played her part."

Seren's brow raised to her hairline. This was a movement she had learned from her photographer husband Madoc who was an eyebrow raising master.

"Wow" was all she could marshal.

A kelpy sea breeze gently drifted around the kitchen, swelled through an open window before racing back to tease the rills on the Irish Sea.

"Our subconscious mind extends beyond our brain. For ease, let's call it our seventh sense. As you and Madoc have a strong emotional bond with Magpie, forged throughout different lifetimes, your thoughts and emotions will resonate with him across vast distances and dimensions. Thus, we are all interlinked."

"Go on" urged Seren.

"This type of communication works at the quantum level. The universe consists of dark matter and dark energy which provides a conundrum for scientists. Most want to have clearly defined evidence, to *quantify* if you will, why quantum particles can affect other quantum particles and even when they are millions of miles apart, they appear to be connected to each other. Entangled so to speak. So, you see, different time dimensions and telepathy are possible. These elements have been tricky to verify for scientists and as yet, no single quantum theory has been found to explain the fundamental forces of life."

Seren pondered for a while until nain spoke again.

"It seems strange that millions of people believe in deities that they haven't seen, but have faith, without proof. And, unless something can be established by scientists, it's considered pseudoscience. Our psychic abilities would be dismissed by many as simply the foolish thoughts of old women. Old women like me, and women like you Seren. Those named Seers, Prophetesses, Sybils or *witches* in bygone ages."

"Hey nain I'm only twenty-seven and that's not old! My past life regressions showed me to be a Sybil in Ancient Rome and I am a white witch now, in 2023" exclaimed Seren, her thoughts following themselves. "Nain, how do you know these things?"

Nain smiled, pleased to share her wisdom, and gently touched her granddaughter's cheek.

"Many people are wiser than they allow themselves to admit. It's all a question of thinking for oneself and not following the crowd. It's about learning the lessons from past lives and this life. Besides, when people are over sixty years of age cariad tlws, they still engage in life you know."

"I know nain." Seren smiled.

"Listen Seren. I have vim, vigour, and lots of adventures to experience, even though taid is no longer in this life to share them with me. See" she said twirling around her kitchen "I've moved into my new bungalow on Bryn Gosol farmland. Who would have thought that I could start a fresh chapter of life … at my age! Besides, I sense taid is always around me."

Silence hung between them like an ethereal silvery cobweb.

"Is it annoying nain, that people might think we are silly to live our lives through the magic and power of prophecy? That we live in the tiny Welsh village of Llanrhos where nothing much happens, but we are Seers and know much more than people would ever believe?"

Nain's determined voice reverberated around the kitchen of Bryn Gosol Bach. A sonorous sound that Seren considered Madoc might have heard as it carried through the open window and across the field which divided nain's bungalow from their farmhouse.

"No cariad tlws. Not at all. Over the years you've seen the numbers of people who have visited me to be *read* when I lived at Bryn Gosol Farm, or those who go to see you for readings and past life regression at your room in Benarth Beach. Some people, especially the younger generation, are more in tune with spirituality, their thinking is evolving, and, thankfully, we are all free to choose our beliefs in this country. Not like in ancient times in some places when women like us would have been burned at the stake. Many people judge it impossible to be psychic, but others know that life is full of infinite potential. It won't be long before what you and I do Seren is accepted as *normal* practice."

"Isn't there anyone in the scientific world who comprehends what we do?" asked Seren "and who can authenticate our psychic abilities?"

"Oh yes. There are some erudite scientists who are trying to grasp our type of communication. By that I mean interaction through space and time. Entanglement. Until enough of them do though, we will quietly go about the business of helping other people to aspire to be their highest self. Remember Seren, that not everything can be seen and any tangible item which illustrates that prophecy is real, must be kept under lock and key. You know what has happened throughout history when the wrong people get hold of prophetic writings?"

"I understand. The ancient mystery of the Sibylline books should remain secret."

"Indeed. Now. Tell me about Magpie. What's he doing *in this life?*"

"Walk home with me nain. I've made a chicken pie for you and Madoc. Rhubarb crumble for dessert. Madoc is home. When I left the farm, he was busy researching for the Historical Society about the Ancient Roman Segontium Sword. I'd like you to explain collective subconscious to him and if you don't blow his mind, I'll be able to tell you both about Magpie after dinner. Does that sound enticing?" Seren questioned.

"It does. We can check on the apiary as we pass. The bee pollen is particularly good this year."

A stripped Devil's Tree, Saint Hilary's Church and the two sodden, uneven hills of the Vardre lay in the distance before them. Nain and Seren strolled arm in arm towards Bryn Gosol Farm where Madoc waited impatiently for their arrival. He could not wait to tell them about a local news item he had just heard. Two metal detectorists had made a huge find of antique coins at the Ancient Roman Fort of Canovium. He knew who had buried them there 2,000 years ago.

***